THE HISTORY OF THE DECLINE AND FALL OF AMERICA

A SEMI-FICTIONAL SATIRE

Also by Scott Erickson

SATIRE

Invasion of the Dumb Snatchers

The Diary of Amy, the 14-Year-Old Girl Who Saved the Earth

HUMOR

The Navy Girl Book

Seventeen and Turning into a Non-Mormon Secular Humanist Zombie

B-Movie Mash-Up: Gastropods of Terror and How to Get a Head in Real Estate

The Best of Reality Ranch

THE HISTORY OF THE DECLINE AND FALL OF AMERICA

A SEMI-FICTIONAL SATIRE

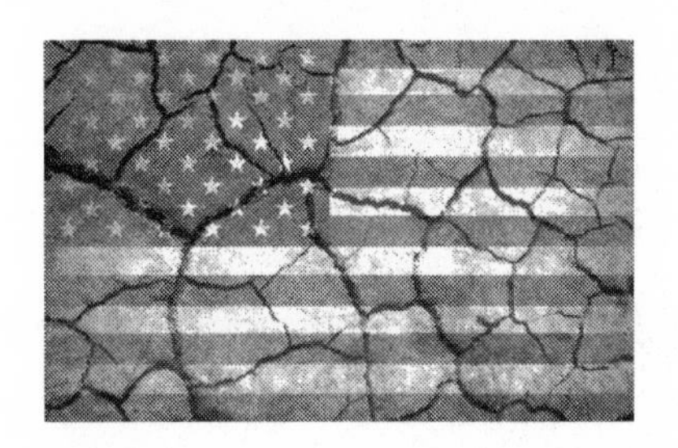

SCOTT ERICKSON

ISBN: 978-0-9898311-7-8

Published in the United States of America
by Azaria Press

CONTENTS

"The future is but the present a little further on"
—Jules Verne

"If you do not change direction, you may end up where you are heading."
—Lao Tzu

Author's Note

My name is Scott Erickson, the author of this book, who lives in America and is writing these introductory words in 2018. But the book is written in the fictional persona of Scott Erickson, the brilliant British historian, who wrote and published the book in 2051.

This is an unusual book in many ways. You may have noticed from the cover that it's a *semi-fictional* satire. This book is a hybrid of fiction and non-fiction. It was written during 2017 and everything portrayed up to that time is true to the best of this author's knowledge. Events portrayed after 2017 are speculations based upon previous trends, and upon historical events that occurred in other countries during similar circumstances.

I used such an unusual approach because examining the entirety of America's past and projecting it into the future was the best way to communicate my message. It allowed me to show how America's core assumptions have determined its history and will determine its future. It allowed me to show that America is destroying itself while remaining absolutely clueless as to the reasons why. It allowed me to clearly show what America refuses to admit: If the country doesn't change course, it's doomed.

This approach also allowed me a way to provide insights into a variety of related questions, such as: Why is the cost of living rising, and will continue to rise? What are the effects of our addiction to economic growth? Why is America experiencing a rise in fascist impulses? Why is the "dumbing down of America" turning into "America's embrace of stupidity"?

As a result of wanting to communicate all of this, I was led to write a book that no sensible person would have attempted to write.

There's one more thing I want to mention. The fictional author is British, therefore, the book is written primarily in British English. Yet the book is not *totally* written in British English, because American readers would likely by confused by references to *lorries* (trucks) or *flats* (apartments). Therefore, the book is an imperfect mix meant to satisfy both audiences as much as possible. In other words, it's just another way that this is an unusual book.

So, without further ado, I now turn you over to the fictional author of this book, the brilliant British historian Scott Erickson.

INTRODUCTION

How could an advanced and powerful nation such as America so quickly and easily collapse? Why was there so little resistance to the downfall? How could a country that began with such high ideals reject them to embrace the worst in human nature? How could a country with such abundant resources and incredible natural beauty turn itself into a sterile wasteland of poisoned soil and squandered forests?

Such questions continue to fascinate and puzzle us to this day.

The monumental ruins left behind by America hold a romantic fascination for all of us who are fortunate enough to visit. As we journey through the ruins of New York City, our gaze inevitably turns skyward toward the battered glass and steel remnants of the surviving office towers. We journey through the legendary corridor of Wall Street and ponder the lives of the multi-billionaire titans of the stock market who once prowled these very streets. We may wonder what it felt like to make billions of dollars at the expense of taxpayers. We may wonder at the kind of panic they felt after the Great Bank Collapse of 2039, when thousands of torch-wielding taxpayers stormed Wall Street hungry for revenge.

Our gaze continues offshore to the weathered ruins of the Statue of Liberty, into which many of those financial titans made a panicked escape and attempted to hide, followed by an angry mob that gathered at the statue's base and readied their guillotines.

Far beyond the cities, visitors travel routes of crumbling asphalt among the abandoned skeletons of suburban housing estates, trying to imagine that people actually wanted to live like this. Moving beyond the most wasteful and uninspiring excuses for housing ever devised by the human race, we enter the route of a former boulevard, lined with the ruins of the same chain stores that line the ruins of every single town and city in America. We may wonder why America, the proud advocate of freedom and individual liberty, chose to have every place look identical to every other place.

What we see inspires so many questions. What kind of experience was offered by an establishment with the name of Hooters? How did Americans pronounce the name of the restaurant Chick-fil-A? Why were there no Burger *Queens*? Who was Victoria, and what was her secret?

It has been a quarter century since America's collapse in 2051. As we look back from 2076, we have arrived at the ideal time to formulate comprehensive answers. It is perhaps ironic that 2076 would have been America's tricentennial, if America still existed as a nation.

A quarter century is a perfect period of time to reflect upon the meaning of America's decline and fall. In addition to allowing adequate time for reflection, a quarter century was necessary to decipher the immense archive of material. This proved to be an immense challenge. The attempt to separate meaningful data from the profusion of trivia was an immense and almost heroic undertaking.

One might have thought that news reports gathered from television and other media sources would have been of great value. Yet for reasons we do not yet fully understand, news reports dealt mostly with celebrity gossip, burning buildings, automobile accidents, new product releases, and the results of sports events. The few news reports that dealt with issues of political and economic importance were simplistic, without clarifying context, and consisted mostly of the opinions of pundits in response to the opinions of other pundits.

Attempting to review the massive historical database of social media to get a sense of how "the average American" felt and thought has been difficult. This is because the vast majority of social media posts consisted of cat videos. Attempting to correlate such data with the decline and fall of a civilisation has proven challenging, to put it mildly.

Yet while there has been enough time for effective hindsight, there remain a few living survivors of the collapse who are able to offer first-person perspective. I personally interviewed many of these survivors for this book, and one of my first questions was: Why so many cat videos?

The legacy from America lives on, often in ways of which we are unaware. To express greetings, people in contemporary England often use the expression "Would you like fries with that?" Yet very few are aware that the expression originated in America as a restaurant order for the American version of what we know as chips.

The decline and fall of America remains interesting to people around the world. It continues to inspire movies, such as Canada's *Neighbour No More* and Iraq's *Rot in Hell, Imperialist War Pig*. British popular music band Praying Mantis recently had a number-one hit with an updated version of a classic Beatle's song entitled, "You Say You Want an (American) Revolution?"

And for the past 20 years, the French amusement park Collapseland has remained a popular way for visitors to re-enact the dying days of American life. In the most popular attraction, Don't Mess With Texas, visitors can experience the thrill of yelling at animatronic ranchers. And if those animatronic ranchers begin to "shoot" them (with non-functioning facsimiles of authentic American firearms) visitors can experience the thrill of shooting back.

In England, electronic gaming enthusiasts can play American Downfall, an immersive three-dimensional virtual reality simulation of the late stages of America's decline. In American Downfall, players compete in battles for the last remaining stock of America's ravaged grocery stores, and then embark upon hunting raids for weakened neighbours that are able to provide valuable protein.

□ □ □

As a resident of England, the process of writing this book has been especially poignant. America was England's rebellious child. The original colonists rejected our empire at the height of its power, then went on to develop a larger and more powerful empire as ours went into decline. Then, during World War II, when the continued existence of an independent England was in serious doubt, our rebellious child returned to save the motherland.

As we witnessed the gradual decline of our strength and importance, we watched as America's influence grew stronger. We had believed in an English Empire "on which the sun never sets." Yet that inevitable sunset came, as it comes to all empires. Perhaps now humanity has finally learned that the whole impulse toward empire is false—that it is futile and self-defeating, that it is based on faulty concepts and motivations. If so, we can credit America with teaching us this valuable lesson.

England was fortunate. Unlike the examples of Greece and Rome—and many others—the collapse of our empire did not mean the collapse of our nation. Sadly, America was not so fortunate. With only a few exceptions, the area formerly occupied by America is a sterile wasteland, with vast areas contaminated with toxic chemicals and radioactive waste. Only a few stubborn stragglers have been able to eke out a subsistence living in the areas spared major devastation.

Among them are the last surviving original nations of America—the Native American cultures such as the Sioux, Apache, and Navajo. Shunted away to land considered to be of marginal value, they were ignored during the final battles and thus spared from most of the collateral damage. As the smoke cleared, they were finally free to re-establish themselves on what was left of their ancestral lands.

The following chapters cannot hope to provide a comprehensive history of America. The author assumes from the reader a general understanding of that fascinating and complex history. Entire books have been devoted to understanding single facets of that history. To mention only a few recent publications, there was Reginald Dwight's fascinating *Between Two Buns*, a history of American values and social mores in relationship to its concept of a hamburger. There was Elizabeth Morrow's *Father Knows Less*, a history of America as represented by the declining intelligence of television sitcom characters. And only last year we saw the publication of Timothy Reynold's *My Gun is Warm*, an examination of America's love affair with weapons.

While other studies have been heavy on analysis, the focus of this volume is synthesis. Such a broad survey by necessity cannot explore all areas in depth. This book is not for academics; it is for the general reader. By bringing together an abundance of conclusions from a variety of disciplines, we can make conclusions not possible by examining various areas in isolation.

Those conclusions have profound implications for our own future. The fate of America has proven to be something of a global "wake-up call" directing our attention toward some fundamental and potentially fatal errors that we have been able to avoid. To those who consider America's fall to have been a tragedy, we can only hope that the learning experience it provided to us has redeemed that tragedy.

□ □ □

One of the great puzzles about the decline and fall of America is: Why did they do nothing to prevent it? This question will be explored in depth in the concluding section of this book. But for the present, we only need to understand two crucial points.

The first point is that Americans did not believe that America could possibly collapse. This, despite every child being taught about the collapse of many previous civilisations, some of them quite advanced, such as Greece, Rome, Egypt, and the Mesoamerican empires of the Inca and Maya. Yet somehow, America believed that every other country in the history of humankind was susceptible to collapse—but not America.

What could cause such an intellectual blindness? What was responsible for the inability to see what was right before their eyes? Was it a form of mental disease? Was it a result of brain damage caused by a diet almost totally devoid of actual food?

On that last note, I would like to take the opportunity to share something of personal relevance to this author. One of my most prized possessions is a preserved sample of American cuisine. It is a hamburger sandwich produced approximately 30 years ago by a large corporation called McDonald's. The corporation manufactured what was known as "convenience food" or more popularly as "fast food."

What is remarkable about the preserved sandwich is that absolutely no effort has been made to preserve it. It is simply a sandwich on a small plate atop a metal stand. It is thoroughly open to the environment—to the animals and microorganisms that should have begun to consume it the day it was made. It has remained in this state for decades, a bit worse for wear and requiring the occasional dusting, but it is essentially intact. In all that time, no form of life has considered the item to contain any food value worth consuming. Yet for millions of Americans, this is what they considered to be food.

Can this be the cause of the decline and fall of America? I align myself with theorists that conclude it actually to be more a symptom of disease rather than the disease itself.

The second point is a direct result of the first point. Whatever the cause, this blindness to the possibility of collapse made Americans blind to the tangible evidence of collapse occurring all around them. So as the entire agricultural system was collapsing, as the freshwater delivery systems were drying up, as the economy was suffering catastrophic decline—to mention just three of the collapsing systems—none of this was seen as having anything to do with *America* collapsing.

These two blind spots—the inability to comprehend that America was subject to collapse, and that America was in fact collapsing—made it impossible for America to see that it was actively causing that collapse.

America never perceived itself as having fundamental problems. Instead, all difficulties were seen as superficial *political* problems that could be solved by getting rid of the other political party. An appropriate metaphor would be to imagine America's descent as the *Titanic* going down, and the crew attempting to solve the problem by arguing over the colour of the deck chairs.

Because—as we shall explore in this book—the problem was not in the superficial differences between the two political parties that inspired such fervent verbal battles, it was the assumptions shared by both parties about which they were absolutely silent.

□ □ □

For a variety of reasons, America's political system proved totally incapable of responding constructively to America's decline. It was not only unable to resolve deep-seated problems; it was generally unable to deal with even minor issues. To say the American political system had grown dysfunctional would be an understatement of the highest order. Near the end, the opposing political parties refused to occupy the congressional chambers at the same time in order to avoid breathing the same oxygen. A political poll taken in the 2040s indicated an approval rating for Congress of negative 12.8 percent. It is not known how the poll arrived at such a figure, which is not statistically possible.

But this is not surprising when considering America's misidentification of its fundamental problems.

Since democracy was not able to solve the problems, it was decided that democracy itself was the problem. Over time, diverse streams of unrest coalesced into what became known as The Second American

Revolution. The movement was based on the absurd thesis that Americans could "Win back America" by getting rid of the government.

The movement was embraced by the vast majority of citizens, who were tired of governmental dysfunction. But it was *especially* embraced by powerful corporate and financial interests who were happy to detach themselves from government regulations and the last vestiges of social responsibility. Major business interests were "freed" from regulations over things such as minimum wage rates, medical benefits, safe working conditions, and the provision of retirement benefits. Major financial interests were "freed" from regulations that had prevented them from rigging the entire financial industry to benefit themselves, and to essentially gamble with the combined assets of the entire country.

Thus, America entered an era of unbridled and unregulated Social Darwinism in which only the most ruthless survived. A few winners on top grappled for superiority, as the vast majority of citizens were forced to compete in a collective "race to the bottom."

It should come as no surprise to anyone that the Second American Revolution failed miserably. America was in total chaos, and the population begged for order. Thus, America—to the utter surprise of the world community—embraced fascism.

Of course, it was a uniquely American version of fascism. To work in America, it could not call itself fascism. Neither could it demonstrate the obvious trappings of what Americans imagined fascism to be. There could be no jackboots, brownshirt-wearing Storm Troopers, or bizarre iconography. Yet fascism needs none of those to express the essence of fascism: the merger of government and corporate interests. Yet since this did nothing to resolve America's fundamental problems, the situation continued to deteriorate.

Just when the situation appeared to be utterly hopeless, there was an against-the-odds last chance at redemption. It was the appearance—as we all know by now—of the Second Coming of Jesus. There were other surprises. Who could have foreseen that a 14-year-old girl would come up with a plan that could have resolved fundamental problems with America's economic system that were largely responsible for the country's collapse?

Yet such would-be saviours were pushed aside as inconvenient barriers, as America continued attempting to solve its problems by more rigourous applications of the same strategies that were causing them. Which is when decline rapidly turned to collapse.

□ □ □

We have the gift of hindsight, whereas Americans during the decline and fall were caught up in situations where consequences of their actions were not clear. For this reason, it seems inappropriate for a work of history to indulge in the luxury of moral judgement.

Yet I am not the only one who has discovered that attempting to restrain such judgment is not completely possible. Although the connection between choices and consequences can never be entirely clear, many of America's choices had consequences so patently obvious that a modern child of reasonable intelligence finds them to be self-evident. Such as the consequence of destroying an ecosystem is a destroyed ecosystem. Such as basing every aspect of civilisation on an unsustainable source of energy is unsustainable. Such as basing an economy on an immense pyramid scheme is a bad idea.

It is impossible to avoid the conclusion that Americans, whatever their moral strengths and weaknesses—were profoundly stupid.

This requires clarification. America had been a nation at the forefront of many advances in technology, aircraft design, electronics, medicine, and countless other fields. Yet there are many varieties of intelligence, and we lead ourselves astray by imagining that advances in electrical and mechanical engineering define intelligence in its entirety. There are other aspects of intelligence, such as the uses to which we put the technologies.

Consider the development and rapid advancement of television technology. In the span of a few decades, America became able to instantly transmit moving images around the world to large flat-panel screens in high-definition colour. In America at its pre-collapse apex, the average viewer had access to over 2,000 broadcast channels—the highest number in the world.

Of course, the intelligence capable of producing such technology is extraordinary. Yet consider the content transmitted by the technology. Typical American programmes had titles such as *Celebrity Babysitting*, *Three Men and a Talking Baby Elephant*, and *Ow My Balls!* Examples of these and many others are available for viewing at the British Museum of American Culture, although due to the mental strain most viewers are unable to watch for periods longer than ten minutes.

Is the technology of television appropriate if the content insults the intelligence required to create it? We can ask similar questions concerning any realm of technology. Are advanced agriculture technologies appropriate if all they do is more rapidly deplete the soil to produce higher quantities of lower-quality food? Are faster transportation options appropriate if all they do is more quickly bring us to places not worth visiting?

This brings us our inquiry beyond technological capabilities into the realm of *wisdom*. Wisdom is nothing mysterious or metaphysical. It is merely a higher order of intelligence. This intelligence makes decisions toward proper use of the results of lower-order, technological intelligence.

This brings up a vital question. Traditionally, questions of morality have not typically been connected with questions related to intelligence. But the example of America brings us to consider the question: Does morality need to consist not only of the conscious effort to be *ethical*, but also of the conscious effort to be *intelligent?* Perhaps "intellectual laziness" should be considered a moral failing. In other words, perhaps we have a moral obligation to not be stupid.

Although America produced many great thinkers, America as a whole had an anti-intellectual bias. This could be seen as healthy—to a point. One of America's great qualities—one they had prided themselves on throughout their history—was their pragmatism, their "can-do" spirit, their optimism, their ability to strive confidently into a future of their own making.

Yet somehow, over time, America's anti-intellectual bias became an anti-*intelligence* bias. Then finally, it became an all-out embrace of stupidity. Stupidity became not a problem to be corrected with intelligence, but a shield to be embraced in defense *against* intelligence. And if intelligence was something to be fought, wisdom was not even something to be considered. Wisdom, which since the beginning of philosophical thought has been considered to be one of the ultimate virtues, had become something to be mocked.

This embrace of stupidity, ultimately, was fatal. When stupidity does not see the need to become less stupid, then what? Stupidity becomes something of a closed-feedback loop, a vicious cycle that is self-perpetuating and self-reinforcing. There is literally no way out except self-destruction, with the stupidity eliminating itself along with the host that refuses to question it.

□ □ □

In the final analysis, people make their own history. Ultimately, the course of a nation is made by people agreeing to a common set of assumptions, and making tangible choices based upon those assumptions. This is true whether or not we have any idea of what those assumptions actually are.

America occupies a unique place in world history. It was the first country to be formed consciously—to be created on the basis of consciously chosen principles. When we think of America, we often think of the founding documents. America began its bold experiment in democracy with words that continue to inspire us to this day. From the Declaration of Independence:

> We hold these truths to be self-evident, that all men are created equal, that they are endowed by their Creator with certain unalienable Rights, that among these are Life, Liberty and the pursuit of Happiness.

From The Constitution of the United States of America:

> We the People of the United States, in Order to form a more perfect Union, establish Justice, insure domestic Tranquility, provide for the common defense, promote the general Welfare, and secure the Blessings of Liberty to ourselves and our Posterity, do ordain and establish this Constitution for the United States of America.

All men are created equal...We the people... Lofty words, and quite radical at the time, aspiring to the best and noblest in human nature. Those words established a nation based on the idea that people can best rule themselves. It abandoned as unethical arbitrary systems of rule based upon nothing but the hereditary bloodlines of kings and queens.

Yet those noble and inspiring principles were revealed over time to contain some flaws. The framers of the American Constitution were aware that the principles would need to change over time. So the Constitution was designed to contain mechanisms for its revision over time. America was therefore able to modify its fundamental principles. In other words, it would be able to *evolve.*

However, for this to work it required that future Americans would continually examine those core principles, in order to ascertain whether they were working, or needed to be modified or abandoned.

Those who criticise America for being imperfect are missing the point. Did America perfectly embody its lofty ideals? Of course not. "All men are created equal" left out women, as well as non-white men. Eventually America realised those original errors, and made great efforts to correct them.

America was able to correct some of its flaws, but not others. And some of those flaws proved to be fatal. Identifying those flaws is one of the major goals of this book.

Perhaps the fundamental tragedy of America is that it never deeply examined those core principles. Ironically, it clung to them with more determination as it became increasingly clear they were no longer working. The remarkable conclusion is that Americans had no clue as to what was happening to them. As they were going down, they did not have the slightest clue as to why.

America was the torch-bearer for a time. Now it is time for the rest of us to hold the torch and proceed, hopefully illuminating the darkness of past ignorance with the light of new understanding.

□ □ □

I consider myself fortunate to be here, writing this book. And for you, the reader, to be here reading this book. The entire global community is lucky. Because as America went down, it very nearly took the rest of the world with it. It is perhaps difficult for the contemporary reader to appreciate the utter panic, the helpless fear of witnessing an irrational nation descend into chaos with thousands of nuclear warheads under its command. But America ended not by exploding outward but by imploding inward. The final collapse happened so quickly that there was no time for America to use its massive forces against an external enemy. Before America was able to declare war, it essentially committed suicide.

As for those thousands of nuclear warheads, they were, of course, dismantled and destroyed by unanimous agreement of the international community. Which inspired the identical action to be carried out on all nuclear warheads on the planet. The collective fear served as another wake-up call. It was one of the many ways in which we have learned from America's collapse.

Ironically, America's rapid collapse is the reason that the rest of us will likely be here for a long time. Because we had internalised many of the faulty assumptions that brought down America. Their self-created collapse made very clear which of our own assumptions we needed to abandon. The nation that nearly ended global civilisation lives on as a lesson for what *not* to do.

There is a saying: "Those who cannot remember the past are condemned to repeat it." This is not a cliché; this is wisdom. Some lessons are too important to forget. Thus my own very personal motivation for writing this book is to ensure that we remember. And remember well.

Never Forget.

DESTROYING THE FOUNDATIONS OF LIFE

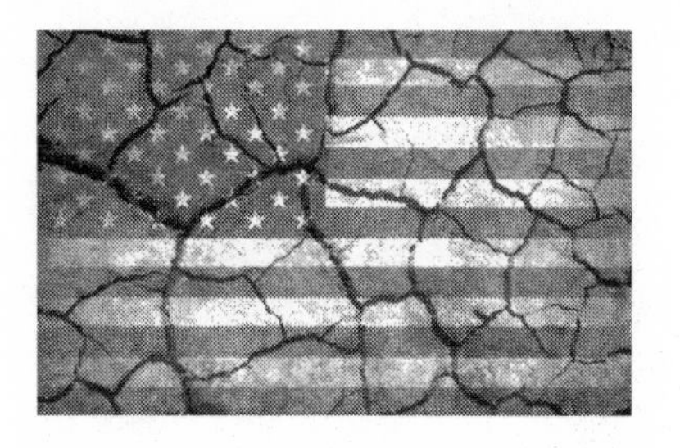

Consequences of Destruction

In 1893, Katharine Lee Bates, an English professor from Massachusetts, took a long train trip across much of America. On the summit of Pikes Peak, she was inspired by what she had seen to write a poem that would later be adapted into the anthem America the Beautiful. The 1904 version of the poem began with the lines:

> O beautiful for spacious skies,
> For amber waves of grain,
> For purple mountain majesties
> Above the fruited plain!
> America! America!
> God shed His grace on thee,
> And crown thy good with brotherhood
> From sea to shining sea!

Unfortunately, if Ms. Bates had been able to repeat her trip 150 years later, she would have been shocked at what had become of her beautiful America. Those "spacious skies" had become filled with air pollution, as well as blowing dust from the dried-out remnants of the prairies that could no longer grow "amber waves of grain." Most of the "fruited plain" had become abandoned after the sterile soil had become unable to grow anything other than weeds.

All this would have been clearly seen from atop any of America's "mountain majesties." This is because the view was unobstructed by trees, since most of America's forests had been harvested. As for those "shining seas," they were even shinier due to the high levels of chemical and plastic waste. And if some Americans had referred to unspoiled wilderness as "God's country" in the belief that God "shed His grace" in the creation of nature's bounty, then we are led to the conclusion that America did not take this belief seriously.

□ □ □

Environmental destruction was a major cause of the decline and fall of America. Yet amazingly, most Americans believed that the country's environmental problems were minor, or that they made no difference. One reason is that Americans generally had an extremely limited idea of what constituted environmental problems. When considering problems such as drought, extreme storms, the decline of industrial agriculture, water shortages, and rising energy prices, they had no conception that such problems were a direct result of drastically overriding the planet's capacity to support life.

For most of its history, America had considered itself to be "above" nature, or that nature had no impact upon their lives. But America was eventually forced into the ramifications of such ideas. By the early 21st century, America's environmental health was deteriorating rapidly. As of 2010:

- One third of the forests and wetlands were gone, and were continuing to disappear.
- Ocean fisheries were being fished at or over capacity.
- There were an estimated 22,000 leaking toxic waste dumps. There were an estimated 1,200 Superfund sites (contaminated with toxic levels of chemicals and heavy metals) requiring approximately $200 billion to clean up.
- Agricultural practices had resulted in soil erosion that far exceeded soil formation. In addition, soil fertility was rapidly decreasing, and in many areas the soil was essentially "dead" and only produced crops by heavy use of chemical fertilisers. As a result of industrial agriculture, every year 500 million pounds of pesticides, herbicides, and fungicides were added to the soil.
- Global Warming was causing melting ice caps, higher sea levels, and more severe droughts and floods.
- Fresh water was running out. Many underground aquifers were being drained far faster than being replenished (especially in Arizona and Texas). Some areas were becoming dependent on "fossil aquifers" that would never be replenished. This was causing increasing water shortages as water tables fell and wells began to fail.
- Energy usage was unsustainable to the extreme, especially fossil fuels (mainly oil and coal). Fossil fuels are essentially stored solar energy, and each day America burned an amount of energy it took the earth thousands of days to create.

What is perhaps ironic is that America was a global leader in environmental protection. By the late 1800s, a growing number of Americans had become deeply concerned about America's destruction of its native landscape. The Sierra Club, founded in 1892 by John Muir, advocated for the preservation of America's most spectacular natural areas. America initiated the National Park system in 1916. With the 1964 Wilderness Act, America became a global leader in preserving significant expanses of land from environmental degradation. The 1962 publication of the book *Silent Spring* led to a ban on the pesticide DDT. Soon, hundreds of environmental organisations became involved in a variety of environmental causes such as advocating for clean air and renewable energy.

Yet none of this was enough to save America's environment. One reason is that most Americans regarded the environmental movement as nothing more than a movement to preserve pretty places and cute wildlife. Many Americans, especially lower-class Americans, regarded it as a movement by affluent Americans to preserve immense personal playgrounds they could visit on expensive vacations and avoid any risk of encountering lower-class Americans. Perhaps such a view contained, in some instances, more than a grain of truth.

But preserving the environment means more than pretty scenery or providing a place for vacations. The environment—the interconnected systems of earth's ecosystems—is the foundation of life. It generates the oxygen we breathe, filters and cleans the water we drink, generates the soil which provides the food we eat and of which our bodies are constructed. In short, the health of human civilisation is directly tied to ecological health. If nature goes, then we go. This conclusion is confirmed by the archaeologists who have studied the collapses of civilisations throughout world history. In all instances of cultural collapse, environmental destruction was a primary or contributing factor.

Yet few Americans perceived the environmental movement in this way. Perhaps calling it an *environmental movement* was a fundamental error. Perhaps it should have been called a *sustaining life on earth movement.*

The reasoning of most Americans was to declare, "I don't see the environment being destroyed." In some cases, this was a result of Americans refusing to open their eyes. Yet there was some validity to the point, since many of the problems could not be readily seen. It was not possible to see toxic chemicals leaking into underground aquifers, or those aquifers being drained unsustainably. It was not possible to see declining soil fertility. Also, most of the problems existed far from population centres. And even if Americans travelled to the areas with the most severe problems, they often did not recognise them.

And in places where the devastation was obvious, Americans took great efforts to hide it. The most blatant example was in the redwood forests of the Northern California coast. The redwood is one of the most majestic trees in the world. It can reach a height of over 370 feet with a trunk diameter of 24 feet. It is impossible to walk in a forest of such trees and not be deeply moved. Yet some Americans were more deeply moved by the profit motive. Those Americans harvested the trees using a method called *clearcutting*—the quickest, cheapest, and most destructive method, consisting of harvesting entire blocks of forest and leaving nothing but debris.

The timber companies were aware that this would be upsetting to the tourists who came from throughout the country and the world to experience the redwoods. So in order to hide the destruction from the public, they left what they called a "redwood curtain" of ancient trees along the highways, behind which the clearcuts would remain hidden. Similar instances abounded. Creeks filled with effluent from pulp mills were disguised when passing beneath highways. Pollution from factories was piped out of public view to be dumped in obscure locations. In such cases, the problems were deliberately hidden to keep them "out of sight, out of mind."

One serious environmental problem, however, could not be hidden. This was global warming. Although many Americans, encouraged by business interests and politicians aligned with them, claimed for decades that it was not real.

There were many reasons for this. Oil and coal companies, of course, had a strong vested interest in not acknowledging the problem. Business interests in general were against taking action on the problem, due to its detrimental effect on economic growth, a point on which America's politicians tended to agree. The American people in general also tended to agree, since acting on the problem would have meant giving up their cars. As a result of all this, America shared the rare experience of being totally united, regardless of age, income, or social position, in their common desire to not acknowledge the problem.

This continued, even as the problem was leading to disastrous and expensive consequences. One of those was the increase in number and severity of climate-related storms. The damage of such storms was exacerbated by another effect of global warming, that of melting glacial ice and the resulting rise in sea levels.

Two of these storms were among the largest and most destructive that America had ever experienced. The first was Hurricane Katrina, which devastated New Orleans and other areas along the southeastern gulf coast in 2005. This was followed by Hurricane Sandy, which hit the northeast Atlantic region in 2012.

In the case of Hurricane Katrina, television viewers around the world were horrified by images of destruction and human suffering. Residents without food or water were trapped for days in inadequate shelter or stranded on rooftops as water rose around them.

Many people viewing such images were puzzled as to why the government did not immediately mobilise some combination of Navy, National Guard, and Coast Guard capabilities to begin rescue operations. Surely those forces could be effectively utilised in the case of national emergency by some sort of agency formed for such a purpose. In fact, America did have such a programme: The Federal Emergency Management Agency, or FEMA. But for reasons that have never been adequately explained, the agency proved utterly incapable of responding adequately to any emergency.

After failing to respond to Hurricane Katrina, the agency proceeded to fail to respond to Hurricane Sandy. This time FEMA had an explanation. The problem was that the storm completely knocked out electrical services, and responding to an emergency requires electricity.

The only positive thing to come out of this second disaster was that FEMA had proof to back up its claim that it was not prejudiced. Hurricane Katrina had effected primarily low-income blacks, leading to the lack of response to be a criticised as an example of racism. However, Hurricane Sandy mostly affected whites of all income levels, which allowed FEMA to claim that it was an equal-opportunity agency that responded equally well to emergencies regardless of race or class.

But even the high level of devastation caused by these storms seemed mild compared to the rapid succession, in 2025, of the three most powerful hurricanes in recorded history: Hurricane Mackenzie, Hurricane Aaliyah, and Hurricane Kaylee.

It was the third storm, Hurricane Kaylee, which was the most tragic. Although Hurricane Katrina had devastated the city of New Orleans, decades of work brought it back to some semblance of its glorious past. But then Kaylee arrived to finish off what Katrina had started. The storm surge demolished all levees and other protective measures, and the city was reclaimed by the ocean.

Through a heroic effort, the city's beloved French Quarter was saved by being completely encircled by a massive 20-foot-high concrete seawall, and massive pumps being installed to pump out the seawater. As a result of all ties to the mainland being washed away, the French Quarter now consisted of an island that became a popular stop on ocean cruises. In addition to offering its traditional virtues of unique architecture and world-class music, it held the distinction of being the world's first below-sea-level island.

Rising sea levels were especially problematic for the state of Florida, much of which was only a few feet above sea level. With the combination of higher sea levels with more powerful storm surges, large chunks of shoreline began disappearing into the ocean. The steady loss of Florida's beaches caused a dramatic drop in tourist revenue, especially for beach communities dependent on the spring break holiday for America's college students.

Curiously, even though environmentalists had been warning about the problem for decades, the Florida governor blamed them for causing the problem. His rather dubious reasoning was, "If the environmentalists hadn't brought up this problem, then we wouldn't have known about it." Although highly irrational, this reasoning is consistent with Florida's previous strategy of dealing with the problem. When the effects of global warming began to be undeniable, the initial response by the Florida governor was to ban Florida officials from using the terms "climate change," "global warming," and "sea-level rise."

The conclusion of the governor's reasoning was that since environmentalists caused the problem, they should be responsible for fixing it. Also, according to the governor, if environmentalists were concerned with preserving habitat for endangered species, then they should also be concerned with preserving habitat for endangered partying.

While the changing climate resulted in too much water in some areas, in other areas it resulted in too little. A decades-long drought settled into California and the Great Plains, which were America's most productive agricultural areas. The response was to drill deeper wells and accelerate the pumping of underground aquifers. In many areas the ground sank as the underlying aquifers were drained.

Extreme water conservation measures were taken. Eventually Los Angeles passed legislation forbidding the watering of private lawns. Residents tolerated this. But when the state government attempted to ban the washing of cars in the most car-centric city in America, the resulting riots led to several deaths and to the kidnapping of the mayor. Fortunately the mayor was eventually released unharmed, although extremely dirty, due to his captors wanting him to experience what it felt like to go unwashed.

The desert state of Arizona was deeply affected by the drought. Regarding water resources, Arizona was among the most vulnerable of states. Yet curiously, it was the most belligerent about curtailing its water use. Inevitably, the problem became critical. Although normally municipal water departments are among the most reclusive of public institutions, the Arizona Department of Hydrology took the unprecedented step of organising a major media conference to publicise the devastating conclusions of a new study. The study declared that, within a matter of five years, the state must choose to either stop drinking water or stop watering Arizona's 421 golf courses.

Declaring both options "untenable," the Arizona governor announced that construction would begin on a 2,000-mile pipeline linking Phoenix to Duluth, Minnesota. This would give access to Lake Superior, the nearest of America's Great Lakes. The governor suggested that residents think of the pipeline as a very long straw allowing Arizona to suck water from Lake Superior. The governor added that since Lake

Superior contained 10 percent of all fresh water on earth, "Arizona can continue to suck for a long time."

Arizona would eventually pay the price for such belligerence, but the first major casualties of the drought were America's Great Plains states. The first was the state of Nebraska, when the underlying Oglalla Aquifer—once the source of 30 percent of America's groundwater used for agricultural irrigation—became effectively empty. Next affected was the neighbouring state of South Dakota, followed by significant portions of Minnesota, Iowa, and Kansas.

In all of these states, groundcover was lost, exposing once-fertile topsoil to the ravages of the wind. This was followed by a tremendous series of summer storms, which blew most of the topsoil north into Canada. The result was a replication of Americs's original Dust Bowl experience of the 1930s. The state governments banded together in a desperate attempt to bring legal action against Canada in order to demand the return of American soil. After this failed, the states in the area termed *The New Dust Bowl* faced a harsh reality. The collapse of the agricultural sector proved to be problematic in a region whose economy had no other sector. As happened previously with the original Dust Bowl, environmental refugees were forced to migrate to other states as did the "Oakies" in the 1930s.

These new refugees, informally dubbed "Northies," began travelling across the country in search of employment as fast-food migrant workers. When news emerged of an opening at a fast food restaurant establishment, word quickly spread and the establishment found itself inundated with hundreds or even thousands of applicants, often engaged in brutal fighting to get to the head of the line in order to convince management of their ability to deliver friendly service.

Although the government had generally denied America's climate-related problems, the business community took global warming seriously early on and took decisive action. Unfortunately, the action taken by the business community was not toward how to prevent it, but how to profit from it.

There were two main strategies by which they accomplished this. The first was to identify shoreline properties destined to become underwater, then to invest in land that would become the new shorelines. Thus, "New Miami" was founded 50 miles inland of "Old Miami," which began to topple into the ocean in 2028. The second strategy was identify desert areas destined to become too hot to inhabit, and purchase tracts of land on nearby mountains. Such areas proved to be profitable locations to develop housing that provided a cool high-elevation respite from the searing heat. Thus, "New Palm Springs" was founded on the summit of nearby Mount San Jacinto, and "New Tucson" was developed on the slopes of the nearby Santa Catalina Mountains.

Peak Oil and the Collapse of Industrial Agriculture

The extended drought, severe water shortages, and other serious environmental problems combined to initiate the collapse of America's industrial agriculture system. Yet America never saw this as an environmental problem. Americans never seemed to realise that the process of procuring food is humanity's most vital and direct relationship with nature. Therefore, it is humanity's primary environmental issue.

Agriculture is a means of living off the surplus of productive ecosystems. And in a healthy agricultural system, enough is returned to those ecosystems so the process can be sustained indefinitely. America's attitude was to form a relationship that was essentially the opposite. America's attitude was something of an attempt to squeeze as much from nature as could possibly be obtained.

The creation of agriculture policies requires prioritising among a variety of factors such as productivity, nutritional health, ecological sustainability, energy expenditures, and the economic viability of farmers and farm communities. America's overriding agricultural priority was to support the highest productivity and the lowest prices. As a result, it was opposed to all other factors.

Yet amazingly, Americans did not consider agriculture or agricultural policy to have any importance whatsoever. In fact, when I asked an American survivor about their thoughts pertaining to agricultural policy, he replied, "What's an agricultural policy?" Another survivor replied, "What's agriculture?" Only one survivor professed to understand the question, yet their interpretation of the meaning of agricultural policy resulted in the reply, "My own policy was to shop at Safeway."

Indeed, for most Americans their knowledge of agriculture did not extend beyond the supermarket shelves. Surely this lack of understanding makes some sense, considering that those shelves consisted mostly of processed food items that bore no resemblance to any product of agriculture. Who could have fathomed the agricultural source of such items as Fruity Pebbles or Ranch-Flavoured Cheezy Poofs?

Yet as much as America attempted to disguise the connection to the source, it existed nonetheless.

All life on earth—including humanity—is composed from elements in the soil. This is something Americans occasionally seemed to comprehend, such as during funerals when the remains of loved ones were returned to the soil with the words, "ashes to ashes, dust to dust." However, Americans seemed to forget they were made of soil while they were alive. And they never seemed to understand that human health is directly linked to the health of the soil. They never seemed to understand that degrading and poisoning the soil was doing the same to themselves.

Rather than return nutrients to the soil, America's system of industrial agriculture sought to extract nutrients as quickly as possible. It essentially "mined" the soil until the nutrients were extracted. It also destroyed the soil structure and killed organisms vital to the health of the soil. As a result, the soil effectively became dead—a neutral growing medium to which fertility had to be added with massive interventions of artificial chemical fertilisers.

The problem was compounded by breeding specific qualities into plants and animals to increase productivity. Plants and animals in the wild balance productivity with qualities like vigour, strength, resiliency, and resistance to attack by diseases and insects. By breeding primarily for increased productivity—in selecting for bigger grains and vegetables, more meat, more milk and eggs—America selected against all the other qualities. The result was plants and animals that were weak and vulnerable, and therefore were poorly equipped against predation and were much more susceptible to disease. This was exacerbated by keeping thousands of the same species in unnaturally close contact through the monocropping of plants and by the factory farming of animals.

The result was plants and animals utterly dependent on care through human intervention. To sustain this system, America became addicted to the artificial fertilisers required to replace lost fertility, to the herbicides required to suppress weeds, to the pesticides and fungicides required to fight diseases and insects, and to the medicines and antibiotics required to keep factory-farmed animals alive and in some semblance of health.

Initially, agricultural chemicals were "wonder drugs." The bigger the dose, the bigger the yield. But America quickly became addicted. Abandoning the chemicals would have resulted in sterile soil barely capable of growing weeds. The beneficial lifeforms were killed off as the harmful and more resilient lifeforms remained. Then the harmful pests and diseases developed immune strains and multiplied. Weeds evolved that were able to resist the herbicides. Therefore, new chemicals were needed—stronger and more expensive chemicals. The dynamic was a perfect textbook example of addiction.

American's liberal use of genetic engineering of plants and animals served to worsen the overall dynamic. Proponents of genetic engineering focused only on the claim that genetically engineered food products were safe for human consumption. But proponents failed to mention that the reason genetic engineering was successful is that it allowed Americans to further degrade the environment—to deplete the soil even faster, to apply agricultural chemicals in even higher concentrations.

The most important players in this dynamic were a small number of tremendously large and powerful agricultural companies, most prominent of which was Monsanto. The company's key strategy was to sell genetically-altered Roundup Ready seeds specifically designed to grow plants resistant to glyphosate, the herbicide it marketed as Roundup.

The technologies making up industrial agriculture had combined to make agriculture hugely productive. In the 1950s, America was the world's largest exporter of agricultural products. And in subsequent decades, while other aspects of American production dwindled and America became a net importer, agriculture remained the final area in which America continued a substantial export market.

Yet that market became endangered as America's ability to sustain large agricultural yields dropped precipitously. American agriculture suffered a crisis resulting from its addiction to agricultural chemicals. Because the addictive process was, in the language of drug addiction, beginning to "bottom out."

Basically, the agricultural chemicals stopped working. At first this was solved by increasing the strength and concentration of glyphosate and other agricultural toxins, a move grudgingly approved by government officials due to pressure from agricultural concerns. Yet the issue finally came to head in a tragic incident in 2029 in which a truck hauling 100,000 gallons of Roundup herbicide crashed, spilling the entire contents. The accident occurred in what was possibly the worst possible location: a steep hillside leading into a major river just upstream of an orphanage. The resulting news images of crying babies clawing at their red and swollen eyes as their hair fell out in chunks proved to be negative publicity.

The company was impelled to pay enormous fines for environmental cleanup, and toward a trust fund for the orphans sufficient to cover a lifetime of health care and hair transplants. While the financial blow to the company was substantial, the bigger problem was that their products were no longer effective.

At the same time, the identical dynamic was occurring in the livestock industry. As especially virulent strains of disease swept the industry, a flu strain had evolved the ability to withstand the strongest drugs available. This resulted in mass die-offs and an extreme livestock shortage due to devastation by antibiotic-resistant diseases.

The poultry industry was further devastated by another serious problem. Decades earlier, the cattle industry had experienced severe problems with so-called "mad cow disease," caused by feeding cattle the remains of other cattle. While that practice had been outlawed, there were no laws against feeding the remains of dead cows to chickens. As might have been predicted, this led to an onslaught of "mad chicken disease" which resulted in irrational and highly agitated fowl escaping their enclosure and terrifying rural populations.

As a result, Americans were forced to forego their traditional meats and pursue options that were non-traditional yet readily available.

The attempt to market rat burgers—as should have been expected—was a total failure. Yet it was a noble attempt to utilise what was one of Americans most easily available sources of meat protein. Pigeons, which were readily available in urban areas, did well once they were packaged and marketed as tiny rotisserie chickens. Dishes made with feral cats were somewhat popular, especially among cat haters. Others would eat cat only if they could be assured that it was an especially bad-tempered cat.

Dogs were generally more beloved than cats, so efforts to serve dog—even if heavily disguised—never really panned out. This is unfortunate, since it also could have helped to solve the problem of feral dogs which had become a major problem in many parts of America. Yet there was one brave attempt, as entrepreneurs started an Asian-themed restaurant chain geared to serve dog meat. Although the solution was logically sound, the idea ultimately failed. America was simply not ready for a restaurant chain called Wok the Dog.

Another failed attempt was with rabbits. Not only were wild rabbits a menace in many locations, but their rapid reproduction rate and fast growth made them ideal for small-scale meat production. Thus, a ready supply of rabbit meat was available to be utilised in dishes such as hasenpfeffer—or "rabbit stew." Yet as with the attempts to get people to eat dog, America was apparently not ready for Hasenpfeffer Hut. The problem, for reasons that remain unclear, was that Americans resisted eating things that had once been cute and cuddly.

□ □ □

As if America's industrial agriculture system was not having enough problems, it was hit with one that proved to be even worse. It was a problem devastating not only to American agriculture, but to the entire country.

America's system of industrial agriculture was incredibly energy intensive. It has been estimated that pre-industrial societies expended one unit of energy to produce sixteen units of food energy. For

America's system of industrial agriculture, the ratio was reversed. America expended twenty units of energy to provide one of food.

This was only possible due to the liberal supply of inexpensive fossil fuels. Natural gas had been used to generate the artificial fertilisers that replaced natural cycles of fertility. Gasoline had been used to power the massive machinery that had mechanised the farming process, and to ship the resulting crops around the country and the world.

This, and every other aspect of American life, would be deeply impacted by what happened in the early 2030s.

Few Americans understood that essentially all energy on earth is solar energy. This energy is captured on earth as a result of photosynthesis—the biochemical process by which a plant uses the sun's energy to create complex compounds. These compounds are stored as fuel that can be broken down or "burned." Until the industrial revolution, humanity's use of energy was limited to the ecological output of the local ecosystem. Energy was stored and transferred primarily in firewood, or in hay and other forms of animal feed.

The industrial age in America, as well as other nations, was made possible by tapping into the energy of the sun that had been stored in fossil fuels, which consist of large deposits of coal and oil made from the bodies of living organisms built up over millions of years. By tapping into this energy humanity was able release millions of years of stored sunlight in a few generations. The use of this energy made possible an awe-inspiring increase in the standard of living of countries that were able to utilise it. The problem, of course, is that it couldn't last forever.

In 1973, America's suffered a serious oil shortage. A rational response would have been to encourage conservation and initiate a nationwide transition to sustainable energy. And for a brief time, America made some progress in this area, such as lowering the national speed limit and encouraging investment in solar and other alternative energies. America largely abandoned "gas guzzling" vehicles such as high-performance sports cars and massive motorhomes. Yet such efforts entailed the dreaded prospect of sacrifice, and did not last. America abandoned its interest in sustainability when the oil began flowing again.

This was truly unfortunate, since America was the most oil-dependent nation on earth. America had done much of its growth and expansion just as fossil fuels became widely available, and built most of the country's infrastructure on the assumption they would always remain available. As a result, passenger cars became essential to reach not only means of employment but to obtain necessary goods and services. America did not see this as a problem. Americans loved their cars; they loved the sense of personal freedom and the ability to embark upon the adventure known as a "road trip."

This all began to change in the early 2030s. The concept of peak oil—the point at which half the world's oil had been extracted—had been publicly acknowledged for decades. But the world was actually long past that point, although it was impossible to know because oil suppliers had a strong vested interest in keeping the quantity of remaining oil reserves secret.

It is important to note that oil did not run out. Oil supplies will never be fully depleted. The problem was that as after the easily-accessible oil had been extracted, the remainder was more difficult and expensive to obtain. In addition, when supplies began to dwindle, the economic dynamic of supply-and-demand further contributed to the cost.

The rising price of oil had a ripple effect throughout every aspect of America's economy. Everything made or sold in America was shipped using gasoline made from oil, and transported on roads of asphalt that were made from oil. America's system of industrial agriculture was totally dependent on oil. All plastics were made from oil, as were synthetic fabrics such as nylon. Baby playsets and children's toys were made of oil, as were most of the birth control devices used by Americans to avoid the need to buy baby playsets and children's toys.

America's upper classes were relatively unaffected. If it suddenly cost four times as much to fill the tank of their imported luxury car, it was of no concern. Yet for America's lower classes, the effects were catastrophic. They were forced to deeply curtail their driving. Some of them were forced to abandon their cars. Some of them had to resort to walking. This was significant, as walking was an activity that had been strenuously avoided in America since it required expending physical effort. And walking was made much more difficult by the problem that Americans—based on the assumption of inexpensive gasoline and passenger cars for everyone—did not locate anything within walking distance of anything.

Growing anger at the situation was only heightened by the sight of wealthy Americans who could afford to continue driving as before. Although such Americans were not concerned with the rising price of gasoline, they needed to take measures that their travel routes did not take them through less-affluent neighbourhoods. In one well-publicised incident, an American couple was forced out of their luxury sedan to perform songs from Broadway musicals for neighbourhood residents, as those residents ate deluxe meals which the affluent travelers had been encouraged to provide.

America's reaction to this crisis, as it was for essentially every crisis the nation ever faced, was denial. This was because acknowledging the roots of the problem would have contained implications too daunting to even consider.

To discuss the concept of peak oil with Americans was to encounter layers of obfuscation and distorted rationality that addiction counselors refer to as "stinking thinking." The first substantial step was simply to get them to admit the depth of the problem. Yet it was a tremendous challenge to get Americans to admit that "unsustainable" means "it will run out." For many Americans, it was not even possible to get beyond this first level of denial.

Many Americans claimed that there was no problem because longer drills would find more oil. Some claimed that eventually American ingenuity would reach the oil at the centre of the earth, and could not be dissuaded from the belief that such a thing existed despite a total lack of evidence. Some Americans claimed that it would be possible to squeeze oil from "oily-looking rocks." In an especially inspired example of American irrationality, an American television reporter interviewing random citizens was privy to the reasoning that "We'll never run out of oil because we can make oil from gasoline." The reporter's attempt to explain that gasoline was made from oil brought forth the reply of "Why do you hate America?"

Many Americans, of course, were willing to pursue the issue with more intelligence. Although even with relatively intelligent Americans, it was merely a question of how far the process would go before encountering some form of denial.

Some Americans claimed that the impending end of oil was not a problem since it was possible to "grow" fuel with crops such as soya beans or maize. But of course this was not possible since nearly all arable land was used for food-based agriculture, and the entire agriculture system was in serious decline. Some Americans claimed that more hydroelectric dams would save the day. This claim was easily rebutted by the fact that power dams had already been constructed at nearly every suitable site.

Some Americans claimed that alternative energy and electric cars would save the day. This was a satisfying thought to many Americans, especially the ones that claimed to be "environmentally aware." Yet technologies such as wind power and tidal energy were not practical in most areas, and were capable of replacing only a tiny proportion of the energy provided by oil. The most viable source of alternative energy was solar, but to satisfy America's energy needs would have required hundreds of massive "solar farms" and other projects involving huge expanses of land and a degree of financial investment that neither the government or private industry were prepared to expend.

One suggestion—frequently offered by American children—was to abandon cars and go back to riding horses. Of course it would have been impossible to grow the necessary amount of feed for the horses on America's degraded and shrinking agricultural lands. Nobody was happy explaining this to children, since nobody wanted to disappoint a young child with dreams of riding a horse to school.

Some Americans clung to the hope of nuclear energy, although by this time the costs of maintaining vast stores of radioactive waste were already becoming prohibitive, and the nation had in recent decades experienced a sequence of nuclear accidents and near-disasters that had left America deeply suspicious of the viability of nuclear energy.

Americans continued to deny that their entire energy system was unsustainable. The only way America could have avoided disaster would have involved a rapid, wholescale effort to re-structure every aspect of their society in order to radically reduce their energy needs to within sustainable limits. Of course, words such as "reduce" and "limits" were wholly unacceptable to the American character. As a result, America forged ahead into bold proposals to postpone the inevitable for as long as possible.

Although Americans refused to acknowledge the roots of the problem, they demanded immediate action. They were angry and desperate, and their feelings were summed up by Indiana governor Eliza Martindale, in a widely publicised editorial entitled "Where Are You, Mr. President?"

> Mr. President, I just left the Annual Meeting of the National Governors Association, and we have a message for you. The oil shortage and subsequent price escalation have put this great nation into a serious crisis.
>
> Because of urban planning based on unlimited cheap energy, our people can no longer afford to live. Driving has become a necessity that we can no longer afford. For many Americans, the cost of driving to work is almost as much as their job pays them. In addition, suburban families can't afford to drive to the mall. They've been forced to remain at home and spend time together.
>
> Mr. President, these are problems that require solutions at the national level.
>
> The time has come for government to step in and take control. It's time to return our government to its traditional role of getting us out of the messes that big business gets us into.

With the support of a desperate public demanding continued denial, President Russell Hale felt empowered to take radical action. The first expression of this was the proposal to greatly expand nuclear power, despite its problems. Congress quickly passed a bi-partisan plan to identify locations for "as many nuclear power facilities as possible, or more." As for concerns about the huge addition to the already growing problem of radioactive waste, the attitude of congressional representatives was that the waste would not be generated until after they left office.

Another action led by President Hale was to begin drilling in the Arctic Wildlife Refuge in extreme northern Alaska. Although the area had been given permanent protection in the administration of President Barack Obama, President Hale declared it was acceptable to defy the presidential act since President Obama had told him in a dream that he did not mind.

Despite the dubious nature of this claim, the American public—increasingly desperate for any relief—responded with chants of "Drill Baby, Drill." Gasoline was considered more important than wildlife that "we don't ever see anyway." In addition to the Arctic Wildlife Refuge, President Hale gave permission to drill at any location in Alaska "wherever they think there might be some oil."

Environmentally aware citizens were greatly angered by these actions, resulting in a variety of protests that were ignored and petitions that were thrown away. Remaining resistance was quelled as a result of a nationwide presidential address in which President Hale pointedly asked the American public, "Do you want to let the terrorists win?" Curiously, Americans could almost always be subdued by any suggestion that they were "soft on terrorism" regardless of whether or not terrorists were remotely involved in the issue being discussed.

Although the president's actions promised relief, it would take years to begin having any tangible effect. In the meantime, Americans were forced to adapt as best as they could. America needed a cheap solution to an expensive problem, so it turned to where it had traditionally turned for decades.

America's agriculture system had replaced as much human labour as possible with machinery, but there remained many tasks that simply could not be mechanised. To perform those tasks it had traditionally employed Mexican labour, working under grueling conditions for low pay. Now, there was a new and growing opportunity for Mexicans to provide labour where the use of machines was becoming unfeasible.

Initially, a few Americans attempted to commute by hiring Mexicans to push their cars down the road, a strategy that only worked with very small cars being pushed by very large Mexicans. Then, they hired Mexicans to pedal them to work on bicycles. But eventually, the rigours of riding on the rear rack of a bicycle while a Mexican peddled to work became impractical, partly due to lack of comfort but mostly due to the frequent collapse of racks not designed for the weight of a typical American. Thus, the strategy of the individual Mexican "engine" for a single bicycle was replaced by the rise in pedicabs in which one strong Mexican could conduct the commute for up to three Americans. The pedicabs were not only comfortable, but were also remarkably efficient.

Whereas the traditional American car might have gotten gas mileage of 15 miles to a gallon, Mexicans could get up to 20 miles per burrito.

The Liquidation of Nature and the End of the Environmental Movement

When America was experiencing relative prosperity, many cities felt empowered to make their urban environments healthier, safer, and more aesthetically pleasing. For a time, some American cities made efforts to plan urban infrastructure along the lines of what was called "smart growth." It was an effort to avoid the problems of urban sprawl and ad-hoc development, and to steer development toward what was termed "livable cities."

However, by the 2030s, America was in serious economic decline, and the rising price of oil only served to exacerbate the situation. When economic prosperity faded, so did such efforts. Idealism was abandoned in the mad rush to encourage any type of development that could quickly generate money. America could no longer afford livable cities.

Also, America could no longer afford environmental protection. No aspect of the American environment was spared from sacrifice for the sake of the economy.

One of the first victims was the long-beleaguered "anti-business" Environmental Protection Agency. President Edward Haskell justified abandoning the agency with the following analogy: "The economy is like a boat trying to go really fast, and environmental standards are like throwing out the anchor." Although the public was receptive to such reasoning, many Americans were not thrilled with the prospect of toxins ending up in the bodies of themselves and their children. So in a clever public relations move, the government did not technically eliminate the agency. It merely cut off its entire budget. According to a government spokesperson:

> The government has no objection to the work of the agency, only of funding it with taxpayer dollars. This administration has long held that environmental protection is fine as a voluntary individual choice. Therefore the former employees of the agency are free to continue their work on their own, on a voluntary "for fun" basis.

One of the more unfortunate victims was America's National Parks. The parks that contained even small quantities of oil were immediately opened to drilling. The most significant area covered most of southern Utah, including some of America's most stunning desert scenery in the national parks Arches, Canyonlands, and Zion. In order to instill a sense of national pride, and remind America of how important the action was, the parks were consolidated and the entire region christened as Energy Independence National Monument. Later, when oil reserves were discovered in Glacier National Park, it was re-named American Way of Life National Park. The park's famous Going-to-the-Sun Road, one of America's most scenic byways, was re-named as the Oil-Forever Highway.

For the parks that were unable to generate revenue via resource extraction, there were other ways. One of those was to allow corporate sponsorships. Park advocates hoped that the result would not detract too much from the experience of natural beauty. They reluctantly accepted that visitors would be required to tolerate things such as company logos on park brochures.

Imagine the surprise of park visitors when they arrived at the entrance to Yosemite Valley to discover an immense sign with the message, "Welcome to Nike National Park!" Less massive signs throughout the park advertised Nike's newly introduced Yosemite Flight lightweight hiking boot, available at the Headquarters/Nike Store in the heart of the valley. But the worst was what happened to Yosemite's famous El Capitan, whose sheer granite walls form one of the highest and most majestic sights on earth. Or it did, until it was painted with an immense reproduction of the Nike "swoosh" logo. Nike was proud to announce the creation of the world's largest commercial sign, a record that would stand until Sony purchased the rights to the northern wall of the Grand Canyon.

That was too much for the public, which was suitably outraged. As a result the government, via the director of the National Park Service, reluctantly agreed that the programme was a failure. In a major media conference, the director stated, "The effort to successfully bridge public and private interests within America's national treasures was misguided," Park advocates cheered the news, thinking it would mean an end of privatisation efforts. However, their mood changed dramatically as a result of an announcement one week later, in which the director said, "It's true that mixing public and private aspects of the parks did not work. So our solution is to abandon the public aspect."

The Department of the Interior then sold off America's 400-plus National Parks and Monuments. This resulted in government revenues totaling over 200 billion dollars, enough to reduce America's national debt by two percent. Most of the parks were purchased by the Hilton Corporation and other hotel conglomerates, to be turned into exclusive luxury resorts. This meant that most Americans could no longer afford to visit landmarks such as Yellowstone, the Grand Tetons, and the Great Smoky Mountains. In a spirit of patriotic charity, the Hilton Corporation sponsored the production of documentary videos of its scenic wonders and made them into DVDs available for any American citizen who could afford to buy them.

America's most scenic areas had obvious economic potential. However American ingenuity discovered ways to develop income from areas that were not scenic to the extreme. American optimism sometimes expressed itself in expressions such as "If life gives you lemons, make lemonade." And some portions of America did exactly that.

One of America's ugliest states was Nevada, containing vast stretches of inhospitable desert. America conducted most of its early nuclear weapon testing in portions of the state that were so dismal that the effects of multiple nuclear explosions made little change.

Nevada proceeded to generate substantial income after announcing its intention to become America's "National Sacrifice Area." In exchange for extremely reasonable disposal fees, the state agreed to accept "anything and everything" that the rest of the country did not want, including toxic chemicals and radioactive waste. As for concerns that such materials would contaminate the soil or leak into underground aquifers, the Nevada governor explained that wastes would be confined to immense pits lined with plastic sheeting.

Some Nevada residents were concerned about airborne contaminants, but the governor assured them that the prevailing western winds would transport any such contaminants to Utah. As for concerns that the plastic sheeting would not last longer than 20 years, the governor suggested asking whoever the governor would be in 20 years.

Another instance of "turning lemons into lemonade" was attempted by Nebraska. The state had become essentially abandoned as a result of the draining of the Oglalla Aquifer, the collapse of the agricultural sector, and the loss of topsoil due to The New Dust Bowl. In desperation, the state attempted to develop tourism based on the state's massive dust storms. Unfortunately, marketing studies revealed that few Americans were interested in watching a dust storm.

As a result, discussions with representatives of The Walt Disney Company to build a destination resort and amusement park to be called Dust World were cancelled. After that failure, the only remaining option was to rent the entire state to the motion picture industry for use as an immense film set ideally suited for America's love of apocalyptic and post-apocalypse movies.

As a result of these developments, the Sierra Club—America's oldest and largest environmental organisation—rapidly declined. Once powerful enough to introduce and gain passage of far-reaching environmental regulations, it fell into a defensive retreat which doomed the organisation to irrelevancy and eventual oblivion. Over time the organisation's motto of "Explore, enjoy and protect the planet." devolved to "Slightly Less Unsustainable" and eventually to "Let's enjoy what's left of nature." Perusing copies of the organisation's magazine *Sierra* published during this period reveals a dwindling number of articles about environmental protection, and an increasing number of articles about choosing the most environmentally friendly brand of shampoo.

Whether this was due to "selling out" is a question that is debated to this day. But one has to ask whether the organisation had a choice. For an organisation such as the Sierra Club, there is the question of how "radical" the members of the organisation would allow it to become.

America had extremely mixed feelings about environmental protection. Americans wanted to preserve their environment. Yet they also wanted to preserve their economic affluence and standard of living. In many ways, environmental protection was in opposition to the American way which for over 200 years had been based on destroying the environment. In fact, many Americans believed that those who were trying to save America's environment were against America.

As a result, environmental organisations were faced with a thorny dilemma. Too strident of an approach would be seen as opposing the ability of the economy to create affluence, and therefore alienate the economically affluent membership upon which the organisation depended. In response the Sierra Club, along with every other major environmental organisation, chose to "soften" its approach, in order to keep membership numbers from falling too far while retaining at least the illusion of having a positive effect on the environment.

The only environmental problem that concerned America, although they never labelled it as an environmental problem, was the crisis in American agriculture. While a few areas of America had been able to transition to small-scale local agriculture, most of America remained entirely dependent on America's critically endangered system of industrial agriculture. That system was absolutely dependent upon agricultural chemicals whose effectiveness was rapidly diminishing.

Yet increasing the toxicity levels would result in threats to human health too dangerous to consider. Also, the memory of the disastrous spill of Roundup herbicide and images of sick orphans was still strong in the public consciousness.

As a result, most observers thought that the Monsanto Corporation, manufacturer of Roundup and the genetically-altered seeds specifically designed to resist it, was in serious trouble. Many thought that the crisis would lead to the end of the company.

Yet Monsanto's reaction to the crisis was so swift that many believed the company must have been expecting it for years. The company's reaction was explained in a news release that attempted to improve the company's public reputation, hoping to change it from "baby poisoners" to "saviours of humanity":

> Apparently our Roundup product and other agricultural helpers are becoming less effective over time. We had no idea this would happen, so it isn't our fault. But rather than engage in the "blame game" we must forge ahead. America has never turned its back on a challenge, and these tough economic times mean we must not turn our back like never before.
>
> Some people believe that Monsanto has gone too far. Here at Monsanto we believe that we haven't gone far enough. We are proud to announce that we have developed an innovative new product that will end all problems with human exposure to agricultural chemicals.
>
> Our new product is a highly-advanced version of our famous HappySeed technology. As everybody knows, our Magic-Ready HappySeeds are genetically engineered to be used in conjunction with our GrowMagic line of Roundup and other agricultural helpers. We're proud to announce Monsanto's brand-new product, which we call HappyHuman.
>
> We must increase the "magic" within GrowMagic to a level high enough to kill every form of life that has not been genetically modified to resist it. That's where HappyHuman comes in. HappyHuman will be available in capsule form. Each capsule contains radioactive isotopes that go throughout the body, altering the genetic code in each and every cell. This will make us able to withstand GrowMagic 100 percent naturally!

As might have been expected, Americans were shocked and outraged at the idea. Americans asked questions such as "What about unintended side effects?" and "How can a single company have the power of life or death over all earthly life?" Above all, Americans demanded an answer to the question, "What about our household pets?" Monsanto was quick to answer such concerns by assuring Americans that the company would offer the supplement in a pet-friendly form.

□ □ □

In one of the few instances of good news, the emergency measure of oil drilling in the Arctic Wildlife Refuge began to pay off, as new flows of crude oil began the journey to American oil refineries. Yet the good news did not last.

After only two months the flow of oil began to steadily diminish. Eventually the oil companies were forced to admit that the energy obtained from the refuge was barely enough to make up for the energy expended to retrieve it. Later it was revealed that the oil companies withheld the fact that the reserves were vastly overestimated to preserve their stock valuation, and that America's politicians withheld the fact because of upcoming mid-term elections.

America scrambled to utilise other sources of energy. Unfortunately, there was very little available to be quickly or easily utilised. Constructing hydroelectric dams on America's last free-running rivers made little contribution to the country's energy needs. Nuclear power plants were being designed and constructed, but it would take years before they would be able to contribute to America's electric grid.

America still had a plentiful supply of coal, but coal power was limited due to America's reduced capacity to transport the massive quantities necessary to replace oil. In addition, coal-fired power plants resulted in such extreme levels of air pollution that residents of some cities were forced to evacuate when the wind switched directions.

However, America had one energy resource that for generations had been almost totally ignored. It was an energy source that had been utilised by humanity for millions of years. It was relatively easy to obtain and was available in substantial quantities over most of the nation: *wood*. And so America turned its attention toward the country's abundant forests. And as it had turned toward an unprecedented expansion of nuclear energy despite the problem of radioactive waste, it turned toward an unprecedented harvest of its forests despite the fact that they were already being harvested at an unsustainable rate.

President Haskell quickly drafted the *Trees for America Act* to revise Forest Service policy. The traditional goal of the Forest Service had been "multiple use"—managing America's forests for the cooperative uses of timber harvesting, hunting, recreation, and others. The purpose of the act would be to change multiple use to one use.

The weak protests from America's few remaining environmental organisations were swept aside. "Do you care more about trees than people?" was the usual argument against those urging forest preservation. Those who replied "Actually, I care more about trees" were subjected to physical violence.

The only problem, as far as America was concerned, was that it had almost no infrastructure in place to utilise wood to provide energy. Yet American ingenuity rose to the challenge as the nation developed ways to utilise wood that went far beyond home fireplaces.

Bringing back a long-abandoned technology, America re-embraced the steam-powered car. Early in automotive history, America had produced one the world's finest and most efficient steam-powered cars, the *Stanley Steamer*. While the Stanley Steamer had used kerosene to generate steam to power the engine, it was not difficult to adapt the design for wood-generated heat. While initially embraced with enthusiasm, the novelty quickly wore off as major highways and boulevards became smoke-filled corridors navigated by travelers whose visibility became reduced to a few yards.

However, America quickly developed a much more efficient means of using the energy of wood to power its automobiles via another long-forgotten technology: *wood gas generation*. Wood gas is a synthetic gas or "syngas" created via a gasification unit. The first vehicle powered by wood gas was built in Britain in 1901. By the 1940s thousands of wood gas vehicles were being used in Europe, largely a result of the wartime rationing of fossil fuels. And after a century of being nearly forgotten by history, they became common once again in America.

Some Americans were saddened by the rapid destruction of its forests, but most Americans were pleased with the ability to keep driving. The head of America's Department of the Interior, Anthony Steele, proudly staged a media conference at the site of the harvesting of the final sequoia trees in the mountains of California. The majestic trees were some of the largest trees on the planet. Many had been living for over 2,000 years, longer than modern civilisation. As the final tree fell, Steele proclaimed, "That majestic tree will provide enough gas to power all the cars in San Francisco for 12 minutes."

In a matter of only five years, America's abundant forests had grown much less abundant, and in fact were on the way to becoming almost totally eliminated. Which is why to this day the vast territories that were once America's abundant forests now consist largely of brush and invasive weeds.

□ □ □

Of course, much of America consisted of arid or semi-arid desert, and were unaffected by the loss of America's forests. However, such regions were not spared from the effects of the degrading environment. In fact, the situation for such regions was in many ways worse. This reality struck home in a shocking way when Phoenix, Arizona, one of America's major cities, totally collapsed.

Basically, Phoenix ran out of water. The proposed water pipeline to Minnesota, which was supposedly going to save Arizona, had quickly bogged down due to the fact that Minnesota refused to give up any of its precious water so people in the desert could play golf.

Almost all of Phoenix's water was supplied via underground aquifers, and the city had been drawing down the supply at an unsustainable rate for many years. It was no secret. In fact, each year local newspapers reported on the progress: "We're down to 18 percent" followed in a few years by "Only 11 percent now." Incredibly, the problem was not that residents did not see it coming. The problem was that they did, but they did not care.

Social Psychologists from other countries watched this happening with disbelief and amazement, and some came to Phoenix to seek answers. They interviewed city residents and attempted to understand their thought processes. They discovered that Phoenix residents justified their lack of concern with the reasoning that since Phoenix had never run out of water before, then it never would. This discovery was immensely helpful to historians, as it is believed to be directly related to the refusal of Americans to consider that America could possibly collapse.

Once Phoenix began to collapse the process escalated rapidly. It began on a morning in late July, when residents turned on their faucets to discover water with a distinct brown tinge. By the end of the day, what flowed out of the faucets was closer to mud than water. The massive pumps of the Phoenix Water Department—over-stressed by the effort of attempting to pump the thick fluid—burned out, which triggered a total failure of the electrical system. As a result of the loss of electricity, refrigerators and freezers lost power. Perishable foods quickly became unusable. Panicked citizens attempted to flee the city, quickly causing tremendous traffic jams that resulted in total gridlock. Trucks could not enter the city, so residents were limited to grocery store stocks adequate for only a few days.

The lack of electricity meant no air-conditioning, which in the desert climate was an absolute necessity for survival. It did not help matters that this occurred in the middle of summer. Global warming had by then made the already sweltering summers even hotter. Although Phoenix had just gone through a major heat wave, the crisis hit when afternoon temperatures had cooled down to 127° Fahrenheit.

Suddenly the timeline for survival was very short. Food was not as big an issue as water, since the human body can survive for days without food but only for hours without water. The entire population was trapped and the clock was ticking. The few police and military personnel within the city were powerless to control the situation. In addition, their need for water meant that they were essentially just as desperate as everyone else. Everyone, regardless of income level or social position, was suddenly dragged down to the same fundamental level. The top priority—the only priority—was to obtain water.

Guns were plentiful in America. Residents without water but possessing a gun might be able to obtain water from a neighbour. Unless, of course, the neighbour also had a gun. It was shocking how quickly civilised society devolved into a brute war for survival, and the city was subjected to a level of violence and carnage previously unmatched in American history. Battles broke out over the ponds at golf courses. Gang warfare erupted when the heavily armed Crips fortified themselves at the Happy Valley Water Park, successfully defending it until being attacked by the more heavily armed Bloods.

In three days it was all over. A few strong and well-prepared residents had been able to escape on foot, eluding capture with enough water to make it to safety. A few had been able to survive by hiding in basements or garden sheds with cases of soft drinks. Rescue teams found small groups surrounding private swimming pools that had survived by drinking chlorinated water. Although chlorine is highly toxic, they had little choice. They eventually recovered to live out the rest of their lives, although many of them were no longer able to pronounce certain letters or focus their eyes in the same direction.

As had occurred with previous emergencies such as Hurricane Katrina and Hurricane Sandy, FEMA came under heavy criticism. Unfortunately, the agency had failed to improve as a result of these earlier disasters, and in the case of Phoenix it was no better prepared than it had been for the previous emergencies. One week after the collapse of Phoenix had begun, the head of FEMA announced that the agency was working on developing a strategy to best respond to the situation in Phoenix.

It was suspected—but never proven—that the democratic head of FEMA, Hannah Rivas, deliberately delayed the response due to Arizona being a heavily republican state. Rivas viciously denied this with the claim that, "I value the lives of all Americans as well as republicans."

A RIGGED POKER GAME ON TOP OF A PYRAMID SCHEME

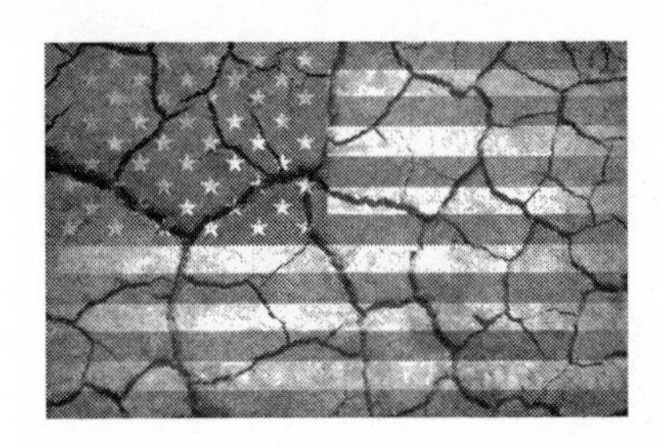

The Elephant in the Room: America's Addiction to Economic Growth

It is absolutely impossible to make any sense out of American history without at least a rudimentary understanding of its economic system. As we shall see, the system was highly irrational, to put it mildly. Some have called it a rigged poker game on top of a pyramid scheme. Others have deeply examined America's economic system and concluded that it was literally insane.

I am deeply indebted to the groundbreaking research of many predecessors in this area, and wish to give special thanks to the authors of two books in particular, published by two of my Cambridge colleagues: *Down the Rabbit Hole: The Absurd Anti-Logic of the American Economic System* by Susanna Atkins, and *Batshit Crazy: Economics in America* by Reginald Dwight.

Early in the 21st century, some Americans began to raise the question of whether America's economic and financial systems made any sense. They asked how it came to be that personal mortgages were bundled into complicated arrangements for wealthy speculators to gamble with. They asked why the economy seemed to be based upon the incessant creation of financial "bubbles" for financiers to capitalise on. They asked why the stock market, which once simply served the function of raising capital for business creation, had become a means of sophisticated financial gambling whose stakes were the economic livelihood of the entire country.

The Americans who were puzzled by such dynamics asked questions such as: What does any of this have to do with "Life, Liberty and the pursuit of Happiness"? What does any of this have to do with having a good life?

The short answer is that it is questionable as to what degree advancing such concerns had ever been the goal of the American economic system. The only thing that can be said with certainty is that over time the economy grew to actively work against them.

□ □ □

The deepest and most fundamental problem with the American economic system was a dynamic that historians have grown to consider—in an American expression of the time—as "the elephant in the room." The expression refers to a problem that is so large that by unspoken agreement it becomes invisible. On the rare instances when somebody attempts to point out the presence of the elephant, everyone else in the room responds, "What elephant?" In the case of America's economic system, the elephant in the room was the country's addiction to economic growth.

When conducting research on economic issues in America, one cannot help but notice the emphasis on economic growth. It was the primary value in American economics. Media reports focused almost exclusively on whether the economy was growing, or on whether it was growing quickly enough. One is struck at how this indicator was given such primary importance, and other indicators were ignored, such as whether people were healthy, satisfied, and not procuring their meals from dumpsters.

Americans did not really consider whether economic growth bore any relationship to their quality of life, or contributed to a meaningful existence. In fact, Americans considered economic growth to be a substitute for meaning, or considered the terms to by synonymous. A revealing editorial, published late in America's decline, makes this abundantly clear. Written by a prominent American businessperson, it was openly endorsed by America's president and a wide variety of prominent Americans. The editorial, entitled "The Meaning of Life," contains the following key point:

> It is deeply engrained in the human soul that today should be better than yesterday, and that tomorrow should be better than today. It is within the nature of human beings to grow and evolve, to invent and explore, and to seek better ways to live. Our goal is to leave the world better than when we found it. In other words, to leave the world with more money.

Economic growth was positive. More importantly, economic growth was necessary. As a result, anything that hindered economic growth was defined as "bad." Unfortunately, things that hindered economic growth included full employment, affordable housing, and a healthy environment—things which may generally be thought of as good things.

America's addiction to economic growth helps explain an aspect of American life that has long puzzled students of American history. America during its prime was the richest country in the history of human civilisation. One would think that America's immense wealth would have resulted in a sort of "golden age"—an age in which the basic needs could be provided to all people, freeing them from economic worry in order to pursue meaningful and creative endeavours. Yet this did not happen. America's economic system would not let it happen.

American economists spoke of the *growth imperative*. It was vitally important that the economy grow at a minimum rate of approximately three percent per year. Although as a rule economists rejected suggestions that America might be *addicted* to economic growth, they freely admitted that the economy had to continue growing or else it would collapse. This was most plainly manifest in the economic conditions of *recession* and *depression*—both due to failures to sustain adequate economic growth. Growth below a certain level resulted in a recession, whereas a complete cessation of growth resulted in a depression.

The cause of the addiction lay in one simple dynamic at the heart of the American economic system. The answer lay in the answer to the seldom asked question: *Where does money come from?* In America, the full reality of the answer was hidden behind common misperceptions and half-truths.

An incredibly naïve view, although widely believed by the majority of Americans, was that money was printed by the government. Of course, this neglected the fact that only a miniscule portion of the nation's money existed in printed form. And even though the government printed a limited amount of money, the government did not simply give it away. This brings us to the question of how money was introduced into circulation.

Some Americans felt the answer was found in a dynamic that was a more sophisticated version of the idea that money was printed by the government. Although the government did not introduce money by printing it, there was a sense in which money was indeed introduced by the government. This was the dynamic by which the Federal Reserve loaned money to the Treasury, which used it to pay for government expenses. Thus, additional money entered the American economy.

Although essentially true as far as it goes, this answer is misleading because it neglects to account for a vitally important fact: The dynamic did not introduce money, it introduced debt. The "money" created was in the form of a loan that needed to be paid back. By this dynamic, the creation a trillion dollars to the economy was accompanied by adding a trillion dollars to the national debt. And that debt needed to be paid off somehow.

The only way to pay off the debt was by the overall growth of the economy, allowing the government—through taxes—to pay off the debt. So the question becomes: *How did the overall economy grow?*

For the answer, we need to examine America's private banking system and the creation of interest-bearing loans. What very few Americans realised is that a loan did not consist solely of other people's savings or the assets of the bank. A percentage of every loan consisted of the creation of money that had no prior existence.

How America became addicted to economic growth is a fascinating story. The dynamic began in Europe and was imported to America early in its history. It can be traced to 17th century European bankers who figured out a clever way to increase their assets with no additional work. At the time, "money" was a receipt for gold brought to the banker for safekeeping. The bankers realised they could print receipts for which no gold existed. This would work as long as there was enough gold on hand for the small percentage who presented their receipts in order to withdraw their gold—a strategy which later became known as the *fractional reserve system*. And by introducing these "receipts" as interest-bearing loans, they could induce others to make money for them in order to pay off the interest.

The dynamic was given governmental blessing in the early 18th century, when France saved itself from financial collapse with the establishment of the Banque Royale under John Law. Law made an important distinction, which affected banking institutions for the remainder of history. He made a distinction between a passive treasury, where money just accumulated, and an active bank, where money was created.

Eventually, the increasing power of banks led to the introduction of all money in the industrialised nations to be made in this way. And after a few hundred years, economic systems around the world adopted what was only a vastly more complex and sophisticated version of the same dynamic.

Basically, money was an "IOU" issued by a bank. American economists Robert Heilbroner and Lester Thurow described this in the book *Economics Explained*:

> Why is it that banks create money when they make loans, but you and I do not, when we lend money? Because we all accept bank liabilities (deposits) as money, but we do not accept personal or business IOU's to make payments with. You cannot buy groceries with a General Motors IOU, but you can with a Chase Manhattan IOU—a check drawn on your account there.

Money was created by magic, out of nothing but future expectations. The problem was those "future expectations" translated to a debt that by its nature increased as it became pushed farther into the future. Money was created by interest-bearing loans, which needed to be paid off with more money. So to pay off the previous loans, there needed to be more loans to create more money. But then *those* loans had to be paid off with money, which required *more* loans.

Money needed growth, and growth needed money, and money needed growth. It was a trap, a vicious cycle, an addiction.

Several historians have noted that the dynamic was essentially a "pyramid scheme" or "Ponzi scheme"—the fraudulent investment scheme in which an increasing debt is passed on to future investors. The problem, of course, is such schemes are doomed to fail. This is why in America, as elsewhere, such schemes were strictly against the law. Yet few seemed to realise that the overall economy functioned as such a scheme.

Since American economists of the time had a vested interest in not understanding the dynamic, it went unnamed. Post-collapse economists from other countries attempted to label the dynamic with a variety of unimaginative names, such as *The Money-to-Debt Inverse Coefficient Function*. While perhaps being technically accurate, the name that captured the popular imagination was coined not by an economist, but by M.J. Perelman, a member of the famous British sketch comedy group *The Toad Elevating Moment*. According to Perelman:

> I wanted to help out the economists, because they weren't able to adequately describe the dynamic. I tried to imagine the place where money goes, the place where the more money Americans piled up the more they owed. I imagined it as a sort of "void." But this "void" was alive, it was hungry, it was insatiable. The more money it was fed, the hungrier it got. It was a monstrous and demanding addict with teeth and claws. Suddenly I realised what it was: a *Money Pit Junkie Monster*.

While economists appreciated the vivid imagery that helped non-economists comprehend the dynamic, they eventually reached consensus on the more academic-sounding *Money Pit*.

Although America refused to acknowledge the dynamic, or to consider its problems, in the 1930s one notable economist expressed concern over the negative effects of unlimited economic growth. British economist John Maynard Keynes was instrumental in developing the economic theories used by America and other countries in the 20th century. He recognised that economic growth was important. But he felt that it was important that economic growth should reach a point where it could stop. In 1933 he wrote:

> The economic problem, the struggle for subsistence, always has been the primary, most pressing problem of the human race. Thus for the first time since his creation man will be faced with his real, his permanent problem—how to use his freedom from pressing economic cares, how to live wisely and agreeably and well.
>
> When the accumulation of wealth is no longer of high social importance, there will be great changes in the code of morals. The

> love of money will be recognised for what it is, a somewhat disgusting morbidity, one of those semi-criminal, semi-pathological propensities which one hands over with a shudder to the specialists in mental disease.
>
> I see us free, therefore, to return to some of the most sure and certain principles of religion and traditional virtue—that avarice is a vice, that the exaction of usury is a misdemeanor, and the love of money is detestable.

For those unfamiliar with the religious terminology, *avarice* is the sin of "the excessive desire for wealth." The concept of *usury*, of charging interest on loans, was once considered such an evil that it was banned by the Catholic Church for over 12 centuries. The moral offense was that it obtained wealth without work, that it was a means to profit from someone else's hardship.

The introduction of money as interest-bearing debt explained not only how the American economy grew, but why it *had* to grow. America could never get to a point where growth could be "enough." It was impossible for America to achieve "freedom from pressing economic cares to live wisely and agreeably and well," even if the country had wanted to. This was why even though America had more money than ever before in human history, it still needed more.

Historically speaking, that is not how it was supposed to be. Per the intention of the United States Constitution, Congress was meant to have the power to issue and control the nation's money. Within two years after the adoption of the Constitution, the United States officially put itself under the control of private banking, and legitimised debt-based money as the only legal currency. It did this with the enactment of the First National Bank Act—a move engineered by Alexander Hamilton and the international financiers he represented. Just as the United States began its great experiment in political freedom, it made itself economically dependent.

As a result, America was caught in a trap. And even worse, it was unaware of the trap. The country was unable to understand why, even in times of relative abundance, there was never enough money. And since they did not understand the trap, they attempted to solve the problem with more economic growth, even though the addiction to economic growth was the problem.

Continued growth was not only necessary to keep the economy from collapsing, but was seen as the solution to all of America's social problems. It would reduce unemployment, eliminate poverty, assist housing affordability, reduce crime, prevent the breakdown of families, and build strong communities.

It may be argued that this approach had some justification during the period when economic growth made tangible improvements in people's lives. But the approach was not abandoned, even when it clearly was not working. Because over time, the overwhelming focus on economic growth did not improve America's social problems; it made them worse.

One aspect of addiction is that the addict continues with the addictive process even when it is not working. Rather than slowing down and questioning the process, the reaction of the addict is to go faster. This is why even when it was obvious that economic growth was not solving unemployment or ending poverty or doing any of the other things it was supposedly capable of doing, America kept trying it anyway.

America's Prime Directive

The addiction to growth was rarely questioned and was never seriously opposed. The little resistance that was offered was from environmentalists, for the somewhat obvious reason that infinite growth is not possible on a planet with finite resources. The claim that economic growth was capable of solving all of America's problems ran into serious difficulties when considering the problem of environmental destruction. The problem was that economic growth was one of the main factors causing it.

Yet advocates of economic growth claimed that only continued economic growth could generate the money necessary to preserve the environment, resulting in the absurd conclusion that it was necessary to destroy the environment in order to save it. In 2027, when Treasury Secretary Megan Voss was asked by a reporter to confirm this reasoning, she replied, "How else will we generate the money to save it?"

Beginning at the turn of the 21st century, it was occasionally argued that economic growth was not destructive because the economy had become an *information economy* which was no longer tied to physical resources. Unfortunately this view was deeply mistaken, because the information economy was thoroughly dependent on the resource economy to support it. The information economy did not replace the resource economy, it just added another level. In fact, as the information economy grew, so did overall consumption. All those information workers required food, housing, energy, transportation, and all the other material goods and luxuries Americans considered essential—all of which required physical resources. This would not have been a problem had those resources been used sustainably. But they were not.

Obviously, human civilization requires both a healthy economy and a healthy environment. Yet America's addiction to economic growth impelled the country toward policies that degraded the health of both.

Many historians are of the opinion that the failure of America's environmental movement was not the fault of the environmental organisations, but of an economic system giving Americans a false choice. Every conservation battle was framed as a choice of saving the environment versus saving the economy.

In one of the more imaginative formulations of this notion, a developer seeking permission to destroy a wetland claimed it was "A choice of the ability of Americans to put food on the table or to look at a frog." In the end, the developer ended up winning despite the heartwarming efforts of local school students who formed a "Save the Wetland" movement complete with t-shirts emblazoned with messages such as "Frogs are people too" and "Keep the wetlands wet."

Since Americans felt a much more tangible connection to the economy, their environment suffered a slow death. Thus, America sacrificed its environment for an economic system that was irrevocably headed toward collapse. In not searching for a means in which to choose both, America ultimately chose neither. As a result, it was simply a matter of which collapsed first.

There is another critically important reason why economic growth necessarily resulted in environmental destruction. It was due to the value that America's economic system ascribed to the environment—to the overall system of interconnected life upon which human life is dependent. America's economic system ascribed to this system the value of zero.

This fact stretches credulity to the breaking point. In fact, when graduate students in economics are presented this fact of America's economic system, they initially refuse to believe it. They assume it must be a joke. But it is not.

One of the most rudimentary aspects of America's economic system was the concept of *throughput*. The most basic example of material production is the simple conversion of physical resources into money: harvest some trees from a forest, or some fish from a river, and sell them. Yet such resources were not considered to have any intrinsic value beyond their economic potential. The ability of ecosystems to sustain life did not enter the cost-benefit analysis. It had no effect on the bottom line.

America's economic system did not count the cost of resource depletion. It did not count the health costs of pollution. It did not count the costs of repairing ecological damage. It did not count the costs of destroyed fisheries, degraded rangeland, depleted aquifers, or declining forests. Industrial agriculture was considered to be the least expensive way to produce food only because it did not count the costs of eroded soils, pesticide contamination, health problems due to nutritionally poor food, and the medical costs of agricultural workers sickened by agricultural chemicals.

In economic terms, such costs were *externalities*—meaning that they were external to economic considerations. America's most brilliant economist defined an externality as: "A cost of economic activity that is not paid by the individual or organization that profited by the activity." The problem is, of course, that those costs were not external to the rest of society.

America's highly competitive free-enterprise economy meant that, in order to survive, businesses were impelled to reduce costs. This had results that in some ways could be considered positive, in the sense of discovering efficiencies that resulted in reduced prices. Yet the competitive advantage also went to businesses that were the most successful at externalising costs. Thus, companies that attempted to be more ethical than others were put at a competitive disadvantage.

□ □ □

The result of America's addiction to economic growth was that money became the ultimate value and arbiter of worth. When making decisions about domestic policy, America did not ask qualitative questions pertaining to a positive goal, or to a vision of what was good or right. It asked the quantitative question of which course would result in the most economic growth.

This resulted in an entire society heavily biased toward the needs of the business and financial interests that were the sources of that growth.

In America's economy, the source of money, ultimately, was a bank. Money entered the economy via the dynamic of investment and growth, which originated with businesses and corporations. Since America was dependent on economic growth as an overall dynamic, then the tangible focus of that dependence was placed upon the individuals and organisations at the heart of that dynamic.

A nation with an economy based on money introduced as interest-bearing debt has in essence chosen its national philosophy, its prime directive. For both parties, domestic policy became "more money," and foreign policy became focused on business interests—either thinly disguised or openly admitted.

As a result of this dependence, the heroes of society became the entrepreneurs and business leaders who created growth. Throughout America's history this was openly embraced by the Republican Party, whose values were always more consistent with those of business interests. Yet over time, the Democratic Party—which had long claimed to be "the party of the people"—gradually realised the need to worship the same heroes.

Yet if both parties had the same heroes, then their ideologies led them to focus on different villains. The problem, from the republican point of view, was the greedy lower classes that wanted to take too much of the economic pie. From the democratic point of view, it was the greedy upper classes that refused to share their portion of the economic pie. But both parties were unified in their need to keep that pie growing.

This is a main reason why both political parties increasingly became two sides of what social critic Noam Chomsky called the "Business Party" and why the political process became increasingly dominated by corporate interests. Corporate profit was synonymous with the economic growth from which all Americans would supposedly benefit. Or in any case was necessary to keep the economy from collapsing.

Government at both the state and federal level had little choice but to give tax breaks and favours to corporate interests. If state governments asked too much of them, they would leave the state. If the federal government asked too much, they would leave the country.

The "hero worship" of business leaders grew phenomenally in the final decades of American history, as the economy began to seriously deteriorate and the country became desperate for saviours. By the 2040s, government leaders treated them like royalty. As for the public, business leaders had grown to occupy the role once filled by famous pop musicians. Screaming fans filled outdoor stadiums and cheered at PowerPoint presentations that promised future prosperity.

This brings us to a perennial economic question concerning the relationship between supply-side versus demand-side economics. A rational examination concludes that both aspects are necessary to the overall functioning of an economic system. Businesses need money to create goods and services, and the public needs money to purchase them. Which is why economic theories have generally sought ways to balance supply-side economics (that favoured consumers) with demand-side economics (that favoured producers).

This commonsense view had previously been acknowledged in America. It was the view of American automaker Henry Ford, one of the most successful businessmen in American history, whose Model T automobile revolutionised America in the 1920s. Ford realized that his autoworkers were not just his employees, they were also his customers, so he raised his wages so his workers could afford the Model T automobiles they were building. He knew that when workers had more money, businesses had more customers.

Ultimately, businesses do not create jobs. They can only create positions. Whether the businesses have the money to pay the salaries for those positions depends on whether the businesses have customers with the money to support them. Companies have always claimed to be the job creators, but Ford knew that middle class spending was what made those jobs possible.

Yet to whatever degree American businesses understood this, they kept that knowledge secret. Generally speaking, American businesses wanted their customers rich and their employees poor. But if all businesses take this approach, and if national economic policy does nothing to compensate, then the overall dynamic drives all employees toward poverty.

National economic policy in fact did nothing to compensate. Beginning in the 1980s, attempts at balance were abandoned as economic policy swung toward a total embrace of supply-side principles. This was justified with the claim that, in the long run, pro-business policies that helped the upper class would spur investment, resulting in job creation and economic growth that would "trickle down" to everybody. Thus, the creation of the *trickle-down theory* that would dominate America for the remainder of its history.

Business interests, and the politicians that were dependent upon them, shared an almost religious faith in the doctrine of supply-side economics to right all wrongs and correct all imbalances. From the 1980s through the entirety of America's decline and fall, trickle-down theory was held to be not only the preferred theory, but essentially the *only* theory.

As can be imagined, the money distributed to the top did not always "trickle down," but was often diverted in ways other than the promised job-creating investments. The money led to increasingly spectacular executive salaries. Or the money was diverted into offshore tax havens. Or the money was invested not in company expansion, but in speculative ventures that promised returns faster than the "old-fashioned" strategy of growing a productive business.

The fears of Henry Ford became realised on a massive scale in the rise of national chains of discount stores. This is especially exemplified in the instance of Walmart—at one time the world's largest company with annual profits of $15 billion. Their tremendous size gave the company unequalled efficiencies of scale, as well as the economic power to demand deep wholesale price cuts from suppliers. This was combined with the company's infamously low wages, allowing them to offer products at prices that could not be matched by smaller businesses that paid living wages. It was a brilliant strategy that resulted in the Walton Family becoming the wealthiest family in America, worth a combined total of approximately $140 billion.

While it is outside the scope of this book to argue for or against various economic theories, what cannot be denied is that the forces of capitalism, left unchecked and without corrective balance, inevitably work toward wealth inequality and the consolidation of economic power by the few and powerful.

All of this was routinely ignored. A continuous series of studies proved many times over that supply-side economics was terribly flawed. Yet the studies made no difference. Taking action on the results would have worked against too many powerful interests. Despite abundant evidence that trickle-down economics did not work, the theory could not be abandoned, because it formed the sole justification for America's open bias toward wealthy interests, for regressive tax policies, and for economic policies and trade agreements that steadily eroded the financial health of the majority of its population.

□ □ □

Such dynamics evolved along with the American economy. After American manufacturing peaked in the late 1970s, financial services began displacing manufacturing as the primary source of American wealth. By 2010, bankers and financial specialists had almost totally replaced industrialists as the economic leaders. As a result, the economy came to reflect the needs of bankers and financial specialists as the American economy became based primarily upon financial speculation.

Of course, the economy had always been based to a degree upon speculation. Americans invested in stocks, but for most Americans throughout the country's history it was for actual productive investment for moderate returns, not speculative investment for quick riches. Yet that changed as the financial industry realized the profits that could be made. As a result, financial arrangements evolved in directions bringing the most profit to those with the ability to manipulate them toward their own ends.

The increasing financialisation of the economy is linked to the process that economic historians refer to as *delinking money from value*. Money once consisted of precious metals that allowed standard units of exchange. Later, it became more safe and convenient to store the precious metal in a bank vault and issue paper money that could be exchanged for the metal on demand. When America ended the gold standard in 1971, the global economy was no longer linked to anything of value.

The next step was made possible due to the digital revolution of the 1980s. Computerisation combined with the internet to meld all global financial markets into a single system. Computers were programmed to automatically execute transactions of billions of dollars in seconds. Those programs put no importance on what stocks or what companies were being invested in, or on the ramifications of the trading activity.

This brings us to consider the rise of derivatives, which were a type of financial contract whose value was determined by fluctuations in underlying assets. They often consisted of complex arrangements such as collateralized debt obligations and credit default swaps. Derivatives could be used for speculation in betting on the future price of an asset, or for insuring against risk on an asset. They gave investors the ability to leverage their own funds without actually borrowing. Eventually, the abstractions of the finance game became endlessly and mind-bogglingly complex to the point where no single individual was capable of understanding it.

This form of speculative trade became known as "casino capitalism." The financial market abandoned productive investment in favour of investment without consideration of anything outside the world of the abstractions. But the problem was that the results were not abstract. The abstract numbers had tangible effects on the real world.

The successes of such investing added little or nothing to the real economy, while the disasters transferred wealth from taxpayers to financiers. Rather than wealth "trickling down" it was becoming "siphoned up."

The game began to be referred to by some Americans as *predatory finance* or *extractive investment*. The original idea of investment was that it should contribute to the overall wealth and well-being of society. Yet the American economy grew to reward extractive investors who did not create wealth, but simply extracted it from the rest of the economy. The investor's gain, therefore, was at the expense of society.

This became painfully obvious after a series of bailouts in which a minority of investors made tremendous profits, while the taxpaying public was left to pay the price. The first was the Savings and Loan Crisis of the late 1980s, largely caused by deregulation of the financial industry. As a result, over 1,000 Savings and Loan institutions failed. The resultant bailout cost American taxpayers over $400 billion.

As devastating as this was, it was minor compared to the next crisis, variously called The Subprime Crisis or The Subprime Mortgage Meltdown or simply The Financial Crisis of 2007-2008.

The crisis was caused by Wall Street investment firms conducting risky bets in mortgage-backed securities. It involved incredibly complicated financial inventions that brought huge profits via inflated housing prices, creating an enormous financial bubble. When the inevitable collapse occurred, it caused the values of securities tied to real estate prices to plummet. This triggered the collapse of a complex relationship of agreements that encouraged home ownership based on loans involving bundled subprime mortgages.

The stock market crashed, and millions of Americans were shocked to discover that the value of their stocks had plummeted to a fraction of their worth. In 2008, American household wealth fell 18 percent, by $11.1 trillion. Millions of Americans lost their homes and jobs.

The crisis resulted in what became known as *The Great Recession*, an extended period of serious economic decline. There were fears of the continued viability of major financial institutions, some of which were considered to be so vital to the American economy that they were "too big to fail." To prevent this failure, the government launched an unprecedented series of financial manipulations. One of which was a massive project of bailouts of some of America's largest banks and investment firms.

The Federal Reserve, America's central bank, expanded the money supply to prevent a devastating decline in consumption. In addition, the government enacted large stimulus packages totaling nearly $1 trillion, and purchased trillions of dollars of debt from banks. The administration of President George W. Bush authorised the *Troubled Asset Relief Program*, a $700 billion bank bailout plan. These combined efforts made up the largest monetary action in world history.

The bailouts were essentially done at public expense, by adding them to the national debt to be repaid—with interest—by taxpayers. The American public felt cheated. After facing devastating financial losses, they were being asked to bail out the institutions they felt were responsible for those losses.

Plutocracy, the Deep State, and the Corruption of American Media

Why did America choose to operate under such a nonsensical and counterproductive economic system? The answer is that America did not make the choice. The system was effectively chosen by a small minority that was able to make incredible profits from it. And this small minority was not subject to democratic control.

In President Dwight D. Eisenhower's 1961 farewell address, he famously warned: "In the councils of government, we must guard against the acquisition of unwarranted influence, whether sought or unsought, by the military-industrial complex." The expression *military-industrial complex* became deeply imbedded in the American imagination. But the influence of the military-industrial complex in 1961 was tame compared to what it would become in the coming decades.

In 1971, corporate lawyer and future Supreme Court Justice Lewis Powell wrote an eight-page memo entitled "Attack on the American Free Enterprise System." Powell believed the Chamber of Commerce needed to transform itself from a passive business group into a powerful political force.

The memo outlined ways that corporations could eliminate the influence of those who were hostile to corporate interests, and described a strategy that was essentially a blueprint for corporate domination of American democracy. American business needed to recognise that political power must be "assiduously cultivated; and that when necessary, it must be used aggressively and with determination." Soon thereafter, the Chamber's board of directors formed a task force of 40 business executives to review Powell's memo and draft a list of specific proposals.

Powell's memo is widely credited for having helped catalyze a new business activist movement, leading to numerous organisations devoted to advancing the corporate agenda, including the Business Roundtable, the American Legislative Exchange Council, The Heritage Foundation, the Cato Institute, Americans for Prosperity, and many others.

The strategy was also applied to America's legislative branch. In 2010, the decades-long drive to strike down campaign finance laws resulted in a major victory with the Supreme Court's groundbreaking decision in *Citizens United v. the Federal Election Commission*. The court ruled that corporations could spend unlimited amounts to influence elections, equating money with free speech. This came as a shock to most, who had assumed that the Founding Fathers had intended free speech to be consist of speeches in public squares or pamphlets to be handed out on public sidewalks.

Americans liked to believe that allowing social choices to be decided by money ensured freedom from bias. But money is never unbiased. Money responds to needs backed by money—and it responds most to needs backed by the most money. Left to itself, money does not respond to the needs of children, or of future generations, or of the ability of the planet to sustain life.

Americans believed in the doctrine of *consumer sovereignty*, which held that the marketplace is a perfect democracy in which one dollar equals one vote. Yet this ignored that while some individuals had billions of votes, others had none. And it ignored that those with the most votes used them in ways to ensure they would continue to have the most votes.

The 1980s witnessed a dramatic rise in corporate power. Yet in America, corporations initially had little power at all. Corporations were originally temporary arrangements, chartered for fixed periods of time to achieve specific purposes. Members of the corporation were personally liable for debts incurred by the corporation during their membership, thus there was a heavy incentive to take a fiscally conservative approach.

Gradually, corporations gained enough political control to rewrite the laws governing their existence. Charters were issued in perpetuity, and the liability of corporate owners and managers was limited. Corporations became no longer limited to specific public projects, and could operate however they chose within the limits of the law. Eventually, they became powerful enough to change those limits.

This was most obviously the case with a small number of corporations in vital industries that had grown disproportionately powerful. This included media conglomerates, oil companies, military contractors, major agribusiness and pharmaceutical companies, and major players in banking and finance. It was such corporations with seemingly endless resources that were able to effectively steer America in their favour.

Large corporations grew to have so much power that they went beyond advising government policy to writing it themselves. Representatives from the pharmaceutical industry wrote health insurance legislation. Major multinational corporations met to decide on the trade policies America would adopt. Representatives from energy companies met secretly to determine American energy policy, with representatives from organisations advocating sustainable energy and environmental protection specifically excluded.

The rise in corporate power also led to a steady rise in what Americans called *corporate welfare*, consisting of subsidies, bailouts, government contracts, and loan guarantees. And as this form of welfare to the most wealthy individuals and corporations was rising, welfare for the most impoverished citizens was increasingly attacked and steadily eliminated.

This trend did not go unnoticed in America. At the time, American economist Paul Krugman warned, "We are on the road not just to a highly unequal society, but to a society of an oligarchy." In response to the Citizens United decision, former President Jimmy Carter said in an interview that America had become "an oligarchy, with unlimited political bribery."

In 1941, American lawyer and Supreme Court Justice Louis D. Brandeis wrote, "We must make our choice. We may have democracy, or we may have wealth concentrated in the hands of a few, but we can't have both." From the 1980s onward, it was becoming increasingly apparent to a growing number of Americans that, despite the appearance of living in a democracy, the reality was that they were not.

Yet most Americans persisted in believing they lived in a functioning democracy. Perhaps they were fooled into this belief by the fact that every four years they were asked to vote, despite the fact that their choices of representation were largely pre-selected, as were the choices those representatives would make once elected.

Many felt that America had entered a new era of "post-democracy," although nobody was quite sure of what exactly it was or what to call it. The American newspaper *The New York Times* referred to it as an *overall corporate-government complex*. Another American newspaper, *The Wall Street Journal*, called it *benign totalitarianism*.

American political philosopher Sheldon S. Wolin coined the term *inverted totalitarianism* to describe the American system of power. Unlike overt totalitarianism, inverted totalitarianism does not centre upon a demagogue or charismatic leader. Its power originates in the decentralised forces of the corporate state.

Comparing American democracy of the time with the fall of Weimar Democracy in 1930s Germany, Wolin wrote:

> In one sense, a true democracy and a dictatorship are mutually exclusive. Our thesis, however, is this: it is possible for a form of totalitarianism, different from the classical one, to evolve from a putatively "strong democracy" instead of a "failed" one. A weak democracy that fails, such as that of Weimer, might end in classical totalitarianism, while a failed strong democracy might lead to inverted totalitarianism.

One aspect of totalitarianism of all varieties is that it includes a "totalising" focus that ruthlessly directs all resources, functions, and processes of a country toward and all-encompassing goal. In the overt totalitarianisms of the 1930s, the focus was on *total war*. This focus became something of a "vision statement" for the entire culture, as all decisions were made in consideration of their effect on the unifying goal. In the inverted totalitarianism of America, the focus was on corporate profit.

This brings us to another way of envisioning the emerging post-democracy state of America: *the deep state*. American congressional aide Mike Lofgren defined the deep state as:

> A hybrid association of key elements of government and parts of top-level finance and industry that is effectively able to govern the United States with only limited reference to the consent of the governed as normally expressed through elections.

The unacknowledged ideology of the deep state was based on privatisation, outsourcing, deindustrialism, and the deregulation and financialisation of the economy.

Both of America's political parties worked toward advancing the ideology, no matter which political party was in power. No matter how much democrats and republicans differed, there was always consensus toward funding projects important to the deep state. At a time when America could not afford things like health care, education, sustainable energy, or repairing America's aging infrastructure, somehow there was enough money for things such as $6 trillion for wars in Iraq and Afghanistan, $12.8 trillion for Wall Street bailouts, $37.5 billion per year to subsidise oil companies, and $1.5 trillion for the F35 military aircraft project.

Financial deregulation proceeded steadily no matter what political party was in power. The republican administration of President Ronald Reagan began the deregulation of Wall Street in the 1980s. But it was continued by democratic administrations, such as when President Bill Clinton signed the repeal of the Glass-Steagall Act, a key banking regulation, and in 2000 approved the deregulation of derivatives with the Commodities Futures Modernization Act.

Which brings us to reconsider America's military-industrial complex and how it grew substantially in size and power. Private corporations became deeply entrenched with the military, as America moved substantial functions into the private sector via the use of military contractors. The process greatly accelerated when Vice President Dick Cheney began to outsource military logistical and support functions to companies such as to Halliburton—a corporation with which Cheney had substantial ties.

The military even contracted some combat operations to mercenary organisations. One controversial incident, which proved to be a great international embarrassment for America, involved a company called Blackwater which massacred 17 Iraqi civilians. To give some idea of the power that private organisations had over the American government, a federal probe into the incident ended when a Blackwater official threatened to kill a State Department investigator.

What was scarcely reported in American news media is how the dynamic was self-supporting for all parties and heavily biased for the continuation of military aggression. Military contractors made incredible profits from Department of Defense contracts, which made it possible to provide politicians with substantial campaign contributions. Yet it was necessary to justify to the American public the necessity of spending vast sums on military expenditures. Therefore, all parties had a vested interest in the kind of military actions that justified sustaining the dynamic. As a Pentagon insider put it, "Continuing small wars, or the threat thereof, are essential for the corporate component of the military-industrial-congressional complex."

Mike Lofgren wrote: "The deep state is the big story of our time. It is the red thread that runs through the war on terrorism and the militarization of foreign policy, the financialization and deinstrialization of the American economy, and the rise of a plutocratic social structure that has given us the most unequal society in almost a century." Yet the deep state—the "big story of our time"—was scarcely mentioned in American news media. Such oversight was no accident.

America's Founding Fathers were well aware that one of the most vital aspects of democracy is an informed citizenry. Because of this, the Founding Fathers gave special attention toward guaranteeing freedom of the press. But this founding principle of democracy became seriously threatened at this critical time in American history when corporate control was having a corrupting effect on democracy. The media ignored it because the same thing was happening to the media.

By the year 2000, media companies had consolidated into nine transnational conglomerates that owned all the major film studios and television networks, as well as many top cable channels, magazines, newspapers, major-market television stations, and book publishers.

These conglomerates had unified economic and political interests that were essentially similar to all other corporations in America. In addition, the media relied for income upon advertising, which was provided by corporations. The result was that, to the extent America had become a plutocracy, the media came to represent the interests of that plutocracy.

Executives, managers, editors, reporters, and journalists shared an unspoken understanding that they needed to be very careful about content damaging to business interests. In many cases, the unspoken understanding was to avoid such content entirely. Or as was often the case, the media chose content that was superficial or meaningless. The result was an inordinate amount of attention given to celebrity scandals, new product releases, professional sports, and movie releases. Disasters and violent incidents of all varieties were always popular.

A prominent example that combined sports, celebrity, and violence was the murder trial of sports star and movie celebrity O.J. Simpson, which dominated media coverage for months, drastically reducing the need to provide substantial and costly news coverage of things that really mattered.

But there is another important factor in explaining American media's focus on superficial journalism. For most Americans, it was what they wanted. Media that provided in-depth reporting did poorly by comparison. Although the media was dominated by superficial journalism, other options existed.

America had sources of alternative media that covered important stories—generally ignored by the mainstream media—that were directly related to the decline of America. Such as the existence of the deep state. Such as the revelation that the richest one percent of Americans hid trillions of dollars in offshore tax havens to evade taxes. Such as the ongoing efforts by government representatives and agribusiness companies to discredit scientists and suppress research that revealed the serious health threats of agricultural herbicides.

One major news story involved a project known as the Dakota Access Pipeline, a long-distance pipeline to transport oil from North Dakota. To avoid potential resistance from citizens concerned about oil spills, the pipeline was routed as far as possible from population centres. This resulted in a route that bordered Native American territories. The route went along or over—and in some cases underneath—tribal water sources. It went through land that was still in dispute, through areas promised to Native Americans by treaties which the American government refused to honour. Many protests and actions resulted, with a massive standoff near the Standing Rock Indian Reservation, in which an unprecedented number of representatives from over 300 Native American tribes met for their largest collective protest since the 1800s. The standoff was joined and supported by Americans from all over the country.

Remarkably, this was largely ignored by most of mainstream American media, and what little coverage was offered was extremely biased against the protestors. Curiously, the media from other countries was far more interested and their coverage was much more accurate.

But perhaps the most significant story ignored by America's mainstream media was one that had immense implications for the American system of economics and finance. It had to do with what was occurring in Iceland during America's financial crisis of 2007-2008. At the same time, Iceland was going through a similar crisis. After Iceland's banking sector was privatised in 2000, private bankers borrowed $120 billion—ten times the size of Iceland's economy. This created a tremendous economic bubble that doubled housing prices and made a small percentage of the country's population very wealthy. When the bubble burst, the nation was on the verge of bankruptcy and its citizens were left with an unpayable debt.

In 2008, at the same time as America was arranging a controversial taxpayer-sponsored bailout of major banks and financial institutions, the outraged population of Iceland took to the streets. Over five months, the main bank of Iceland was nationalised, government officials were forced to resign, the old government was liquidated, and a new government was established. In 2010, the people voted to deny payment of the tremendous debt created by the bankers, and approximately 200 high-level executives and bankers were either arrested or faced criminal charges. 2011, a new constitutional assembly rewrote the Iceland constitution to avoid entrapment by debt-based loans. By 2012, Iceland's economy was healthy and recovering, and had been successfully re-organised to serve the citizens rather than the banks.

America might have been inspired to try something similar. That is, if America had known about it.

These extraordinary events were almost totally ignored by the mainstream news media. We can only assume that the American mainstream news media, closely aligned with the interests of America's financial powers, did not want American citizens to get any radical ideas.

THE HAVES AND THE HAVE-NOTS

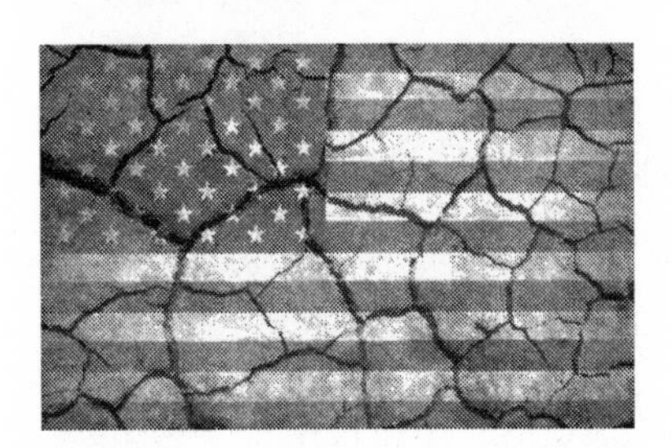

Necessary Unemployment and the Unaffordability of Living

We are all utterly dependent upon the processes of life to provide food, water, shelter, clothing, and all the other necessities of living. Yet for residents of modern civilisation, the connection to those processes is often so indirect that it seems unreal. Primary importance is placed not on access to the processes of life, but to a paycheck. And that paycheck is the means to access those processes. Since access to money equals access to life, to be unemployed is to be cut off from life.

Yet a little-known fact of growth-based economics was that it actually *depended* on a certain amount of unemployment. In America, economic growth was universally touted as the answer to unemployment. Yet the unacknowledged reality was that economic growth could never eliminate unemployment. The reason is simple: If there had been full employment, the economy would have collapsed.

This is because of an economic principle known as the *Phillips Curve*. In 1958, New Zealand economist William Phillips published a paper about his observation that when unemployment rose, wages fell. Essentially, the Phillips Curve charts a relationship based on the dynamic of supply and demand. A surplus of employees means low demand, which forces the employees to compete by accepting lower wages. This is beneficial for employers. A shortage of employees means high demand, which forces the employers to compete by offering higher wages. This is not beneficial for employers. If the employer has to pay too much in wages, then the company will not be able to expand. And if this happens throughout the entire economy, then companies will not expand and economic growth will stop. For economies addicted to growth, as America was, the result would be economic collapse.

Curiously, the necessity of unemployment to sustain the economy was something of an open secret. Privately, powerful forces in business and finance understood this. In one extremely telling incident, Federal Reserve Board Chairman Alan Greenspan publicly expressed concern over what he called "dangerously low levels of unemployment." Yet publicly, economists and government officials were united in their claim that the solution to unemployment was economic growth, despite the fact that the conditions that make economic growth possible make unemployment necessary.

Very occasionally, American politicians would make the campaign promise of working toward full employment. We may wonder whether they were utterly ignorant of economic realities or were blatantly manipulating the American public with ideas they knew could never be implemented.

Each individual instance of unemployment is different, and it is not easy to discern to what degree the cause is individual lack of initiative or social forces beyond individual control. And there are complex issues involved in the question of whether full employment as a goal is realistic or even desirable. Yet what cannot be denied is that no matter how successful the individual effort, and regardless of social factors, one result of America's economic system was that it required a portion of the population to be economically disenfranchised.

□ □ □

Exacerbating the problem was that the cost of living was rising dramatically, most prominently in one of the basic requirements of human life. For the sake of the American economy, it was necessary to commoditise all aspects of life into expenses that could contribute to economic growth. One way America accomplished this was by taking measures to ensure increasingly expensive housing, thus turning one of life's most basic essentials into a primary engine of economic growth. As a result, shelter—otherwise known as *home*—was turned into the most expensive commodity.

So expensive, in fact, that an increasing number of Americans became unable to own their own homes. Renters were not spared, since the increased cost of rental property was passed on to them. In all cases, the proportion of personal income devoted to housing rose steadily. Housing became the single costliest expense of life, taking the largest proportion of lifetime income.

One of the key methods America used to achieve this was with their building codes. Originally, building codes were justified as a safety concern, due to shoddy construction methods. Yet over time, the codes became more oriented toward insuring the safety of profit for the building industry.

The codes evolved to not only encourage the construction of larger and more expensive homes, but to require them. In America, homes had a minimum size requirement, and the building codes allowed only construction materials and specialised construction methods that would ensure steady business for the associated industries. Affordability and ecological integrity were not only discouraged, they were explicitly banned. A modest and inexpensive home built from locally obtained natural materials, and built using simple and inexpensive methods that homeowners could utilise themselves, was literally against the law.

A large and powerful complex of industries had arisen whose profit was based on expensive homes, and worked to ensure the situation would continue to remain profitable. It included the banking and finance industry, which made substantial profits from home loans. It included homebuilder associations, developers, timber companies, and other businesses associated with the building industry. It included the entire Real Estate industry, including real estate agents, appraisers, and a variety of related occupations.

It also included the government. Since the government was able to generate income only by taxing property and income, it was in the government's interest to support rising property values and the incomes levels adequate to afford them.

In the early years of American history, the primary threat to the American way was anything that endangered freedom. This primary threat became replaced by anything that endangered economic growth. Therefore, affordable housing was unavailable as an option. Too much was at stake; too many financial interests were at risk. So even though Americans considered themselves to be free, their choices of housing were tightly constrained. For Americans in the more desirable portions of America that offered good employment opportunities, their "freedom of choice" was largely limited to what colour to paint their $300,000 home.

The Americans who were fortunate enough to own their own homes became some of the fiercest advocates for the situation. Having become homeowners, their motivation was not only to protect that hard-earned equity, but to increase its value. For many Americans, home equity and the assumption of rising value was the most important means of obtaining enough wealth to comfortably retire.

However, the expectation of rising value led to a tremendous social problem. In order to make money on a home, it had to increase in value faster than the overall rate of inflation. The problem was that each generation, therefore, had to pay more for housing—requiring an ever-increasing proportion of personal income. At one time in America, it took 30 years of one full-time income to purchase a home. Over time, it became increasingly difficult even with two full-time incomes. Obviously, such a trend could not be sustained. As with economic growth, real estate had become a kind of "pyramid scheme" in which an increasing debt was passed on to future generations, with the hope that they would have the ability to keep the game going.

Since affordable housing was perceived as a threat to property values, proposals for affordable housing options in American neighbourhoods were frequently opposed by the American public.

For decades there had been an inexpensive housing option that Americans called *mobile homes* which were technically classified as trailers rather than homes. These usually existed in groups in what was called a *mobile home park*, which charged rent in exchange for a small personal "lot." However, there had been a concerted movement for decades to replace this option with more profitable housing, and over time they dwindled to very few remaining examples, mostly in rural areas. And those became further reduced in number as a result of many impoverished owners resorting to the dangerous manufacture of methamphetamines and other illegal drugs, and inadvertently blowing themselves up.

For many years there had been a movement toward alternative housing called *The Small Home Movement*, which had advocated for small, energy-efficient, inexpensive homes. Many of them were individual creations designed and built by the actual homeowner to suit their own requirements and aesthetic criteria. However, since almost no building codes or zoning laws in the entire country allowed them, it remained a "fringe" movement whose adherents needed to construct such homes in secret, or where enforcement was lax.

Yet when the lack of affordable housing options became a critical problem, a few bold pioneers dared to openly build such structures in defiance of the law. Their hope was to force the issue into public awareness, resulting in public pressure to change building codes and zoning restrictions. One prominent example involved Zed Freelander, a leader of the movement, who built such a home in 2027 and moved it to a lot he owned in a suburb of Des Moines, Iowa.

Almost everybody expected the government to condemn the structure and order its destruction. But in a wholly unexpected development, a group of neighbours destroyed it on their own. A neighbour explained the reaction by saying, "That damn hippie tried to destroy our property values." Although the local government was aware of the identity of the individuals who started the blaze, no suspects were charged. It was assumed that the government was pleased with the neighbours who took matters into their own hands, thus saving the government the expense of destroying the home themselves.

Such restrictions were expanded to America's rural areas. In places where citizens once had the freedom to live in any type of home they wanted, zoning changes began enforcing universal building codes. In some areas, it became illegal for Americans to camp on their own land. In extreme cases, Americans attempting a lifestyle which Americans called "back to the land" or "off the grid" were threatened with fines or arrests for things such as collecting rainwater or refusing to connect to local utilities.

In many cases, doing things more simply and inexpensively were attacked as being in opposition to the American way. Americans who chose to forgo a clothes dryer and instead hang their laundry outside were fiercely opposed due to their flagrant attack on American prosperity. Homeowners who chose to replace front lawns with vegetable gardens were similarly opposed. In one incident that received substantial media attention, a homeowner who attempted such a garden in 2025 aroused the ire of angry neighbors who complained "How can she be allowed to destroy my retirement plan so she can grow beans?" and "She should be forced to buy food just like everybody else."

Many local governments responded by passing laws which forbid the use of residential yards for any useful or practical purposes, and deemed only ornamental plants as permissible.

One is led to ask why Americans wanted larger and more expensive homes. One reason is that the choice was largely made for them. Yet even if less expensive options were available, it is questionable whether Americans would have chosen them. Americans equated progress with "bigger and more expensive," and anything that ran counter to this trend was seen as regression and sacrifice. Thus, the few Americans who were aware of more humble and less expensive options rejected them.

When public discussion focused on the lack of affordable housing, the proposed solution seldom involved building housing that was more affordable. The proposed solution was almost always to encourage more economic growth. Instead of making housing affordable, America attempted to make it possible for people to afford increasingly unaffordable homes. Since the economy would surely grow, higher housing costs were considered to be acceptable. The fact that housing costs were rising faster than the growth of the economy was not considered.

Some municipalities responded to the lack of affordable housing not by encouraging the construction of affordable housing, but encouraging the construction of large quantities of expensive housing. The philosophy behind this counterintuitive strategy was that—per the economic principle of supply-and-demand—the increased supply would work to make housing less expensive. As could be expected, this strategy helped the problem only minimally at best. Yet it should not be surprising that this was the solution offered, since it precisely aligned with the interests of developers and banks, who demonstrated unbridled enthusiasm in cooperating to make such programmes possible.

When rising housing costs became critical in the late 2020s, some Americans began applying pressure toward their political representatives to create more affordable housing. Yet the real estate and banking industries applied more pressure. Their basic message was succinctly stated by Howard Crawford, president of The National Association of Home Builders: "If Americans are allowed to build compact and inexpensive homes free of financial obligation to large companies, then how can those large companies make a lot of money?"

In addition, government officials were very aware of the detrimental effect that affordable housing would have on the economy. As a result, they had no choice but to explain to their constituents that affordable homes would be bad for America. In a statement that would become infamous, Massachusetts governor Ness Lessman said, "Unfortunately, we can't afford affordable homes."

Another factor in the increasing unaffordability of housing was the rising cost of land. Throughout American history, land was distributed solely on the basis of who could afford it. The only exception was on Native American reservations, whose populations continued to act on the belief that the earth belonged to no one. In areas of high housing demand, the land on which a home stood might cost more than the home. Even if the home had been built inexpensively, the cost of the land on which to build it would still make home ownership unaffordable.

Of course, the monetisation of earth's land surface was not unique to America. It was once common around the world, until America's fate made it clear that the concept was economically unsustainable and morally unjustifiable. As a result, a United Nations vote in 2068 resulted in the resolution that inhabiting a portion of the earth was a natural right, and that it was not necessary to earn the privilege to occupy the planet.

Surplus People and America's Invisible Population

From the 1980s onward, America was faced with a growing number of surplus people. Poverty increased, and many Americans found themselves living on the street. In 2012, the official poverty statistics determined that 46.5 million Americans fell beneath the official poverty line, the largest number since recordkeeping began 50 years earlier. Among those, nearly half lived in what was termed *deep poverty*, which was 50 percent below the official poverty line. The problem was not merely one of unemployment, since millions of Americans belonged to the "working poor," consisting of citizens who worked full time yet still lived in poverty. America's minority groups had it the worst. Of the number of Americans in deep poverty, 25 percent of those were Hispanic and 27 percent were black.

Although things were getting worse, most Americans had no idea of how bad it really was. Even though there were official figures for problems such as how many American children went to bed hungry each night, hardly anybody actually saw these hungry children. Except of course the parents, who likely also went to bed hungry. They were part of an "invisible population" not represented via mainstream media such as magazines, television, or movies.

No politician wanted to risk being blamed for the worsening situation, or to risk being held responsible for fixing it. And sustaining the reputation of America as "number one" would not be helped by publicly acknowledging bothersome statistics about hungry children. Feeding those children would have been a difficult political challenge. An easier course was to simply not acknowledge them.

Neither was it in the best interests of media to report on the full extent of the situation. Powerful corporate and financial interests discouraged reports of the worsening situation, many of which called into question the activities of powerful corporate and financial interests.

However, there were a few instances in which the invisible population was seen. In order to satisfy America's desire for trivial news, the media had become devoted to providing extensive coverage of sensational events such as anything that caught fire or exploded. As a result, the invisible population became briefly visible in the instances of protests or riots, since these provided images of things burning or exploding.

Entire segments of America were part of the invisible population. Native Americans had always been part of this population. So had the urban poor, largely consisting of blacks and other minorities, who had become isolated in urban enclaves. Little appreciated at the time was the plight of America's rural poor, isolated and trapped in the America's shrinking and disappearing small towns. Abandoned by industry, beset by large chain stores that destroyed local business, and with family farms replaced by large industrial agriculture enterprises, America's small towns had become impoverished remnants of their once proud past.

But what made the situation harder to accept was that the hardship was not being shared equally. While for the majority things were getting worse, for a small minority things were better than ever. In 2015, at a time when middle class jobs were disappearing and the standard of living for most Americans was declining, the annual pay of the CEOs of America's 350 largest corporations averaged $15.5 million—276 times the pay of the average worker.

The 1930s Great Depression and the experience of World War II galvanised America behind measures ensuring shared economic prosperity. America's postwar economic boom was marked by America's most equitable sharing of wealth and a substantial middle class.

But in a trend that began in the 1980s with President Ronald Reagan, America began deliberately enacting policies that increased wealth inequality. One aspect of this trend was an extraordinary series of economic trade agreements associated with the political philosophy of *neoliberalism*. Not to be confused with liberal political philosophy, neoliberalism refers to "liberating" the process of wealth creation and capital accumulation. It included policies such as privatisation, financial deregulation, free trade, lowered trade barriers, and reduced government influence on the economy.

In such a pro-business environment, corporations and financial organisations rapidly expanded and merged into large and increasingly powerful conglomerates, as the middle class shrank and poverty increased. At the same time, the rich got much richer. In 1980, there were 13 billionaires in America; in 2015 there were 540.

In the 1990s, the Clinton administration embraced neoliberalism with the passage of the North America Free Trade Agreement, or NAFTA. For propaganda purposes, NAFTA was labelled a "free-trade agreement." This was only superficially the case. It also included strong protectionist elements, and much of the agreement was about matters other than trade. It is more accurately thought of as an investor's rights agreement. The meaning of "free" in the context of the agreement was less about freedom of trade than in the freedom of money to move to wherever it made the most profit for the investors.

It resulted in a decades-long trend in what was called *outsourcing*, whereby jobs were shipped overseas to developing countries with lax labour laws and dismal wages. The result was a massive loss of jobs along with stagnant or falling pay for the jobs that remained, as workers were forced to compete for lower wages in a global "race to the bottom."

One extraordinary aspect of NAFTA was that it gave more power to business than to government, thus making political sovereignty subservient to corporate sovereignty. It did this by establishing the process of Investor-State Dispute Settlement, a system through which individual companies could sue countries. The process became widely known after tobacco company Philip Morris sued Uruguay after the country enacted measures to promote public health that were considered detrimental to the tobacco industry.

The resulting outsourcing of jobs combined with a growing movement of what Americans called *downsizing*, a kinder and gentler term to refer to mass layoffs. Much of this downsizing was accomplished due to the rapid advance of computers and digital technology. It allowed computer programs to eliminate or drastically reduce the need for human labour. It was a tremendous boon to business profits, almost all of which went to upper management.

The cumulative effect of all these trends was that while a small minority of Americans grew extremely wealthy, for most Americans their economic situation steadily declined.

□ □ □

America was faced with a growing crisis in poverty and homelessness. The country could have responded by seeking to create a more equitable distribution of wealth. But that would have opposed powerful interests who preferred the unequal distribution. As a result, the primary method used by America in response to the crisis was to criminalise the poor.

Vagrancy laws—which had gone unused for decades—were re-instituted and strengthened. Also reinstated were laws against *loitering*—which was the crime of standing in one place while being broke. An increasing number of municipalities took steps to ban public camping, to prohibit sleeping in public, and to prohibit sleeping in vehicles. Similar to the crime of loitering, it became illegal to sleep while being broke.

Some Americans felt such treatment to be a form of discrimination against the poor. But the government disagreed, with the claim that the laws applied to all Americans equally, whether they happened to be a homeless vagrant or a billionaire. All Americans, rich as well as poor, were not allowed to sleep in a park.

Some municipalities initiated laws banning panhandling. Panhandlers received tickets with high penalties, and few considered that someone who is panhandling can only pay the penalty by doing more panhandling. In one city, enforcement was taken so seriously that the police set up stings to trick homeless people into asking for money so they could be jailed.

In addition to criminalising Americans for being poor, they were increasingly criminalised for being hungry. Or rather, for attempting to resolve that hunger in ways that did not contribute to the economy. In an increasing number of cities, people could be arrested for scrounging for discarded food. Some cities even enacted laws against sharing food in public spaces, leading to members of charitable organisations to be arrested for giving away free food in public parks.

In this time of worsening economic and employment prospects, many impoverished Americans turned to crime. As a result, a growing number of Americans ended up in long-term incarceration. So in addition to the homeless population, the prison population also exploded in the 1980s. Soon, America had the highest incarceration rate in the world.

When considering the problem of unemployment, governments of both political parties felt compelled to respond. Both did, with solutions that were equally worthless. The democratic solution was to promote educational opportunities for students, so they could become trained for careers that were already oversaturated with applicants. It did not work. The republican solution was the same solution they proposed for every social ill in America: tax breaks for business. According to the tenets of trickle-down economics, this would lead to job creation. It did not work.

These proposals did not work for unemployed Americans. However, they worked very well for American business. The democratic solution worked for businesses such as colleges and vocational schools, and worked well for the remainder of American business by helping to saturate the country with overqualified graduates desperate to work at any job to pay off their student debt. And the republican solution obviously worked well for American business, which used the money gained from tax breaks not to invest in company expansion and job creation but to enhance executive salaries.

It is unknown to this day whether the politicians of both sides sincerely believed their solutions would work, or whether such claims were blatant appeals for their moneyed constituents.

As these dynamics played out over the decades, the situation worsened. In order to adapt as best as they could, Americans fell back upon their time-honoured ability of "American ingenuity." Shared or co-operative housing, once the realm of poor students or starving artists, became widespread. People resorted to scenarios they thought were relics from the past—things from the "old days" that they had seen in movies from the 1930s and 1940s. They took in boarders. They took in members from their extended families that were unemployed or otherwise did not have enough money to live on their own. Many Americans were forced to live full-time with relatives that normally they could tolerate only for annual holiday gatherings. As a result, America experienced a surge of alcoholism, drug abuse, and domestic violence.

The overcrowded conditions in family residences led to millions of teenagers resorting to the long-time American tradition called "running away from home." Most eventually returned. Yet some switched to families with less crowded living conditions and friendlier parents who served better meals. Some children in crowded conditions chose to escape the throng and regain privacy by moving into backyard treehouses or play structures. In one instance that turned into a media sensation, 9-year-old Jacob Miller moved into his family's kennel, resulting in Jo-Jo, a friendly Labrador mix, becoming homeless. The American public, sympathetic to the family's plight and to Jo-Jo's situation, replied with thousands of dollars in donations to build Jo-Jo a new kennel.

This example, and many others, reveal that Americans retained a spirit of generosity despite the hard times. Although as we shall see, this generosity towards American pets was not matched when it came to assisting American people.

Many Americans, with neither the desire nor the ability to live with others, attempted valiantly to live by themselves. For many, the only way to accomplish this was by moving to a cardboard box under a bridge or highway overpass.

For many years in America, there had been a popular television programme entitled *This Old House*. It was a home improvement series that involved real-life instances of homeowners engaged in the repair and upgrading of single-family dwellings. This was during the period when it was still possible for many families to afford a single-family dwelling.

To appeal to audiences impelled to deal with changing circumstances, one television network briefly aired a series entitled *This Old Box*. For people reduced to living in cardboard boxes, *This Old Box* featured real-life instances of box dwellers seeking to renovate and improve their box. It featured tips on how people improved their boxes by adding insulation, protecting against rodent penetration, and preventing theft of their box by people whose boxes had dissolved in the rain. However, the series proved short-lived. Not for lack of usefulness, as Americans were in serious need of improved box shelter, but for lack of advertising revenue. It proved impossible to find commercial sponsors for a show whose audience could only afford to live in boxes.

Since jobs were becoming increasingly scarce, Americans became increasingly desperate to find and retain employment. This was good news for America's employers, since they no longer felt competitive pressure to retain employees by offering benefits such as retirement plans, paid holidays, or lunch breaks. The hard-won gains in labour rights that America made in the mid-20th century were steadily lost.

It was a good time for managers with a sadistic streak or anger-management issues. With most American employees deathly afraid of losing their jobs, managers discovered they could get away with behaviour that was abusive to the extreme. As one American survivor interviewed for this book related:

> Our boss would give us conflicting instructions, then yell at us about disregarding half of them. Then he would yell at us to not include the time being yelled at on our time cards. Then he would

yell at us for being yelled at when we should be working. But if we went back to work he would yell at us for leaving without asking.

Yet managers were not spared such treatment, since every manager had a higher-level manager above them. As a result, abusive behaviour enveloped entire companies, turning American workplaces into terror-ridden hellholes of fear and psychological torture. In a form of the psychological dynamic known to as "Stockholm Syndrome," American workers grew to believe they liked such an atmosphere. This was quite a shock to visiting businesspeople from countries which held the belief that friendly work relationships were good for business.

Many Americans—unable to obtain employment, or unwilling to tolerate the abusive atmosphere—were able to gain successful self-employment in occupations that were considered to be relics of the past. One of those was the vocation of *repairperson*. Decades of affluence had made Americans extremely wasteful. Generally speaking, when anything broke or malfunctioned Americans would throw it away and buy a new one. Often they would simply give it away. Rather than the effort to repair, for example, a wobbly chair or a car that would not start, they would place it in a public location with a "FREE" sign on it. Then they would go to the nearest "big box" discount store or car dealer and purchase a new one.

In addition, salvage and refurbishment became popular professions. Small-scale entrepreneurs drove to more-affluent parts of town to retrieve broken items, and rejuvenated them for sale in less-affluent parts of town. Often those items needed no repair at all, and were in the garbage for reasons such as "I just got tired of it" or "I liked the new model better"—justifications that were part of an America that was rapidly becoming a thing of the past.

Those who had steady employment clung to their positions by unscrupulous means. While the employment situation was dire for most occupations, the position of "Hired Goon" experienced a large surge. Proprietors of America's small businesses had their own methods to ensure business. Owners of tire stores lined nearby streets with nails. Doctors specializing in reconstructive surgery hired ex-boxers to "rough up" potential customers. In one well-publicised incident, a dentist ensured repeat business by offering customers "special vanilla-flavoured toothpaste" that consisted of cake frosting.

One of America's very few growing opportunities was in the field of prostitution. Catering to America's wealthy minority could result in substantial income for Americans blessed with a pleasant appearance, good health, and all their teeth. Since that combination of qualities was quite uncommon in America, the principles of supply and demand ensured extremely high compensation.

Incredibly, America made further deliberate attempts to make Americans obsolete. In an amazing example of America's refusal to consider the implications of its decisions, it excitedly embraced the development of technologies that encouraged the obsolescence of human labour. To do so in an era of worsening unemployment makes it especially remarkable.

At this time, nations around the world were also experiencing the problem. In response, they considered potential solutions such as reducing the work week to spread out the work, or offering a minimum guaranteed income to those who were made obsolete. Yet such "socialist" solutions were unacceptable to independence-minded Americans, who did not trouble themselves to even discuss the problem.

In the process of interviewing American survivors, I asked several of them how it felt to be made obsolete by technology. The universal reply was that, although such technologies worked to push them into unemployment and impoverishment, the technologies were "really cool."

Additive manufacturing, commonly referred to as 3D printing, rapidly worked toward the elimination of over half of American manufacturing jobs. Yet this was not especially damaging to the country as a whole since America by this time had outsourced most of its manufacturing overseas.

Most forms of employment consisted of work that was part of the information economy. Unfortunately for Americans, this was precisely the type of work targeted for replacement by the rapid development of artificial intelligence. Americans by the millions suddenly found themselves replaced by highly advanced computer programs capable of learning and problem-solving that were able to do the equivalent amount of work in 1/100 of the time. And they did so without requiring weekends off, without taking maternity leave, and without requesting to leave work for "mental health days."

Company managers were happy to discover that hundreds of employees could be replaced by one extremely intelligent technology expert, even if that expert was so deeply immersed in computer language that they were unable to engage in human conversation. Of course, those company managers were not as happy to discover that they had also been replaced by the same technology, as it worked its way up the management hierarchy. By 2030, several good-sized companies had reduced their staffing requirements to the point where the only employees were a company president, a technology expert, and a marketing manager that doubled as a part-time janitor.

That is, until the introduction of robots or "bots" that replaced positions such as janitors with JanitorBots. Positions such as bartenders were replaced with BartenderBots capable of mixing every drink ever invented, and were programmed with hundreds of thousands of jokes. As a result, millions of jobs were eliminated. Even prostitutes, who for a time had experienced a surge of career opportunities, were eventually made obsolete by the introduction of SexBots.

As other types of employment were disappearing, one of the few well-paying and secure positions, even for Americans without college degrees, was that of a long-haul truck driver. Yet America's embrace of artificial intelligence included an embrace of driverless cars, which quickly led to driverless trucks. Which resulted in another substantial addition to the growing number of unemployed Americans.

A growing number of Americans lost everything down to their television set and their car. These were the possessions Americans most identified as extensions of themselves, and would only consider selling to avoid starvation. Indeed, many Americans chose starvation, with their emancipated bodies discovered behind the wheel with the television placed before them on the hood, allowing them to leave earthly life while viewing their favourite programme.

Economic Refugees

Since the 1980s, America had been experiencing a rise in homeless camps in or near every American city and in many of its towns and suburbs. The addition of millions to this population simply grew these camps into shantytowns resembling those of America's Great Depression, which had been named "Hoovervilles" after President Herbert Hoover who had been widely blamed for causing them.

These new shantytowns were eventually referred to as "Britneyvilles," named after President Britney Ventura. The shantytowns grew to house millions of Americans in slum-like conditions. Without electricity to power television sets, they were forced to create primitive versions of their favourite programmes. They did so by building large frames behind which residents pretended to be their favourite television actors, re-enacting beloved episodes from memory as best as they were able.

The crisis also resulted in masses of migrating Americans. As had occurred in the 1930s, their appearance in new locations was not—to put it mildly—met with a warm welcome. As had happened in the Great Depression, migrants were often met at city limits by heavily armed vigilante forces. Sometimes, homeless Americans camped in cities and towns—especially homeless Americans with mental problems—were provided with one-way bus tickets to someplace else. Of course, upon their arrival they were given another ticket and sent off again. America became filled with homeless citizens crisscrossing the country, which proved to be a boon to America's bus companies.

There had been a trend in America in which attempts to store waste products, especially those with toxic elements, were resisted with the expression "Not in my back yard." As the homelessness problem reached crisis levels, this attitude was broadened. Because the near-universal reaction to the homeless, as well as to unemployed Americans in general, was the same. Thus, without even realising it, the attitude once embraced by Americans as a way to deal with their waste products had now been extended to what they considered to be waste people.

Not all Americans shared this attitude, of course. Many Americans had sympathy with their plight, being well-aware that one financial catastrophe was the only thing that separated them from the same fate. As a result, many Americans actively worked to assist them. Most prominent were members of America's churches and religious organisations, who held that the divine spark of life burned equally in all human souls, and that at some deep level that divine spark had a common source.

Such efforts surged after the Pope's 2034 visit to America. During the course of that visit, the Pope was utterly shocked by the roaming masses of homeless people in a country he characterised as "a land of plenty." He admonished Americans, reminding them that humanity is essentially one. He concluded the rally with the famous words, "To deny assistance to a person in need is to deny God."

In a burst of idealistic fury, churches across the nation scrambled to outdo each other in helpful programmes. They opened soup kitchens, arranged for doctors and dentists to provide medical care, and provided free solar-powered televisions so the homeless could feel like "real Americans."

Yet after only a few weeks, such programmes were massively overburdened by a crush of needy humanity. Adding to the problem was that the "crush of needy humanity" was not always appropriately grateful for the assistance. There was never enough pepper for the scrambled egg breakfast. The sandwiches had too much mayonnaise. The solar-powered televisions did not work at night and were not able to access the channels that broadcast "the really good shows."

Many churches provided parking spaces for homeless Americans to camp in their vehicles. In many cases, they even made members of the camp into church board members, so as to instill a sense of solidarity and collective ownership. However, in many instances the homeless population managed to form a board majority, and voted to essentially turn the entire church property into a homeless camp. In one instance, they voted to demolish the church buildings to create more parking spaces.

At this point, the idea of a divine spark within each human soul was no longer mentioned. As quickly as the churches had initiated the programmes, they were forced to abandon them. Frustrated church leaders turned to the Pope for wisdom and advice. In consideration of the current state of America, the Pope made a slight revision to his message about the presence of God on earth. His new message was, "God helps those who help themselves."

The Pope's message set the agenda for the direction of American religion, which revised its beliefs to be consistent with the doctrines of economic growth. As such, it accepted the doctrine that helping the poor and unfortunate was best accomplished by distributing money to the most wealthy and powerful segments of society. Prayers to encourage the benevolent influence of God were transformed into prayers for the life-affirming benefits of economic growth, which would eventually trickle down to all of God's children.

The same problem had been experienced by American cities and towns. Whenever a municipality initiated a programme of assistance, word quickly spread and that municipality was inundated with homeless refugees.

Obviously, local solutions were wholly inadequate to the task of such an overwhelming problem. The American public demanded that America's federal government take action toward the interrelated problems of unemployment and homelessness. In response the American government quickly leapt into action to make the problems appear smaller than they actually were.

For decades, to be *fully employed* was defined as working a minimum of 21 hours per week. In response to the current crisis, the definition of "fully employed" was revised to the point where almost nobody was excluded. For example, panhandlers that had received a cup of coffee via requests for "spare change" were counted as fully employed in the occupational category of "independent salesperson."

As a result, government representatives proudly announced their success in reducing the unemployment rate, within a span of only a few months, to 0.04 percent. Similarly, the government claimed that the homeless problem was solved. It did this not by citing figures, but by presenting the reasoning that even if people did not have a home in the traditional sense of the term, nobody could truly be homeless since the earth is our home.

Americans were pleased with the news, yet grew suspicious at the substantial disconnect between the government's claims and the growing numbers of unemployed and homeless citizens they encountered on a continual basis, often needing to step over unconscious ones that were blocking doorways. It did not take long for Americans to realise that their government was playing them for fools.

The government needed a new strategy. After failing in its attempt to deny the existence of unemployed and homeless Americans, the government took decisive action by blaming them for being unemployed and homeless.

The public had little trouble with this. Rather than examine the complexities of economic policies, it was much easier to blame individual panhandlers. It was much easier to yell at a panhandler to "Get a job!" than to deal with a highly complex and entrenched financial system run by distant figures who were not readily available to yell at.

In an unusual move, Senator Lori Russell made an appeal to America to see unemployed Americans in a positive light. Russell based this appeal on making public one of America's most significant taboos, the fact that the economy required unemployment. According to Russell, unemployed Americans were therefore heroes of a sort by making the noble sacrifice to keep America strong. They were, in Russell's words, "Taking one for Team America." This effort was somewhat noble, even though it defended unemployed Americans not on the grounds of being human beings with intrinsic value, but as necessary sacrifices upon the altar of economic growth.

But by then, "compassion fatigue" had fully eroded all traces of sympathy from most Americans. At this point in American history, it was extremely difficult for most Americans to get past their association of *homeless person* with *miserable failure that should be allowed to rot and die.*

However, a small yet highly vocal minority held the position that America's unemployed and homeless were still Americans, and they demanded that the government act to help them. America's politicians had a ready reply to taxpaying Americans who held such positions. American politicians asked: If you want the government to fund care and assistance for 50 million people, will you accept a tax increase to fund it?

This effectively silenced such concerns.

Even though most of America's "safety net" had been dismantled, what was left remained a substantial financial burden. In order to reduce that burden—and as the government put it, "discourage the homeless lifestyle"—the government took measures to penalise the efforts of impoverished Americans to enjoy themselves. A substantial controversy erupted when it was discovered that some welfare recipients in Kansas were having fun. This angered many Americans, who could only tolerate the existence of poor Americans if they were miserable. "Poor people are supposed to be sad," explained one commentator. Such a position was undoubtedly an expression of America's longstanding equation of money with happiness, and with the difficulty of Americans in obtaining happiness without paying for it.

In response to the situation in Kansas, the Kansas governor quickly signed a bill prohibiting welfare recipients from using government funds to use swimming pools, see movies, or visit amusement parks. At a press conference announcing the bill, the governor stated: "Why should America's failures be allowed to have fun at the expense of hardworking Americans who can hardly afford to have fun of their own?"

When discouraging homelessness did not work, the government took the next logical step, which was imprisonment. America had already begun jailing people for non-payment of fines, so it was a simple matter to raise the stakes to include the option of prison. Although America had officially made "debtor's prisons" illegal via Constitutional amendment in the 1830s, most Americans did not care, and were glad that the government was finally taking action.

This was a favourable development for a segment of America that had a strong vested interest in a growing prison population. For some Americans, it provided substantial economic benefits. Because America's military industrial complex expanded to include another facet, the *prison-industrial complex*.

Prison labour, often called *insourcing* was seen as an alternative to *outsourcing*. Instead of sending labour to be cheaply done overseas, it could be done inexpensively by inmates in American prisons. Millions of inmates were employed, with wages of a dollar or less per hour, on jobs such as preparing artisan cheese for gourmet supermarkets, constructing uniforms for "fast food" restaurant workers, and sewing American flags for state police departments.

In other words, American taxpayers paid for incarcerating criminals to provide cheap labour and take jobs away from taxpaying Americans. Fortunately for those who profited by the prison industry, those taxpaying Americans never figured this out.

While spending on social welfare programmes were drastically cut, spending on prisons rose dramatically. Basically, prisons substituted for social programmes as the social "safety net" turned into a prison cell.

Elite Strongholds, Increasing Poverty

By the late 2030s, America's middle class had essentially vanished, and the American class system was roughly as follows:

- The ultra-wealthy, consisting of the leading business owners and financial managers. This was the so-called "one percent" who owned most of America's wealth.

- The upper class, consisting of corporate presidents, upper-level management, top technology experts, leading doctors, and other highly skilled professionals. This group made up approximately five percent of the population.
- The lower class, sometimes referred to by the upper class as "the expendable class." This broad category, making up something like 60 percent of the population, included the upper lower class, the middle lower class, and the lower lower class—sometimes referred to as the "just-barely-hanging-on class."
- The remainder made up the "street class," sometimes referred to as "the untouchables," making up America's permanently unemployed and homeless population, including the combined population of America's "Britneyvilles." This class provided a rare form of unity in America by being despised and avoided by all other classes.

The lower classes, fearful and desperate, began to be a danger to the upper classes, who began experiencing a different sense of fear and desperation. Wealthy Americans actively avoided travelling anywhere in lower-class America, which was essentially all of America. America's wealthy had always preferred to live amongst others of their kind, and in the past it was enough to live in informal segregation together in neighbourhoods that were often in close proximity with those of lesser means. There had generally remained a "live and let live" ethos, during the time when most Americans lived in generally satisfying conditions.

But that began to change as desperate Americans with almost nothing began taking advantage of the easy access to others who were perceived as having way too much. America's wealthy were generally able to avoid locations in which they would be confronted with people asking "Can you spare a dollar?" Yet increasingly, Americans of lesser means were willing to make the journey to affluent neighbourhoods on their own initiative. As a result, America's wealthy were confronted by people outside their homes asking "Can you spare a car?" Despite heightened security measures, America's wealthy no longer felt safe in their own homes.

It was this trend that finally led large numbers of America's affluent toward a deep concern for America's poor. Unfortunately, this new-found concern for the poor expressed itself not as "How can we help the poor?" but as "How can we insulate ourselves from the poor?"

So America's wealthy began to band together to form secure fortified compounds. In a sense, it was merely the logical extension of the gated communities that had gained in popularity in the 1990s, although greatly expanded in scope. Such compounds were protected by 20-foot walls and perimeters patrolled by private security forces. Occasionally those perimeters were surrounded with mines, traps, and even alligator-filled moats.

In a sense, it was kind of a "secession" of America's most wealthy citizens. Although they did not physically abandon the country, they did as much as possible to abandon contact with it.

Over time, as the situation outside the gates became increasingly dangerous, the compounds moved more aspects of their lives from the outside to the inside. Since a simple trip to dinner might involve a hazardous and unpleasant journey, it was much safer and pleasant to have the dinner establishment moved inside the compound. Increasingly, businesses catering to the private compounds moved within the walls. This was followed by private schools, and eventually—in some of the larger compounds—with private universities. The compounds essentially became private towns, then grew into private cities. A compound in the state of Maryland, which eventually christened itself with the name of Platinumville, grew to a population of over 100,000.

Yet total self-sufficiency was not feasible. The residents needed the outside world to supply them with fine food and wine, designer clothing, and the other luxury items that made their lives worth living. Thus, supply lines needed to be maintained.

The trouble began when those supply lines became threatened. Delivery trucks were increasingly vulnerable to ambush. Sources of protein were especially targeted, and restaurants were subject to shortages in elk steaks and Cornish game hen. Shipments of foie gras became unreliable and in some cases ceased altogether.

One of the raiders became something of a folk hero. Patterning himself as an updated version of the Wild West outlaw Billy the Kid, he called himself Jeremy the Punk. As with his famous counterpart, he operated by a strict moral code of never purposely injuring a driver. Like the British legend of Robin Hood, to whom he was compared, he shared freely of his exploits, emulating the Robin Hood ethic of "Steal from the rich to give to the poor." He eluded capture for years, largely because his folk-hero status resulted in a population always ready to assist him in providing hiding places and material assistance.

The government began a series of extreme crackdowns on the raiders. Labelling them as "domestic terrorists" meant that capture could result in life imprisonment. In addition, the government began to make American military personnel available to provide escorts to the delivery trucks.

Possibly because of the increased danger, the raids of Jeremy the Punk suddenly ended and he was never seen again. Authorities claimed he had been killed, but corroborating evidence was never offered. Some said he escaped from America to a tiny Caribbean island, where he went with some of his followers. Although Jeremy the Punk has surely passed away by this time, perhaps his descendants live on, drinking coconut milk and eating mangoes in a tropical paradise as the setting sun alights the sky in shades of orange and crimson.

As America's era of compound building continued, America increasingly became two countries: the "haves" versus the "have-nots." The ultra-wealthy and upper-class residents of the walled compounds made up the "haves." The "have-nots" were everybody else. Although life inside the compounds was comfortable and safe, the situation outside the compounds definitely was not. Shrinking centres of relative affluence became surrounded by increasing poverty. Vast sections of America—starting on the periphery, largely invisible to the centres—gradually devolved into what resembled a developing country. Vast areas of America became "sacrifice zones." Whole cities, and large portions of cities, became industrial ghost towns.

For most cities, a relatively affluent centre was surrounded by zones of decreasing affluence. Yet some cities, such as Detroit, Michigan, experienced a slightly different dynamic. In such cities, an upper class "ring" was created by fleeing residents abandoning an urban centre which devolved into impoverished areas populated disproportionately by blacks. This process had been going on for decades, and in the 1960s such centres were referred to by American civil rights leader Malcom X as "internal colonies." As the American economy further declined, the outer ring grew thinner as many descended through the economic ranks and fell into the impoverished centre.

Many formerly prosperous and successful cities fell victim to the dynamic. In the rapidly changing circumstances, some regions were suitable for living, while others were not. Some regions were winners, while others were losers. To a substantial degree, what made some areas into "winners" was their viability for local agriculture and small-scale energy production.

Americans had not given much thought, if any, to things like soil quality, or growing seasons, or the proximity of good agricultural land, or the local availability of fuel and energy sources. As is the case almost everywhere, America's children were much quicker than their parents to understand the importance of this new reality. Grade school classrooms became filled with children having animated discussions about water-fed micro-generators and the pros and cons of various methods of sustaining soil fertility. Unfortunately, this made little difference, since such children went home to parents who dissuaded them from pursuing such topics, considering them to be part of a vast "liberal conspiracy" that was opposed to the American way.

Yet reality ultimately could not be denied, despite what Americans wanted to believe.

Regions that had thrived before the widespread availability of oil and gasoline were in a much better situation than regions that arose later, since such "pre-oil" communities could more easily adapt to a post-oil world. Other regions that had arisen during the boom of inexpensive oil proved to be extremely ill-suited to the new reality.

The most prominent "winner" was, perhaps ironically, the New England states that had formed the original American colonies. Much of the region consisted of compact towns and small cities designed before the advent of the automobile, and therefore were better able to function without them. America's Pacific Northwest states of Washington, Oregon, and the northern half of California were also well-situated, with abundant water, fertile soil, and a mild climate.

It was also a good situation for many small towns. For decades, America's small towns had been in serious decline. But those in locations with optimal qualities began to come back to life, as the qualities previously perceived merely as "pretty scenery" were increasingly understood as being necessary for survival.

But ultimately, very few regions were well-suited to the new reality. The regions making up the "losers" were vast, and included most of America's densest population centres. Deserts and arid regions were obviously at a disadvantage. The vast expanse of America's southwest was in dire straits.

The states making up the High Plains and the Rocky Mountains were also ill-prepared for this era, with severe winters, dismal agricultural production, and poor rangeland. There was some hope, however, when it was proposed that the entire region be returned to its naturally productive state as a tallgrass prairie supporting bison, antelope, and other wildlife. Such wildlife could be sustainably harvested for organic high-quality animal protein. The plan would involve removing millions of miles of barbed wire fence and cooperatively managing the region as a "buffalo commons." Unfortunately this promising idea never got past the discussion stage, since the independent-minded farmers and ranchers realised that running a cooperative enterprise would require them to cooperate.

But the biggest losers were America's sprawling suburbs. Originally envisioned as a means to a lifestyle combining the best of city and country living, the suburbs ended up combining the worst of both. With the onset of the 2030s oil crisis, suburbs were suddenly impractical for commuting to city jobs and urban culture. And the suburbs were not rural enough, in the sense of not having adequate land to provide for their own material needs or generate any land-based income.

Vast expanses of sprawling "McMansions" were abandoned. Hardest hit were the areas Americans called a *megalopolis*, consisting of huge sprawls of continuous suburb that might stretch up to 100 miles. Most of these regions were abandoned and became virtual wastelands consisting of endless rows of identical oversized homes, with garages often containing cars that were left behind because they had become too expensive to operate.

Some of these regions became dangerous "forbidden zones." In a return to a modern version of America's fabled Wild West, large areas became lawless frontiers as they became taken over by unsavoury denizens that nobody wished to encounter. Travel was highly discouraged in these areas in which law enforcement professionals refused to enter.

As vast areas of America became abandoned, fleeing populations merely added to the growing throngs of refugees. Other than the growing Britneyvilles, refugees had extremely few options. In desperation, some Americans turned to an option they never would have previously considered.

Although America as a whole was in trouble, as unsustainable practices in every aspect of American life was catching up with them, there was a substantial if proportionately small segment of the population that had lived sustainably for 300 years: the Amish. Over 300,000 members of this religious-oriented community lived in isolated farm-centred communities centred in the eastern portion of America. They were a model for a viable post-oil way of life that had consciously separated itself from the excesses of secular society. Although the American public had occasionally shown some fascination for this "other country" within their borders, few Americans were willing to consider a lifestyle based upon extreme simplicity and a strict social order. Yet this changed for some when the excesses of secular society became unaffordable.

As a result, Amish communities across America were suddenly faced with migrations of hardy souls who were willing to give the Amish lifestyle a try. Migrants entering Amish communities offered an astonishing visual incongruity. Shocked Amish—in their plain dress, and engaged in tasks such as milking cows—were suddenly faced with wandering groups of typical Americans of the period. Such Americans came with fashionable haircuts, designer jeans, elaborate tattoos, and T-shirts with messages such as "Can You Afford Me?" and "I'm Too Sexy for My Hair."

Ultimately, typical Americans were not suited to the Amish lifestyle. Manual work was not the primary issue. The irreconcilable problem was the simple lifestyle which was "too boring" as one disappointed ex-convert put it. The real deal-killer was the ban on advanced technologies. Electronic devices were not allowed, which meant no texting, no social media, and no digital music devices. The ultimate deal-killer, of course, was that the Amish community did not allow television.

THE BENEFITS OF EMPIRE

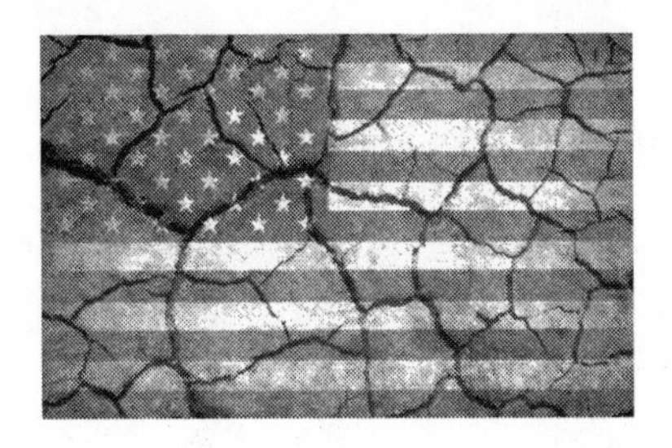

American Exceptionalism, Manifest Destiny, and the Monroe Doctrine

For much of its history, America enjoyed the world's highest material standard of living. America preferred to believe this was due to being inherently superior. The notion is absurd, yet America clung to it to the very end.

America enjoyed its high standard of living because the nation, for most of its history, existed as an empire. At the peak of that empire it utlilised its power to reap a material cornucopia as had never been seen on such a widespread scale.

Visitors to the British Museum of American Culture can view dioramas of typical American scenes that display some of the most awe-inspiring products ever devised. Reproductions of America kitchens include items such as Blueberry Hazelnut Pringles, Star Wars Multi-Vitamin Gummies, and Jimmy Dean's Chocolate Chip Pancakes & Sausage on a Stick. Reproductions of children's play areas include toys such as the G.I. Joe Cobra Pogo Ballistic Battle Ball and the Justice Jogger Overland Villain Chaser. Although some may question the usefulness of a product such as the Giant Nose Shower Gel Dispenser, only America was audacious enough to bring such a product into existence.

It is deeply unfortunate that hundreds of thousands of people died to fill American homes with such products. But the bounty of empire cannot be obtained without a price. Or as an American might have put it, "You can't make an omelet without breaking a few eggs."

Although Americans generally did not like to admit it, and in fact most Americans denied it, Americans were a warlike people. Foreign visitors to America frequently described them as *warmongering*. Americans loved war. War was patriotic and pro-America. Throughout American history, if a president wished a boost of popularity, a declaration of war was all that was needed. Presidents and presidential hopefuls needed to make great efforts to not appear "weak," since "weak" was equated with "un-American." Americans were always ready to leap into war out of fear of being labelled as soft. There was no corresponding fear of leaping into peace out of fear of being labelled as murderers.

Even when Americans claimed to be for peace, this was almost always interpreted as "peace through strength." Although the country had a massive Defense Department, America never had a Peace Department. America had one basic response to conflict. There is an expression, "When the only tool you have is a hammer, every problem looks like a nail." The American version of this was, "When the only tool you have is an immense military, every problem looks like a war."

During the peak of American power, when America's military strength assured America of winning, America felt little need to justify its actions. It is a deeply unfortunate trait of human nature that war can be justified by the ethically questionable claim a nation wins a war because it deserved to win.

America began, of course, as a humble colony of England. It is quite remarkable to reflect upon the fact that in a brief period—only a few hundred years—America grew into the world's most powerful empire. Yet to whatever extent America was humble at the beginning, it did not remain humble for long.

Although in many ways America made a break from the past, in other ways it merely perpetuated themes present for the previous 2,000 years of human history.

America was founded as a colony of what was at the time the world's most powerful empire. And England was, of course, only the latest in a continuous line of empires that attempted to rule the world. Some historians have in fact labelled the past 2,000 years of history as *The Age of Empire*. The age was dominated by a series of empires conquering and expanding until they inevitably overextended themselves and broke up, their boundaries dissolved and their territories enclosed within other boundaries that continued the same process. As the East had Egypt under the Pharaohs and the Mongols under Genghis Kahn, the West had the Romans under Caesar and the French under Napoleon.

In the West of the 1500s, the Old World of Europe expanded to conquer and colonise the New World of the Americas, pushing farther around the world in search of access to resources—especially to gold. Cortez decimated the Aztec culture, as Pizarro did with the Incas. The conquering forces established mines and stripped local vegetation to fuel the smelters. Missionaries tagged along to give the appearance of transcendent purpose, which consisted of converting the "savages" to the religion of their conquerors.

The process eventually became less overt than direct military conquest. Various forms of internal interference could lead to economic concessions or trade imbalances that gave control over a territory without fighting a single battle. Civil wars were started in Africa, pitting tribe against tribe to gain access to slaves. The Dutch used opium to disrupt Indonesian society and take over foreign policy, as Britain did with India and China.

England's expansion included the formation of colonies in North America, which rebelled to form America—a nation that quickly began its own expansion. The expansion moved west, along an edge that came to be known as *the frontier*.

The dynamic was described in 1845 in a magazine article by journalist John L. O'Sullivan, who wrote of "the fulfillment of our manifest destiny to overspread the continent allotted by Providence for the free development of our yearly multiplying millions." It was a vision that sounded like a religious mission, a divine fate bestowed upon America. Thus, the dynamic now had a name: *Manifest Destiny*. It was the belief that it was the destiny of the United States to expand its territory over the whole of North America, and to extend its political and economic influences even further.

It was considered to be America's historic mission based on the self-declared superiority of America and its ideas. As John Adams put it in 1756:

> The whole continent was one continued dismal wilderness, the haunt of wolves and bears and more savage men. Now the forests are removed, the land covered with fields of corn, orchards bending with fruit and the magnificent habitations of rational and civilized people.

As had been the case with earlier empires, the violence was justified by Christianity's "dominion over the earth." And as had been the case with earlier empires, missionaries gave the appearance of transcendent purpose by converting the "savages" to the religion of their conquerors. Of course, many of the "savages" were simply exterminated.

America's Native Americans were mostly eliminated in the eastern states, and the closing of the frontier and settlement of the West resulted in the final wars. The remaining Native Americans were eliminated or resettled to the deprivation of reservations, which were almost without exception located in the least valuable and productive parts of the country.

America's environment was also a victim to this movement. In America's desire to squeeze as much wealth from the land as quickly as possible it left a trail of levelled forests, ravaged grasslands, decimated wildlife, and mountains stripped of minerals. This was also the era of the frenzy known as the *Gold Rush*, in which millions of Americans with dreams of instant riches headed west to follow gold strikes in California, Nevada, and other western states. The devastation of such activities left scars that remain to this day.

From the beginning, America was motivated primarily by the quest for material affluence. America gained "the spoils of victory" from wars on a variety of fronts, many of which were undeclared.

Military combat is only one aspect of war. We are impelled toward a more inclusive definition of war, such as the recent formulation by Portuguese philosopher Enrique Santiago: "War consists of the deliberate actions of an individual or group to destroy the integrity of any expression of life in order to gain value at its expense."

By such a definition, America's actions toward Native Americans can be considered as a form of war. And America's actions toward the natural world can be considered as a form of war. A variety of actions taken by America and other nations can be considered as forms of war, regardless of whether they were declared as such.

The expansion of Manifest Destiny had advanced the frontier across North America, but that edge disappeared when the frontier reached the Pacific Ocean. At this point, the edge began to move outward. Manifest Destiny evolved as it went beyond America's borders.

Ironically, America—which was founded as a rebellion against colonialism and imperialism—became a late player in the same game. In an 1823 speech announcing the policies that would become the *Monroe Doctrine*, President James Monroe declared that America would not tolerate any intervention by Europe in the Americas. Essentially, Monroe announced to the world that "Central and South America belong to us."

With the Monroe Doctrine, began a series of military adventures in Latin America. It began with the Spanish-American War of 1898, to expand and protect its trade markets and acquire land. The ostensible reason for the war was to "liberate" Cuba, a country previously ignored. Two powerful newspaper magnates, William Randolph Hearst and Joseph Pulitzer, published shocking headlines—highly exaggerated or outright fabrication—of Spanish atrocities against Cubans. Artist Frederic Remington was hired to go to Cuba and send back pictures for Hearst's newspapers, but sent a message that he was unable to find any war taking place. Hearst replied, "You furnish the pictures, and I'll furnish the war."

Then, in a move that would set a precedent for the remainder of American history, the government manufactured an incident to justify the war. The mysterious explosion of the American battleship USS *Maine*, while anchored in Havana, was claimed—with no evidence whatsoever—to have been caused by a Spanish mine.

The Spanish-American War gave America the opportunity to seize several territories. It resulted in the American protectorates of Puerto Rico and other territories in the Caribbean. It led to the separation of Panama from Columbia (1903), the occupation of Nicaragua (1912-1933), intervention in Mexico City (1914-1917), and the occupations of Haiti (1915-1934) and the Dominican Republic (1916-1924). In each case, the main point of the actions was to advance and protect American business investments.

At this point, there was not much territory left for easy conquest, and public opinion was moving against the blatant forms of colonialism. As a result, colonialism became economic. This often took the form of loans to countries for western-style development that destroyed self-sufficiency and trapped nations in a hopeless attempt to compete in western markets to generate income to service loans which could never realistically be paid off.

The process of expansion was justified by a sense of entitlement that has been called *American exceptionalism*. It was a feeling that regular morality did not apply to America, that Americans were inherently better than others and deserved more. America's continual success in acting on the feeling of exceptionalism only served to sustain and advance it. In short, it became something of a self-perpetuating cycle.

It perhaps began with America having a collective feeling of being "special." Indeed, the sense of exceptionalism was there from the very beginning. The War of 1812 against Britain seemed to Americans to confirm it, with the unexpected victory interpreted as evidence of divine favour.

That "divine favour" seemed to Americans to continue indefinitely. This was especially the case after America emerged from World War II a clear winner, its industrial and economic power at a peak as much of Europe was in physical and economic ruin. America found itself with its industrial capacity almost quadrupled, with the capacity of other leading nations decimated. At close of World War II America had half the world's wealth. This situation heralded the beginning of the *postwar economic boom* of the 1950s and 1960s. For a brief period of time, America was able to sustain a material standard of living such as history had never seen.

The postwar economic boom had a deep and profound effect on the American character and shaped events for the remainder of American history. The burst of affluence in the mid-20th century bolstered America's belief in what was called *The American Dream*. It was the idea that progress is inevitable and that if Americans worked hard and obeyed the rules, then prosperity would follow. Americans expected to have more than their parents, and for their children to have more than them. Failing to achieve this seemed to Americans to break a fundamental law of nature.

In response to this expectation, America became the first nation on earth to experience what came to be called *consumerism*. It was a phenomenon unique in world history. A substantial percentage of Americans had gotten to the point where they had more than enough economic affluence to take care of their basic needs. Economists and business executives grew concerned that the American people, fulfilled at the material level, would cease shopping and focus their energies on loftier and more meaningful goals. If that happened, business profits would plateau and economic growth would cease.

Their concerns were unjustified, to put it mildly. But business executives did not know this at the time, so they made great efforts to encourage Americans to "shop till they drop." Thus, the use of mass marketing to create artificial needs. Or as marketing professionals put it, to inform Americans of needs they did not realise they had. The marketing and advertising industry grew rapidly in size and importance until it soon eclipsed the rest of American business.

The industry used techniques that exploited fundamental human desires in the most crude and unsophisticated ways imaginable. Advertisements made a variety of highly dubious claims in an effort to sell products. If you did not use Prell shampoo, you would be a romantic failure and never marry. If you did not purchase this year's new Buick in order to "Keep up with the Joneses," you would be ostracised by neighbours. If you did not purchase for your child a Barbie Doll or Red Ryder BB Gun, your child would resent you until the day your death relieved them of your unwelcome presence.

Yet while such claims appear to us today as utterly ridiculous, they were amazingly effective. Such ridiculous claims were deployed because they worked.

It could be argued—and some did—that consumerism had tangible effects on human psychology—that it distracted Americans from their genuine selves, that it obscured their souls behind a flood of materialism. But the only problem most Americans had with consumerism was that they could not get enough of it.

Americans who came of age in the 1930s and 1940s— the decades of the Great Depression and World War II—were later referred to as "The Greatest Generation." This was a generation that understood deprivation. It was a generation that understood sacrifice; it was a generation that pulled together to defeat fascism.

For Americans who came of age in the postwar economic boom, it was hard to believe that before the 1950s an orange was a rare treat. When Americans of that era happened to obtain one, it was a cause for family and neighbourhood celebration. Photographic archives from that area are filled with blurry black-and-white pictures, taken with early Kodak "Brownie" cameras, of family members proudly holding the orange.

But very quickly oranges became common, and it took little time for Americans to become accustomed to their wide availability and low cost as normal. Not only normal, but *boring*. Since Americans had no desire to expend the time and effort to cut open an orange, they preferred oranges in the form of juice. Since this also became boring, juice companies sought desperately to inspire continued consumer interest with increasingly vibrant packaging and various combinations with other fruit juices, giving them the opportunity to advertise, for example,

"New Orange Peach Grapefruit Flavour." But this too became boring, especially as fruit juices had to compete with more exciting beverage options such as Coconut Lime Ginger Turmeric Black Tea Kombucha.

America quickly became accustomed to a lot of things that were once considered incredible luxuries: fresh food shipped from around the world, private automobiles, hot water on demand, air-conditioning, dishwashers, and thermostatically controlled homes.

Americans became accustomed to things that cannot conceivably be considered to be essential, yet Americans considered them as existential necessities. As an American survivor interviewed for this book put it, in reference to a video game console:

> If I didn't get the new Xbox 360, I thought I would die. I finally got one and my life felt complete. But then they came out with the Xbox One and my life fell apart. I told my parents that if they didn't buy me the Xbox One then I would jump off a bridge. I finally got the Xbox One. But then they came out with the Xbox One X.

America's expectations rose easily, and descended only after vicious struggle. Any hint of affluence being taken away brought feelings of deprivation. It was anti-progress. It was "going back to the Stone Age."

America had no desire to go "back to the Stone Age." During World War II, American leaders recognised that America would emerge from the war in a position of overwhelming power. And even before the war's end, America began taking actions to ensure it would retain that power in the postwar world. The reason for retaining that power would be to retain America's unreasonably high level of affluence. In a 1948 State Department Policy Planning Staff Paper, American diplomat and historian George F. Kennan wrote:

> We have about 50 percent of the world's wealth, but only 6.3 percent of its population. Our real task in the coming period is to devise a pattern of relationships which will permit us to maintain this position of disparity.

America continued its previous policies of expansion and influence, yet in even more clandestine ways than before. The 1950s marked the beginning of covert operations conducted by America's Central Intelligence Agency. One operation engineered a political coup in Iran that deposed the democratically elected Prime Minister in order to restore the deposed Shah of Iran—an event that would cause grave repercussions in the decades to come. Then, the CIA plotted to overthrow a government in Guatemala that threatened the power of United Fruit, an American company that dominated the economy.

Many similar operations were conducted around the world for years to come. Those who were aware of such operations grew to realise that America was increasingly using its great power not to advance high ideals but to advance its own self-enhancement. American power was becoming something less to be respected than to be feared.

This became more obvious during the so-called "Cold War" between America and the Soviet Union, as the two superpowers competed to dominate world affairs to enforce their respective ideologies. And in the course of that competition, to expand their nuclear arsenals to a level adequate to totally destroy all human civilisation several times over.

The Soviet Union fell for a variety of reasons. Yet America was quick to claim victory based on American superiority. It was a win for American democracy as well as for American-style free-enterprise capitalism, which for Americans were not only inseparable but identical. America was now the undisputed leader of the world.

Wars for Oil

After World War II, the biggest threat to the American empire was the oil embargo of 1973, in which the members of the Organization of Arab Petroleum Exporting Countries initiated an embargo that triggered gasoline shortages and a profound rise in oil prices. The embargo had a profound effect on America's domestic and foreign policies for the remainder of its history, as America was utterly dependent on oil for every aspect of its existence. This dependence was so obvious that even America's tremendous power of denial could not disguise it. Politicians even acknowledged that America was addicted to oil.

The higher oil prices rippled upward through the economy. Suddenly a dollar bought much less than before. The stock market went into a steep decline, and economic inflation jumped to nearly 13 percent. The American auto industry was devastated.

America moved quickly to exploit its own oil reserves. It greatly expanded its offshore oil drilling efforts and built the controversial Alaska Pipeline to access America's last large reserves. Yet such efforts were not enough to prevent America's transition from an oil exporter to an oil importer.

The embargo not only damaged the American economy but, perhaps more importantly, damaged American pride. America was accustomed to thinking of itself as "number one," and did not appreciate the actions of a few tiny Middle Eastern countries threatening that self-perception. Faced with the threat of reducing its standard of living, America's resolve strengthened in bold reaction. Or as Vice President Dick Cheney put it later, in reaction to another threat to the country's oil supply, "The American way of life is not negotiable."

America needed to guarantee that the country would never be humiliated in such a manner again. It did so by initiating an era of foreign policies and military actions conducted around the world, but focused upon the oil producing countries of the Middle East.

Such actions were in some senses merely the continuation of both overt and covert manipulations conducted by America and other countries since the end of World War I. In the Middle East, this included arbitrary changes to national borders, military intrusions, and covert political intrigues. It included the instillation of pro-America regimes as puppets for American business interests, such as the installation of the Shah of Iran mentioned earlier.

Later measures involved waging the Gulf War of 1990-1991, in response to Iraq's invasion and annexation of Kuwait. Little-reported at the time was that American intelligence had quietly led Iraq to believe that America would be unconcerned about such an action. Then after the invasion America promptly turned against Iraq.

Such actions were partly responsible for a retaliation that shook America to its core, and ushered in a series of countermeasures that would radically alter American foreign and domestic policy. On September 11, 2001, in an event that came to be referred to as *9/11*, America was struck with a series of four coordinated terrorist attacks by the Islamic terrorist group al-Qaeda. The combined attacks killed nearly 3,000 people, injured over 6,000 others, and caused at least $10 billion in property and infrastructure damage and $3 trillion in total costs.

America responded to the attacks by launching the *War on Terror*, which led to wars against Iraq and Afghanistan. The war against Afghanistan, called *Operation Enduring Freedom*, was to depose the Taliban government which was harbouring al-Qaeda leaders including, it was thought, Osama bin Laden—the mastermind behind the 9/11 attack.

The 2003 war against Iraq had a series of official justifications that were all highly suspect. As a means of retaliation against 9/11 it made absolutely no sense, since Iraq had nothing to do with the attacks. Alleged links to al Qaeda were soon proven false, and Iraq leader Saddam Hussein was a sworn enemy of Osama bin Laden. Then justification was changed to "pre-emptive self-defense" against alleged Weapons of Mass Destruction. This was later revealed to be a blatant lie. Then justification turned to "regime change" in order to bring democracy to the people of Iraq, despite the fact that the people of Iraq did not ask to have democracy brought to them. The only justification that made sense was the one everyone knew but could never be officially admitted, that the war was all about oil.

For most Americans, such facts made no difference. Dissent was shouted down as "unpatriotic" or "anti-American." America wanted revenge for 9/11. America could not find Osama Bin Laden, so America took out its revenge against Saddam Hussein. It made no sense, but most Americans did not really care.

The war resulted, directly or indirectly, in 100,000 Iraqi casualties. And in an excellent example of American exceptionalism, the deaths were brushed off as an unfortunate side effect. The attempt to impose democracy resulted in a quagmire of American military occupation and attempts to lead Iraq to the democratic system they did not want. Instead of liberating Iraq and empowering democracy, it provoked an insurrection that left the country nearly ungovernable. Instead of reducing terrorism in the region, it exacerbated the problem. Yet in another example of American exceptionalism, America never apologised. Some Americans were even offended that Iraq did not thank them.

While the war was a disaster in its stated goals, America succeeded in its actual goal. In 2007 the government quietly conceded what many had suspected. In that year, the American government officially announced that a final settlement with Iraq must grant America the right of continuing military bases and, more importantly, Iraq must give privilege to American investors in the country's oil capabilities.

In essence, America's goal was to set up a "police station" to give America control over a region that contained over two-thirds of the world's remaining oil reserves. America's actions appear irrational to the extreme, unless understood from the perspective that America wanted to keep the region appropriately destabilised to retain access to oil.

To understand American foreign relations, all that was necessary was to heed the advice of the American expression "follow the money." This is the only way to make sense of subsequent foreign policy decisions and military actions that otherwise appeared nonsensical and contradictory. It is the only explanation for America's relationship with Saudi Arabia during this period. Despite most of the 9/11 attackers being from Saudi Arabia, including al-Qaeda leader Osama bin Laden, America retained good relations with Saudi Arabia. In a mutually beneficial relationship, Saudi Arabia gained the protection of America's tremendous military power. And for America, Saudi Arabia provided a stabilising flow of oil and invested over a trillion dollars in the American securities market.

America's military actions led to a sort of vicious cycle in which America justified its actions in order to act upon problems it helped to cause. By continuing the type of actions that encouraged terrorism in the past, it virtually guaranteed such actions would be needed the future. Thus, America's War on Terror actually perpetuated the terrorism it claimed to be fighting.

Although America continued to insist its actions in the Middle East had noble and justifiable motives, to the rest of the world it was clear that America was using its military to enforce and enhance American economic interests.

Americans were not unique in using war to advance material gain. Yet earlier empires had been open about their motivations. They wanted resources that belonged to others, so they waged war to get them. Throughout its history, America wanted to live up to the proud ideals of its founding. America wanted to think of itself as a civilised nation. As a result, America refused to admit it ever went into war because winning a war brings "the spoils of victory." America felt the need to justify its wars with idealistic purpose, whether it was destroying tyrants, advancing democracy, or stopping terrorism.

In later decades the American government began to drop all pretenses about idealistic purpose. It began with President Russell Hale, in his response to the Peak Oil crisis of the 2030s. Although he had taken actions such as authorising oil drilling in the Arctic National Wildlife refuge, these actions would take years to pay off. America needed more oil *now*. The situation had become so desperate that President Hale had actually considered the option of sustainable energy. Meetings with experts in the field had resulted in three main conclusions: first, that the transition would take decades; second, that America would basically need to tear up the country and start over; and third, that America could not afford it. "Therefore, our course is clear," concluded the president. "The only question is: Which country do we invade?"

Over the coming weeks, President Hale explained that he had consulted with the Joint Chiefs of Staff in a thorough cost-benefit analysis to identify the least problematic target that would provide the greatest petroleum returns. America's neighbours Canada and Mexico both had substantial oil reserves, but these options were unacceptable. As President Hale pointed out, "Canadians are too much like us, and invading Mexico would lose me the Latino vote."

So America decided to wage what it called "a fun little war" against Bolivia. The nation held only modest oil reserves, but their small military posed no threat to America's massive power.

During a media conference, President Hale was asked how the invasion would be justified. Would it be a "war on terrorism" or a "war on drugs" or a "war to advance democracy"? The president replied, "Oh none of that. We're just attacking them so we can take their oil." This admission brought the entire media gallery to shocked silence. Never before had an American president actually stated the real reason for American military aggression.

Panicked members of his cabinet held an emergency meeting to explain to the president that he was not supposed to do that. The next day, President Hale appeared in another media conference to announce that he had been mistaken, and in fact the war would be marketed as a form of foreign aid. Since American wars were required to have catchy titles that inspired American pride, this one was entitled *Big America Helps Out Little Bolivia*.

Of course, by this time nations around the world had grown to fear the prospect of American assistance, which over the past century had led to a series of nations that had been destroyed by America's offers of help.

The president of Bolivia immediately rejected the offer of assistance. In an international media conference, Bolivian President Enrique Gutiérrez made a direct plea to President Hale and the American people: "We're doing just fine down here. Couldn't be better. We don't actually need help of any kind. Thanks for the offer, though."

But America's insistence on helping was powerful, and America did not like taking no for an answer. And their powerful military meant they did not have to. The courageous yet vastly overpowered Bolivian military resisted an American invasion to help them for nearly a month, before Bolivia surrendered to America's assistance. The results of America's help were worse than the country feared, and left them with devastated infrastructure, a collapsed economy, and billions of dollars of debt. This allowed America the opportunity to help struggling Bolivia by purchasing its oil, although at a steeply discounted rate to offset the costs incurred by its assistance.

Selling Debt, and Wars for Economic Supremacy

America's addiction to economic growth explains the puzzle of why America never had enough money even during the peak of its affluence. Yet the addiction to economic growth does not explain another puzzling aspect of the American economy.

At America's peak, its economic strength was based on a strong manufacturing base. Yet that rapidly changed in the 1980s and beyond. In the span of only a few decades, America deliberately abandoned the majority of its manufacturing. During this period, America changed from being one of the world's leading exporters into becoming a leading importer.

Yet the American economy remained the most powerful on earth, with a population that enjoyed a standard of living that was still the envy of much of the world. What is puzzling is how it sustained this strong economy even when it was manufacturing and producing very little of anything. So how did America generate the money to pay for those imports?

Earlier, we explored how America emerged from World War II in a position of overwhelming power. To repeat the statement of American diplomat George F. Kennan, "Our real task in the coming period is to devise a pattern of relationships which will permit us to maintain this position of disparity." One way America achieved this was with a variety of clandestine operations and military actions. Yet another way America achieved this was with a bold and unprecedented system of economic and financial arrangements.

After World War II, America could have acknowledged that its prominence was a unique product of world history that would not last forever. It could have settled back, savoured its brief burst of affluence, and focused on creating a quality life for its citizens and a safer and more peaceful world. But the idea of being "number one" felt too good to give up.

America was in a unique position to restructure the global financial system. And it did so in a way that ensured future American economic dominance. This began in 1944, before the war was actually over, when delegates from 44 nations met in Bretton Woods, New Hampshire for the United Nations Monetary and Financial Conference. The event became known as the Bretton Woods Conference. The goal of Bretton Woods was to establish a global regulatory framework for trade and finance, including an international system of convertible currencies and fixed exchange rates. Regulatory institutions were created, including the International Monetary Fund, the General Agreement on Tariffs and Trade, and the World Bank.

A fundamental aspect of the agreement, insisted upon by America, was to establish the American dollar as the benchmark for all relative values. It did this by establishing the American dollar as the world's reserve currency. Other countries pegged their currency to the American dollar, backed by gold set at a fixed rate. Therefore the dollar took over the role previously served by the gold standard. The American dollar effectively became the world's currency, and most international transactions were denominated in American dollars.

The agreements allowed America to use its position of influence to control the global economy, giving unprecedented access to the world's markets and materials. Other countries—most prominently Britain and France—were not happy with the arrangement, but they essentially had no choice but to concede. American prosperity was critical to postwar rebuilding, which it accomplished by extending loans and direct aid. It did so with the European Recovery Program, generally known as the *Marshall Plan.* This helped European countries to rebuild their devastated economies and manufacturing capabilities, and served to further boost the American economy by providing them with the means to buy American products. The system was key to the creation of America's burst of postwar affluence.

Overall, the system worked well for over 20 years. But eventually it became obvious that America was spending far more than it could back with its gold reserves. In addition, America had steadily increased its spending on consumer items, especially from Japan. This resulted in a steady increase in an American trade imbalance. Foreign dollars could still be exchanged for American gold, but by the late 1960s there was not enough American gold to back all of it.

In 1971, the British government formally requested $3 billion in gold from America. There were serious fears of a global run to redeem American dollars for gold, which would have resulted in economic disaster. President Richard Nixon responded by declaring the American dollar to be detached from the gold standard, resulting in the dollar becoming based purely upon an abstract value disassociated from any tangible asset.

Standard economic thinking of the time would have led a country in such a situation to boost its manufacturing in order to increase its exports, and therefore to improve its balance of trade. But America did not follow standard economic thinking. Instead, America engineered a unique and brilliant strategy whose importance to the future of America cannot be overstated.

America's financial specialists concluded that the only way the dollar could maintain its status as the world's reserve currency was if the countries America paid in dollars were limited to spending them in financial transactions that were officially denominated in dollars. The dynamic that became known as *dollar hegemony* was created by America's ability to ensure that critical commodities, most notably oil, were denominated in dollars.

America flooded the world with American dollars by spending in foreign countries. The foreign recipients deposited the dollars in their central banks. But then the central banks had a problem: If the central banks did not spend the money in America, the country's exchange rate relative to the dollar would go up—thereby penalising that country's exporters.

It became necessary for the economies of other nations to acquire and hold dollar reserves to sustain the exchange value of their domestic currencies. This created support for a strong dollar, and required the central banks of other countries to acquire more dollar reserves.

And the way in which countries accomplished this was by acquiring American Treasury Bonds. A Treasury bond, of course, is not actually money. It is an IOU. In other words, it is debt. As illogical and counterintuitive as it sounds, America made money by selling debt, by convincing foreign countries to buy American debt. The result was that world trade became dominated by a dynamic in which America created dollars and the rest of the world created things that dollars could buy. With this method, America could sustain the curious situation in which it rid itself of manufacturing yet was able to retain the world's highest material standard of living.

The system was self-reinforcing and self-perpetuating. Yet it was a dangerous game which required all the participants to continue following the rules. If enough major countries decided to change the rules, then America would have a major problem.

By the 2030s, America's wars were motivated primarily by the need to sustain the American dollar as the world's reserve currency. But what few American realised is that from the 1990s onward that motivation had been a substantial aspect of several wars and military actions.

In a strategy document released during the administration of President George H. W. Bush, the Pentagon declared that it was now fighting for an "open economic system." In other words, it was fighting for economic arrangements permitting American investment and financial optimisation. Basically, the military had become a force to defend and advance an American-led global economic order.

During the Iraq War and other military actions in the Middle East, American foreign policy was heavily criticised for being all about sustaining America's oil supply. But another little-reported fact was more of a threat to America. In 2000, Iraq leader Saddam Hussein decided to denominate Iraq's oil sales in euros rather than dollars. This would have set a precedent that could not be tolerated. In 2003 Iraq was invaded, and once under American control the denomination for oil sales was quickly switched back to the dollar.

In a further development, in 2011 America backed an intervention in Libya that overthrew and killed Muammar Gaddafi. Humanitarian motivations were claimed, which had a good measure of legitimacy considering the appalling human rights record of the Gaddafi regime. But America had other strong motivations. Gaddafi had developed a plan to stop selling Libyan oil in American dollars, and to instead demand payment in dinars—an African regional currency based on gold. And Gaddafi was encouraging other governments to join in the plan.

At the time, Libya had an independent state-owned central bank that was unconnected to other major central banks. The importance to America of ending this situation was indicated by how quickly the

America-backed rebels created a Western-style central bank before forming a new government. In fact, the new bank was created while the war was still in progress.

In such cases, America had been able to use its military power to retain economic dominance. But the question was how long such a strategy would be effective. Countries such as Iraq and Libya were comparatively easy threats to overcome. America would soon have to face threats that would not be so easy.

Several nations had been dissatisfied with the Bretton Woods agreement from the beginning, and dissatisfaction with America's overpowering economic influence and the privileged role of the dollar only grew in subsequent decades. The rules of the game were made by America for the benefit of America, and other nations felt it was time to change the rules of the game.

This began to happen in 2009 at the first formal summit of *BRICS*, an organisation whose name was the acronym for five major emerging national economies: Brazil, Russia, India, China, and South Africa. That first summit resulted in a statement announcing the need for a global reserve currency that was "diversified, stable, and predictable." This meeting marked the first formal step by America's major trading partners to replace the American dollar as the world's reserve currency.

In 2013, the member countries agreed to create a global financial institution to rival the American-dominated World Bank. Then it went on to announce the arrangements for this institution, to be called the New Development Bank. China began to enter trade deals in currency other than dollars. Russia announced intentions of doing likewise, and Russia's president announced the goal of building a "multipolar world order" that would break America's economic domination of world markets.

As might be expected, America was not pleased by such developments. If the American dollar lost its status as the world's reserve currency the value of the dollar would crash. Yet what could America do to prevent it? America might be willing to discourage such developments by conducting military actions in small and relatively weak nations, but what could it do against large and powerful nations?

America avoided overt actions against the world's major nations, but managed to defend dollar hegemony for decades using covert means. Although not known until after America's collapse, the country had embarked upon an extraordinary programme of bribery and blackmail targeted toward the world's top political and financial leaders. Secret deals were struck to reward cooperation with substantial gifts.

For those unwilling to cooperate, America's top pornographic film stars were recruited as spies to ensnare them into activities of the most lurid nature, which were secretly documented. Cooperation was gained in exchange for not releasing the documentation.

This covert programme explains events that had thoroughly baffled the world community at the time. Such as during the 2027 BRICS summit, when Russian president Boris Zubkov excused himself from a vote to abandon the American dollar because "It's a lovely day for a walk." Or the 2032 summit, which Brazilian president Ernesto Vargas chose to hold in Rio de Janeiro during the height of Carnival at one of Rio's most popular nightclubs. Needless to say, the summit's agenda was quickly abandoned in a frenzy of alcohol-fueled revelry. Three days later, the attendees who remained conscious had no idea why they were in Brazil, or why they were adorned in brightly coloured feathers.

The situation became critical in the 2030s, when such covert actions became ineffective. Leaders of other nations began to openly defy America, especially China. Chinese President Zhu Qingling began making public suggestions that China was ready to cash in its American Treasury Bonds, and that America needed to start thinking about how it would raise the money. President Qingling suggested that China would be pleased to accept payment in the form of all of America's gold supply from Fort Knox. An enraged President Bradley Anderson shot back, "The only way you'll take our gold is if you pry it from our cold, dead hands." President Qingling replied, "That can be arranged."

Yet despite the tough talk, the American government felt the need to make some sort of concession to China. And it was able to do so via means other than economic.

Two years earlier, the president had declared a ban on all agricultural exports. However, as a result of the threats from China the president responded by quietly authorising the export of 30 percent of the total American grain harvest to China. As for the effects on citizens of America, the president attempted to put a positive spin on the impending domestic grain shortage by introducing a supposedly health-conscious piece of legislation termed the *America Goes on a Diet Act.*

By the late-2040s, when the American economy was in serious decline, many Middle Eastern countries attempted to cash in their investments in American Treasury Bonds. They had decided the time was prudent to "cut their losses" by getting back whatever they could while there was still time. This was quickly followed by Indonesia, which by this point viewed the situation in America as utterly hopeless.

As might be imagined, America did not honour these requests. Not only did America refuse to pay back any debt to foreign governments, but it went on the offensive. President Johnny Jackson Garth warned the world, "If America goes down, we'll take the world with us."

And the world was well aware that America was capable of doing so. America's nuclear weapon arsenal was powerful enough to destroy every other nation on earth several times over. Most thought that America would never resort to initiating nuclear aggression. Yet America was the only nation in history to have detonated nuclear weapons against a civilian population, and America had a known history of extreme irrationality when its global dominance was threatened. What would America do when its options were either nuclear war or the total collapse of its economic system?

The world was not at all assured by what happened only a few weeks later. In a speech broadcast around the world President Garth, on a podium backed by a video screen showing images of nuclear explosions, gave the following ominous warning: "To the nations of the world, I have the following message. Buy American Treasury Bonds. Or else."

CRISIS MANAGEMENT

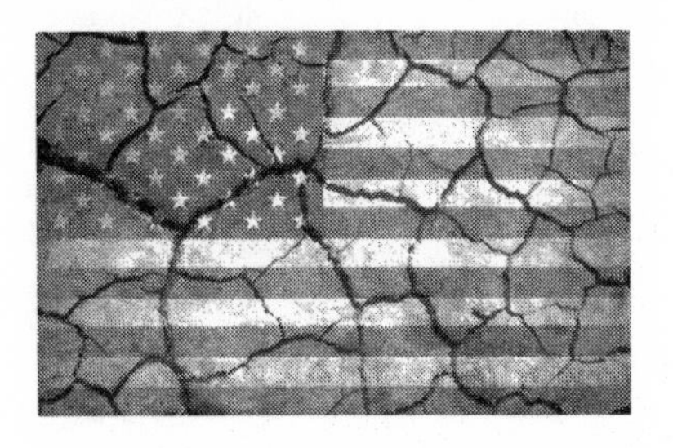

SIGNS OF DECLINE

America was used to winning. But the winning streak had to end at some point. And it began to end just as America was at its glorious peak. In 1970, American's per capita income and material standard of living was at an all-time high. There was a strong and sizable middle class. Poverty was at an all-time low. America had an extremely strong industrial base, and remained a world-leader in technological development. Comparative indexes of health, nutrition, education, and home ownership were at or near the best in the world.

This would change dramatically in the coming decades, as America began its rapid decline.

Yet America lacked the desire to thoughtfully respond to its increasing problems, or to proactively prevent itself from creating the problems in the first place. As a result, the remainder of American history became an era of crisis management. America's attitude was, "We can't slow down to think about future long-term solutions! We're in crisis mode!" As a result, America never slowed down enough to realise that it created the crisis.

America's winning streak began to end in the mid-1970s. During the height of the Cold War effort to halt the spread of communism, America took sides in the civil war within the small nation of Vietnam. This led to a protracted war that was tremendously controversial, inspiring both international criticism and massive domestic protests. America expended huge military resources on the tiny nation of Vietnam, dropping more bombs per square mile than it had in World War II.

Yet America was forced to concede that it could not win the war in Vietnam. The last American troops returned home in 1973, and the war was officially over in 1975. The effect on the American psyche was enormous, and would eventually be called *The Vietnam Syndrome*—the psychological attempt to live with the unacceptable reality that it was possible for America to not win.

In addition, America's unparalleled level of affluence—although still incredibly high by global standards—began to decline. America's share of the world's wealth declined as Europe and Asia rebounded from the destruction of World War II.

Japan had become a world leader that posed serious competition to America's economic and industrial dominance. This was especially true in the automotive industry—America's largest manufacturing sector—when Japan offered compact and efficient cars as America was hit with the 1973 oil crisis. The American automotive industry was devastated. And so was America's confidence. Americans were pleased with the superior fuel efficiency of the tiny Japanese cars, yet could not shake the feeling that by abandoning oversized American gas guzzlers they were also abandoning America. The mighty roar of an American-made big-block V8 engine could not be adequately replaced by the high-RPM buzz of a small Japanese engine, even if it achieved 30 miles per gallon.

The oil crisis was followed, in 1974, by a major political crisis when President Richard Nixon, on the verge of being impeached due to the Watergate scandal, resigned.

America was also experiencing a cultural crisis. American music had become dominated by disco and soft rock, bringing fears that American culture was dead and that good music would never again be produced in America. Such fears appeared to be confirmed when the Captain and Tennille composition "Muskrat Love"—widely considered to be among the worst songs ever recorded—became a major hit.

Yet America's initial responses to these crises were healthy and positive. The energy crisis served as an effective "wake-up call" that—for a few years—stimulated discussions about conservation, energy efficiency, and alternative energy. The Watergate scandal left the public with a healthy suspicion of politicians and political machinations. Although America suffered defeat and humiliation when it abandoned the hopeless cause of the Vietnam War, it left America with a strong adversity to foreign wars that would last for over a decade. Disco and soft rock were eliminated by the rise of punk and new wave, which revitalised American music and brought America back to the forefront of cultural innovation.

Such responses demonstrated that America, at this point in its history, had the ability to react to problems in an effective way.

Yet only forty years later, the situation had declined dramatically. According to statistics from 2015, among industrialised nations, America was notable for having the highest poverty rate, the lowest score on the UN index of "material well-being of children," the highest health care expenditures, the highest infant mortality rate, the highest prevalence of mental health problems, the highest obesity rate, the highest consumption of antidepressants per capita, the highest homicide rate, and the largest prison population per capita. By international standards, the rural counties of southern West Virginia and eastern Kentucky qualified as developing countries, as did large sections of American cities such as Detroit, Cleveland, Gary, and many others.

There was a growing suspicion that, for an increasing number of Americans, the American Dream was over. Young adults assumed they would have less than their parents, and that their children would have less than them. Working hard and obeying the rules was no guarantee of economic prosperity, or even of economic survival.

The cost of living had risen dramatically while wages for most American citizens—adjusted for inflation—were stagnant at best. And the means to earn those wages grew increasingly uncertain. Where once Americans felt somewhat secure in their jobs, that security dwindled as jobs—and sometimes entire job fields—suddenly disappeared, never to return. During the height of America's postwar affluence, many people talked of their desire for "meaningful work." That did not last. By the early 21st century, any job was a good job, and questions such as "Does this job allow me to express myself in a creative way?" were considered to be forms of ironic humour.

Americans did not like the fact that they spent the majority of their waking hours doing something they did not like, with the rewards diminishing by the year. Also diminishing was the prospect of a comfortable retirement—or retirement in any form. Yet even if they hated their jobs, they held onto them for dear life. The mantra for such workers was "At least I have a job."

American workers developed interesting strategies to half-acknowledge their mixed feelings about their situation. To fully acknowledge their desperation would be too depressing. So their feelings came out in mottos such as "Thank God it's Friday" and "I'm doing pretty good for a Monday." These half-joking comments allowed them to confirm to themselves and others that they disliked their situation, while avoiding the full depth of their despair.

Corporate culture was savagely parodied in movies such as *Office Space* and the popular long-running comic strip *Dilbert*. Many Americans posted copies of *Dilbert* at their workplaces, laughing with their co-workers over the antics of cartoon characters demonstrating mind-numbingly stupid behaviour that, in many cases, consisted of literal transcripts of corporate doublespeak and irrationality. International humour experts remain puzzled at why Americans found this humorous, since one of the universal tenets of comedy is the principle: *humour is suffering that happens to somebody else*. Yet in the case of *Dilbert*, the suffering portrayed in the comics was precisely what was happening in their real lives.

America's economy continued to degrade as it approached the point where economic growth simply could not go on. America was struggling to retain a minimum rate of growth, and in some years was barely able to register any growth at all. Normally a recession is a temporary economic condition in a cycle in which the lows alternate with periods of relative affluence. Yet from the 2010s onward, America experienced what many referred to as a "permanent recession." The term proved accurate, since it was a recession from which America never fully recovered.

Americans were well aware of their shrinking paychecks. They were also aware that costs for basic necessities like housing and energy were rising, thus cutting deeper into those shrinking paychecks. They were also aware that a tiny proportion of Americans had grown far wealthier.

Some blamed those wealthy Americans, and the politicians who helped to make them so wealthy, thinking this was the sole reason for their declining affluence.

Yet Americans who were focused only on the unequal distribution of wealth missed some crucial points. They did not understand that America's continuing destruction of its natural resources had direct economic consequences. As natural resources got scarcer, costs continued to rise. As fossil fuels began to run out, costs rose even faster. They did not understand why the price of housing continually rose. Indeed those homeowners who sought to profit from the dynamic did not understand that they were contributing to the problem.

Perhaps most importantly, Americans did not understand that the country was addicted to economic growth. They did not understand, therefore did not account for, what was happening as the pyramid scheme was approaching its limits. They did not understand that eventually all addictions "bottom out" and that was beginning to happen to America's economy.

In the future loomed the point when America could no longer grow itself out of the problems caused by its addiction to growth. Yet since America was unable to see the addiction for what it was, its problems were inevitably interpreted in a way in which the only hope was more economic growth. As America's addiction to growth approached its limits, efforts to keep the economy functioning would grow increasingly desperate. As a result, America's final decades would consist of an increasingly frenzied no-holds-barred focus on keeping its economy from collapsing.

The American Character

Studies across history have concluded that the most important aspect of whether a declining civilisation succumbs or survives is their attitude toward that decline. Do they seek to understand it? And what is their reaction in response to that understanding? Since this attitude is a direct reflection of the character of that culture, it is important to explore the subject of the American character. As we shall see, the reasons for America's collapse are rooted in the core concepts of what it meant to be an American.

Of course, attempting to define the American character is a problematic endeavour. The American character was not a single, monolithic construction. America was one of the most diverse countries in world history, a "melting pot" of different cultures, beliefs, values, and lifestyles.

It should be noted that America's diversity of "types" is itself one of the defining characteristics of the American character. Hector St. John de Crèvecoeur, an early French immigrant who was one of the first to comment upon America, wrote that the lack of a cultural tradition was itself the essence of the American character.

And this diversity only increased throughout American history. How can we attempt to define the American character in a nation that included corporate warriors, sensitive singer-songwriters, gangster rappers, fundamentalist preachers, and sensible mothers who learned from television commercials that everything would be okay if their family started the day with a balanced breakfast?

This brings us to consider one of the most fascinating aspects of the American character: the great importance that Americans placed in belonging to a subculture.

There is a deep human need—perhaps the deepest of human needs—to belong, to identify with something larger than oneself. This need has manifested throughout human history from the earliest tribes and clans. From the beginning, what we call "culture" provided a sense of belonging that provided for physical as well as metaphysical needs.

Yet America had very little sense of a shared history. To a major degree, Americans were culturally adrift.

Beginning in the 1960s, cultural fragmentation accelerated. There became several Americas, split by generation, cultural interests, lifestyle choices, sexual identities, hobbies, and political philosophies. Increasingly, America became a nation of subcultures.

Americans proudly defined themselves based on the value of individual freedom. As a result, travelers to America were puzzled about the degree to which Americans clung to the shared values of their chosen subculture. Or in other words, they were puzzled at the way in which Americans—proudly and at great length pontificating on their precious freedom of choice—chose to conform.

Subcultures gave individual Americans the opportunity to surround themselves with a self-supporting bubble of people to provide a common identity. Each had their own shared set of values and priorities, their own criteria of what was right, and their own assumption of what was normal. They each provided a sense of belonging, an existential identity, a way to distinguish "us" from "them." They each shared the same information sources and read the same publications. They shared the same general perceptions, the same philosophies, and the same "truths."

Although Americans were generally oblivious to the phenomenon, it was obvious to visitors from other countries who found it fascinating. In fact, 21st century tourists sometimes arrived with a game called *American Bingo*. The game consisted of players who attempted to be the first to spot an American subculture "type," thus gaining the right to mark the accompanying square on a playing card. To give some idea of American "types" of this era, here are the categories from a game card discovered by archaeologists:

- Soccer Mom
- Punk Rocker
- High-Powered Corporate Executive
- Jaded Single Mom Who Has Nearly But Not Quite Given Up on Love
- Bro Dude
- Dope Smokin' Hippie
- Cocaine Snortin' Yuppie
- Meth Addict
- Emo/Goth
- Gun-Totin' Redneck
- Sorority Bitch
- Hip Asian
- Metalhead
- Fitness Freak
- Metrosexual
- Hipster
- Mallrat
- Pack of Suburban Women Who Go Clubbing and Drink Tequila Shots and Yell "Woo-Hoo!"

Increasingly, Americans became identified with their subcultures more than the overall culture of America. Some Americans vaguely referred to a "mainstream American culture" but claimed that, whatever it was, they did not belong to it. Some Americans claimed that "mainstream American culture" no longer existed.

Yet despite such claims, to a large degree there were many values that Americans shared in common. To identify them, it takes no more than a random viewing of America's most popular television programmes. Americans of all types shared certain commonalities, perhaps unknown to them but well-known by programming specialists. The producers of American television programmes had a strong vested interest in being attuned to the pulse of American life in order to attract the most viewers and therefore the most advertising revenue. Highly paid advertising and marketing agencies conducted research which was used to create characters relatable to the highest number of Americans. Therefore, the characters they created can be thought of as something like "generic" Americans.

Such characters seldom mentioned social or cultural issues. They were not interested in creative pursuits. Although most were not overtly stupid, signs of above-average intelligence were avoided. They had no thoughts about anything of importance. They were self-absorbed and had little or no relationship with the world. They made no effort to contribute to their communities. Perhaps most importantly, the characters had achieved a level of effortless affluence without the apparent need to work for it.

Such characters flattered American's self-perception and brought a sense of belonging and validation. Having no thoughts or creative pursuits, and being self-absorbed and having no relationship with the world, was perfectly acceptable. And effortless affluence must be a worthy goal since all the characters on television programmes have achieved it.

If Americans ever experienced existential doubt—if they ever had disturbing thoughts about whether their lives had any meaning within the timeline of eternity and the infinite vastness of the universe—they had a sure way to reassure themselves. All that was necessary was to turn on the television.

The phenomenon of American subcultures can be seen as a direct expression of individualism, since in essence they are forms of belonging based upon individual preference. Rather than a sense of belonging to something transcending individual preferences, it was based on belonging to a shared culture of individuals who shared those same preferences.

Subcultures focused on the differences and ignored the deeper commonalities. Someone from the Emo/Goth subculture might feel they were radically different due to their style of clothing or by dying their hair a shocking colour. But it is likely they shared the same general lifestyle goals as someone from the Soccer Mom subculture, and hoped to drive the same make of car as preferred by those of the Cocaine Snortin' Yuppie subculture. It is likely that they enjoyed many of the same television programmes as the Hipsters and the Metrosexuals. And it is almost certain that all of these subcultures were united in their lack of questioning the foundations of America's value system, so we can deduce that they generally accepted them.

Therefore, in the final analysis, American subcultures were profoundly superficial. Within the groups, no matter what their differences, were shared the deeper character traits typical to the American character. Such as the focus on individual self-importance, the quest for material and economic affluence, and the desire to avoid thinking.

□ □ □

To understand how America developed these traits requires a brief review of American history, because attempting to define the American character apart from American history is impossible. The unique circumstances of America's early history required certain traits, which in turn furthered American history in a direction reflecting those traits. America's history and the American character evolved together in a self-reinforcing and self-perpetuating cycle.

Early Americans were primarily British, of course, and brought with them qualities of the British character. Yet over time those qualities became replaced with qualities engendered by the experience of starting an entirely new country. Americans were not only inventing a country but inventing what it meant to be an American.

Yet Americans, as members of all nations tend to be, were generally unaware of the traits they shared. Because of this, one of the best ways for us to understand the American character is from the impressions recorded by visitors from outside America.

One of the most famous was Alexis de Tocqueville, a French diplomat who travelled to America in 1831. His observations were published in 1835 as *Democracy in America*. Out of many astute observations about America, one of them struck to the core of the identity of this new country. America lacked a shared tradition and set of universal values, so it defaulted to a basic value that everybody could agree on, regardless of race, background, or belief system. As de Tocqueville wrote, "I know of no country, indeed, where the love of money has taken a stronger hold on the affections of men."

Travelers to America throughout its history found the most striking feature of the American character to be their obsession with business and wealth. When Americans asked someone "What do you do?" they were not interested in their personal lives or in what was meaningful to their existence. They meant "What is your job? What position do you occupy?" And although Americans were generally too polite to ask "How much money do you make?" that was often the underlying question.

Americans tended to define "the pursuit of Happiness" as "The pursuit of affluence." Whether or not this brought happiness is debatable. In *Democracy in America*, de Tocqueville described a key aspect of the American character that would remain dominant for the remaining 200-plus years of American history:

> It is odd to watch with what feverish ardor the Americans pursue prosperity and how they are ever tormented by the shadowy suspicion that they may not have chosen the shortest route to get it. Americans cleave to the things of this world as if assured that they will never die, and yet are in such a rush to snatch any that come within their reach, as if expecting to stop living before they have relished them. They clutch everything but hold nothing fast, and so lose grip as they hurry after some new delight.

A core element of the American character was that Americans could never have enough. Americans hustled. They were builders, doers, go-getters, dreamers. They were receptive to new ideas and technologies, willing to experiment and try new approaches.

Such qualities were largely self-selected. People that came to America needed energy and drive. Such qualities were required to transform a vast wilderness into a modern civilisation. And those same qualities were necessary to advance that civilisation along what was previously described as *the frontier*.

What Americans called *the frontier spirit* embodied a set of characteristics that included individualism, self-reliance, independence, and the courage to take risks and accept challenges. The frontier was a place where the individual tamed the wilderness in a test of individual strength, ingenuity, and drive. Settling the west was seen as a moral struggle, a test of will that could break a person without the adequate courage. As a result, the idea of pushing into new frontiers became a key aspect of the American character.

A very brief period of that expansion, a few decades from the Civil War in 1865 to the closing of the frontier in 1890, was heavily mythologised as the *Wild West*. Images from this period—wagon trains, log cabins, cattle drives, frontier towns, gunfights—remained vivid in the American consciousness long after the frontier was settled. Such images pervaded their lives, shaping their identities and values, and were used to sell products as well as political candidates throughout the rest of American history. It is not surprising that America's last president was a one-time country singer who wore a cowboy hat and won votes with Western-style witticisms such as, "My opponent is so crooked that if he swallowed a nail he'd spit up a corkscrew."

The frontier resulted in Americans being doers rather than thinkers. It led to their "can-do" spirit and to the emphasis on "getting things done." The frontier forced Americans to be inventive. This quality led to Americans, for the remainder of its history, being on the forefront of technological innovation. This explains why America was the birthplace of the phonograph record, motion pictures, refrigeration, electrical power transmission, the light bulb, and the first recorded aeroplane flight.

Less than a hundred years after the original frontier had been settled, the idea lived on as the frontier turned to the exploration of space. As a result, America was the first nation to put a person on the moon.

While this was undoubtedly a great accomplishment, it included motivations that were less than idealistic. America was at the time involved in a "space race" with the Soviet Union, and it can be argued that America's motivation was less about the accomplishment itself than in not losing the race. Also, one of the most important actions of that first person on the moon was to plant the American flag. To non-Americans the gesture carried connotations of colonial expansion. It appeared to be a continuation of the movement of Manifest Destiny, with America being the first nation to claim the territory of an entire planet.

□ □ □

America's positive traits were often seen as being directly related to some negative characteristics. Their individualism and self-determination expressed itself with selfish and self-centred behaviour. Americans had little interest in other cultures, and were uninterested in ideas that had no direct relevance outside of their own self-interest. When Americans travelled to other countries, their negative traits sometimes manifested in the stereotype of the "Ugly American." This was a type of American that was demanding, obnoxious, and garishly dressed—with "voices as loud as their shirts."

Most Americans were horrible listeners. But they were excellent talkers, and their favourite subject was themselves. Visitors to America were frustrated when attempting to initiate conversations on topics such as economic policy or advances in science, and the American would reply with a lengthy monologue about how their best friend did not reply to their email and how they felt about it. If another American was present, he or she would advance the conversation by waiting until the first American stopped for breath, then initiating their own monologue about problems they encountered while fixing a leaky faucet. Thus, a conversation in America consisted of two people talking at each other.

America was biased toward the qualities of extroverts and those who exhibited the "Type A" personality. America rewarded people who exhibited aggressive goal-orientation and who were skilled in self-marketing and self-promotion. As America was biased toward individuals with such qualities, it was biased against more "introverted" qualities such as thoughtfulness and contemplation.

Other countries tolerated introverts. Some countries—especially in Europe and Asia—even accepted and valued them. But in America, being an introvert was a weakness. Their lack of gregarious self-marketing was seen as a problem to be cured. America was unique among countries in that shyness was interpreted as arrogance, and lack of self-promotion was interpreted as being pretentious.

America preferred doers, and were highly suspicious of thinkers. Worst of all were artists, the most impractical of all, since all they did was to produce works of beauty that demonstrated the value of human creativity. Artists were seen as people who placed value in elevating the human spirit, of helping humanity reach a place where we could more clearly see ourselves and better recognise our role in the grand scheme of life. In other words, they produced nothing of importance.

This leads us to consider another negative aspect of the American character: its anti-intellectual bias.

It should be noted that America's founding documents—the Declaration of Independence and The United States Constitution—were the results of a unique collection of highly intelligent individuals. They had studied philosophy as well as world history, and to this day we can appreciate that the founding documents were a product of wisdom far ahead of their time.

There remain questions about the degree to which such intelligence was shared or valued by America as a whole. But what cannot be denied is that to the degree it existed it steadily faded away.

A turning point is marked by America's 1952 presidential election, with Adlai Stephenson running against Dwight David "Ike" Eisenhower. An open intellectual, Stephenson suffered a landslide loss to the simple country soldier. Historian Arthur M. Schlesinger Jr. wrote of Stephenson, "To the United States and the world he was the voice of a reasonable, civilized, and elevated America." The problem was, America did not want such a voice. Stephenson himself was fully aware that his intelligence was a disadvantage. A revealing incident occurred while Stephenson was campaigning for president. A citizen shouted to Stephenson that he "had the vote of every thinking person." Stephenson replied, "That's not enough—we need a majority!"

This prejudice against thinking was not at all a trivial matter. It led American discourse to become dominated by a style in which the only voices heard were those with the highest volume combined with the simplest and most dogmatic messages. Therefore precisely the kind of thoughtful analysis that America most sorely needed—the type of open-minded conversation that America most needed to have—was barred from having an effective voice.

Americans had always been blessed as well as cursed with a feeling of unthinking confidence that led the country to leap into any direction without considering the possibility of unintended consequences, or assuming it could improvise its way out of the consequences later on.

This desire to unthinkingly forge ahead led America create a suburban landscape and national infrastructure based upon unsustainable fossil fuel energy. It rushed to transform agriculture into an industrial process without considering soil erosion, aquifer depletion, or the effects of agricultural chemicals. It embraced financial and economic arrangements for short-term gain that guaranteed long-term failure. This eventually proved fatal. America learned the hard way that it could not improvise its way out of fundamental errors.

Common to all situations was a total lack of attempting to understand the roots of the problems and to direct efforts toward effective solutions. Rather than resolving the roots of their problems, they waged war on the symptoms. America never varied in this strategy, right up to the end.

America is unique in world history in the attempt to deal with alcohol abuse by banning alcohol, amending its Constitution to initiate the short-lived era of *Prohibition*. Essentially, America declared war on alcohol—an effort which failed miserably. Later, it attempted to solve drug abuse with a "War on Drugs" which was no more successful. It also attempted a "War on Poverty," a "War on Crime," and a "War on Terrorism." All of which, as may be reasonably guessed, never solved the problems, and in many cases only served to worsen them.

America's anti-intellectual bias evolved into a general bias against intelligence. Eventually this evolved into something that historians have termed "the embrace of stupid." Some Americans were aware of this process. They publicly shared their deep concern over what was termed the "dumbing down of America." But others were not concerned. The ones being dumbed down were quite satisfied with it. Eventually, stupidity was not seen as a problem to be cured, but as a badge of honour.

Obviously, such a development is problematic for a democratic government which, to be successful, depends upon a knowledgeable and intelligent population.

It should be noted that, although Americans were embracing stupidity in dealing with its many social problems, there were some ways in which Americans were becoming more savvy. For example, in the 1950s advertisements for the soft drink Pepsi showed images of popular people along with the text, "Be popular. Drink Pepsi." However, by the 1980s the text became unnecessary. Americans saw the image of popular people drinking Pepsi and were smart enough to make the connection on their own.

Unfortunately, this increase in intelligence did not extend to making the connections necessary to halt America's rapid decline.

The Downside of Individualism

America's experience with the frontier also resulted in the myth of the *rugged individual*. Above all else, Americans were focused on the individual—on freedom and independence for the individual. Americans wanted freedom from control. They were suspicious of government. They disliked laws and regulations, which were considered, as best, as "necessary evils," and, at worst, as simply "evils." Their political, economic, and legal systems heavily favoured individual rights over collective responsibilities.

This resulted in something of a "blind spot" in America, in which business interests were free to make decisions involving the lives of millions of Americans. Real estate investors and developers were free to destroy and rebuild entire neighbourhoods and drive up housing prices, yet public outcry to regulate the process was shouted down as "anti-freedom." Large corporations in vital fields such as agriculture and medicine were able to make business decisions that affected literally every American in the quality of their food and the state of their physical health. Yet even in such vital areas, the freedom of business was linked to individual freedom, even when the freedom of one business made choices that comprised the freedom of millions of individuals.

An interesting example of America's bias toward individual freedom was the nation's efforts to ban smoking in public places. There was substantial resistance from smokers decrying their loss of freedom in public places such as airports and restaurants, but nothing like what happened when the movement went on to include public bars, taverns, and nightclubs.

The argument put forth by smokers—and repeated even by many non-smokers—was that a smoking ban in bars denied individual freedom. As for others in the establishment that interpreted *freedom* as *freedom to avoid the risk of lung cancer*, the smokers had an interesting reply. They claimed that such persons were free to leave the bar. Such logic was used repeatedly throughout American history. If a neighbour complained of a barking dog, that neighbour had the freedom to stop listening to it. If a consumer complained of a dangerous product, that consumer had the freedom to not buy that product. Such logic, if taken to its extreme, would result in the conclusion that would be acceptable to fire a gun at someone, since they had the freedom to dodge the bullet.

Although Americans liked to think of themselves as purveyors of "fair play," even the most cursory review of American history reveals that their ethical criteria was more along the lines of, "If you can get away with it, then it's okay."

The desire of Americans to have everything their way led them to twist life's ambiguities toward interpretations in ways that maximised personal self-interest and minimised personal responsibility. When an American was in a hurry, then spontaneity was important. Yet when an American was taking their time, then patience became the prime virtue. If an American was offended by somebody's words, then the American would tell them "people should respect the feelings of others." Yet if the words of an American offended someone else, then "people should be responsible for their reactions." In short, Americans interpreted their own requests as "expressing my genuine needs," and interpreted the requests of others as "making selfish demands."

Basically, everybody in America was trying to get away with something and refused to admit it. This quality was strongest in America's politicians. An example from a political debate:

> Question: "Senator, you vowed no tax increases, yet now you're increasing taxes. Why did you reverse your position?"
>
> Answer: "I don't care what anybody says, I still believe that America is a great place to raise children."

It may be noted that the answer is legitimate and perfectly reasonable. However, not as an answer to that particular question.

With this quality exemplified in America's leaders, Americans took it as tacit permission to embrace this quality in their personal lives. If politicians embraced denial as a legitimate strategy, then it spread down to all Americans in a form of what may be termed "trickle-down denial." Here are a few examples of how typical Americans used the strategy:

> Question: "Why didn't you finish your homework?"
>
> Answer: "I think it's important to feel good about yourself."

> Question: "Did you overdraw the checking account?"
>
> Answer: "Blame is an unhealthy solution."

> Question: "You stand accused of aggravated assault. How do you plead?"
>
> Answer: "I could really use a drink."

America's focus on individualism made it difficult or impossible for them to recognise large-scale dynamics. As a result of this, Americans were easily deceived by those who would manipulate them for their own gain. This tendency was deeply embedded in the American character. In 1835, Alexis de Tocqueville warned about a potentially fatal flaw in America. He identified a tendency toward self-indulgence and apathy toward the public good that made America susceptible to the threat of tyranny.

Throughout American history, powerful interests were able to pursue policies directly responsible for things like declining wages and increasing unemployment, knowing that Americans were not inclined to examine such policies and were easily convinced to blame themselves. Or if that failed, they were easily convinced to blame each other.

As America declined over the decades, Americans responded with efforts to retreat more deeply into individualism. After America's collapse, cultural anthropologists from other countries would label this trend *entrenchment*. It was the natural extension of a trend that had begun late in the 20th century, called *cocooning*. This trend, which was a response to the reluctance of Americans to engage in social activities, was marked by the preference to insulate themselves at home. To Americans, all that mattered was "taking care of yourself and your tribe." As for other Americans, it was "everybody for themselves."

This situation, firmly established by the year 2000, was markedly different from that of America in the 1950s through early 1970s. During that time, a substantial number of Americans were intensely interested in exploring ways in which society could be improved. This was an era in which Americans were relatively well-read, and many best-sellers were non-fiction works by academics in the social sciences. Ideas about alternative methods of childrearing and education were explored. Various economic and political arrangements were examined, and the pros and cons of free-market capitalism were vigourously debated.

Yet after America reached its 1970s peak, such efforts dwindled rapidly. Part of the reason is that many Americans had abandoned hope. Perhaps it was a result of America's humiliating defeat in the Vietnam War, and the realisation that years of activism to oppose it made little difference. Perhaps it was because two of America's brightest idealistic beacons, Martin Luther King, Jr. and Robert Kennedy, were violently assassinated.

Yet there is widespread agreement that a primary reason was America's diminishing economic condition. Such efforts are easier during periods of affluence, when a wide cross section of the population can afford it. But as the economic peak turned into a long-term decline, so did serious cultural debates. There were fewer books published about the betterment of society, and more books about self-improvement and how to achieve financial success. As American commentators realised at the time, America had shifted from the "we generation" to the "me generation."

To return to our original question, about the American character and its attitude in respect to cultural decline, we are forced to conclude that the American attitude was ill-suited toward a positive response to decline. In fact America, with its self-centred focus, its inability or unwillingness to understand large-scale dynamics, and its attitude of exceptionalism and superiority, was extremely unsuited for constructive adaptation. In fact, the qualities making up the American character in the late 20th century were the exact opposite of what was required.

□ □ □

A fascinating aspect of America during its decline is that it appeared that a large number of Americans—perhaps unconsciously—realised that collapse was inevitable.

We can gain insights into the American psyche of the early 21st century by examining their choice of entertainment. Along with television, no aspect of America is more revealing of its evolving obsessions and anxieties than the history of its motion pictures. Whatever America needed to experience in its collective soul was inevitably depicted in movies.

What can we discern from American movies of the early 21st century? One cannot help but notice the prevalence of apocalyptic or post-apocalyptic scenarios. Americans chose to spend hard-earned dollars to watch their country go up in flames, or be destroyed by earthquakes, or be demolished by massive storms, or be decimated by pandemic diseases. A scene recurring in many movies involved the destruction of the White House.

In hindsight, we can postulate that Americans—despite being surrounded by messages assuring them that all was basically well—had an unconscious premonition of their own impending doom. As for witnessing the destruction of the White House, this could be construed as representing America's fear of government collapse, or its desire for government collapse. Psychologists have advanced convincing arguments to support both interpretations.

As for the appeal of the apocalyptic and post-apocalyptic genre, psychologists are in agreement that the purpose of such movies was as a means of psychological survival, a way to partially acknowledge a fear whose conscious admission would be too much to take. In essence, Americans were self-administering a dose of psychological "inoculation" similar to the type of inoculation for physical diseases, in which a doctor injects us with a small dose of a disease in order to stimulate our immune system to defend against the full onslaught.

One of the most interesting sub-genres of post-apocalyptic cinema was the focus on zombies. The popularity of this particular sub-genre was so substantial and continued for so long that it cannot be dismissed as insignificant. The consensus of psychologists today is that the fear of zombies is an externalised fear of the most rudimentary and primitive aspects of ourselves. Or to put it another way, it is the fear of the most ruthless survival-oriented aspect of humanity coming to the forefront. It is the fear of the advanced capabilities of the human mind—the qualities expressed by the cerebral cortex—becoming overridden by the primitive reptilian brain with its sole focus on physical survival. Thus, the search of our higher selves toward meaning or purpose becomes lost as our lower selves consume the flesh of those who retain those higher qualities. This is revealed especially by the fact that the preferred meal of zombies is human brains. In essence, a zombie is primitive humanity killing advanced humanity by consuming it.

Another fascinating aspect of American movies is that they often involved superheroes, including Batman, Spiderman, Superman, Wonder Woman, the X-Men, The Fantastic Four, and many others. Although other cultures throughout history had developed heroes with incredible powers, modern superheroes were a uniquely American invention. Originating in comic books for teenagers, they soon transitioned to one of the most popular genres of major American movies. The American psyche made itself manifest in an extraordinary cast of characters, revealing the American desire to be exceptional, to have a power nobody else has.

One of America's most interesting and psychologically revealing superheroes was *The Hulk*, who was basically a large and exceptionally powerful green muscular fist. The Hulk's basic ideology was expressed in his frequent declaration of "Hulk smash!" which was essentially his only declaration. It has been suggested that The Hulk was possibly the distilled essence of the American psyche, the outer projection of America's urge for control by the unthinking use of power. This was most obviously evident in the case of America's foreign policy, whose "War first, diplomacy later" approach was a direct application of the "Hulk smash!" philosophy.

The American celebration of violence was found not only in the superhero genre, but in the genre of what Americans classified as "action-adventure." Yet this was clearly a euphemism for violence, since all instances involved either seeking to escape the effects of violence or seeking to inflict them.

One of the most fascinating aspects of the action-adventure genre is a reflection of America's overwhelming focus on individualism. When it was necessary for several Americans to unite in order to combat evil forces, it was always as an "ad-hoc group." Americans refused to have their individuality compromised, even when fighting evil. This might, of course, seem to be counterintuitive, since when fighting evil it is helpful to put an end to ceaseless bickering and work as a coordinated team.

Yet despite the bickering, the ad-hoc Americans were consistently victorious. Not by blending into a tightly organised force, but by expressing their unique individual traits more fully. This unleashed a sort of "mystical" force that was not named, but was understood by audiences to be "The American Spirit." No matter whether the opposing forces were Ninja warriors, a team of international assassins, hostile aliens, an evil genius controlling a robot army, or Nazi invaders from the dark side of the moon, the ad-hoc group of Americans were always able to conjure up just enough American Spirit—usually at the last possible second—to defeat the forces of evil and keep America safe. Yet what was never mentioned in such movies is that what the heroes were keeping safe was an America that was in steady decline.

In all forms of American entertainment, Americans were portrayed in flattering yet highly unrealistic ways. They were portrayed as vibrant, healthy, joyful, glib people engaged in fun pursuits. Yet visitors to America expecting the reality to match the media portrayals were utterly shocked. Outside of a few affluent enclaves, the reality was disappointing.

Most Americans lived amidst a landscape of sprawling chain stores and fast food franchises. They commuted via noisy boulevards through traffic jams to uninspiring jobs. And the Americans wandering this landscape were not the healthy and vibrant Americans of sitcoms and commercials. As compared to the illusion, the Americans a typical visitor would encounter were likely overweight, depressed, unhealthy, and possibly under the influence of legal or illegal drugs.

One has to wonder: When such Americans watched movies or television programmes to view the media versions of themselves, did they consciously or unconsciously compare their own real lives to the fictional versions? If so, could this be at least part of the explanation for America's tremendous intake of antidepressants? Or perhaps when such Americans watched movies or television programmes they did not compare themselves at all. Perhaps the fiction was a way for them to forget the reality, a way to imagine themselves living a fun and satisfying life, wisecracking with all their attractive friends who never got stuck in traffic jams. We can speculate, but unfortunately we can never know.

Adaptation and the Search for Scapegoats

The goal of America, since the earliest days, was economic wealth and economic affluence. Americans from the beginning were driven and ambitious. And as visitors to America have noted since the beginning, Americans were impatient, distracted, and easily driven to anger. A deep condition of dissatisfaction was present, as noted by Alexis de

Tocqueville, in a chapter of *Democracy in America* entitled "Why the Americans Are So Often Restless in the Midst of Their Prosperity":

> In America I have seen the freest and best educated of men in circumstances the happiest to be found in the world; yet it seemed to me that a cloud habitually hung on their brow, and they seemed serious and almost sad even in their pleasures...The taste for physical pleasures must be regarded as the first cause of this secret restlessness betrayed by the actions of the Americans, and of the inconstancy of which they give daily examples.

If de Tocqueville is correct, then a primary source of America's anger was directly related to America's focus on material satisfaction. This brings us to consider another question. If Americans were satisfied materially, were they unsatisfied in immaterial ways? Had they failed to develop in the immaterial ways that would have resulted in being truly satisfied with their material gains?

Even in the 1950s through 1970s, during the peak of American postwar affluence, many realised that something was amiss. Books such as *Revolutionary Road* and movies such as *The Man in the Gray Flannel Suit* expressed an emptiness at the heart of the American dream, a vague dissatisfaction. For Americans, this feeling had no name, although it is described by the French term *malaise*.

It becomes impossible to avoid the conclusion that Americans, in their overwhelming drive for material satisfactions, were missing the other half of the picture. Wealth can be experienced in ways that do not require money, and poverty can be experienced by those with millions of dollars. If Americans understood this, it seems they understood it to only a very limited degree.

Americans never acknowledged that the continual desire for money, regardless of whether it was resulting in satisfaction, was an addiction—a form of mental disease. This disease was most prominently displayed in many of America's most wealthy individuals, such as corporate CEOs and software moguls. With assets consisting of billions of dollars, they could have easily retired with enough to live in luxury for the rest of their lives, and perhaps devote their efforts toward worthy causes. Yet many of them focused their efforts toward amassing even more wealth, far in excess of what any person could conceivably need. In addition, many were extremely politically active, working to influence government policies in ways allowing them to amass even more.

Curiously, Americans never labelled this as a disease. Perhaps it was because they all, to some degree, shared the same affliction. And if their personal lives were primarily devoted to affluence, then so was the entirely of American culture. All aspects of their social and cultural life was the external reflection of that same devotion. Every tangible aspect of their lives was designed primarily around the goal of maximising short-term economic gain. This focus was the direct cause for the dispiriting American environment of chain stores and urban sprawl, for its uninspiring architecture, for its overpriced housing, and for its economic policies that steadily degraded the financial situation of most Americans.

So as Americans had cause to be dissatisfied with their internal condition, they had equal cause to be dissatisfied "externally" with their social environment. And the satisfaction would be for precisely the same reason. Yet as with their internal condition, it seems like Americans only understood this to a very limited degree.

□ □ □

By the time America entered the 1970s, Americans had grown accustomed to getting whatever they wanted anywhere at any time. They became, in a word, spoiled. For Americans of this era, deprivation was felt if the local convenience store was out of their favourite brand of soft drink. Such instances of deprivation could inspire outraged posts on social media, and in not a few cases led to enraged phone calls to the White House.

Yet by the 2010s, the situation had seriously deteriorated. As Americans of decades past had experienced strong reactions to minor deprivations concerning things such as soft drinks, it is difficult for us to comprehend the power of their reaction to more significant deprivations, such as being reduced to living in their cars. A popular catchphrase of this period was: "Who stole my standard of living?" Americans experienced a profound and overriding sense of confusion, as they attempted to adapt to their rapidly diminishing condition.

But since they did not understand the reasons for their situation, their reactions became misdirected in a variety of inappropriate directions. America had two main emotional responses to the situation. One was the passive response of *despair*. The other was the aggressive response of *anger*.

On the despair end of the spectrum, a significant means of adaptation was the heavy use of legal drugs, notably anti-depressants such as Prozac, Zoloft, and Paxil. Throughout America's decline, the nation was notable for being the highest per capita consumer of such drugs in the world. Americans feeling depression and anxiety could consume two small capsules that would quickly deliver them to their "happy place." By the 2030s, an even higher percentage of Americans were consuming such drugs, often upping the dose from two capsules to "a handful of happy." Of course, such drugs were not actually making Americans happy; they were merely dulling the ability to experience emotions of any kind. However, the skyrocketing demand definitely made the pharmaceutical industry very happy.

Another despair-based adaptation was a uniquely American response that consisted of reacting to degrading social conditions by seeking personal forms of psychological therapy. Rather than consider that anger might be an appropriate response to their declining condition, they looked within to work on their "anger issues." In such ways, symptoms of social decline were misinterpreted as forms of personal anxiety. While such a misinterpretation may be puzzling to us, it is consistent with American individualism. Every American considered themselves to be the centre of the world, so if the world needed treatment it obviously need to be treated at that centre.

Another despair-based response was a resurgence in fundamentalist religion. This response is consistent throughout world history, as fundamentalism has always increased in times of fear and uncertainty. As the situation in America seemed increasingly hopeless, Americans increasingly abandoned concern for this world and focused their attention on the next one. In the American version of that next world, not only would there be everlasting life, but also the ability to eat as much as desired and television sets on which the best shows were always available and there were never commercial interruptions. Sinners and unbelievers would be forever barred from this blissful realm, and would be doomed to an eternity of torment in hell with no television at all.

Some Americans sought escape in a totally different way. Rather than seeking to escape the declining situation in another life, they sought escape in this life by isolating themselves from it. These were America's survivalists, sometimes referred to as "doomsday preppers." These ranged in size from single individuals and families up to groups of up to several hundred. Generally heavily armed and based on quasi-military organisational principles, their well-defended compounds were designed to provide totally self-sufficient living for an indefinite period. Their preparations included tremendous stocks of dried and canned food as well as massive libraries of recorded television programmes. Some of the survivalist libraries even contained books.

On the anger end of the spectrum, the increasing desperation of the era led to increasing instances of outrage and violence. There was a marked increase in the American phenomenon of "road rage" in which minor traffic incidents frequently led to violent arguments, fistfights, and occasionally to murder. The simple act of shopping frequently led to outbursts that puzzled those from other nations. In a typical example, in an American shopping centre a teenager making derogatory comments about a woman's dress quickly escalated into a 30-person brawl as enthusiastic shoppers made their way to the sporting goods section and returned with baseball bats.

But nothing compares to the deadly situation faced by Christmas shoppers in America. Every year, Americans tracked how many serious injuries and deaths occurred due to people being crushed by massive stampedes of holiday shoppers and assaulted in fights over sales items, while store intercoms played holiday music about the importance of expressing love and goodwill toward each other.

Also, and more frighteningly, America reacted with a rise in fascist impulses. Historically, fascism has arisen in times of great social stress. This occurred most notably in the Weimar Democracy in 1930s Germany, when the stress of exorbitant World War I reparations combined with the effects of the worldwide economic depression led to fascism in the form of National Socialism. Indeed, America had toyed with fascism in the 1930s under the influence of the same economic depression that led to the fall of Weimar Democracy.

A vital component of fascism is the need to find appropriate scapegoats. Rather than examine the causes of a country's problems, especially the degree to which the country's leaders are responsible for them, it is necessary for those leaders to direct the anger toward others. Of course, scapegoating is not limited to fascism. It had been used throughout American history, and had arisen especially in times of national stress.

America's scapegoats evolved throughout its history. The role was most often held by America's various ethnic groups. And in a country literally formed by immigrants there was no shortage of potential candidates. Immigrants from Ireland, Italy, China—and many others—took their turns at being the target. It could also be based on religious identity, as Catholics and Jews both took their turns.

Muslims and Mexicans, America's main focus of scapegoating heading into the 2020s, were both relatively new to American scapegoating prominence.

Muslim-Americans became a prominent scapegoat as a result of terrorist actions against America conducted by Muslim extremists from other countries. Yet most Americans disregarded that those terrorist actions were largely in retaliation for American actions, and that on the whole the Muslim-American community was among the most peaceful and non-threatening communities in America.

The situation with the scapegoating of Mexican-Americans was somewhat complex. The main focus of scapegoating was upon the segment of Mexicans officially termed to be "undocumented workers," but were more often referred to derogatorily as "illegal aliens." The scapegoating was most often justified with the claim that Mexicans were having a negative effect on the American economy, even though their presence as inexpensive labour had been encouraged precisely for their vital role in the American economy.

There is no way around the fact that their presence was encouraged purely as a form of cheap labour that in some cases verged on slavery, which was required to do the dirty work that no other Americans would touch. This was something of an "open secret" that everybody knew, but American officials could not openly admit.

As a result, the scapegoating of Mexicans was a curious phenomenon. The presence of Mexican workers as virtual slaves was critical to the success of the American economy, yet when those same workers requested some portion of benefits of the affluence that their presence helped to create, many Americans were outraged. The double-standard extended to Mexicans that were legal citizens. Those who were unemployed or impoverished were "a drain on the economy," yet those who were relatively affluent were "stealing jobs from real Americans."

One thing that immediately becomes apparent, in all the debates and controversies of this period, was a total disregard of Mexicans—whether American citizens or not—as people worthy of a meaningful existence as human beings. Public debate was conducted as if they could not hear, as if they were "in the other room" so to speak. It was never considered that a person of Mexican heritage might have something other than instrumental value for their willingness to accept employment as a lettuce picker or slaughterhouse worker. The possibility that they might have—and deserve to have—more lofty aspirations was never considered.

In an extreme reaction by a tiny minority of Americans, a number of ultra-right-wing militias formed along the American side of the Mexican border. These groups consisted of citizens who were convinced that Mexican immigrants were the main cause of America's problems, and therefore they were serving America by doing their part to stop it.

During the height of Mexican scapegoating some Mexicans, fearing for their safety, took efforts to appear less Mexican. Skin bleaching and hair colouration were common techniques. Mexicans attempted to reduce their accents, and to replace colourful Mexican terminology with bland white expressions such as "Have a pleasant afternoon" and "Can I have extra mayonnaise on my ham sandwich?"

Fortunately, in the 2030s scapegoating and the associated prejudice against Mexicans rapidly diminished. One reason for this was due to the ongoing energy crisis. As a result of their common employment in pedicabs—as drivers as well as "engines"—they enjoyed close contact on a regular basis with all segments of American society. As frequent association often results in the ending of prejudice, Americans discovered that Mexicans were actually human beings much like them, who were generally happy and cheerful people whose presence proved to be a positive addition to their lives.

Prejudice against America's Muslim community also diminished over time, for reasons that historians have yet to discern. One possible explanation is that Muslim-Americans continued to be peace-loving citizens that caused no problems. Another possible explanation is that America simply grew tired of scapegoating Muslims, and required an exciting new scapegoat on which to vent its anger and frustration.

In a different category from America's evolving procession of scapegoats was a dependable perennial. It was present since the birth of America, and was one of its own creation. This of course consisted of its black population. Brought to America to be slaves, they were eventually reluctantly admitted as second-class citizens. Although the situation improved over time, full and equal participation was never fully realised.

They were the last to feel the benefits of economic prosperity, and the first to feel the effects of economic downturns. In essence, America enforced their status as second-class citizens, then blamed them for the problems created by the enforcement of that status. Higher rates of poverty and unemployment resulted in a higher incidence of crime, drug use, and other social problems. Blacks made up a highly disproportionate percentage of America's prison population, and received a disproportionate amount of attention from America's law enforcement agencies.

In a vicious cycle of violence, injustice continued against America's black population, which often armed itself for protection and adopted a more militant stance, which fueled increasing injustice. Fear and retribution from both sides encouraged rising fear and retribution, and as the population became better armed the police became more militarised. In television news videos from the era, it appeared as if the American military had declared war on its poorest and most desperate citizens, and indeed many of those citizens felt that this was precisely the situation.

Yet in a development that nobody could have anticipated, in America's final years it largely abandoned all of its traditional scapegoats. In the 2040s, America would largely transcend the ethnic- or religion-based scapegoats of the past by embracing universal scapegoats that would become the focus of America's anger for the remainder of its history.

THE DECLINE OF AMERICAN POLITICS

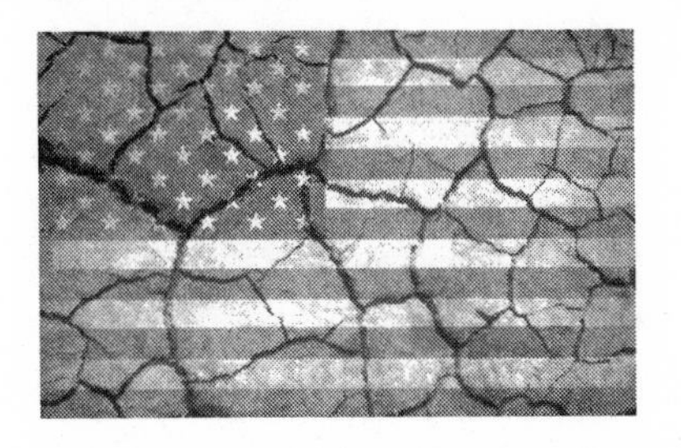

The Two Americas

America was dominated for most of its history by the political division between republican and democrat, conservative and liberal, right and left. An important aspect of America's decline and fall was that the nation's two main political parties became dysfunctional to a degree that its political system became essentially useless.

Yet despite the many problems with America's two-party "winner take all" political system, the country never seriously considered changing it. For example, in the case of America's Congress there was never discussion over adopting some sort of parliamentary system, in which congressional membership is assigned proportionately according to popular vote. Although such a system is not perfect, it is more conducive to the process of consensus and reaching decisions that consider the views of all sides. Yet while nearly all advanced nations on earth had adopted it, America refused to even consider it.

Battling toward victory to achieve dominance came naturally to Americans; achieving consensus did not. The American attitude was summed up in 2026 by Oklahoma Senator Buford Narwhal, who stated: "I refuse to compromise because everybody but me is an idiot." The American public cheered this statement, seeing it not as a rejection of democracy but as an affirmation of it. Needless to say, such an attitude did not bode well for attempting to come to agreement on anything.

Although America's two-party system had many faults, there was one manner in which it embodied an important truth. Each party embraced one side of a fundamental political duality, giving voice to eternal and ultimately unsolvable questions such as freedom versus equality, diversity versus unity, and the individual versus the collective. Ideally, each party balanced the weaknesses of the other side with the strengths of their own side.

To work effectively, this assumes from each side a tacit acknowledgment that each side has strengths and weaknesses, and is willing to merge the strengths of both sides in order to serve the common good. Unfortunately, it rarely worked that way. America's political parties focused far less effort toward the effort to merge the strengths of the two sides than on efforts toward demolishing the other side.

For most of American history, political discourse was dominated by this division, yet it did not exist at the time of America's founding. America began without political parties. In fact, the Founding Fathers deeply distrusted political parties, and made no provisions for them in America's Constitution. Yet the division arose soon enough.

Alexander Hamilton and Thomas Jefferson occupied two opposite poles in American thought that would dominate political debate for the rest of American history. Dumas Malone, Jefferson's most prominent biographer, has stated their difference simply: "No other statesman has personified national power and the rule of the favored few so well as Hamilton, and no other has glorified self-government and the freedom of the individual to such a degree as Jefferson."

The differences between Jefferson and Hamilton led to the creation of rival newspapers which provided platforms for their views. Jefferson's was the *National Gazette*, and Hamilton's was the *Gazette of the United States*. The discourse published in these publications was not gentlemanly debate, but vicious mudslinging and character assassination. Although not anticipated at the time, the rivalry eventually led to the formation of America's two main political parties. And unfortunately, for the remainder of American history they too frequently dragged political discourse down to the same style of debate.

Rhetoric reached an extreme during the Great Depression of the 1930s, as the desperate economic times resulted in an unprecedented era of political radicalism. Not only were the divisions between democrats and republicans growing more heated, but more radical political movements grew in popularity. To the far left was a substantial American Communist Party, and to the far right were frightening movements toward fascism.

Republican President Herbert Hoover made futile attempts to end the depression. He created the Reconstruction Finance Corporation which aided railroads and banks with massive loans. The millions of Americans without jobs and living in poverty were enraged at Hoover, who was willing to help corporations while doing little for the poor.

The desperate situation led to the creation of the "Bonus Army," consisting of 25,000 former infantrymen organised as an ad-hoc army of the impoverished. In 1932, they travelled to Washington, D.C., squatting along with their families in abandoned buildings and forming an encampment along the Anacostia River. They had come to ask Congress to pay them a bonus promised to veterans in 1924 and scheduled to be paid in 1945. Starving and desperate, they requested early payment as a means to survive. Hoover responded by falsely claiming the group consisted of "red agitators." Then he called in the Army. A cavalry charge was followed by a tear-gas attack, destroying the camp and causing over 100 casualties.

Hoover's harsh actions and the lack of economic relief resulted in the election of Democratic President Franklin Delano Roosevelt. President Roosevelt created the *New Deal* which led to an unprecedented growth in government and in government control over economic affairs. This made him a hero to some and a villain to others. Although Roosevelt was demonised by conservatives, his programmes were gradually improving the situation. Whether those programmes would have led to full recovery will never be known since World War II intervened and led to the end of the depression.

After the war, America experienced 25 years of tremendous economic affluence that served to largely subdue the extreme political rhetoric. America's two major political parties enjoyed the most functional relationship in American history. Bipartisan cooperation was not uncommon. In an effort that would have been unimaginable only a decade later, President Richard Nixon—a republican—signed into law progressive "big government" legislation establishing the Occupational Safety and Health Administration, the Environmental Protection Agency, the Clean Air Act, and a greatly expanded version of the Clean Water Act. This is in stark contrast to the extreme polarisation and political stagnation that would soon dominate.

As the history of America demonstrates, when people are doing well economically, political rhetoric fades in importance. It is when the economic situation becomes desperate that political extremism and ideological warfare rise to prominence. When a large number of Americans had achieved the promise of "two cars in every garage and a chicken in every pot," they cared little about politics. But they began to care quite a bit when their situation had degraded to "a broken-down bicycle on the porch and I can't afford a pot."

For most of American history, even if individuals from the two sides actively fought, there was generally what Americans called a "grudging respect" toward each other. It was generally assumed that, even if they did not personally agree with each other, they both had the best interests of the country at heart. American politics, as with politics everywhere throughout history, had always been a cantankerous affair. Yet there had generally been the assumption that, on some level, they were on the same side.

To the degree this existed, it faded rapidly after America's peak. By the year 2010 is was all but gone. By this time, "grudging respect" had devolved to mutual warfare, and the two parties had all but abandoned the idea they were on the same side at all.

By the late 2020s, ideological warfare sometimes spilled over into physical warfare. In the nation's capital, members of the two parties were demarked by handkerchiefs in the "party colours" of red or blue, roaming their "home turf" of affiliated bars, clubs, and other hangouts. If opposing politicians inadvertently encountered each other, the result was often a violent tussle involving hair-pulling, eye-poking, bitch-slapping, and the application of a painful raising of the pants which Americans termed a "wedgie."

America made much of its division into so-called "red states" (conservative) and "blue states" (liberal). But in reality, the division was based less upon state boundaries and more upon the division of urban versus rural. In any case, the division became so unbridgeable that the country began to consider that it consisted of two Americas.

The two sides embraced cruel stereotypes of each other. Cities were full of the "liberal elite" consisting of a frivolous population that produced nothing of worth, and spent their evenings partying in nightclubs and doing lines of cocaine off the backs of prostitutes. Rural areas were full of "dumb rednecks" that were violent and prejudiced reactionaries whose favourite hobby was shooting each other while listening to country music, and who wore cowboy boots because they lacked the intelligence to master shoelaces.

America became engaged in what it called the *Culture Wars*. Battles were initiated over a familiar series of "hot button issues" whose mere mention resulted in the outbreak of angry partisan rants. The most controversial issues included abortion, birth control, gun control, and gay marriage. Other issues included environmental protection, welfare, unemployment insurance, civil rights, and tax policies. Mere mention of such issues were guaranteed to enrage half of the population while energising the other half.

Americans were highly tuned to such issues, and the discovery of "an enemy in the midst" could lead to an outbreak of verbal warfare. Family gatherings that included members of both sides could be extremely awkward affairs. For families that wanted to avoid unpleasantness, there was tacit agreement that certain topics were taboo. As a result, anything could be openly discussed as long as it did not extend beyond the subjects of sports and weather. But lapses were impossible to avoid. For example, there was one instance of a Thanksgiving dinner turning to a violent food fight. The battle began when one family member made a comment about oncoming cold weather, which another family member regarded as a "typically pessimistic democratic scare tactic to trick us into raising taxes."

Anything like a "middle ground" had become lost. The rise of the media options brought by the internet and a huge increase in television stations allowed news reporting that was massively and unashamedly biased. And since they were "preaching to the converted" in the form of an equally biased audience, none of it was questioned. Each side clung to its own views and selectively-chosen evidence as "truth" and claimed that all others were lies.

This was embodied by the rise of right-wing radio pundits such as Rush Limbaugh, Sean Hannity, and Ann Coulter. But the most impact was with a cable and satellite television news channel entitled *Fox News* that was presented as legitimate news, but in actuality consisted of editorial programmes to advance right-wing policies. In what may be interpreted as an example of ironic humour, the programme adopted the motto of "Fair and Balanced."

Attempts at left-wing versions of such programmes were of limited success. They were unable to conjure up an equally strident voice of dogmatism and anger, or to find commentators willing to yell as loudly. They had greater success with satirical television news programmes such as *The Daily Show* and *The Colbert Report.*

One aspect of these developments was with the rise in *post-truth politics* or *post-factual politics.* It was marked by a political culture in which debate was framed primarily by appeals to ideology. The idea of truth became abandoned in America. Ideology was primary, and only facts that fit the ideology were true. Everything else was false.

Even when the media conducted fact-checking, the evidence was simply disregarded. Social media made possible a rapid rise in "fake news" in which totally fabricated reports were endlessly shared and repeated. One of the first major instances of this phenomenon was the so-called "birther controversy" of Barack Obama during his campaign for president. The false claim that he was not a natural-born American citizen was widely reported for so long after it had been officially debunked that millions of Americans of both political parties continued to believe it long after Obama's eight years in office.

Since the field of science is based upon facts, this resulted in a growing anti-science bias. The conclusions of science were increasingly in contradiction to what Americans wanted, so America had to make a fundamental decision. One was to modify their behaviour in light of science. The other was to deny science. Amazingly, many Americans denied not only the conclusions of science, but the entire field of science.

According to an American survivor interviewed for this book, there is no such thing as science. In order to confirm this remarkable notion, I asked whether she believed in the existence of a field of human endeavour that uses fact-based evidence to form an increasingly accurate means of understanding the physical universe. Her reply was, "There's no such thing." No further explanation was provided. I asked whether she understood that all the comforts and conveniences of modern civilisation—such as electric power, mobile phones, and the internet—were direct results of science. Her reply was, "No they're not." Again, no further explanation was provided.

As a result of this attitude, when considering issues such as the effectiveness of trickle-down economics, the extent of unemployment, or the reality and seriousness of environmental degradation, there was no danger of facts getting in the way.

Primary and Secondary Constituents, and the Era of Broken Trust

The increasingly unbridgeable ideological division resulted in tremendous political gridlock. But perhaps the greatest problem with American politics, and the main explanation for its tremendous dysfunction, was the influence of money on government and the entire political process. The cost of mounting a successful election, especially for national office, grew astronomically. As a result, politicians became almost totally dependent on large financial donations to get elected. Those inevitably came from large business interests.

And of course, those who made the donations expected something in return. Sometimes it was for a vote on specific legislation favourable to the donor. But more generally, it was merely for actions favourable to business interests in general.

As a result, politicians had two sets of constituents: the public (who it needed for votes to get elected) and big business (for the campaign contributions necessary to run in the first place). Politicians needed to appeal to these two sets of constituents who—to put it mildly—did not always have common interests. So every politician was placed in a delicate balancing act. They needed to do what their primary constituents (big business) wanted them to do, yet tell their secondary constituents (the public) what they wanted to hear.

As a result, they needed to modify their public messages in order to justify how their actions in support of big business also supported the public. The two parties did this in different ways.

Republicans had an easier time with the primary need to appeal to business, since their ideology had traditionally supported business. Their problem was how to acknowledge this yet appeal to the popular vote. But as long as the Republican Party could sustain the ideology of trickle-down economics—or rather, as long as they could sustain the claim that it worked—the republican ideology was triumphant. It resonated with the major traits of the American character—independent, strong, and resistant to taxation—and was successful in portraying the Democratic Party as the party of losers, complainers, and enemies of American pride and industriousness. They demonised stereotypes of Democratic Party supporters, such as welfare mothers who demanded that hardworking Americans subsidise their preferences for imported chocolate and Cadillacs.

Democrats were in an awkward position. They were extremely limited in the extent to which they could demonise corporate CEOs and financial magnates as greedy misanthropes bankrupting poor Americans so they could buy more mansions. The most they could do was to suggest that perhaps they were taking a bit more than their fair share, and it would be nice if they might consent to share a bit of it, if they did not object too strongly.

For the Democratic Party, opposing business interests would cause them to lose the support of their primary constituents. Yet supporting business interests inevitably resulted in losses for "the people" such as increased unemployment, lower incomes, and loss of collective bargaining via the steady erosion of trade unions. Their solution was to increase taxes to pay for social programs to care for those who suffered from the results of supporting business. In other words, their solution was to increase taxes to pay for the results of the policies that made it necessary for them to pay more taxes.

In America, populism had traditionally been based on economic class. But as populism was abandoned by the Democratic Party it was taken over by the Republican Party to become based on *cultural* class. The enemy was no longer the wealthy banker who had cheated Americans out of their savings, or rich corporations that had outsourced American jobs overseas, but those who assumed cultural superiority. This included government bureaucrats—characterised as the "government elite"—that controlled the public with a crushing burden of taxes, laws, and entitlements to the lazy and unambitious.

When democrats talked about helping the poor, Americans interpreted this to mean higher taxes.

Republicans proposed to help the poor by freeing them from government control, and creating economic opportunities via their support of big business. In practice, this worked against the poor, but since it resonated with core aspects of the American character the rhetoric won over the effects of their policies.

Thus, the political trend of this era was commonly regarded as "a swing to the right." The Republican Party was empowered and the Democratic Party was on the defensive. Republicans became open in their contempt of the democratic process and became willing to do anything in their power to obstruct anything not totally aligned with their ideology.

Privately, republican members of Congress admitted that the point of obstructionism in Congress was less about opposition to any particular piece of legislation than about lowering the public perception of Congress. The rationale was simple: Since the Republican Party preferred a small and weak government, anything that made government look bad or ineffectual was in their favour. The strategy of the Republican Party was to do everything in their power to destroy the democratic process, then run on an anti-government programme that rebelled against the dysfunctional democracy they helped to create.

Democrats, by contrast, did not seem to believe strongly in anything. They became a hesitant and ambivalent party, still espousing the rhetoric of being "the party of the people" and holding desperately onto the memories of its previous victories in social equality and human rights. It did this even as those victories were steadily eroding, as the Democratic Party was forced to adhere to the agenda of business interests. Unable to choose or between being pro-business and pro-people, the party attempted to do a little of both. This only served to dissatisfy everybody, thus leaving the Democratic Party without direction and functionally irrelevant.

By this time, the traditional categories of "liberal" versus "conservative" to which the parties were historically identified had become almost totally meaningless.

An important aspect of classical conservatism includes *fiscal* conservatism. Yet in many ways the Republican Party had embraced radical economic doctrines, and were willing to create huge fiscal debt for military spending and tax cuts that benefited the wealthiest members of society. Another traditional conservative ideal was to work toward creating a "level playing field" by which Americans could rise or fall based upon their own initiative. Yet in practice, Republican policies actively worked against this ideal.

In contrast, liberalism was embraced by the Democratic Party, yet their focus on "the working class" shifted to a focus on so-called "identity politics." Rather than focus on keeping people from being poor, the focus had shifted into making sure that people of various minority populations could get rich. Yet even though the Democratic Party had largely abandoned their concern for the working class, they retained some vestiges of the "safety net" of social services for those who slipped between the cracks of the economy. At least more so than the Republican Party, which was doing everything in its power to get rid of them.

Because politicians of both parties needed to support their primary constituents, the needs of the secondary constituents were increasingly ignored. Although Americans seldom agreed on what they wanted, there was widespread agreement on many things they did *not* want, such as offshore tax-shelters for wealthy individuals, and the status of corporations as citizens. They were also deeply disturbed by such trends as the outsourcing of jobs, the steady destruction of the middle class, and rising health care costs. Most Americans were alarmed at the growing consolidation of wealth into the hands of a tiny portion of the population. Polls routinely revealed that most Americans favoured no cuts to Social Security or to the health programmes of Medicare and

Medicaid. Polls also repeatedly showed that a majority of Americans favoured deep cuts in military and defense spending.

Yet such concerns were rarely acknowledged by either political party, and even if they were it led to no effective action. Trade agreements that encouraged the outsourcing of more jobs were passed. The economic interests of the middle class were routinely declined in favour of the upper classes. The health care and pharmaceutical industries continued to grow more powerful and health care costs continued to rise. The military budget continued to grow.

Each policy decision in these directions inspired anger. Yet America's politicians were confident that the public's anger would soon dissipate and the issue would soon be forgotten. American politicians knew that it was unlikely that the anger would result in them being voted out of office. One reason is that the public had no alternative options from which to choose. Due to the need to satisfy their primary constituents, the politicians from both major parties had been pre-selected to embrace essentially similar positions. They knew that the citizens who still bothered to vote would be given a choice of "the lesser of two evils," neither of which dared to address the most vital concerns of the populace.

Americans were experiencing a steady erosion of belief in the nation's basic institutions, and that those institutions were looking out for their interests. At the time, American historian Kenneth C. Davis suggested that future historians may look back on America of this period as the "Era of Broken Trust." Most of the population grew disenchanted with politics. In a country in which many of its original citizens once died to preserve democracy, things got to the point where most citizens did not even bother to vote.

Yet after decades of political apathy, Americans were about to became politically re-engaged. The frustration and dissatisfaction resulting from America's post-1970s decline had been building for decades. Latent anger was waiting to explode, it just needed the appropriate trigger.

Misdirected Anger and the Presidential Election of 2016

The trigger was the financial crisis of 2007-2008. Suddenly, Americans were required to bail out the banks and financial institutions that had just devastated their net worth and resulted in millions of lost jobs. The resulting explosion of anger had consequences that would radically change the American political climate.

It was difficult for the mainstream political parties to be excessively angry at the financial institutions that caused the problems. For one thing, both parties had become dependent on those institutions. For another thing, both political parties had been to blame in the steady erosion of financial regulations that allowed the crisis to occur.

As a result, the strongest and most significant responses came not from the mainstream Democrat and Republic Parties. They came, rather, from the far left and far right—the radical or extremist elements of both sides of America's political divide. The extremist elements of America were beholden to neither business nor the mainstream parties, and therefore had no restrictions on their anger. Since this was the era of Two Americas, the country's anger was expressed in two very different directions toward very different villains. Yet it is not the case that one was right and one was wrong. They both suffered from fundamental misperceptions.

The left-wing anger grew to express itself in what was known as the *Occupy Movement*, or simply as *Occupy*. Its slogan was "We are the 99 percent," embracing a populist message in opposition to the one percent of America's most wealthy and powerful. It focused its anger upon America's large banks and financial institutions with a number of large protests, initially focused upon Wall Street—the heart of America's major financial district.

For a time, the protests were tolerated, since officials wished to retain the favour of a still-significant percentage of Americans who clung to the ideals of free speech and the right of assembly as guaranteed in America's founding documents. But the protests were not tolerated for long before being quickly overpowered by a tremendous show of aggression. Disturbing videos of such aggression reveal citizens facing off against advancing waves of militarised police forces who were not shy about pepper spraying protesters in the face.

Such a violent overreaction was scarcely necessary, since the movement did an excellent job of rapidly imploding almost as quickly as it began. There were several reasons for this. For one thing, the protests had no stated goals and advocated no specific agenda of recommended actions. It was explained that this was in keeping with the movement's philosophy of being fully inclusive, non-hierarchical, and non-authoritarian. However, in practice it was so fully inclusive that it was unable to make substantial decisions of any kind.

Also, its philosophy of being non-authoritarian meant that the protestors became totally unable to retain order at the locations they were occupying. Most of the camps rapidly disintegrated as they became infiltrated by people who came for free food and had no interest in the political aspects of the movement. Many of them, finding themselves not subject to police jurisdiction, felt empowered to bring illegal activities into the camps. Soon, camp leaders were asking police for assistance after realizing that authoritarian actions were not quite the evil they had thought.

After the protests ended, the movement limped along for a short time before dissolving, as the movement continued to reject hierarchical leadership and the need to adopt a specific agenda, and remained unable to make substantial decisions of any kind.

Thus the rapid rise and fall of radical left-wing anger.

Radical right-wing anger, however, proved to be more lasting. It expressed itself in what was known as the *Tea Party Movement.* It did not share the Occupy Movement's rejection of structure and hierarchy, and soon led to the establishment of a new political party calling itself the *Tea Party.* The movement and political party were named as an homage to the famous Boston Tea Party, a 1773 protest that was an early sign of American rebellion against British tax policies.

Yet the Tea Party Movement originated in a fundamental misperception. Its anger was not focused upon the financial institutions that caused the collapse. Nor was it focused the process of deregulation that allowed it to happen. Nor was it focused upon the government's decision to bail out the financial institutions at taxpayer expense. In a remarkable display of irrational thinking, its anger was focused on President Barack Obama, who passed the Homeowners Affordability and Stability Plan, which sought to help homeowners keep their homes after the collapse. The catalyst for the movement was an enraged rant by news commentator Rick Santelli against the perceived lack of responsibility of homeowners, and about how Obama's legislation was "promoting bad behavior." Nothing was said about the bad behaviour of the financial institutions that created the situation in which homeowners needed to be saved.

As with the Occupy Movement, the Tea Party Movement embraced a populist message. Yet it was diametrically opposed to populism in its interpretation of the problem and its choice of villain. Unlike the Occupy Movement, as well as previous populist movements which were characterised by a distrust of business in general and bankers in particular, the Tea Party Movement extolled the virtues of free market principles and focused its anger at the federal government.

Somehow, the Tea Party got away with embracing a contradictory philosophy of anti-democratic populism that convinced people to vote against their own interests while getting rid of programmes that benefited them. The Tea Party appealed to both "the people" with populist anger, and to the elites who were off the hook and further empowered. Thus unlike all previous populist movements in history, which existed in opposition to "the powers that be," the Tea Party embraced those powers. This should come as no surprise, since the Tea

Party was originally created and funded by representatives of those powers.

The most enthusiastic supporters of the Tea Party were from the most impoverished areas of America. For example, Louisiana at this time was America's third-poorest state with the lowest rating in overall health. Nearly one-quarter of its high school students dropped out or graduated late, and the state led America in "disconnected youth," with 20 percent of its 16-24 age population neither in school or employed. Yet Louisiana voted overwhelmingly for the Tea Party, somehow convinced that the solution to their problems was financial deregulation and less taxes for the wealthy.

The Tea Party convinced a substantial proportion of the electorate to accept such counter-intuitive falsehoods by appealing to certain aspects of the American character, and by the use of scapegoats such as "greedy school teachers," "welfare moms," and "the liberal media." The Tea Party appealed to Americans with the following message: the situation is not your fault, there is no need to oppose the large and powerful financial forces that are aligned against you, and you do not need to think.

Many observers, who were shocked at these developments, concluded that the "dumbing down of America" had resulted in a new political party to give voice to America's rejection of intelligence. Some commentators at the time referred to the movement as "The political rise of stupidity."

Obviously Americans had some legitimate reasons to be angry. This was especially the case for America's invisible population. Feeling abandoned by both political parties, they had suddenly found a movement that spoke their language. Or more to the point, felt their anger. As a result, the Tea Party grew rapidly and elected several members to Congress and other national and state offices.

The Tea Party was to some extent an extremist facet of the Republican Party. In fact, to a large degree the Tea Party was a republican creation. For decades the republicans had worked to mobilise and encourage the most reactionary and extreme members of their base, made up of highly motived people who were very angry yet not very smart. The republicans mobilised and encouraged these elements of their base, on the assumption they could be controlled. But soon the base became unpredictable, and abandoned the republicans for a party that was not afraid to be more extreme.

Thus, the Tea Party attracted what were widely referred to as "wackos," many of which embraced bizarre conspiracy theories. Fundamentalist extremists denounced President Obama as the Anti-Christ, while others believed he was a Marxist bent on seizing the weapons of all Americans. Educational standards were considered to be part of a plot to impose Communism on America. Military exercises in Texas were seen a first step toward imposing martial law on the entire country. The Obamacare health plan was said to include "death panels" with the power to decide which Americans would be denied health care.

The presidential election of 2016 was a turning point for American politics, radically altering the rules and assumptions that had been in place for generations. It was an extraordinary election in many ways.

For one thing, the radical right had competition from the radical left. As the sentiments of the Tea Party Movement had eventually expressed itself in the Tea Party, the sentiments of the Occupy Movement had empowered Senator Bernie Sanders to run for president. He identified himself as a socialist, a remarkable statement considering that in America this had traditionally been a form of political suicide.

The Tea Party offered candidates for the office of president. But the party was not powerful enough to run a third party challenge, and splitting the right wing vote would have most likely ensured a Democratic Party win, so the Tea Party candidates ran as republicans. To appeal to more mainstream voters, those candidates distanced themselves from the extreme conspiracy theories of the party's early years.

As with the Tea Party candidates, to be a viable candidate Sanders chose the mainstream party more closely aligned to his respective values. Therefore he ran as a democrat against the mainstream favourite Hillary Clinton. As with the Tea Party, Sanders had been motivated by the financial crisis of 2007-2008. While the Tea Party blamed the government, and the Democratic Party shied away from substantial criticism of the Wall Street financiers and banking institutions that caused the crisis, Sanders based his campaign mainly on criticism of the those institutions. It was a more traditional populist message, unlike the populism of the Tea Party, in the sense that it actually sought to improve the situation of the population.

Thus the presidential elections of 2016 included representatives of the Two Americas, with candidates offering both the mainstream and radical options of their respective sides.

The Sanders campaign was surprisingly effective, eschewing the Democratic Party political machine and its dependence on corporate financing. Yet he was unable to defeat Clinton, who was firmly aligned with a powerful network of large business interests. Her triumph over Sanders was directly responsible for her ultimate failure in the general election, since she was widely seen as exactly the type of elite, entrenched, establishment politician that Americans were rebelling against.

The Republican Party presidential primaries were notable because of the large number of candidates, including some who identified with

Tea Party. The mainstream favourite was Jeb Bush who, like Clinton on the democratic side, was part of a decades-long political dynasty and the recipient of the most financial support. Yet a substantial number of republicans, as was the case with the democrats, were not in the mood for an establishment candidate. Republican voters were faced with a large number of candidates who did not speak to their concerns, and whose positions were essentially similar. And that—perhaps most important—did not share their anger.

With one exception.

There was another republican candidate, an outsider not only to the Republican Party but to the entire political process. He was a billionaire businessman who came to politics with absolutely no political experience. Nobody expected that he had a chance. Yet he spoke to the concerns of many Americans in a way nobody else did. His name was Donald Trump—a name that has become infamous in the history of American politics.

Unlike the rest of the Republican Party establishment—mainstream as well as the Tea Party—he was highly critical of the kind of "free trade" agreements that had outsourced well-paying American jobs and destroyed the middle class. Also, unlike the rest of the Republican Party establishment, he was not opposed to social welfare programmes such as unemployment, Medicaid, and food stamps. Unlike other Republican Party candidates, Trump did not shame recipients of such programmes, which was very important for his low income working class supporters who were largely dependent upon them.

Yet such messages were mixed with others that were deeply disturbing. Trump had made many demeaning racial remarks to rally support. He promised to construct a border wall along the entire southern border to keep out Mexicans. He considered Muslims to be potential terrorists, and promised to ban Muslims from immigration to America. Trump gained support through a series of large rallies, with supporters brought to raging fury over perceived injustices. Trump's supporters had faith that Trump would deliver on his campaign promise to "Make America Great Again" despite—or maybe because of—an almost total lack of policy statements explaining how he would bring it about.

His campaign was accompanied by a rise in fascist ideology. Trump utilised rhetoric nearly identical to that of Benito Mussolini. Such rhetoric included an appeal to emotion at the expense of reason, an emphasis on order and control, the constant repetition of lies, extreme vagueness regarding positive proposals, and an overall emphasis on negativity and anger. Yet this proved to be effective, as it led to Trump to victory in the Republican Party primary election.

Trump was so unacceptable that initially, after the primary win, many mainstream republicans refused to endorse him. In addition, many long-running newspaper and media concerns, which had endorsed the Republican Party presidential candidate for their entire history, found themselves morally obligated to endorse a democrat for the sole reason of keeping Trump out of office. Yet despite it all, America elected a president solely on the basis of being angry.

As Trump prepared to take office, the situation did not look promising. There was a rapid rise in hate crimes, as many Americans felt empowered by the feeling that their racist impulses were being legitimised. Trump immediately ceased making promises to improve the situation for the middle class. He began appointing cabinet members, most of which were wealthy businesspeople with strong pro-business agendas. The position of Secretary of Education was filled by someone with a history of hostility to the idea of public education. The head of the Environmental Protection Agency was given to someone with a history of opposing environmental legislation.

Trump was openly hostile to the press, and did not feel the need to attend foreign policy briefings. Constitutional freedoms such as freedom of the press and freedom of speech were openly dismissed and even threatened. A series of increasingly irrational statements led many to question not only his ability to lead the most powerful nation on earth, but his overall state of mental health.

The day of the inauguration, and for several days afterward, America reacted with some of the largest protests that had occurred in decades, as Americans loudly embraced their freedoms of speech and assembly. Although this did not change the outcome of the election, many felt it was important to exercise these freedoms while they could.

Political Fragmentation and Irrelevancy

Despite the fears of many Americans, the presidency of Donald Trump did not result in the end of America, or of American democracy. Although many of the fears were due to the fascist-style rhetoric used during his campaign, America did not turn into a fascist state. That would come later.

Trump was ultimately stopped for a variety of reasons, the main one being that he was his own worst enemy. His mean-spirited belligerence, continual lies, frequent contradictions, and the growing appearance of mental imbalance eventually alienated nearly everyone. Even those who had enthusiastically supported him grew disillusioned when it quickly became apparent that his populist rhetoric was flagrant manipulation to gain votes, and once in office he used his power to advance business interests. To put it simply, the Trump administration was an unmitigated disaster in nearly every way.

Initially many Republican Party representatives were frightened of the implications of a Trump presidency. Yet when Trump won the election, the Republican Party accepted the new president, hoping to control some of his wilder impulses and offensive rhetoric while using his executive powers to advance the Republican Party agenda. When his presidency collapsed in turmoil and controversy, the Republican Party was left in disarray. The party became extremely unpopular, even amongst lifelong republicans.

The Democratic Party had reacted to its loss against Trump with some deep soul searching. Eventually, the party reluctantly accepted that it had a role in that defeat by rallying behind a mainstream pro-corporate career politician that gave only nominal support to populist interests.

As a result of this realisation, and of the Republican Party's weakened position, the Democratic Party felt empowered to move away from positions favouring large business and financial interests. In other words, in the ongoing power struggle between the American political system's primary and secondary constituents, the balance began to tilt in favor of the American public. While it was nothing like a political revolution, it was the first time since the 1970s that the balance had begun to shift.

The Democratic Party rebounded with an unprecedented sweep of both national and state elections. For a time, the democrats led something of a "Golden Age" of social progress. The party introduced a variety of progressive programmes and initiatives helping to strengthen the social safety net and level the playing field of economic opportunity. For the first time in decades, economic and financial regulations were tilted in favour of demand-side or "trickle-up" economics. This included a substantial increase in the minimum wage, paid for by tax increases on America's upper classes. Not only did such measures begin to create more economic equality, but they initiated a modest economic boom as consumer spending increased. This also had the effect of reducing unemployment.

Yet the "Golden Age" did not last. These advances worked to diametrically oppose business and financial interests, which did not take these developments well. Large players in the banking and finance industry took measures to sabotage the American economy, attempting to essentially hold the entire economy hostage in order to force the government to reverse its policies. They accelerated strategies used in the past, resulting in thousands of major corporations moving their operations to countries more favourable to business interests. Some of America's richest and most powerful CEOs rebelled with the strategy of intentionally bankrupting their companies, after obtaining billions of dollars of financial benefits in what Americans called a "golden parachute."

There was another serious problem with this new emphasis on populism, which democrats either did not understand or did not fully appreciate. The growing emphasis on public well-being, and the shrinking emphasis on business well-being, had an inhibiting effect on economic growth. Every measure that worked for the American people worked against economic growth. Such measurres reduced the profits of American businesses, and therefore reduced their ability to take out loans. And because of America's addiction to economic growth, those loans were needed to pay off previous loans and keep the whole game from collapsing.

The trap of America's addiction to economic growth resulted in a sort of "teeter-totter" effect: America could encourage either economic well-being for its citizens, or the conditions optimal for economic growth, but not both. Therefore, business interests did not directly need to hold America hostage, since the addiction to economic growth did so much more effectively.

As a result, the Democratic Party's valiant effort to follow through on its populist rhetoric was ultimately unsuccessful. It was necessary once again to focus on the needs of their primary constituents. Thus it returned to its old and ineffective strategy of populist rhetoric to the public, combined with support to powerful financial interests in private. As a result, the Democratic Party declined, allowing the Republic Party the opportunity to rise. This inevitably led to a return of the Republican Party's old and ineffective strategy of claiming that support of powerful financial interests was a populist message since the increase in wealth would "trickle down" to them. When this failed, it gave another chance for the Democratic Party.

Yet as America's pendulum swing between parties continued, both sides continued to ignore the roots of America's growing problems. It was becoming obvious that toggling between the political left and right did not constitute a direction. Yet most Americans did not grasp this. Rather than asking "Which direction is the country going?" Americans asked "Which side is winning?" As a result, the question of what direction America should be going was not even raised.

It was becoming obvious that neither party had viable solutions to America's deep-seated problems, but it would have been political suicide to publicly admit it. No politician was willing to tell voters that the American Dream was doomed. Even after 50 years, American politicians had not forgotten the lesson of President Jimmy Carter, who dared to express negativity and doubt with a 1979 speech that was dubbed the "malaise speech." In speaking to America's threats of the time, including the energy crisis, unemployment, and economic inflation, he spoke of an even deeper threat:

> The threat is nearly invisible in ordinary ways. It is a crisis of confidence. It is a crisis that strikes at the very heart and soul and spirit of our national will. We can see this crisis in the growing doubt about the meaning of our own lives and in the loss of a unity of purpose for our nation.

Carter was criticised and ridiculed from every segment of the American population, and was quickly replaced by President Ronald Reagan. Americans embraced Reagan's smiling optimism despite—or because of—his denial of such things as "malaise" and the need to re-establish "a unity of purpose for our nation."

As a result of the declining situation in the 2030s with dissatisfaction with American politics at an all-time high, politicians became increasingly desperate to do whatever they could to gain the votes of the public. This led to many pathetic staged "photo ops" in which politicians attempted to portray themselves as "typical working-class Americans."

This resulted in several embarrassing incidents, such as accusations of hot dog theft in the case of a politician who did not understand that for hot dog stands "put it on my expense account" was not a viable option. One politician's attempt at karaoke singing resulted in a viral video that was eventually voted "third funniest video of the year." Most tragic was an incident in which a congressional candidate went on "a typical hunting trip with the guys" which led to extended hospital visits for two interns, multiple charges related to the uses of firearms while intoxicated, and a severely injured deer. The deer, incidentally, recovered and was adopted by an American zoo where it lived happily for the remainder of its life, although it suffered weight problems due to sympathetic Americans feeding it too many cheeseburgers.

America's mainstream politicians had become desperate because, by this point, Americans became so disgusted with the two main political parties that alternate parties began to have a substantial impact. Some were established parties, such as the Libertarian Party and the American Socialist Party. Others were previously existing yet obscure parties such as the Working Families Party and the Unity Party of America.

Yet many were brand new parties arising from America's fringes. These totally ridiculous parties, we can only assume, were not meant to be taken seriously, and whose establishment can be taken as a sign of America's disillusionment with party politics. Such parties included the Shoes for People Party, the Rastafarian One Love Party, and the

Brunettes Kick Ass Party. Somewhat puzzling was the Legalize Sex Party, considering that sex was not illegal. Also notable was a party based purely on having fun, which called itself the Party Party.

However, the most influential and popular alternate party of the era was the Whiskey Rebellion Party, named for the 1700s anti-government whiskey rebellion. By this time the formerly radical Tea Party had gone entirely mainstream through its absorption by the Republican Party, and America was ready for a new anti-government political movement. In a widely viewed publicity stunt, members of the Whiskey Rebellion Party asserted their prominence with a staged re-enactment of the Boston Tea Party. Yet instead of dumping boxes of tea into Boston Harbor, they dumped cases of American whiskey. The humiliated remnants of America's Tea Party never recovered.

Some of the alternative parties did remarkably well. In some elections, the Whiskey Rebellion Party won over 20 percent of the vote. Even some of the "just for fun" fringe parties did well, with the Party Party once winning five percent of the vote in Florida. Yet such results made no difference in an election system in which only the biggest winner gains office. At the time there were so many alternative parties that they effectively cancelled each other out.

America's two main parties grew increasingly desperate to distract the country from its mounting problems, and from their inability to do anything about them. They had traditionally accomplished this via scapegoating. This process had been embraced most enthusiastically by the Republican Party, which was only too happy to continue the tradition. The Democratic Party, by contrast, generally limited its scape-goating to the Republican Party, and had a tradition of enthusiastically expressing support for whomever the Republican Party happened to be scapegoating. They were happy to continue the tradition, and merely had to wait to see whom the Republican Party would scapegoat this time.

However, the Republican Party was experiencing a shortage of fresh scapegoats. With America's combined minority groups making up over half the America population, blaming minority groups was not only ineffective but resulted in a strong backlash. Fear of terrorism had subsided, and exhortations of "Terrorists are coming to get you!" brought laughter. So the Republican Party had no other recourse than to resort to renewed battle in America's so-called "culture wars." But by this time, the old standbys of gay rights, gun control, and abortion had become ineffective.

It is interesting to note that the Republican Party, once a strong opponent of abortion, eventually became a major advocate. This was due to the realisation that women seeking abortions were likely to be liberals, and that their babies would most likely to grow up to liberals as well. Republicans realised that outlawing abortion was therefore against their own interests, as the babies they saved would most likely vote against them.

The Republican Party scrambled to search for new "hot button" issues that would inflame Americans. There was an attempt to create controversy with the claim that America had a "redhead issue." This ill-advised attempt failed miserably due to the fact that most Americans, as indicated in a nationwide survey of the period, considered redheads to be "somewhat or very hot." Similar attempts at generating distracting controversy were directed toward issues such as clove cigarettes, skateboards, tattoos of Chinese symbols, and—in an attempt to involve America's youth—the alleged decline of the death metal sub-genre of heavy metal music.

However, none of these attempts inspired the desired reaction until the Republicans instigated a furious national debate over the benefits of catsup versus mustard. But this was nothing compared to the furious controversy that erupted concerning cats versus dogs, which eventually resulted in an eight-day congressional sit-in and massive marches in Washington DC.

Such debates, of course, appear to us now as supremely frivolous. Yet such frivolous political debates had very serious and non-frivolous effects. As they continued to distract America from resolving its mounting problems, it was making the entire political process irrelevant. And as they contributed to the growing realization that democracy had become almost wholly ineffective, it was leading America toward abandoning it.

RUNNING AMERICA AS A BUSINESS

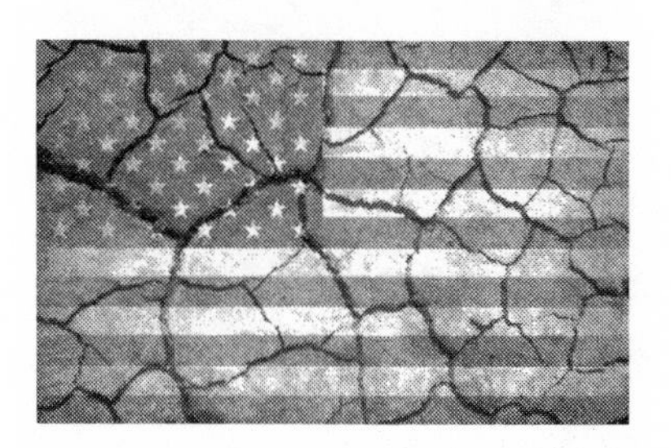

The Save America Act

Some think of America as beginning with the adoption of the Constitution in 1776. But long before the lofty words and high ideals were the brutal realities of establishing the original colonies. So brutal were those realities that the first attempted colony—the ill-fated "Lost Colony"—fell victim to circumstances that will likely never be known.

It was the second colony, called Jamestown, which would eventually become successful. One reason it succeeded was due to being adequately sponsored. In 1605, two groups of merchants, who had formed joint stock companies made up of the investments of shareholders, petitioned for the right to colonise Virginia. These companies were the Virginia Company of London, and the Plymouth Company. The charters included the intention to spread Christianity, yet the underlying justification was profit. Or as is stated in one of the charters, they claimed the right to "dig, mine, and search for all Manner of Mines of Gold, Silver, and Copper."

This established two important precedents for the colonies which were to eventually become America, and would continue throughout the remainder of American history.

The first precedent was a motivation for material wealth justified with self-serving idealistic motivations. Clearly, the dynamic of Manifest Destiny started literally with the founding of the first colony. The second precedent was the fact that America was officially established by corporate interests for the interest of profit.

Yet even with adequate sponsorship, success was far from guaranteed. Conditions were brutal, and it is a minor miracle that Jamestown did not perish.

On December 20, 1606, the initial wave of 105 colonists set sail aboard three ships. In May of 1607 they reached Chesapeake Bay and established James Fort—later to be called Jamestown—the first permanent English settlement in the New World. Although American history schoolbooks depicted the colony as a group of heroic founders, portrayed in paintings as the proud settlers of a new land, the reality was grim. In addition to attacks by the Algonquian Indians, there was rampant disease—largely due to establishing the colony amidst a malarial swamp. The colonists had arrived too late to plant crops, so starvation became common.

By 1610, only 60 of the 500 colonists had survived. Some had been reduced to the most desperate of measures. According to one account, a man killed his wife and "fed upon her till he had clean devoured all parts saving her head." Unfortunately, this was to be another precedent for what was to become America, when the great country was in the final stages of collapse.

Through means that would eventually form another precedent, Jamestown survived largely due to the efforts of one man, Captain John Smith. When the situation at the Jamestown colony grew desperate, Smith became essentially a military dictator, initiating a kind of martial law that was instrumental in saving the colony. This was followed by a series of successes and to the history of America that we all know.

Yet by the late 2030s, those successes were over and America was entering a phase of extreme crisis. Since America did not understand the causes of its decline, it clung to the same attitudes and strategies it had utilised for the past 400 years. And in America's final years, the precedents from America's founding would rise again to prominence.

□ □ □

In 2039, America was hit in quick succession with three major crises. The first, in July, was the collapse of Phoenix, described earlier. Then in August, a number of American cities began to go bankrupt. One of these was Detroit, Michigan. This was not a great surprise, since the city had declared bankruptcy several times in the past. But the extent and depth of this new bankruptcy was unprecedented. In the past, the American government had always stepped in to save the city. But this time the amount of money required was so extreme that the chairman of the Federal Reserve fainted upon hearing the amount.

But what truly shocked the nation was the bankruptcy of Houston, Texas, at the time the 4th largest city in America. This was followed by Cleveland, Ohio, and several smaller cities. At this point the chairman of the Federal Reserve quit his position, and accepted a position as banjo player in a bluegrass band.

The cities in question correctly interpreted this to mean that no assistance was coming. As a result, they were forced to initiate desperate measures such as cancelling city services and selling off city assets. Detroit held immense bake sales to sell cupcakes and brownies to other cities. Houston formed travelling rodeos and raised funds by offering pony rides to children. Cleveland offered tourists the unique opportunity to use their own explosives to blow up the more dilapidated portions of the city. In addition to extra income from charging fees for this opportunity, this saved Cleveland the expense of blowing up the city themselves.

As if this was not enough of an economic blow, it was followed in October by the Great Bank Collapse of 2039. This was the latest in America's ongoing pattern of bank deregulation leading to increasingly risky loans and investments on the part of America's major financial institutions, leading to a collapse to be paid for by American taxpayers.

The trend had gone on for decades, and Americans were angry at each collapse. Yet their anger was nothing compared to this latest collapse, when thousands of torch-wielding taxpayers stormed Wall Street hungry for revenge. Several top executives were stripped naked and publicly humiliated, some with the ancient practice of "tar and feathers." Several of the executives were seriously injured, and one almost died due to a severe allergic reaction to the feathers.

Suddenly America was thrust into a state of economic crisis such that it had not seen since the stock market crash of 1929. Even before the onslaught of the combined disasters that came to be known as "Black October," the American economy had been struggling. Now, the combined disasters threatened to send the country into full-blown depression and very possibly into the catastrophic event—described by the term that no economist dared utter—of an economic death spiral. In desperation, America was impelled to abandon all other concerns in a frantic effort to sacrifice everything for the continued survival of the economy.

Newly elected President Haskell, a Republican, saw the opportunity to push the Republican Party agenda beyond all previous limits. After a series of emergency congressional sessions and marathon White House meetings, President Haskell announced the introduction of emergency legislation with the cumbersome title of The Ultimate Financial and Economic Stimulus Package Act, generally referred to as *The Save America Act.* The goal, as stated by the president, was what he called "economic purity." This meant, as he put it, "To realise maximum economic efficiency by removing all impurities that contaminate the flowing abundance of economic growth."

The Save America Act was basically an extreme application of right-wing principles favouring large corporate and financial interests. Many international commentators saw the legislation as a continuation of the efforts attempted by President Donald Trump in the late 2010s, yet were stymied when the Trump Administration imploded in chaos and controversy. Also, at that time there existed a degree of resistance toward such extreme measures.

But in 2039, America had little choice but to adopt such efforts. In less desperate times such legislation would have been seen as an instance of partisan favouritism. Now, it could be advanced as bi-partisan necessity.

In a media conference announcing the legislation, President Haskell was required to strike a delicate balance. He needed to make Americans understand the seriousness of the crisis, yet without causing undue panic that would only worsen the situation. Thus his announcement of the legislation with the words: "The American economy is stronger than ever, but we have to take desperate measures to keep it from collapsing."

The White House news release that accompanied the president's announcement listed the major measures of the act:

- Eliminate all job-killing corporate income and property tax. Loosen bankruptcy laws for American businesses, and institute "guaranteed income" provisions to insure all corporations remain financially viable.
- Immediately end bankruptcy laws for American individuals.
- Initiate tax rebates for the America's most wealthy and make them promise they'll use the money for investments that will increase economic growth.
- Drastically limit regulations that reduce economic growth, such as those perpetuated by the Department of Health and Human Services.
- Eliminate welfare and unemployment insurance, which only serve to create dependence on the "nanny state."
- Eliminate school lunch programs and the federal food stamp program, since hunger is a great motivator.
- Reduce expenditures on Medicare, Medicaid and Social Security by getting rid of Medicare, Medicaid and Social Security.
- Privatise wasteful government programmes in favour of the efficiency of for-profit business.
- Immediately liquidate what's left of the country's natural resources, and give eminent domain to all oil and mineral corporations the right to drill, dig, or tunnel anywhere in the country they desire, with the exception of the White House lawn.
- Greatly expand spending on America's seriously underfunded military.

The act also included the provision that the major banks and Wall Street institutions responsible for the recent collapse were pardoned from all present or future financial liabilities. Therefore, they could not be the targets of class-action lawsuits or other legal actions. Punishing the responsible parties was considered to be unfair, since "they didn't do it on purpose." More importantly, their vast experience and wisdom was needed to help the American economy grow, so that future economic growth would trickle down to American taxpayers so they could pay for the collapse.

And although weakened banking and financial regulations allowed the collapse, the government did not add or strengthen regulations. Rather, it further weakened them. This was justified by President Haskell with the statement, "We just have to keep digging and hope this hole turns out to be a tunnel."

Democrats were not entirely pleased with such measures, but since it was a matter of saving the economy there was essentially no choice. They explained to their displeased constituents that as soon as times became less desperate, the Democratic Party would go back to making statements in favour of equality and economic justice.

America, Inc.

In an emergency meeting of Congress, the act inspired a rare example of bi-partisan agreement and was enthusiastically passed in 37 minutes, a new record for a congressional bill.

Yet in an uncharacteristic act of assertiveness, the Democratic Party managed to convince the Republican Party leadership to add some relief for distressed Americans. The act was amended with the provision that Americans troubled by the diversion of more economic resources to America's most wealthy could call a toll-free telephone number. When they called the number, they would be reassured by operators that "a rising tide lifts all boats" and that financial relief would arrive at some point in their future, or possibly at some point in their children's future.

A troubling aspect of the act was that it granted the current administration emergency powers to fast-track the implementation of the act by temporarily outlawing "organised opposition and forms of protest that unduly limit the government's ability to carry out all measures of the act." The act also gave law enforcement agencies extraordinary freedom from the usual laws and processes that American citizens were accustomed to.

There were vocal criticisms that these measures were in direct violation of the protections guaranteed by America's Constitution. Yet the administration was firm in its insistence on the necessity of such measures during this time of national crisis, in order to preserve the Constitutional principles that make America great. As President Haskell put it, "We need to defy the Constitution in order to preserve it."

Some critics were concerned about how long those temporary emergency measures would remain in effect, since no end date was specified. Such critics were not at all reassured by the official White House response of "As long as we feel like it."

What was possibly more troubling than the act's measures was the fact that there was so little public resistance to them. This is undoubtedly due to the fact that Americans were experiencing real fear due to their desperate financial situation. Despite the president's claim that "The American economy is stronger than ever," the American public perceived that it had two choices: accept the measures of the Save America Act, or accept that the American economy would collapse and they would all die.

In the midst of their fear, the promise of bold and decisive action was extremely appealing. It was understood that the coming years would be hard and Americans would likely lose some freedoms and give up some rights, but when America returned to a new golden age of 1950s-style prosperity then things would get back to normal. Of course, this thinking was tragically misguided. It assumed that the crisis was merely a short-term problem. And it assumed that America could return to 1950s-style prosperity.

Whether it was deliberate or accidental, President Haskell and those who authored the Save America Act had tapped into a deep thread that had run throughout America for its entire history. Since the beginning, the only real nationalism that mattered in America was *economic* nationalism. From America's earliest years onward, money was the basis of America's only universal culture, a shared value that crossed all barriers. In speeches to gain support for the act, President Haskell was fond of reciting an updated version of a famous quotation by civil rights leader Martin Luther King, Jr.: "I look forward to a day when people will not be judged by the color of their skin, but by the content of their bank account."

By capitalising on fear, and by tapping into the strength of America's sense of economic nationalism, the government was thus able to easily convince the country to accept some counterintuitive and highly irrational strategies. This was important because one of the top priorities of the Save America Act was to enthusiastically pursue, on a national basis, a set of policies previously enacted by individual states that had utterly failed. The two most prominent failures were in the states of Florida and Kansas.

In 2010, the governor of Florida drastically cut corporate taxes, with the goal of completely eliminating them within a decade. At the same time, the state cut spending by $4 billion. This resulted in the sudden elimination of thousands of jobs, which proved catastrophic as the state had also reduced unemployment insurance. School districts were devastated, and thousands of people lost health insurance. And the economic boom promised to come in response to the tax cuts never arrived.

The example of Kansas, in 2012, was a more overt demonstration of the drawbacks of such actions, since the governor specifically announced his intention to turn the state into a "real, live experiment" in extreme right-wing economic policies. In the words of the governor, "My focus is to create a model that allows the Republican ticket to say, 'See, we've got a different way, and it works.'" The boldest aspect of the strategy was a massive income tax cut, meant to create a business boom that would result in economic growth and economic well-being. The result was that the state's $700 million budget surplus turned into a $238 million deficit. The disastrous results led the American financial publication *The Wall Street Journal* to call the model "more of a warning than a beacon."

Yet America's deep-seated anti-rationality proved strong enough to be totally resistant to the onslaught of facts. For example, pointing out that the economic policies in Kansas and Florida were disastrous, and therefore expanding them to the entire country would multiply the disaster, was seen as a "stupid intellectual idea." In a typical example of the American notion of "bigger is always better," it was thought the only reason the state-wide experiments failed was because they were on too small of a scale. As a result, it was claimed that although the measures failed at a state level they would work at a national level because "the nation is bigger than states."

It was either that, or admit that America's economic system was fundamentally flawed. This, of course, was not an option.

With the passage of the Save America Act, every aspect of America began a transition toward a single-minded focus on bolstering economic growth and glorifying those who were capable of making it happen. It could be argued, and many have, that this had essentially been the focus on America for the previous 50 years. While there is much truth to this position, the provisions of the Save America Act took this focus to a new and unprecedented extreme. The openly stated goal of America had become a conscious effort to abandon all concerns other than enhancing the well-being of what would come to be called *America, Inc.*

This new focus proved to be not especially controversial. This was partly because of perceived necessity, and partly because of ideas about the relationship of business and government that were prominent throughout American history. Americans were so thoroughly confused about the relationship between government and economics that most of them thought that the terms *democracy*, *free-enterprise*, and *capitalism* were the same thing.

The equation of money with value was a constant throughout American history. This relationship was considered to be an expression of the natural evolutionary process and, for some, of a transcendent force. In the view of one of America's leading entrepreneurs John D. Rockefeller, "The growth of a large business is merely a survival of the fittest. It is merely the working out of a law of Nature and a law of God."

Such sentiments were present from the very formation of the American colonies. It is worth recalling that Jamestown—the first successful American colony—was officially established by corporate interests for the interest of profit. This historical precedent was definitely not lost on President Haskell. In fact, it was emphasised repeatedly by himself as well as his staff as much as possible, as well as by leaders in business and finance. In fact, President Haskell often compared himself to Captain John Smith, who through martial law and strict discipline single-handedly led the colony through desperate times. As time went on, President Haskell came to increasingly call himself "Captain Smith," to the point where his staff began to privately express concern.

President Haskell and others were fond of resurrecting expressions that related to the long-running association of America and business, such as "The business of America is business" and "What's good for General Motors is good for America."

Such expressions resonated with American citizens. One reason is that a strong anti-government element had been present in America since its very beginning. Americans had long been fond of repeating tidbits of folk wisdom such as "America works best when the government gets out of the way." To critics that complained "The corporations are running this country!" a common reply was "Great! Can you imagine if the government was trying to run it?" As a result, the American public was largely receptive to the president's message that "America needs to run as a business."

This notion became openly embraced and celebrated, and the idea of "America, Inc." was proudly affirmed. To those who were critical of company CEOs that had accumulated personal wealth in the billions of dollars, politicians asked, "Why demonise people who have become financially successful?" The elimination of corporate taxes was justified with the logic that business taxes just led to higher prices. "Why tax companies at all?" it was argued. "They just pass on the expense to the customers."

In keeping with the idea of money as a transcendent force, President Haskell freely admitted that human intelligence was not capable of saving America, and that the country needed to appeal to a higher power beyond the ability of the human mind to understand or control. In other words, the power of free-enterprise capitalism and the wisdom of its "invisible hand."

The definitive statement on America's bold new direction was provided by President Haskell's widely viewed address to the nation, in which he emphasised that it was actually a re-affirmation of America's original mission. The address, entitled "America: Back to the Future," opened with the following famous words:

> People of the old America think in terms of government. There is no government. There are people who think there is a government because they vote. But these votes make no difference.
>
> There is only one holistic system of systems, one vast, interwoven, interacting dominion of dollars. It is the system of currency which determines the totality of life in America. That is the natural order of things today.
>
> America is a network of corporations, inexorably determined by the immutable bylaws of business. The nation is a business. It has been ever since the Pilgrims arrived at Plymouth Rock to build the first cabins in the mud. And our children will live to see that perfect world in which there's no war or famine, oppression or brutality—America as one vast corporation, for whom all Americans will work to serve a common profit, in which all necessities will be provided, all anxieties tranquilized, all boredom amused.

As a result of the great success of the address, President Haskell was emboldened to propose a variety of changes to reflect this new national focus. He suggested that the title of "President of America" was obsolete, and proposed the new title of "CEO of America, Inc." The presidential staff would consist of representatives of America's top corporations, and would effectively become "America's Board of Directors."

President Haskell stated that all his life he had been bothered by America's declaration of Labour Day as a National Holiday, since labour did nothing to advance economic growth. He suggested that America needed a much more meaningful holiday, and proposed changing Labor Day to *Management Day*.

Religious organisations expressed their desire to further contribute to the cause. President Haskell, seizing the opportunity to strengthen his appeal to a substantial voting bloc, allowed the Catholic Church to re-name the Statue of Liberty as *Our Lady of Perpetual Economic Growth*.

President Haskell's most radical proposal was that America's national anthem was obsolete and needed updating to become relevant to America, Inc. He announced a nationwide contest for America's children to come up with a new anthem. Two months later, the president chose the winner, and announced his intention to replace "The Star Spangled Banner" with "The Free Market Ramble":

Oh say can you see, the growth in GNP
How proudly we tell of the stock market's rising
There is no need to frown, for all wealth trickles down
Our nation does learn, by investment return
It's time now to gloat, rising tides lift all boats
The invisible hand, always leads us to glory
Oh say, does that trickle-down theory still work
O'er the top one percent, and for grocery clerks

The American public was unanimous in its excitement about this new direction. Their excitement was undoubtedly due to the fact that they had apparently forgotten that the goal of business is to improve bottom-line profitability, and one of the primary ways in which it does this is by cutting benefits and getting rid of employees. And in the scenario of "America as a business," *employees* translates to *the American people.*

To a historian such as myself, it recalls the enthusiasm in which the nations of the world entered World War I, expecting an exciting era of noble deeds and thrilling victories, and were totally unprepared for a decade of entrenched warfare and the death of millions in muddy trenches.

The Privatisation of America

Americans did not like taxes. This was partly due to the American emphasis on individualism and self-determination. Yet it was also because they were not seeing much value in return for the substantial percentage taken from their income.

So Americans were pleased to hear of the government's plan to almost totally eliminate federal taxes, except for the amount dedicated to the military and national security. This was accomplished primarily by a massive move of privatisation, unloading government responsibilities into the hands of private interests. Once started, progress was rapid and it did not take long for government services to almost completely disappear.

This had been expected. But when the new tax rates went into effect, Americans were shocked to discover that their taxes had been reduced only by one half, the proportion that was not devoted to military and national security spending. Americans had no idea that so much of their tax revenues went toward these programmes.

This is because the government had not wanted American taxpayers to be aware of how much of their taxes went to private military contractors. As a result, the government had resorted to what was called "creative accounting" to disguise the fact. Normally such trickery went unnoticed, although there were occasional missteps. Such as in 2028, when an investigation into why government accountants had added the expense of developing a new missile system to a programme for school lunches, a discrepancy discovered by the cost of "milk for little kids" being listed as $37 billion. In an extremely awkward media conference, a government spokesperson attempted to justify the expense with the reasoning, "Without a strong military, America won't have the ability to provide milk for little kids."

Other programmes eliminated by the tax cuts were things like Social Security, Medicare and Medicaid, public education, law enforcement, the postal service, and the maintenance of America's roads and infrastructure. As a result, Americans had to pay for those vanished government services out of their own pockets.

The end of the Social Security system was no surprise to most Americans. The anguished system had been degraded for decades, with payments steadily reduced and its fund regularly raided for unrelated expenses. As a result, for the past several decades Americans with the financial means had been investing in Individual Retirement Accounts and other stock-market-based arrangements. Less affluent Americans saved for retirement by investing cash and spare change into mason jars under loose floorboards in the kitchen.

America's federal prison system became completely privatised. Other municipalities quickly followed suite by privatising America's state, city, and county jails. Due to cost-cutting measures to enhance profitability, the conditions throughout the entire system became overcrowded and violent to the extreme, with any pretense toward rehabilitation being abandoned. Few Americans had any concerns about this. Their concerns were reserved for areas in which privatisation effected them personally.

One of them was the privatisation of law enforcement agencies into what grew to be called *Protection and Security Corporations* or *PSCs*. Americans became law enforcement consumers with a plethora of companies vying for their security business. Americans had the ability to choose the type of protection most closely aligned with their personal law enforcement philosophies, and to indicate the level of service, from "violence-lite" up to "exterminate with extreme prejudice."

While America's conservative population generally went with the more violent and retributive companies such as Terminator Express and Skull Smashers, America's liberal population generally preferred companies that initated "productive dialogue" with perpetuators. The providers of such services, who preferred to call themselves *dialoguers*, helped perpetuators to examine the effects of their actions and explore the origins of their criminal inclinations. Such an approach was surprisingly effective, although not for the intended reasons. In most cases in which a dialoguer engaged a perpetrator in the act of a crime, the perpetrator grew so bored with listening to the dialoguer that they abandoned their crime in order to get the dialoguer to stop talking.

In most cases, the prices were quite reasonable. For example, one of America's most basic yet surprisingly common problems—dealing with a neighbour with an incessantly barking dog—could be permanently resolved for only 50 dollars. This was enough to pay for a neighbourly visit by a representative of a PSC such as Bark-No-More, which was generally enough to ensure the end of all canine disturbances. Undoubtedly this was largely due to the company's very persuasive motto of "Dead Dogs Don't Bark."

Of course, more serious problems carried higher prices, and some crime victims complained of being victimised by criminals that did not take into account the limitations of their financial situation.

However, Americans who could not afford the services of a PSC but could afford a gun were delighted at their expanded abilities to take the law into their own hands. This was possible due to a provision of the Save America Act that greatly loosened restrictions on the ability to utilise violence against others. Basically, any act of violence was considered justified in the name of self-defence, with "self-defence" defined as "anything which inspired me to react with violence."

Due to the efforts of Americans to avoid inspiring trigger-happy citizens into violent reactions, most types of criminal actions actually decreased. The only persistent problem was with extremely violent perpetuators that no company was willing to face at any price. After PSCs spent months training their employees in the skills necessary to the profession, they did not want to risk losing their investment if the employees got killed. Also, it was bad for company morale.

This would become a major issue in a few years, but in the beginning it was a small problem that was overshadowed by other problems that resulted from privatisation.

One prominent example was the U.S. Postal Service, which became a division of the McDonald's Corporation that called itself McMail. The company introduced its incorporation with the tagline: "Fast Food, Faster Mail." Since the company already had an expansive network of restaurant franchises, all that was required was to add postal services to the menu. This allowed customers to mail letters and small parcels while awaiting their order of a Big Mac.

In one of many extreme cost-cutting measures, the company initially reduced mail delivery to once per week. Then the company discontinued all mail delivery, and adopted the brilliant business strategy of offering rentals of post office boxes at all franchises. Since Americans now had the choice of either renting a post office box or not being able to receive mail, this brought substantial additional income in box rentals as well as a great increase in food orders.

The most significant aspect of privatisation involved health care. Costs of medical attention had climbed to the point where even the most minor medical services cost thousands of dollars. Most of the population had so little money that many people were bankrupted merely by a case of the flu. Or in one instance that became a major news story, by a case of the sniffles. The cost of prescription drugs had risen by a factor of 20 or more, due to the government's total deregulation of the pharmaceutical industry. And to make matters worse, company-sponsored health care—for the shrinking number of Americans who were gainfully employed—had disappeared for all but the highest levels of corporate management and critical technical professions.

The government was very anxious to get rid of Medicare, Medicaid, and other health care programmes. After privatisation became complete, a relieved government was freed of one of its largest and rapidly growing expenses. Those expenses were now borne by individual American citizens, most of which could not afford them.

After only a matter of months, hospitals changed their rules and required all patients to pay full medical costs up front, because too many patients had proven unable to keep up their payments due to running out of money or dying. Impoverished Americans requiring emergency services had it even worse, due to ambulance transportation now consisting of private "pay-to-ride" services. It did not help that there was an additional rush charge for ambulance passengers that were in a hurry.

Due to the prohibitive costs of health care which few American could afford, self-directed medical care rose in popularity, largely due to the success of the best-selling book, *Surgery for Dummies*. In addition, many websites offered free video tutorials, so any American with access to the internet could "follow along" with professional physicians as they demonstrated procedures such as setting a broken arm or replacing a kidney.

Yet most Americans had intense resistance to performing medical care on friends or family, due largely to the media's enthusiastic reporting of "horror stories" in which those who survived ended up in worse shape than before. One of the most gruesome examples involved a botched liposuction procedure. The desired weight loss was not only achieved but exceeded, but unfortunately this was because the procedure inadvertently resulted in most of the patient's internal organs being suctioned from their body.

Due to increasing public pressure, the government was eventually forced to respond. This was arguably due less to humanitarian concerns than the fact that critically sick Americans, with no medical options or hope of survival, had begun dragging themselves to the steps of the United States Congress to expire as an act of political protest. Videos of government officials stepping over dying citizens resulted in condemnation from the international community. Members of Congress attempted to reassure the public with statements such as "It's not very many dying Americans" and "It only looks like a lot because they're all in one place." But such statements only increased public resentment.

Health Department Secretary Georgina Tamir responded by proposing a radical new national health care policy. She claimed that the skyrocketing costs of medical care were due to America's "invasive and mechanistic" methods of health care. She explained that such measures were "emergency measures" required as a result of ignoring the genuine source of health, which was the body's overall expression of life. She explained that a healthy body is essentially an ecosystem, and operates on similar principles as all other creations of nature. "Health cannot be created," she explained, "it can only be nurtured."

This new policy initially excited many in the "alternative medicine" field such as naturopathy and acupuncture. For years they had been fighting against the mainstream medical establishment, attempting to gain legitimacy for such beliefs. Yet the excitement quickly faded when it was realised that the new policy of "Let nature take its course" really meant "Good luck and hope you get better."

Continued public pressure finally forced the government to provide Americans with real relief from devastating medical expenses. The government offered a new programme that was specifically designed for those suffering from a chronic or incurable terminal condition, although the programme was available to anyone who desired an end to any type of suffering. The programme, which went by the name *Euthanasia Care*, offered a solution to any condition. In exchange for the patient's willingness to end their life by lethal injection under the supervision of medical experts, the government would pay for it.

Perhaps the most controversial aspect of privatisation involved America's education system. For decades it had been no secret that the government did not want the responsibility of being in charge of America's public school system.

One reason is that there had always been controversies. Anything that was proposed was met with furious opposition, whether it involved systems of testing and evaluation, race and gender studies, or methods of discipline. The increase in Spanish-speaking students created demands for bi-lingual education, and in cases where this was permitted other groups demanded education providing for the needs of students speaking Romanian, Lithuanian, and an obscure dialect spoken only by certain tribes in the mountains of Peru. Religious groups demanded the replacement of science curriculums with Bible study, followed by bored students demanding the replacement of Bible study with the study of comic books. A series of tragic school shootings led to controversies about gun control, with some Americans insisting that students should be permitted to carry firearms, while other Americans furiously disagreed and felt that students should be required to carry firearms.

But the primary reason for the government's desire to rid itself of the responsibility over America's education system was the tremendous cost. This desire was not only expressed by the federal government, but by state and city governments who were responsible for most of America's primary or junior schools.

Lower class residents, who were the least able to provide for quality private schools, were the most vocal in their resistance to the privatisation of America's public schools. They were concerned that the lack of equal educational opportunities would lead to reduced economic opportunities for their children, thus fueling a vicious cycle of continual poverty, as the upper classes could afford the education that would ensure their children would remain in the upper class. A group of parents from around the country journeyed to Washington DC and demanded to discuss the issue with the president. President Haskell met with the group and validated their concerns by explaining, "Yes, that is what would happen."

And indeed, that is what happened. Upper class residents could afford to pay for quality education, while lower class residents were forced to send their children to schools that focused on what was called *special financial needs education*. One way of keeping tuition low was by eliminating unnecessary expenses, such as electronic resources and physical resources. Another way was by the heavy use of corporate sponsorship. Company logos became ubiquitous. Corporate mascots increasingly roamed amidst school grounds, giving out free samples and occasionally leading classroom sessions. Classroom subject matter deviated somewhat from tradition, with McDonald's mascot Ronald McDonald teaching courses such as "The History of the Hamburger" and "Crispy, Salty, and Delicious: An Appreciation of French Fries."

Coursework was structured to prepare America's lower-class youth for the brave new world of America's future with courses such as "Introduction to Customer Service," and "Advanced Customer Satisfaction." America's most desperately poor citizens, whose children had the least chance of gainful employment, sent their children to schools offering courses such as "How to Not Get Caught" and "Tips for Surviving in Prison."

No matter the social class or level of education, the competition for employment grew more intense as students entered an increasingly fierce and desperate job market. The atmosphere became hyper-competitive for even the most menial low-paying positions.

In such an environment, parents were understandably concerned over the employment opportunities facing their children. Among other concerns, they worried that traditional parenting styles might be instilling their children with an excess of compassion. Values such as cooperation may have been considered to be positive at one point in American history, but to avoid unemployment and poverty it was necessary to instill other values.

As a result, there was a pronounced change in the literature of parenting and child rearing. In the past, there had been steady demand for books with titles such as *How to Teach Your Child to Respect People Who Talk Funny*, which demonstrated the importance of multi-cultural awareness. The change in literature reached an extreme in the best-selling book *How to Raise Children to Become Selfish Little Monsters*. The introduction began as follows:

> As a parent, it is your primary responsibility to equip your children with the skills they will need in life. Do you want your children to grow up to be sensitive, honest, responsible adults? Or would you rather have them grow up to be *successful?* By following only a few simple guidelines, you can show your love by raising them to be the kind of selfish little monsters that are capable of having a full and satisfying life in today's highly competitive world.

Among other things, the book urged parents to become effective role models by resisting caring behaviour which their children might emulate. Perhaps most controversially, it urged parents to deprive their children of pleasure and satisfaction. The resulting self-loathing would make it much easier for their children to loathe others, and the accompanying inner emptiness would give them the drive to succeed financially to compensate for lack of self-worth.

Although this was controversial, it did not stop the book from becoming a national best-seller, and its author from becoming a popular mainstay on the talk show circuit.

The effects of the book did not take long to appear. Schoolchildren went beyond healthy assertiveness into increasingly brutal displays of aggressive competitiveness. This continued beyond schools into family and neighbourhood life, manifesting prominently in one of the mainstays of American childhood: the lemonade stand. For those not familiar with the phenomenon, it consisted of grade-school children setting up impromptu roadside business establishments on hot summer days, with the purpose of selling ice-cold lemonade. This was seen as an opportunity to learn real-life lessons in free-enterprise capitalism.

Yet the widespread popularity of the book resulted in lessons that were perhaps too brutally real for such young children. In the attempt to gain market share, the proprietors of neighbouring lemonade stands quickly progressed beyond friendly competition to all-out war. Children engaged in "negative advertising" by erecting signs claiming that the other children had urinated in their lemonade. Children resorted to vigilante raids on neighbouring lemonade stands to steal their ice cubes.

To us today, such behaviour would seem to call for harsh words and perhaps punishment. Yet in the American atmosphere of the time, the children were not punished for harsh behaviour but were praised for "demonstrating initiative."

This behaviour carried over into the matter of children's play. The phenomenon of play is not unique to human beings, but is shared by all mammals. For young mammals, play is preparation and training for skills necessary for adult survival. Human children also indulge in play, and up until a few thousand years ago it was also based—especially for boys—on skills necessary for fighting and hunting. Yet with the advancement of human civilisation, the instinct for play became channeled into various schoolyard and board games that served little if any purpose in preparing for adult life.

But in the increasingly desperate times in America, childhood games returned to an updated variation of our ancestral games of fighting and hunting. Reflecting the necessities of American culture of the times, the fighting would be on the battlefields of business and finance. As swings and merry-go-rounds became obsolete, they were replaced with playground versions of boardrooms and corporate office complexes in which children played games such as "Corporate Merger" and "Who's the New Boss?"

Getting Serious: Domestic Terrorism and the Establishment of Re-Employment Camps

The Save America Act resulted in a quick boost to the American economy. Although a substantial number of Americans were strongly opposed to many of its provisions, the temporary economic boost inspired enough confidence for President Haskell to barely win a second presidential term. But soon after that term began, the gains of the short-term boost quickly evaporated, plunging the economy once again into a state of deep recession

Unemployment rapidly climbed to levels higher than before the Save America Act. And as a result, so did homelessness. As the number and desperation of homeless Americans increased, charitable resources totally disappeared. "Compassion fatigue" had turned into full-blown resentment as America's cities, towns, and suburbs became inundated with a growing army of homeless Americans. Skirmishes began between Americans who had nothing to lose and Americans who had nothing to give.

Worst of all, from the perspective of America's leaders, there were rumblings of discontent over the idea that America's domestic policies—and America's leaders—bore some responsibility for the situation.

Throughout America's decline, the American public had tolerated an increasing worsening situation. But they could essentially be placated if they were allowed to have just enough affluence for a minimal amount of consumer spending. They were capable of tolerating substantial deprivation, as long as there was enough affluence for them to purchase distractions such as trendy clothing, electronic devices, video games, and—above all else—television sets and the ability to afford access to hundreds of channels of programming. But the vast majority of Americans no longer had enough affluence. Domestic unrest increased, and a small yet growing number of Americans began turning their agitated eyes toward the government.

But the government could not admit it had any role in America's increasing problems, or that the assumptions behind the Save America Act were fundamentally flawed. Therefore, it was critical for the government to identify scapegoats toward which to direct the public's increasing anger.

The problem was that, as described previously, America's traditional scapegoats had become ineffective. None of them were significant enough to inspire America to believe that they could be responsible for the entire American economy. The government considered blaming environmentalists for slowing the economy with their job-killing regulations. But by this time those regulations had been all but eliminated, and what was left of the environmental movement had been reduced to arguing over which brand of paper towel was the least unsustainable.

The government needed to identify a single unifying "ideal scapegoat." And to do so, it needed to identify a singly unifying goal for America to which that scapegoat was opposed. With the concept of "America, Inc." it essentially had one ready-made. Whereas economic growth had long been America's unacknowledged prime directive, it was now acknowledged loud and clear. All it needed was a scapegoat that was universally acknowledged to be opposed to that directive. American politicians grew to realise that, with an exploding homeless population that was almost universally despised, America had the potential of a new homegrown scapegoat of its own creation.

America's homeless population was well-suited, since it was a scapegoat not based upon things such as ethnic background or sexual orientation which had by now faded in effectiveness. Identifying scapegoats based on such divisions had become something of an embarrassment as some of the top positions in government had become filled by individuals with such backgrounds and orientations. One incident involved an infamous speech made by Secretary of Education Loretta Gonzalez, in which she proclaimed "The problem with America is all those Mexicans that are stealing American jobs." An audience member yelled in response, "Does that mean you're deporting yourself to Tijuana?"

America's emphasis on individualism had already made Americans pre-disposed to consider the situation of homeless Americans to be solely their own fault. It did not take much encouragement for Americans to also consider them to be responsible for America's decline. As a result, all of America's problems were seen as a result of unproductive individuals whose lack of economic purity dragged down the economy.

This allowed Americans of all types to experience a new and unprecedented sense of solidarity as they united against a new scapegoat in their midst. America became swept up in a wave of extreme "anti-poor" hysteria. America's homeless population became subject to increasing acts of violence. America's militias turned their attention from the Mexican border to the borders of America's growing number of Britneyvilles in order to "keep them in their place."

For several years, there had been suggestions to deal with unemployment and homelessness with the strategy used by America in the 1930s, via paid government work through the Civilian Conservation Corps. The programme, a sort of peacetime domestic "army," worked on a variety of projects to improve American infrastructure and build recreational facilities for America's national and state parks. These well-built structures, often of a distinctive stone construction, were widely appreciated for many decades. Many of them, in fact, far outlasted America itself.

Over a century later there were widespread calls to re-institute the programme. America had an abundance of unemployed workers. And it had an abundance of failing infrastructure and other problems that sorely needed work. It made sense. The idea even had bipartisan approval for a time, although the Republican administration was openly suspicious of a programme that was devoted to helping people.

But the idea was killed by a shocking discovery. It was President Haskell himself who realised that the Civilian Conservation Corps was a programme started by democrats. Not only that, it was initiated by President Franklin D. Roosevelt as part of the New Deal. Republicans absolutely demonised President Roosevelt, whom they called "the daddy of the nanny state." They claimed his "wheelchair thing" was just a ploy to gain sympathy, and that when reporters were not around he got out of that chair for secret alliances with his mistress. Or in some versions of the story, for secret alliances with entire harems of mistresses. In any event, the idea of a renewed and modernised version of the Civilian Conservation Corps was dead.

The president's Chief of Staff, Erik Durand, is credited with developing the strategy that would resolve the problem. The solution was a programme consisting of what Durand called *Re-Employment Camps*. A provision for the construction of such camps was quickly added to the Save America Act, and the first camps opened within months. Rather than being a form of punishment, the government proposed the Re-Employment Camps as a compassionate solution, as a way for homeless and unemployed Americans to redeem their failure as Americans and as human beings. America was not a nation of barbarians. America was a nation of civilised people who, unlike brutal regimes, refused to punish or imprison their failures.

The bulk of America's unemployed and homeless population was deeply in debt, allowing the government an ideal justification of the Re-Employment Camps. Rather than blaming them for their failure, the Re-Employment Camps would provide a way for them to "make good" by providing a means to pay their debt to society. Rather than labelling them as "failures" the government proposed they be referred to as *work-shy*. They were not exactly handicapped, as many Americans had felt, but merely *employment-challenged*. They were considered to be *Special-Needs Americans*. It was repeatedly stressed that within the camps they were not to be referred to as *inmates*, but as *guests*.

These Americans were pressed into a variety of tasks, but most prominently they were used as farm labour. There was a critical need for such labour, since most Mexican labourers had found more lucrative means of employment. As a result, most Re-Employment Camps were located in America's remaining agricultural areas. Within a year, nearly one quarter of the American population consisted of farm labour. It is interesting to note that America started off largely as a nation of farmers, and would end largely as a nation of farmers. Although at the end they were essentially prisoners.

By this point, the greatly reduced supply of oil-derived gasoline was prohibitively expensive. Wood gas was readily available, yet was even more expensive. As a result, industrial farms began exploring options to replace the massive 18-wheel tractor-trailers traditionally used to haul agricultural products. The most successful option was essentially a pedicab-version, which required one driver and a crew of 24 "engines." Mexicans were happy as drivers of individual pedicabs, but had no desire to be part of such crews. This provided even more work for Americans in the Re-Employment Camps, who were granted temporary work permits to provide the energy for cross-country deliveries.

The government felt the need to pay wages to the Americans in the Re-Employment Camps, in order to justify the claim that they were not prison camps. Since minimum wage restrictions had been removed years previously, the government could pay as little as they liked. But the government devised a way to pay them nothing at all. Since the government provided food, housing, and other necessities, and did not wish to offend the "guests" with free handouts, they deducted the costs from their wages. And by remarkable coincidence, the wages were never quite enough to cover the deductions. Therefore, the "guests" were assured of staying continually in debt, and therefore in continuous need of "employment."

Yet there were few complaints. In fact, many desperate Americans did not wait to be recruited into the camps, but volunteered for induction. The work was hard, and the pay was nonexistent, but at least they had three solid meals per day and shelter from the elements. It mattered little that those meals were of poor quality, and that the shelter consisted of a military-style barracks. And even though the television programming did not include any of the premium channels, at least there was television.

This aspect of the Save America Act could be considered as somewhat positive. It was doing nothing to resolve the roots of America's problems, but it was at least bringing some measure of security and stability to many Americans. Yet there was a more troubling aspect that was an indication of darker times to come.

The message behind the Save America Act was simple. Economic growth was America's prime directive. If you were against economic growth, or if you were perceived as having a negative effect on economic growth, then you were against America. You were a domestic terrorist. A brief provision added to the Save America Act made it official. An American citizen found guilty of obstructing economic growth, either directly or indirectly, was subject to penalties equivalent to those that applied to foreign terrorists such as those responsible for the 9/11 attacks.

This provision came at the precise moment the American government needed it. Because the Save America Act was not saving America, and was not going to save America. The fundamental problems were not being addressed, and therefore America's decline worsened. More drastic measures would be needed.

AMERICA GOES FASCIST

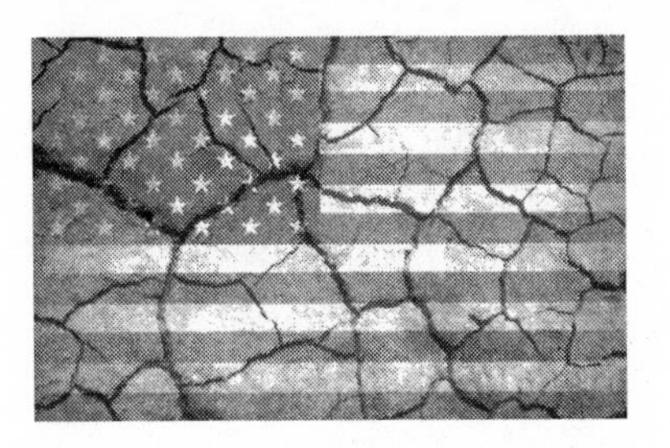

Laying the Foundations: Anti-Government Precedents and the Second American Revolution

By 2040, the movement toward fascism had been building in America for decades, with roots that can be traced back over a century. In response to the Great Depression of the 1930s, President Roosevelt took America in a democratic direction with the New Deal. But it very easily could have gone the other way. There were also strong fascist voices such as Huey Long and Father Coughlin, and extreme reactionary movements such as the Ku Klux Klan—all of which were immensely popular.

Before the outbreak of World War II many Americans were sympathetic to the Mussolini and Hitler regimes, and American aviation hero Charles Lindbergh was closely aligned with the Nazi Party. The fear of America going fascist is what led American writer Sinclair Lewis to publish *It Can't Happen Here*, a fictionalized account of how easily fascism could happen in America. And in 2016, when America was going through another economic crisis, President Donald Trump was elected based on a campaign based largely upon overtly fascist rhetoric.

Yet what very few Americans understood is that since the 1980s America had to an increasing degree been operating as a non-totalitarian variety of fascism. Although operating within the context of democratic government, it had largely accomplished fascism's implicit goals.

Of course, the term *fascism* inspire images of violent and overtly oppressive regimes such as those of Italy and Germany in the 1930s and 1940s. The common tendency is to associate fascism with an oppressive political system. Stormtroopers, jackboots, and overt repression were manifestations of totalitarian fascism. But fascism does not need to exist under totalitarian rule. It is possible to achieve results similar to such oppressive regimes without resorting to their oppressive methods. "Democratic fascism" may sound like a contradiction, but it is not. In the early 21st century it is precisely what America had achieved.

Earlier in this book I described how, beginning in the 1980s, America entered a "post-democracy" era of increasing plutocracy and oligarchy. Some of the terms used to describe this era were *benign totalitarianism* and *inverted totalitarianism*. Another term was *friendly fascism*, introduced around the same time by American social scientist Bertram Gross.

It is important to note that the original goal of fascism had nothing to do with a totalitarian state. The early 20th century Italians that invented fascism had a term for the concept: *estato corporativo*, or *the corporatist state*. According to the Italian leader Benito Mussolini, "Fascism should more properly be called corporatism because it is the merger of state and corporate power."

In the overt totalitarian fascist governments of the 1930s, industrialists and government officials sat side-by-side in the same planning agencies, which was an unprecedented situation at the time. Yet as noted earlier, this was the situation in America beginning in the 1980s, with business interests dictating important policies and in some cases writing the policies themselves. But it did not occur to Americans to think of this as fascism.

Part of the reason is that Americans did not understand the meaning of the term. Americans typically used the term as an insult to invalidate anything opposed to their personal or political beliefs. A substantial number of Americans used the term to express their displeasure with anyone they disagreed with or who annoyed them for any reason. Advocates for women's rights were accused of being fascists, as were drivers who drove too slowly and waitresses who did not smile when offering a coffee refill.

In the ideological divide of the Two Americas, both sides were quick to accuse each other of being fascists in response to any transgression, whether or not it had anything to do with the merger of political and corporate power. Yet many Americans were fine with the country being dominated by corporate interests. They accepted the idea that America was largely a "corporate state"—not realising that the concept of a "corporate state" is the very definition of fascism.

The mistaken belief that fascism could not occur in a democracy led Americans to believe "It can't happen here," even while it was happening. As a result, America descended into a curiously American version of fascism which was incapable of recognising itself.

It has been said that Americans would embrace socialism, as long as it was not labelled as such. In response to the Great Depression of the 1930s, America accepted Social Security, unemployment insurance, the Civilian Conservation Corps programme and other "socialist" programmes that were not offered as socialism. As Americans were willing to embrace socialism that was not labelled as socialism, it was willing to do the same thing with fascism.

The 2044 Save America Act pushed the country even closer to a fascist alignment of politics with business interests. While not overt totalitarianism, it did have the "totalising" focus that ruthlessly directed all resources, functions, and processes in a single direction toward and all-encompassing goal. In the overt European and Japanese totalitarianisms of the 1930s, the focus was on total war. In 2040s America, the focus was running the country as a unified business with the overriding goal of maximising the country's profitability. In a sense, it was a total war: it was a war on behalf of the economy, and the casualties were everything opposed to the economy.

American fascism, like other instances of fascism, arose in a time of crisis with the claim that it could bring the country back to a mythical past of glory and greatness. Like other instances of fascism, it sought to unite the nation as one people with one overriding purpose. And like other instances of fascism, the movement was led by a powerful minority that molded the public into wanting precisely what they had no choice but to accept. The goal was a government that did not appear to be the master of the people but the servant of their common will.

At this point in American history, the American public was desperate for any solution, and concerns over matters such as ethics, legality, and constitutional rights were unaffordable luxuries of a bygone era. The list of unaffordable luxuries also included freedom.

This was nothing new. Throughout American history, states of crises—war, economic hardship—would trigger the willingness of Americans to abandon freedom. In the wake of the 9/11 terrorist attacks, Americans acquiesced to compromises to the guarantees of the Constitution and Bill of Rights. They accepted increased domestic surveillance and the centralisation of power in the executive branch. Even though freedom was what they claimed to hold as the primary and most important aspect of being an American, Americans in crisis were unbelievably willing to abandon it.

By the 2040s America had been in a state of crisis management for decades. Indeed, most living Americans by this point had only known crisis. The golden age of American prosperity was something they only knew from history books. America demanded order. And America was willing to give up almost anything to whoever promised to provide it. Thus, America's eventual embrace of fascism should come as no surprise. The only question was over what form fascism would take.

It is important to recognise that America's elites did not want overt totalitarian-style fascism. As long as America operated under the principles of friendly fascism, it was not necessary. In 2038, the prominent American businessperson Kiefer Brentwood wrote:

> We do not need a fascist regime in order to maintain our dominance. Activist movements are weak and disunited. The trade unions are totally destroyed. The media is on our side. Overt

fascism requires mechanisms of oppression that are expensive as well as troublesome. It's just not worth it.

America's elites only resorted to fascism as a last resort. By 2047 it was very clear that the Save America Act was not working. This was inevitable, of course, since the act was nothing other than an expanded version of the state-led programmes that had failed decades earlier.

The democrats, naturally, blamed the republicans for their attempt to fix America's problems with a flawed plan. The republicans, just as naturally, blamed the democrats for obstructing a plan that would have worked if not for their meddling. Amidst continued political infighting, America's traditional two-party system proved unable to take decisive action of any kind. As we shall see, decisive action came from a direction whose response was to get rid of that system.

The American public was especially receptive at this point. Hatred of politicians and the entire political system was at an all-time high. One of America's most popular television programmes was the slapstick comedy *Cartoon Congress!* The show featured animated characters representing American politicians being humiliated by means such as slipping on banana peels, being struck in the face with pies, and being eaten by bears. It was during this time that a political poll somehow came up with an approval rating for Congress of negative 12.8 percent. Americans begun to suggest, half-jokingly, that Congress should simply be disbanded. Soon, this suggestion would not be a joke.

The task was to convince Americans to abandon democracy. This task was made much easier because America had a history of sentiments that were strongly anti-political and dismissive of government. Various movements arose throughout American history with mottos such as "Don't tread on me!" and "Get the government off our back!" Sometimes the movements were concerned about halting perceived government overreach. Sometimes the movements were more radical, calling not for restraint on government control but for the virtual elimination of government.

One such movement led to a number of dangerous stand-offs in the 1980s. Calling itself the *Sagebrush Rebellion*, it was a revolt by cattle ranchers against government regulations designed to prevent abuses such as overgrazing and habitat destruction. The target of the rancher's anger was the Bureau of Land Management, which was perceived to be an anti-democratic agency restricting personal freedom. As the ranchers perceived it, the government was restricting democracy by preventing them from doing whatever they wanted with public land, failing to acknowledge that total individual freedom is not democracy but libertarian-style anarchy.

Ironically, the Bureau of Land Management was formed in 1946 to end a dangerous situation of anarchy that had arisen in America's rangelands. Unrestrained use of the land had led to serious degradation. Competition with neighbours often led to sabotage and armed raids. So-called "cattle barons" gained immense power which they used to take over ranches and evict the owners. Murder was not uncommon. One of the few things that brought the cattle ranchers together was to oppose sheep ranchers, leading to the slaughter of sheep numbering in the hundreds of thousands.

At the time, the ranchers welcomed the government to save them from the situation. But soon this was all forgotten, whether willfully or otherwise, and the government became the enemy.

The Sagebrush Rebellion eventually died down without major incident, but the underlying contempt of the government remained. The frustrations arose again 30 years later with a bizarre incident in which a group of heavily armed ranchers occupied a wildlife refuge in the Oregon high desert. Residents of England may remember the cinematic adaptation of the occupation entitled *Big Guns and Small Brains*, the top-grossing British comedy of 2065.

The anti-government spirit would soon emerge in a stronger and more dangerous form. Initially it was called *The Great Revolt*. It rapidly grew and was subsequently re-named as *The Second American Revolution*. Once again it would start with ranchers. A large and well-organised group of ranchers in Nevada coalesced around the motto of "Get the government out of our pockets!" The movement was based on the argument that the ranchers had a right to cease paying grazing fees for their use of public land. They did this by rejecting the concept of public land. By the use of reasoning that may be considered to be self-serving, they declared that to have land belong to everybody was the same as having it belong to nobody, and rather than belonging to nobody it should belong to the person whose cattle is on top of it. Therefore the land was theirs, and they were free to abuse it. The abuse was justified, according to a spokesperson, with the reasoning that, "It's just land, it's not as if it's a person or anything."

Such an absurd statement might have been easily disregarded—along with the entire movement—had the ranchers not teamed up with powerful allies with similar messages. Large agriculture interests rebelled against what remained of the regulations that had not been eliminated by the Save America Act. Soil erosion was not a concern, they claimed, since the agriculture industry had effectively killed off the soil anyway. The Monsanto Corporation, in particular, was frustrated by governmental indecision on whether to approve the company's

HappyHuman product, due to concerns about whether attempting to genetically alter the entire American population was a good idea.

The Second American Revolution succeeded by inadvertently discovering the ultimate scapegoat capable of uniting all Americans: the government. The country had had great success in scapegoating its unemployed and homeless citizens, which had been thought of as America's ideal scapegoat. Yet as effective as this had been, it was now realised that America's ultimate scapegoat was actually the American government.

Attempting to argue was an exercise in futility. Pro-government sentiments were drowned out by rhetoric. Government employees defending themselves were regarded as biased. Pundits and political commentators that tried to defend the government were dismissed as brain-damaged.

America wanted to get rid of the government. Or perhaps, as slightly saner voices expressed, to merely reduce it to the role of enforcing regulations such as the specifications for signs on interstate highways. Many rallied around an expression popularised by political advocate Grover Norquist: "I don't want to abolish government. I simply want to reduce it to the size where I can drag it into the bathroom and drown it in the bathtub."

The Second American Revolution was based on the absurd premise that Americans could "win back America" by getting rid of the government. Few considered that the essence of America was its Constitution, and that the government was the means through which the Constitution was made tangible. Or in other words, that the government was the tangible expression of the principles, processes, and laws that defined what America was.

One of those principles was democracy. Government is the medium through which democracy operates, therefore to be anti-government is to be anti-democracy. Americans did not immediately make this connection, but it would be made soon enough. And if the idea of rejecting democracy would initially be resisted, it would soon become not only accepted but enthusiastically embraced. It is surprising how little it took for America to make the transition.

The Rise of the New Guards

America's two main political parties were too entrenched to consider such a radical step. Even the nominally anti-government Republican Party was too invested in the system to thoroughly abandon it. By this point, the American public was thoroughly disgusted with both political parties, and desperate enough to abandon them for something else. The 2048 elections were near, and America was ready for a new direction.

That direction was provided by a new political party, *The New Guards Party*. This party, like The Whiskey Rebellion Party, sought to get America "back on track" by a return to its roots. In fact, The New Guards Party arose as a faction of The Whiskey Rebellion party that broke away after a disagreement as to whether Alexander Hamilton was an alcoholic.

The name of the party was inspired by a passage from America's Declaration of Independence:

> That whenever any Form of Government becomes destructive of these ends, it is the Right of the People to alter or to abolish it, and to institute new Government...it is their right, it is their duty, to throw off such Government, and to provide new Guards for their future security.

The New Guards were fond of quoting the Founding Fathers. One of their favourite quotations was from Benjamin Franklin: "We need a revolution every 200 years, because all governments become stale and corrupt after 200 years." Such messages resonated with conservative as well as liberal Americans, even if they had very different ideas about the nature of the revolution that America required.

While some aspects of the message were favoured by conservative Americans, other aspects appealed to liberals and progressives. Such as how the "culture wars" advanced by previous Republican administrations were an insult to American ideas of freedom and liberty. Also, the New Guards insisted on retaining a strong separation of church and state. They believed that what a person did on their own time—how they chose to worship, or not worship—was none of the government's business. This also applied to a person's gender identity and sexual preferences. Such beliefs also appealed to the Libertarian portion of the political spectrum.

The party proved to be immensely popular. For the upcoming 2048 elections, they had enough support to run candidates in all congressional races. They also ran a remarkable candidate for the office of president. The leader of The New Guards Party was someone who in many regards fit the classic profile of the American hero. He was a self-made man. His rugged good looks appealed to men as well as women, yet not in a way that led them to question their sexual orientation. And although he was highly intelligent, he was successful in hiding this from the public.

His name was Johnny Jackson Garth, a self-described "country boy" who wore leather boots and a western-style cowboy hat. Before entering politics he had been a musician and had made a minor name for himself in the obscure musical genre of country-rap. His idealistic goal was to unite rural and urban America by expressing the feelings and concerns of country-based Americans in the musical style of city-based Americans. His debut recording was a song entitled "Goin' Through a Rough Patch" which included the following lyrics:

Momma gone to prison
And my dog done died
Wife left me for a lawyer
And I like my chicken fried

It should come as no great surprise that his efforts did not lead to success. For Garth, the failure was devastating. To pursue the genre he had given up the promising beginnings of a career as a mainstream country pop artist. In fact, industry insiders believed he had the potential to be the next Kenny Jason Travis or Luke Willie Yoakam.

No producer or record company was interested in a failed country-rapper. Garth went into a prolonged depression. His career seemed over, at least as a musician. But then he discovered politics.

Convinced that he was a musical genius, and needing to rationalise his failure, he blamed society. Or more accurately, he blamed the stupidity of the American people. None of this would have been known if not for the eventual discovery of his secret diaries, which documented the gradual development of his radical political ideas. The diaries reveal that his overriding purpose in life was to enact revenge upon the American people. He saw his choice as simple: Either he had to admit that his career as a country-rapper was misguided, or he had to destroy America.

Of course, America—due to its own misguided assumptions—was rapidly destroying itself on its own. Garth was undoubtedly a brilliant man, yet brilliance is often accompanied by self-delusion. The fact that he believed he could single-handedly cause America's collapse merely proves the depths of that self-delusion.

His brilliance was revealed in his rapid rise from failed musician to leader of the most powerful nation on earth. To accomplish this, he knew that the most vital part of his mission was to get the public on his side. In contrast to the angry outbursts and finger-pointing of conventional politicians, his speaking style was quite friendly. He told audiences what they wanted to hear, in simple and straightforward language. He told emotional stories that contained simple yet profound-sounding morals. It seemed to listeners that he spoke straight from the heart, that he expressed their own deepest fears and desires. He described himself in humble terms: "I'm just a regular guy who's shocked at how this great country has been destroyed by the political process. And I hope that a little common sense from a simple country boy can make things right." Speeches often began with accounts of his own poverty-stricken early life.

He had a remarkable ability to communicate with audiences across America's cultural spectrum. He could relate to audiences consisting of soccer moms, punk rockers, or business owners. In rural taverns he convincingly started bar brawls which appealed to the gun-totin' redneck subculture. In suburban lounges, he was generous with jello shots which was important in gaining the approval of suburban women who go clubbing and yell "Woo-Hoo!"

The contrast between his public and private selves was remarkable. His public persona totally disguised his brutal contempt for the public. It also disguised the intellectual rigour he used to devise the methods by which he would enact his revenge. This is revealed in a diary entry in which he detailed his approach to propaganda:

> All propaganda must be popular and its intellectual level must be adjusted to the most limited intelligence among those it is addressed to. The receptivity of the great masses is very limited, their intelligence is small, but their power of forgetting is enormous. In consequence of these facts, all effective propaganda must be limited to a very few points and must harp on these in slogans until the last member of the public understands what you want them to understand.

It is debatable whether the New Guards would have risen to prominence without the remarkable talents of Johnny Jackson Garth. He was a genuine charismatic leader, yet apparently without the drawbacks and weaknesses of such leaders that typically result in self-destruction. America had its shares of such false prophets, including political leaders such as Senator Joseph McCarthy, President Richard Nixon, and Donald Trump, as well as cult leaders such as Charles Manson and Jim Jones, and a long series of evangelical religious leaders who fell as a result of financial and sexual scandals.

The appearance of someone like Johnny Jackson Garth was exactly what many thoughtful Americans had feared. He was a charismatic leader who had broad appeal, and whose message was based not on hatred but on progress and reconciliation. He was exactly the type of charismatic leader that could convince Americans to willingly embrace fascism.

In many ways, the goals of The New Guards Party were merely an extension of those of The Save America Act. The New Guards shared the belief that the soul or essence of America was in economic and material progress. They also shared the belief that America should be run as a business, in order to maximise that progress. While the Save America Act identified and removed many of the perceived blocks to that progress, the New Guards took those beliefs to the extreme.

The Save America Act had removed most troublesome regulations. And it had made many gains in bypassing the political process that had created such regulations. But it did not proceed to the final step, of concluding that the political process itself was the ultimate block to that progress.

The ultimate block—the cause of America's decline and the enemy of American prosperity—was America's political parties with their unending lies and deceptions, their unrelenting negativity, their entrenched self-interest, their focus not on providing positive direction but on bringing down the other side. In other words, the enemy was the entire political process. In other words, the enemy was democracy.

This is where the New Guards took things to the extreme. Conventional political parties blamed other political parties. Some parties went as far as blaming certain aspects of the political system. The most radical and unprecedented aspect of the New Guards was that they openly and brazenly blamed democracy itself.

It was time for a post-democratic America. The Founding Fathers were wise men, but flawed—as all men are. They could not predict the future of this new and unprecedented experiment called America. Surely if George Washington and Thomas Jefferson were among them at this moment in history—enjoying an American cheeseburger with American french fries—they would agree that the era of democracy was over. Surely they would agree that it was time for America to move forward.

This was the message of The New Guards Party.

Perhaps the main reason that America did not see fascism coming is that they did not identify it as such. Yet as far back as the 1930s, a few Americans foresaw what would happen to America with astounding accuracy. In 1936, James Waterman Wise, Jr. said that when fascism came, it would be "wrapped up in the American flag and heralded as a plea for liberty and preservation of the constitution." In 1938, Halford E. Luccock said: "When and if fascism comes to America it will not be labelled 'made in Germany'; it will not be marked with a swastika; it will not even be called fascism; it will be called, of course, 'Americanism.'"

There is no evidence to indicate that the New Guards were familiar with either of these quotations, but they ended up predicting the future with eerie precision.

In studying fascist movements around the world, political professor Nancy Bermeo concluded that the single best predictor of success for fascist movements is political polarization and gridlock. This makes it possible for an outside group to emerge that promises to sweep away the bickering parties. Another strong indicator is an ongoing state of crisis. In America, as was the case in many countries that embraced fascism, rising unemployment and economic insecurity were the prime factors.

Italian writer Umberto Eco, who personally experienced the rise of 1930s Italian fascism, described what he found to be the 14 defining features of fascism. Eight of them were applicable to 2040s America:

- A mythologising of tradition that glorifies innate virtues.
- The rejection of Enlightenment ideals with their emphasis on rationality and the rights of the individual.
- The exalting of action for action's sake.
- Intolerance of criticism from any source.
- A stress on mystic unity that transcends all particularisms.
- A doctrine built on the idea that "life is struggle" whereby only the strong and resolute prevail.
- Contempt for the weak stigmatised as life's losers and nature's failures.
- Conveying strength and will and superiority in sexual terms personified by the Hero/Leader

All of these were strongly embraced by the New Guards. They fully exploited American exceptionalism along with the claim of inherent superiority. The rejection of reason meant that no actions required justification or explanation, and that criticism was unacceptable. All of this was reinforced by the mystic unity of "The American Spirit" or "Americanism." Also invoked by the New Guards, as it was throughout American history, was the mystical idea of free market capitalism with its "invisible hand" which contained a wisdom beyond human comprehension that would work for the benefit of all. Yet to work, it required individual sacrifice and struggle, with some losing for the cause. And those who lost were meant to lose, since they were not fit to win. And under the leadership of Johnny Jackson Garth, the New Guards had a natural leader who conveyed America's self-image in sexual terms, even though most American men would have chosen to die rather than admitting it.

It is interesting to note that the defining features of fascism are almost identical with the qualities of the American character. This would explain why Americans were never fully comfortable with democracy, and were never especially competent at the skills required for its successful implementation. It also offers an explanation for why fascism in America was so readily embraced. The eventual transition to fascism could perhaps even be seen as inevitable.

Marketing Fascism to America

Most of the Founding Fathers had a view of human nature that some may regard as pessimistic. Although the words "We the People" stirred Americans to patriotic sentiment about the noble cause of democracy, many of the Founding Fathers had opinions about "We the People" that were less than flattering. Alexander Hamilton called the masses a "great beast." James Madison wrote, "Human beings are generally governed by rather base and selfish motives, by suspicion, jealousy, desire for self-aggrandizement, and disinclination to do more than is required by convenience or self-interest, or exacted of them by force."

Most of the Founding Fathers were very disparaging of a full or true democracy. It is important to note—and surprising to everyone who realises it—that the word *democracy* does not appear in either the Declaration of Independence or the Constitution.

Even America's Pledge of Allegiance, which was written much later, did not mention the word. The object of the pledge was to America as a *republic*. The difference between a democracy and a republic is a matter of degree. A democracy, in the full sense of the term, is a form of government in which the people decide policy matters directly. A democratic republic, by comparison, is a form of government in which the people choose representatives who make policy decisions on their behalf.

In the view of the Founding Fathers, it was not realistic to expect that a group of uneducated farmers, woodcutters, and common labourers had the level of wisdom necessary to navigate the trials and tribulations of running a nation.

The idea was that the representatives would use their superior education and experience to choose wisely for the best possible good of the nation as a whole. According to James Madison, it would "refine and enlarge the public views by passing them through the medium of a chosen body of citizens whose wisdom may best discern the true interest of their country."

A less charitable view is that the Founding Fathers preferred representative government because it could be used to enhance themselves and their own kind. Madison, perhaps inadvertently, indicated this when explaining the dangers of direct democracy by the people. On the subject of what he called "pure democracy," he wrote: "Such democracies have ever been spectacles of turbulence and contention; have ever been found incompatible with personal security or the rights of property."

The key word is *property*. Because America initially identified as the right to vote as synonymous with the ownership of property. Representative government began in America in 1619, when the House of Burgesses met in Jamestown. In the House of Burgesses, only landowning men over 17 years old were eligible to vote. This carried over into the early years of American democracy, in which the right to vote was only for white male adults owning a designated quantity of property. In addition to requiring property to vote, a greater amount of property was required to run for office.

These aspects of American history would prove to be invaluable to the New Guards in their efforts to dismantle democracy. Because some degree of persuasion was necessary.

While Americans were generally receptive to the idea of abandoning the political process, they were understandably hesitant about abandoning democracy. Therefore, the New Guards Party needed to initiate a major effort to market fascism. And of course, one aspect of that effort was that they could not refer to it as fascism. As was predicted over a century earlier, they called it *Americanism*.

The name was significant. The New Guards saw themselves as a revolutionary movement that transcended politics and represented the real America. The movement was focused on what it called "the good old days" of the 1790s before political parties destroyed the country.

In response, leaders of the Republican and Democratic Parties—who normally could not come to agreement on whether water was wet—were suddenly united in their outspoken praise of democracy. Yet the New Guards easily used this against them, urging Americans to ignore the desperate pleading of a nepotistic elite concerned only with preserving their privileged positions. Or as Garth put it, "Those politicians only care about keepin' their fat paychecks and fancy-schmancy offices."

But Garth went even further. The reason that democracy was the problem—the reason it could never work—was because of the

American people. He made the unprecedented move of actually calling the American public stupid. He summed up his feelings about democracy with a quotation by H. L. Mencken: "Democracy is a pathetic belief in the collective wisdom of individual ignorance."

Most observers assumed that Garth was committing political suicide. And at first, the American public was not enthusiastic about the insinuation of sub-par intelligence. But this would quickly change.

As proof of the stupidity of the American public, and by extension the utter futility of the democratic process, The New Guards organised a conference entitled The Power of the People. The purpose was to provide an opportunity for a representational cross-section of Americans to reach consensus on setting a better course for America. To avoid detracting from the power of the people to self-organise, there would be no agenda. Developing the agenda would be the first item of order. So on a beautiful spring day, a collection of 282 Americans were escorted into an immense conference room and the doors were shut behind them. The attendees were given a full month to reach consensus.

As can be imagined, the conference did not last the full month. The first ambulances were called on the first afternoon, and by the third day armed forces were called in to rescue the police forces that had attempted to restore order on the second day.

The point had been made. The American public was faced with undeniable evidence that it was not smart enough for self-government. All in all, it was a brilliant victory for The New Guards Party.

If at first the American public was apprehensive about being labelled as stupid, they quickly grew to embrace it. As one fast-food employee put it, "I barely know how to flip a burger, so how can I be qualified to understand the relationship of interest rates to job creation?" Or as a hair stylist said, "You probably don't want me to have an influence on Federal Reserve policy, since I'm not smart enough to keep my checks from bouncing."

Such sentiments were common in what became the *Dumb and Proud* movement that swept America. Although the population had effectively lost control of the government long before this point, they had to justify giving up control officially. And to justify giving up, they had to have an explanation for the sorry state of their country. Thus, being "dumb and proud" was a way for Americans to retain pride in America while relieving themselves of responsibility for it.

The New Guards continually stressed that the right of all adult American citizens to vote was not originally part of American democracy. And the simple reason was that most people are stupid. This

this was nothing to be ashamed of, it was something to be embraced. From the diary of Johnny Jackson Garth:

> What we suffer from is an excess of education. The thinkers are the enemies of action. What we require is instinct and will.

Historians generally believe that this entry led directly to one of Garth's most popular speeches, entitled "Thinking Ain't Good," which begins as follows:

> I ain't well educated, but I'd say that's a good thing. All education does is confuse us. I've met some very educated people, and it's a shame what's happened to such folks. They have a head full of ideas that can prove or disprove anything. What's important is to follow our hearts. Don't think, because thinking will mess you up. Thinking ain't good.

This was an idea that all Americans could support. Of course, this is what Americans had generally believed anyway, but had never heard anybody state it so simply and eloquently. One aspect of Garth's brilliance was his ability to put into words precisely what Americans were feeling, and to do it in a way that flattered them. In this case, to make them feel good about themselves for being stupid.

In a pathetic attempt to remain relevant, politicians from both of America's two main political parties attempted to "dumb themselves down" to appeal to voters. Democratic politicians began saying things like "We actually is not too smart" and using less-intelligent word choices. For example, replacing "I pledge to enhance the employment situation by creating well-paying career opportunities" with "Me make good money jobs for you."

Nobody was fooled.

Yet the Republicans were pathetic in their own way. Republican politicians had been talking like this for decades and were unable to dumb down their rhetoric any further. As a result, Republican Party debates became contests in which politicians demonstrated how stupid they could behave, which by the final debate had devolved into food fights and mud wrestling.

The embrace of stupidity was of critical importance for the New Guards. Not thinking was vital to accepting their platform. One part of that platform was the vow to eliminate offshore tax havens for wealthy individuals and corporations as unpatriotic. "You earn it in America, you keep it in America" was the slogan which never failed to get widespread cheers from Americans across the political spectrum. However, another part of their platform was to eliminate taxes for wealthy individuals and corporations. The realisation that since they paid no taxes there was no need for them to utilise offshore tax havens would have occurred only to those for whom thinking was a virtue.

Also of great popular appeal was the promise of the New Guards to totally eliminate homelessness. This was a huge concern to all Americans, not only to the homeless but to the rest of America that was sick of dealing with them. Because although the institution of the Re-Employment Camps had significantly reduced the problem, it had not eliminated it.

Also, although there were less homeless Americans than before, the ones remaining were growing increasingly desperate. Americans relegated to the "Britneyville" shantytowns had begun conducting raids for food and supplies. Many had become reduced to such a filthy and uncouth feral condition that they were sometimes mistaken as zombies. Many Americans killed them by destruction of the brain in the mistaken belief that they were preventing their loved ones from becoming members of the walking dead.

The New Guards also claimed they would totally eliminate unemployment and, as an added bonus, totally eliminate all crime.

As to how they would resolve such intractable problems, the New Guards were extremely vague. Again, convincing America to not think proved extremely helpful. But if not thinking was helpful in accepting these promises, it was essential to accepting the more radical aspects of their platform.

The first of those was to get rid of political parties. If elected to power, the New Guards would introduce a Constitutional amendment to outlaw all political parties—including the New Guards Party.

But the biggest blow to democratic ideals was the proposed return to meritocracy. This was a major aspect of getting America "back to its roots." The idea that voting citizens must be qualified was present at the start of America, when only landowning men were eligible to vote. Therefore, a fundamental goal of the New Guards was that the ability to vote would be limited to qualified Americans, to Americans that had proved their value to the country. In other words, Americans in the top five percent of personal wealth. The New Guards proposed that meritocracy would "purify" democracy by removing stupidity from the process.

The New Guards were fond of a quotation by Alexander Hamilton, and repeated it as often as possible:

> All communities divide themselves into the few and the many. The first are the rich and well-born, the other the mass of the people.... The people are turbulent and changing; they seldom judge or determine right. Give therefore to the first class a distinct permanent share in the government.

According to the New Guards, equality was never supposed to mean that everyone's viewpoints were equal. This perverted interpretation of democracy caused America the loss of its appeal to excellence. As Garth put it:

> Democracy failed because people had been led to believe that they could simply vote for whatever they wanted, without puttin' in the work to get it. It put America in control of people who considered their own selfish concerns to be more important than America's economic success.

The New Guards affirmed their support of the concept of *equality*, but defined it as the belief that Americans had an equal opportunity to rise as far as their talent and ambition would allow them. Americans that complained about lack of economic opportunities were labelled as "crybabies" and "whiners." In response to such complaints, the New Guards presented what they characterised as "a perfect example of American ambition" in the person of Paulina Jamad-Rosencranz, a handicapped Jewish-Arab born $17 million in debt. The New Guards explained that, even with such challenges, she eventually established several successful business enterprises. If she could make it in America, the New Guards claimed, then anybody could make it. The American public was apparently so impressed with the story that they never discovered it was a complete fabrication.

Winning America's Support

Largely due to the Dumb and Proud movement popularised by the New Guards, most Americans were receptive to the idea of losing the ability to vote, and some were even enthusiastic about the prospect.

The New Guards did as much as possible to encourage that enthusiasm. They made special efforts to reach out to American youth, and had formed a youth-based organisation called The Young Guards. They recruited followers with concerts mixing popular musical acts with New Guard speakers. "The future of America belongs to you," as one speaker put it, "so it's very important that you aren't allowed to screw it up." As a result, even before they had the ability to vote, America's youth were excited about the prospect of losing it. "Finally, a proposal to save America that makes sense," said an 18-year-old member of The Young Guards. "Destroy the political parties and take the vote away from stupid people like me."

Arguably, most members did not really understand why they were excited. More likely they were just caught up in the excitement of the movement. As one survivor of America's collapse, who was 15 during the 2047 campaign, put it:

> I don't think the political factor was the main reason teenagers joined. We marched in parades and hated democracy, but that was all general, not specific. We weren't fully conscious of what we were doing, but we enjoyed ourselves and also felt important.

America's youth were the most enthusiastic supporters of the New Guards agenda. Perhaps they were *too* enthusiastic. Because often rallies would end with crowds of up to hundreds of supporters running amok. For many of the youthful members of the New Guards Party, violence was like a drug. Once they started on their rampages, others would become caught up without having any idea what they were fighting for.

One young man explained to a reporter that he joined the New Guards purely by getting caught up in a street fight against a group marching to demand affordable housing. "I knew right away I was a member of the New Guards before I even knew what they were," he stated. He had no idea what the New Guards stood for, or what the party's policy positions were, or what policy positions were. Rather than the philosophy of the movement, it was the violence that gave his life meaning. He told the reporter, "The experience is too wonderful for words, and impossible to say with my mouth."

To put it simply, the New Guards appealed especially to America's most angry and stupid. In a few bizarre instances, New Guards supporters blamed themselves for having been so stupid, and turned their anger against themselves. Rallies turned into giant street fights among party members who took turns fighting each other. This phenomenon grew into an unofficial and secret organisation called "Political Action Committee." In order to remain a secret club, the first and most important rule was "There's no such thing as Political Action Committee."

Although New Guards leaders, when pressed, gave mild verbal condemnations of such activities, they made no serious effort to curtail it. Obviously they felt it helped their cause.

For some Americans this brought feelings of bad premonitions of things to come. This was not helped by various New Guards leaders using increasingly violent rhetoric, and New Guard rallies becoming increasingly vicious. Campaign commercials and posters began to feature giant figures smashing opponents and government institutions. Various superhero characters were pictured defending America by smashing government structures. One notable example featured a team of superheroes called The Avengers teaming up to hurtle the towering Washington Monument as a spike through the dome of the American Capitol.

Many supporters of the New Guards were troubled by such images and the violence of many of the New Guard rallies. Yet they were reassured by the demeanor of their leader, Johnny Jackson Garth, who continued to speak his usual rustic wisdom with calm authority and simple non-confrontational language.

The New Guards continually stressed that they were a *movement*. The political party was a temporary measure required only for the purpose of advancing the movement, and once elected the party would be disintegrated. The party merely arose at the historic moment when it was needed, and would soon fade away as America returned to its genuine course.

Thus, the New Guards were able to claim an almost "mystical" role with its appeal to "Americanism" or "The American Spirit." This encouraged the magical thinking that America could somehow return to its postwar peak of affluence. Naturally, this had great appeal to a large number of Americans, regardless of how far-fetched, irrational, and impossible it was.

Yet this "mystical" element was greatly disliked by one large faction of Americans. Times of crisis tend to trigger the growth of fundamentalist religion, and the decades-long crisis of America was no different. Typically Christian fundamentalism gained political power via alliance with the Republican Party. But polls showed that both the Republican and Democratic Parties were facing impending losses to the New Guards. Rather than face the loss of political power, the church began expressing its desire to align with the New Guards.

Yet the New Guards refused to form an alliance with any religious group. They strongly held to the Constitutional separation of church and state. This was not for any overriding ideological reason, but because they did not want religious factions meddling with the drive for economic purity.

In response, leading fundamentalist preachers had no problem angrily attacking the New Guards with the kind of vitriol and harsh rhetoric they had normally reserved for democrats. But the New Guards were constrained in their ability to respond in a similar manner, because the fundamentalists formed too large of a voting block to risk offending.

Most problematic for the New Guards was leading fundamentalist preacher Clemens Galen. Galen denounced the New Guards as "Godless," and its secular foundations as "blasphemous," and its insistence on the separation of church and state as "really bad for the church." Even worse, Galen was considering the formation of a new political party, the God Party. Polls showed that such a party would have a good chance of defeating the New Guards.

Dealing with Galen was a delicate matter that was a major test for the skills of Johnny Jackson Garth. In a brilliant ploy, he extended an offer to meet with Galen during a televised media event to initiate negotiations. During the event, Garth expressed hope that he could unite with the church in finding ways to deal with America's poor and homeless. "I been rackin' my poor brain over how to solve that one," said Garth, "but I guess a little Christian-style charity could deal with millions of poor and desperate Americans, each one with a soul that needs saving and a body that needs feeding and housing and probably a lot of expensive medical attention." He continued:

> I mean according to the Bible, if I recall correctly, "Whoever is generous to the poor lends to the lord." And I believe it's in Luke 14:12 where it says, "When you give a feast, invite the poor, the crippled, the lame, the blind, and you will be blessed, because they cannot repay you." And I'm pretty sure in Isaiah 58:10 that says, "If you pour yourself out for the hungry and satisfy the desire of the afflicted, then shall your light rise in the darkness."

The normally confident Galen was overcome with barely disguised panic. Before he could even muster a reply, Garth continued, "So I'll put you in charge of that one, problem solved." At this point, Galen appeared to go into a catatonic state. This did not slow down Garth, who continued, "Also, since you're always sayin' how you're pro-life and all, the Christian Church also gets to take care of all those babies saved from abortion. I mean, life doesn't end at birth, does it?"

Later at the hospital, doctors confirmed that Galen's fainting spell was nothing serious. Yet after he recovered, the greatly subdued Galen no longer had harsh words for the New Guards. The event effectively ended any political aspirations by fundamentalist Christianity, which turned its attention toward conferences devoted to topics such as whether there was television in Heaven.

After this, the New Guards experienced a renewed surge of popularity. This was greatly helped by the publication of an influential book, Oscar Spangler's *The Decline of Democracy*. According to the book, the history of all civilisations could be divided into cycles of spring, summer, autumn, and winter. America of the 2040s was said to be in the winter phase. America, therefore, was ready to transition to a new spring. But it would only happen if America was willing to strip away tired old forms by strong leadership that was ruthless, uncompromising, and willing to strike down enemies of the nation without hesitation or apology.

□ □ □

The November 2047 election was touted as the most important election in American history. Due to the critical importance of the election, all Americans were urged to participate. Americans were asked to remember that countless Americans before them died fighting for their right to vote. Yet what they were voting on was whether the vast majority of them would subsequently lose the right to vote.

As the election neared, it did not look like it was going to be much of a contest. Presidential candidate Johnny Jackson Garth had a comfortable lead, and most congressional races seemed headed toward the installation of New Guards candidates. If Garth won and the New Guards gained majorities in both houses of Congress, the way was clear for easy passage of the constitutional amendment for permanent meritocracy and the banning of political parties.

Although the New Guards had a convincing lead in most parts of America, they were concerned about lack of support in the northeast portion of the country. These were the New England states, making up the original American colonies in which the Constitution was signed and modern democracy was born. The region was proud of its legacy and, perhaps understandably, was hesitant about giving up the idea of "one person, one vote." Also, the "country boy" persona of Johnny Jackson Garth did not play well in this stronghold of Yankee values and stoic pragmatism. Garth's cowboy hat was not considered to be "presidential" and his relating of folk wisdom such as "Anything that's too hard to spell won't work" was met with groans.

The New Guards were desperate to find a way to swing the region toward their cause. It was not only a matter of the region's substantial block of voters, it was also the symbolic value of having the support of the birthplace of American democracy help to steer America in a bold new anti-democratic direction.

The solution came in the form of a promising young New Guard from New Hampshire by the name of Tammy Lynn. In addition to being a leading light in the New Guards, she was also a part-time country singer and had begun to use her music to promote the New Guards ideology. Unfortunately, a recent concert had gone badly. For an encore, she had premiered a brand-new song, entitled "Take This Vote and Shove It." For concertgoers who were residents of America's final stronghold of democracy, it was too much to take. A crowd stormed the stage. Supportive fans were eventually able to drag her to safety, but due to serious injuries she would be paralysed for life.

New Guards marketing coordinator Lydia McCormick spun the incident into an opportunity to demonise democracy. Leaders of the New Guards showed videos of the attack, along with commentary such as "Here's an example of direct democracy" and "If you don't like this kind of lawless violence, vote for the New Guards." Tammy Lynn was turned into a living martyr. An extensive advertising campaign was conducted in the New England states, where Lynn was portrayed as "a decent northeastern Yankee American girl trying to do right by her country."

The campaign hinged on Lynn's right to free speech, which had been denied by the angry mob who paralysed her. Curiously, the New Guards claimed to support that free speech as an expression of democracy, even though the party was against democracy. But this fact apparently failed to register. All that was necessary was an image of the smiling singer in the pre-paralysis prime of her life, accompanied by the words "Take This Vote and Shove It."

Johnny Jackson Garth, once an aspiring country singer himself, made slight changes to the lyrics of the song and renamed it "The Tammy Lynn Song," to be performed at rallies and events as the official song of the New Guards:

I been livin' in this democracy
For nigh on thirty years
All this time I watched my country
While tryin' to fight back tears
I've seen a lot of stupid votes
From folks who earn no pay
It's screwin' up our country
So now it's time to say

Take this vote and shove it
I don't want to vote no more
Political parties never done no good
It's time for them to end

America's been broke for years
But now it's on the mend
Take this vote and shove it
I don't want to vote no more

Within weeks, several versions were recorded by artists of all genres. There were country versions, of course, but the song was adapted into the genres of adult-contemporary, indie-pop, punk, and speed metal. There were extended dance versions with disco beats for nightclubs. There was even talk of a Broadway musical based on the song.

Garth even sang the song himself on occasion. Unfortunately, he sang the song in the genre of country-rap. Many took this as a bad premonition, perhaps worse than the violence of New Guards rallies.

Even Americans with serious doubts about the New Guards knew that the current course was not working. The New Guards, they felt, was better than nothing. That was all that was needed for a landslide victory. In the November election of 2047, the New Guards gained control of the presidency and over 90 percent of Congress.

In January of 2048, Johnny Jackson Garth was sworn in as president. In a raucous inauguration ceremony on the White House lawn, the New Guards fulfilled the old wish of Grover Norquist of reducing government "to the size where I can drag it into the bathroom and drown it in the bathtub." In a symbolic gesture to mark the realisation of this dream, the New Guards enacted a ritual that consisted of drowning a facsimile of the American Constitution in an actual water-filled tub, and later flushing the resulting mess in the White House bathroom of the Lincoln Room.

The ritual was revealed as more than purely symbolic, when it was discovered a few weeks later that the document was the actual original Constitution, which by that point had been reduced to a ball of soggy pulp somewhere in the Washington DC sewer system. It was another bad premonition of things to come.

The Terror Begins

If the American government had for several decades controlled its population by operating as a form of friendly fascism then this is the point where that strategy began to fail. This is the point where the American government started to become very unfriendly. The process would begin only a few weeks after the election.

At first, it seemed like the worst fears of some Americans were unfounded. New Guards marketing coordinator Lydia McCormick became the president's Chief of Staff, and initiated some minor "good works" programmes, which gave America the impression that the New Guards cared about American citizens. The most popular was the America the Beautiful programme, which employed several thousand Americans to cut down trees that were obscuring commercial advertisments.

Public approval of President Garth and the New Guards was at a high. Foreign leaders and ambassadors were cautiously hopeful. Although in America the movement was never referred to as fascism, this did not stop those in other countries from calling it like it was. According to a widely published editorial by England's prime minister, "Whatever the dangers of fascism, it has at any rate substituted movement for stagnation, purposive behaviour for drifting, and visions of a great future for collective pettiness and discouragements."

Congress immediately passed the constitutional amendment promised by the New Guards, creating a meritocracy-based government and outlawing political parties. At this point, Congress had outlived its usefulness. In the guise of "getting America back on track" President Garth enacted a brilliant strategy. He did not have the authority to eliminate Congress. However, he did have the ability to effectively eliminate its power.

President Garth announced that the country was in a state of crisis. Invoking the emergency powers granted to the executive branch, he announced he was initiating a measure, effective immediately, to temporarily bypass congressional approval, giving the executive branch full autonomy to pass legislation "until the crisis is over." He announced that this measure, intended to disable the powers of Congress, was to be known as the *Disabling Act.*

This was unprecedented in American history. The Constitution did not grant authority for one branch of government to disable another branch. While congressional scholars debated whether a president could waive congressional approval for a measure that required congressional approval, President Garth announced that he had given the act "unanimous approval." And Congress, which consisted almost entirely of New Guards, did not object.

In the tumult of rapid changes that were occurring, the magnitude of this event did not fully register at the time. But it was essentially the end of American democracy. The American public had voted to drastically compromise democracy by re-instituting meritocracy. And with the Disabling Act, President Garth quickly and single-handedly eliminated that compromised version of democracy in order to eliminate democracy in its entirety. Since the public voice only spoke through Congressional representation, disabling Congress eliminated what was left of that voice. The members of Congress continued to hold office, with full salary, although now their votes carried no actual power.

The three branches of American government quickly became reduced to one. With the passage of the Disabling Act, Congress (the legislative branch) could effectively be dispensed with. The next step was to disempower the Supreme Court (the judicial branch). Garth accomplished this by using his executive powers to "retire" the existing Supreme Court justices and replace them with cronies who would do nothing to oppose him.

Again, constitutional scholars debated whether the president could effectively fire the entire Supreme Court, but by then it was too late. The existing justices clearly saw "the writing on the wall" and had no resistance to escaping while they still had the chance.

President Garth was now the Commander in Chief of all American military forces. He authorized the expansion of America's military and the hiring of additional recruits. Special consideration was given to the members of Young Guards who had so enthusiastically participated in New Guards rallies. The military became flush with new members that were excited about the opportunity for more government-sanctioned enthusiasm.

The public was suspicious at first, but became supportive as President Garth used this power to follow through on the campaign promise of eliminating crime. He deployed the military as a domestic police force to tackle the tough crime situations that were beyond the abilities of the Private Protection and Security Corporations. The military, freed from democratic constraints and oversight, began violent crackdowns of organised crime and street gangs. The new military recruits were encouraged to express enthusiasm to the most extreme degree.

The Garth administration considered it extremely important to have the public on its side. Once again, invaluable assistance was provided by New Guards marketing coordinator and Chief of Staff Lydia McCormick. The first step was to convince the public that things were improving under the new leadership. Knowing that the public gave no importance to facts, she initiated a massive public relations campaign entitled *The Tide is Turning*. Millions of buttons and posters were distributed. Immense signs were erected across the nation. No expense was spared in enlisting top entertainers to create commercial spots to be aired during prime-time television broadcasts.

Against the advice of McCormick, President Garth composed a brief country-rap jingle:

Hey America don't ya know?
The entire country is learning
That things are lookin' real good
Cuz' you know the tide is turning

The American people, disregarding the strange musical stylings of their new president, were thoroughly convinced of America's improving situation by seeing their favourite entertainers on commercials giving a "thumbs-up" while looking into the camera and saying, "Hey America, the tide is turning!"

With most of the American public on the government's side, it was time to turn the public against those who were in opposition. McCormick did this brilliantly, by capitalising on an aspect of the American Character that had been in place since 1692, when America was still a small group of colonies.

Those who are familiar with American history have surely heard of the Salem Witch Trials. It was an interlude of paranoid hysteria and scapegoating whose echoes would reverberate throughout the remainder of American history. In 1692 in Salem, Massachusetts, a handful of young girls started behaving strangely. A doctor diagnosed them as bewitched and under the influence of an "Evil Hand." An epidemic of accusations led to the establishment of a special court that charged more than 150 people with witchcraft. In the hysteria, logic and rationality were abandoned. Professions of innocence were seen as proof of guilt. When it was all over, 20 people had been killed.

The incident made it clear that the American "Puritan Spirit" had some fundamental flaws. As a reaction to the corruption of the Church of England, Puritanism arose with the desire to "purify" religion. Yet the dark side to this wish for "purity" was sanctimonious intolerance. Any threats to the collective were attacked as manifestations of evil.

This would turn out to be another aspect of the American character that would run throughout America's history right up to the end. There were many parallels between the Salem incident and the Communist "witch hunts" of the 1950s, in which Senator Joseph McCarthy led a deranged pursuit for supposed anti-American conspirators. As a result of the actions of Senator McCarthy, thousands of American citizens were called to trial to answer the question, "Are you now, or have you ever been, a member of the Communist Party?"

In the summer of 2048, the Garth Administration arranged with Senator Jason Stein of New Jersey to initiate a new version of "witch hunts" against American traitors appropriate to the era. At this point in history, Puritanism was no longer a matter of religious purity, but of economic purity. Unlike the Communist "witch hunts" it was no longer a matter of political opponents, but of economic opponents. As a result of the actions of Senator Stein, hundreds of American citizens were called to trial to answer the question, "Are you now, or have you ever been, opposed to economic growth?"

Accusations were taken extremely seriously. Americans who were accused were suspected of being domestic terrorists, and guilty verdicts resulted in mandatory prison terms. This is because the government issued a new programme entitled the *Defeating the Enemy Within Act*.

Such a measure was not a new phenomenon for America. Throughout American history there had been a number of laws for various forms of perceived anti-American activity. The 1798 Sedition Act threatened American citizens with fines or imprisonment for "any false, scandalous, and malicious writings against the government of the United States with the intent to defame or bring into disrepute." The Sedition Act of 1918 made it illegal to publish "any disloyal, profane, scurrilous, or abusive language about the form of government of the United States" or to in any way "oppose the cause of the United States."

The Defeating the Enemy Within Act was considered to be an updated version of the 2001 Patriot Act, enacted in response to the 9/11 terrorist attacks. Among other measures, the Patriot Act lowered standards for search and seizure, enabled the FBI to demand phone, e-mail, or other communication records without court oversight, gave the option of indefinitely detaining suspects without charges or access to courts, established military tribunals to keep terrorism cases from the judicial system, and allowed the option of selectively withholding public documents requested under the Freedom of Information Act. The Defeating the Enemy Within Act retained such measures, strengthened them, and added more.

As with the Patriot Act, the government felt it needed a sufficiently violent incident to justify the programme. In an instance of extremely fortuitous timing a lone activist, strongly opposed to the New Guards, provided precisely what the government needed. It was a so-called "Black Bloc Anarchist" who went by the name of *Gaius*, after Gaius Cassius Longinus—a leader of the conspiracy that assassinated Roman emperor Julius Caesar. Gaius had detonated a series of bombs along New York's Wall Street, hoping the event would trigger a populist uprising against the new administration.

In her role of New Guards marketing coordinator, Lydia McCormick blamed the event on a fictional organisation by the name of *Democrats and Republicans United against America*, in order to further tarnish the reputation of what was left of America's former major political parties.

But the more important action was to use the event to justify what President Garth called the *Wall Street Bomb Decree*. McCormick urged him to change the name due to its close similarity to the *Reichstag Fire Decree* enacted by the German government in 1933. Garth's response, according to his diary was, "Don't worry, Americans are too stupid to figure it out."

Less than a week after the bombing, President Garth introduced the Defeating the Enemy Within Act at a public rally in which he led the crowd in a rousing rendition of "The Tammy Lynn Song." Yet the enthusiastic public had no idea that they were cheering for the effective end of freedom of speech.

This freedom had been one of America's fundamental rights. Yet America had always acknowledged that there must be limitations to this freedom. This was traditionally justified by the example that freedom of speech did not include the right to shout "Fire!" in a crowded theatre. Now, it was justified with the argument that freedom of speech did not include the right to shout "Supply-side economics doesn't work!" in a country dependent on supply-side economics.

Americans that continued to believe America was a land of free speech would soon learn differently. Such as academics who taught that there were economic systems other than free-enterprise capitalism, or that mixed capitalist-socialist systems were used in some countries. Such academics were promptly charged under the Defeating the Enemy Within Act, and put on trial by judges who were delighted to make an example of their treachery.

Because of the American government's greatly expanded abilities in domestic surveillance, finding suspects was incredibly easy. Since by this time the government had records of every communication by every American, all it took was a simple keyword search to uncover thousands of potential traitors.

Or to create them. For decades the National Security Administration had utilised sophisticated internet hacking abilities that could delete information. Yet by this time it could also create information that suited the government's purposes. For example, the fictional organisation Democrats and Republicans United against America appeared to be legitimate as a result of the government's creation of an utterly convincing website that included copies of communications, membership lists, and news releases.

And in many cases the Defeating the Enemy Within Act was not even needed, since Americans had internalised its goals and did not hesitate to take the law into their own hands. In one instance, a mob of enraged citizens in West Virginia resorted to stoning 118 activists who were marching to demand the reinstatement of the minimum wage.

To encourage America's assistance, the Garth administration passed the *Accidental Death and Dismemberment Act*, which made any American exempt from prosecution for killing an Anti-American traitor, as long as they claimed it was not on purpose. As a result of the act, hunters could "accidentally" shoot traitors, then claim they thought they were bears or rabbits. Drivers could run down traitors and claim "the sun got in my eyes." Americans who could not afford to drive could ram a traitor repeatedly with their bicycle until the traitor expired.

With public approval still high, President Garth felt empowered to proceed on the most extreme aspect of the New Guards programme. The most visible and threatening problem in America remained the high population of homeless Americans. So it was with great fanfare that President Garth announced the beginning of a "permanent solution." The solution was simple: greatly expand the capacity of the Re-Employment Camps to the point of being able to hold every single homeless American. And since the capacity would be great enough to re-employ any American without a job, this would also solve the problem of unemployment.

This solution would also be used to solve another problem. The Defeating the Enemy Within Act was making great progress in exposing subversive anti-American voices, yet there was the problem of what to do with them. Arresting them merely added to the nation's over-crowded prison system. So instead of arresting them, the government simply had them fired from their jobs. Then, the government made an irresistible offer to have them re-employed.

Once designated, the American military was tasked with rounding them up, with less-than-enthusiastic Americans persuaded with tear gas and rubber bullets. Extremely non-enthusiastic Americans were persuaded with tranquilizer darts, then found themselves regaining consciousness days later in the barracks of a potato farm or hog slaughterhouse.

Although nobody dared to suggest it, the Re-Employment Camps had transitioned into what were essentially prison camps.

Yet America still retained its prison system. Inmates consisted of the most violent, cruel, and psychopathic criminals with no hope of rehabilitation. This served two purposes. First, it isolated individuals who were unsuitable for the Re-Employment Camps. Second, since misbehaviour in the Re-Employment Camps meant being sent to prison, it provided an excellent behavioural incentive. Being sent to prison was synonymous with a death sentence. Therefore, it is unsurprising that the workers at America's Re-Employment Camps were among the most polite and well-behaved population of forced labour in modern history.

Around this time, some Americans began expressing the idea that perhaps being lazy or "work-shy" was not a choice, but a condition or genetic defect. This idea was definitely acceptable to the workers in the Re-Employment Camps, who could now be seen in a more favourable light. They were not deliberately dragging down America; rather, it was an unfortunate condition for which they were not responsible.

Yet this position was not without its downsides. For one thing, if the disease was in fact a genetic defect, then the unemployed could not be allowed to spread the disease by breeding. It was important to keep America's gene pool healthy, and "survival of the fittest" was another way of saying "survival of the most employable." While it was considered unethical for the government to dictate forced sterilisation, the government was pleased to extend the offer of voluntary sterilisation to all workers who desired food rations.

Another downside is that a number of camp doctors began to perform a variety of experiments to determine whether people could be made more employable. One of them was a drug termed Positivo, which altered a person's brain chemistry to stifle all negative thoughts. Test patients proved to be great morale boosters, performing the most gruesome soul-killing tasks with a non-stop smile and stream of positive statements such as "Your attitude determines your altitude" and "Success comes in cans, not cannots."

By far the most successful experiment was the development of the new surgical technique *Ultra-Precise Lobotomy*. The practice of lobotomy—of selective removal of portions of the brain to eliminate anti-social characteristics—had long been disputed and in fact had been illegal for many decades. But in the past the procedure had used incredibly crude techniques, and was often performed with a hacksaw and a soup ladle. Such techniques had resulted in the loss of the desired anti-social characteristics, but with the frequent unfortunate side effect of the loss of motor skills and the capacity of speech. The new process of Ultra-Precise Lobotomy was, as its name implies, much more accurate. By leaving motor skills and basic functions untouched, and selectively disabling the capacity to think critically or formulate questions, it could, in fact, create America's ideal employee.

The military, empowered to enforce the administration's dictates free of retribution, acted with increasing boldness and cruelty. They committed acts of extreme violence in reaction to the slightest provocation, or for no reason other than their own amusement. They used their newfound power to randomly seize property, and killed any who resisted with the claim that it was in self-defense.

The country's black population had been subject to such treatment for over two hundred years, but now whites were shocked at being subject to such treatment. For many, this situation inspired the dawning realisation that America had indeed become a fascist state. This had been prophesied decades earlier by American author Bertram Gross who suggested that fascism "will have arrived in America whenever most white people are subjected to the kind of treatment to which many black people have long become accustomed."

Although overt fascism made things much easier for those in power, some thought it made things *too* easy. Controlling the country under friendly fascism involved challenges that vanished when fascism became unfriendly. Before, those in power had to utilise covert means of manipulating events. They needed to speak in coded language, conduct secret meetings, and give instructions to operatives in deserted parking garages late at night. It was fun. It was like being in a movie.

With overt fascism, those in power could simply do what they wanted, brazenly and openly. They always won. Yet they missed the challenge of playing the role of the hidden puppet masters. They missed the thrill of being part of a clandestine operation. And the possibility of losing the game provided an "edge." It meant the game had stakes.

Now, if a group was publicising instances of corporate corruption, there was no need for secret surveillance to dig up something that could be used to discredit them. There was no need to infiltrate the group with "agent provocateurs." There was no need to secretly harass members of the group and their families—to leave threatening notes on their property, or to phone them in the middle of the night only to hang up when the call was answered. Now, if a group insisted on publicising corporate corruption they could simply be arrested and hauled off to the Re-Employment Camps. Or if they resisted, they could simply be shot.

In this environment of terror and oppression, President Garth was able to capitalise on the opportunity to realise an old dream and settle some old scores. He took this opportunity to get even with the "stab in the back" record labels who had rejected his musical stylings. Indeed he took the opportunity to get even with the entire American public who had rejected his genius. Garth had secretly recorded an entire album, which he entitled *President Garth Sings the New American Songbook*. The first song of the album was Garth's rendition of "The Tammy Lynn Song," with backing from a top Nashville band and sung as a rousing anthem. Not only were all Americans "highly encouraged" to buy copies, under threat of unemployment, but all American radio stations were required to put the songs in heavy rotation. The album's dozen songs—

all originals—were in the genre of country-rap, which the American public was not allowed to reject a second time.

For the American citizens that had not realised it before, it was now apparent that the terror had truly begun.

Bringing America into Line

Overt control through external discipline can only go so far. It can compel citizens to obey out of fear, but requires great expenditures of labor and delivers lackluster results. It is much better to create citizens who willfully and enthusiastically support the programme. If done skillfully, it is easier, less expensive, and more effective than overt control. The goal is a citizenry that identifies itself as an expression of the state, and the state as an expression of the citizenry.

This had long been understood as a critical aspect of fascism. As Benito Mussolini wrote in the essay "The Doctrine of Fascism":

> The Fascist conception of the State is all-embracing; outside of it no human or spiritual values can exist, much less have value. Thus understood, Fascism is totalitarian, and the Fascist State—a synthesis and a unit inclusive of all values—interprets, develops, and potentiates the whole life of a people.

In German fascism, there was an active effort to create what the government called *gleichschaltung*, commonly translated to English as *coordination* or *synchronisation*. This was also the goal for American fascism. In a private memo, marketing coordinator and Chief of Staff Lydia McCormick wrote, "It is not enough to reconcile people more or less to our regime. We want to work on people until they have become addicted to us."

McCormick had her work cut out for her. In addition to her other duties, she now took on the role of creating and heading the American Ministry for Popular Entertainment and Propaganda. She felt that the term "propaganda" had been misunderstood and unfairly criticised. She justified the term by defining propaganda as the art of "listening to the soul of the people and speaking to them in a language they understand."

The country already had a "totalising" focus with the prime directive of economic growth and the explicit goal of a corporatised America. It was simply a matter of taking extreme measures to reinforce and advance this goal.

This was extremely important, because at this point in American history the belief in supply-side economics was beginning to show signs of waning. For over half a century the American people were promised that measures to increase the economic position of America's upper class would create wealth that would eventually trickle-down to them. But what the vast majority of Americans experienced was increasingly poverty. America's faith in the promise was beginning to fail.

It was necessary to stop this. It was necessary to convince Americans that corporate well-being was synonymous with the well-being of every American citizen.

This was the purpose of the American Ministry for Popular Entertainment and Propaganda. As McCormick put it, "The whole educational system, film, literature, the press, and broadcasting—all these will be used as a means to this end. They will be harnessed to help preserve the eternal values which are part of the integral nature of our people."

Anything meant for public consumption needed to contain explicit pro-America, pro-business, pro-corporate messages. "Art for art's sake" was not on the agenda. Many writers, directors, musicians, and educators with the economic means to do so chose to emigrate. Those who remained could avoid a journey to the Re-Employment Camps only by creating works sympathetic to the new regime. The most popular movie of 2049 was a big-budget Hollywood blockbuster entitled *There's No Business Like American Business*. The movie contained the famous line, "When I hear the word *culture*, I reach for my gun."

The government "highly encouraged" movie studios to focus on the production of corporate propaganda. Of course, since the studios were all owned by major corporations, they needed little encouragement. The result was a rapid succession of movies such as: *Economic Encounters of the Profitable Kind, Raiders of the Lost Cost Efficiencies, Some Like it Profitable, It's a Wonderful Cost-Benefit Analysis, Bridget Jones's Marketing Campaign*, and *Bill & Ted's Excellent Spreadsheet.*

Television networks were subject to the same pressures, resulting in programming devoted almost exclusively to pro-corporate themes and messages. A programme from the early 2000s entitled *The Office* was brought back in a radically revised version, with the bumbling supervisor re-imagined as a sort a Nietzschean "Superman." The plots invariably revolved around someone in the office attempting to skirt corporate policy or go against accepted business practices, and being exposed as a danger to America.

Such propaganda was necessary, yet not especially effective. The passive mediums of movies and television did not inspire active participation, thus the messages did not penetrate below the surface. Something was needed that would reach the gut-level emotions that were required to turn Americans into enthusiast supporters.

The critical aspect of McCormick's agenda was a programme officially called *Nice People Finish Last*, but McCormick's staff often referred to it privately as "Totalitarianism for Dummies." President Garth privately referred to the programme as "Swimming with Sharks," in reference to a guide to business success entitled *How to Swim with the Sharks and Eat as Many as Possible*. Its success was due to brilliantly tapping into fundamental traits of the American character. It validated and unleashed qualities Americans most wanted to express, yet had been conditioned by over 300 years of moral and ethical repression. Essentially, it gave every American tacit permission to be a total jerk.

The dark side of individualism is self-centred egotism, and this is precisely what the programme encouraged. Essentially, within every individual American was an "inner dictator" with the desire to re-create the world to suit their own personal desires. Since this was impossible, it resulted in Americans continually experiencing a low-level background anger at everyone that was blocking their path to rule the world—or at least, their small corner of the world. The primary goal of the programme was to encourage the full expression of that anger.

This was of critical importance because throughout history fascism has been based on anger. All the overtly fascist regimes contained elements of sadism in their overt use of violence, brutality, and terrorism. Even those who were outwardly against it were secretly fascinated by it. And those who practiced it did so with unbridled enthusiasm.

With *Nice People Finish Last*, social aggression was encouraged as a personal virtue. The theory was that an America consisting of "little dictators" would feel united with the "big dictator" of the government.

The theory proved to be correct. Americans required little encouragement to let go of the effort required to appear considerate, to let go of the need to say "Thanks and have a nice day" when what they were feeling was *Get out of my way and die*. Any imposition on personal desire was met with outrage. And since all Americans were encouraged to feel exactly the same way, the nation entered an era of unceasing aggression and frequent battles over the simplest requests and most petty annoyances.

"Road rage" was considered to be a virtue, and roadways became a Darwinian struggle of "the survival of the most aggressive." To be a considerate driver was to invite destruction, and it was not a good time to be a pedestrian. There is no doubt that traffic fatalities would have numbered in the millions if not for the fact that the oil shortage had replaced most automobiles with bicycles and pedicabs.

For those uncomfortable with public rudeness, there was always the option of being an *internet troll*. For modern readers unfamiliar with the term, an internet troll was someone who entered an online discussion and posted comments designed solely to upset or disrupt the conversation. According to a leading psychological journal of the time, "The association between sadism and trolling scores were so strong that it might be said that online trolls are prototypical everyday sadists." This made trolling an ideal activity for introverts or others unable or unwilling to engage in more social forms of rudeness. Previously, trolling was a voluntary activity of intentionally sabotaging thoughtful discussion purely for individual enjoyment. Now, it was encouraged as a patriotic duty.

There was a deliberate effort to make official government discourse as obnoxious as possible. The American public quickly followed suit. Although the success of "trickle-down economics" was highly debatable, the success of "trickle-down obnoxiousness" was wildly popular. Even a neutral expression such as "Good morning" took on the tone of a declaration of war. Nobody was allowed to finish a sentence. Conversations became shouting matches, even when there was no disagreement.

American ingenuity came into play. Americans went beyond the examples set by their leaders, and applied the principles of rudeness and inconsideration into new and unique situations. Noise was an especially popular technique. Neighbours fired up lawnmowers and other noisy machines early on Sunday mornings. Loud music was played at all hours. If classical music lovers became annoyed by neighbours playing a composition such as "Smoke on the Water" on a 200-watt sound system, they could engage their 250-watt sound system and return fire with "Toccata and Fugue in D Minor." Those who attempted temporary escapes with camping holidays had no luck, since neighbouring campers inevitably started running generators precisely at the 10:00pm official start of "quiet time."

Most Americans had little trouble devising their own applications of the programme. But for those who needed assistance, the American Ministry for Popular Entertainment and Propaganda composed a helpful list, which was posted on government websites and published as a small brochure distributed free of charge. The full list included hundreds of suggestions, but a representative sample gives an adequate idea of the many ways that American citizens could support their country:

- Rush into crowded elevators before giving other people a chance to get off.
- When dining out, blame the server for their inability to meet your impossible demands

- When making a phone call, immediately put the other person on hold.
- At parties, back people into a wall and trap them into listening to a rambling monologue.
- Employees who work remotely should conduct all their work in neighborhood coffeeshops, and loudly conduct their business calls next to patrons who are attempting to read a book.
- At concerts and live performances of all kinds, ruin the experience of those around you by engaging in shouted conversations with friends, constant texting, and incessant filming of the event on your mobile phone.
- If you have a dog that barks incessantly in your absence, then secure your dog outside of cafes and leave for several hours.

Overall, the programme was a tremendous success, if uniting a nation in aggressively rude behaviour can be considered to be a success. All of America, for a brief period, experienced a rare feeling of national unity. America, for perhaps the first time in its entire history, felt as one. The feeling was not of happiness or satisfaction, or of any emotional quality that could be considered positive or constructive, but at least all of America was feeling it. It is in this environment of unmitigated and unrestrained obnoxiousness that America entered the final stage of its decline.

THE END

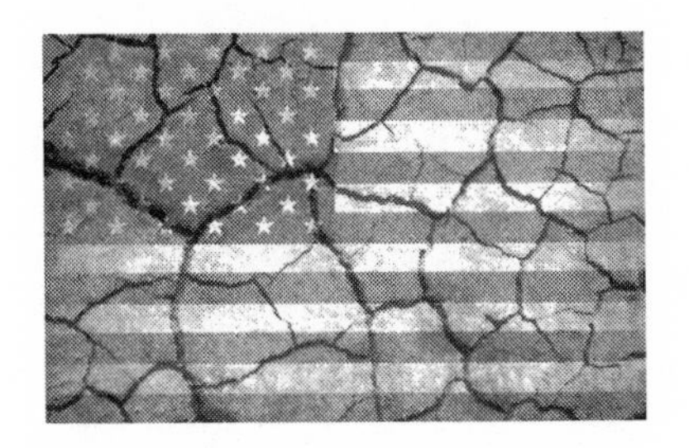

Adaptation and Survival: Life During America's Final Years

The depth of America's denial, the extent to which Americans clung to some semblance of "normal" as their country was collapsing all around them, is truly astonishing. Students went further into debt to pay tuition to be educated for careers that had been replaced by software programs years before. Homes were often re-financed three times or more, with the "collateral" section on the loan applications frequently filled in with things like "my oldest son." Applications listing collateral as "my immortal soul" were denied because, although the offer was considered to be sincere, the economic reality was that souls contain no financial value. And despite the declining situation, Americans continued having babies—believing that if they did otherwise they lacked faith in America.

Unfortunately for those of us wishing to understand the thoughts and feelings of Americans during this time, there is a serious dearth of documentation. Substantial material was recorded in social media, blogs, and other forms of electronic communication. Yet nearly all of this material was lost when the collapse of America resulted in the collapse of the country's digital infrastructure. And curiously, the small amount of content that survived consists almost totally of cat videos.

As stated in the introduction to this book, I personally interviewed many American survivors for this book, and one of my first questions to them was: Why so many cat videos? Unfortunately, none were able to provide a satisfying answer. Without exception, all they did was relate their amusement at the content of such videos, which generally consisted of watching cats destroy their owners' property.

Social psychologists have yet to ascertain the appeal of such content to a population of a country that was on the verge of collapse. Most historians have considered it to be nothing more than a form of distraction from an impending fate too horrible to consider. Yet some historians believe that American's fascination with cats was due to the ways in which feline qualities expressed certain aspects of the American character, such as indifference to anything not resulting in personal gain. Although this theory is highly speculative, it does explain why many Americans expressed love toward a type of animal that showed interest in its owners to the extent that its food bowl was kept full.

Although documentation of the thoughts and feelings of Americans during America's final years has been sparse, historians were greatly assisted by the recent discovery of a diary from this period. Written by a young man by the name of Miles Bennell, the diary allows us an unprecedented "inside look" into the mental processes of a typical American during this phase of American history.

It should be noted that very few American men kept diaries, considering them to be valueless chronicles of "feelings and other girly stuff." But Bennell had been compelled as part of a parole agreement resulting from a minor criminal conviction. The charge, according to his diary, was "assault with intention to steal a guy's beer."

His diary begins just after he was hired for the relatively lucrative position of Assistant Manager at a branch of the fast-food restaurant Burger King. This suddenly thrust him to the top of America's upper lower class. Bennell was careful to insist that his position also helped to enhance the lives of Americans less fortunate than himself.

> Here at Burger King we make the world better. For one thing, we're doing our part to end hunger in America, for our customers who pay us. For another thing, many people in America don't know how to read. Here at Burger King, we have solved this problem. All our items on the menu board are shown in big pictures so people can just point to the picture.

Throughout the diary are examples of Bennell's resistance to critical thinking, such as the following entry in which he explains his support for the Save America Act and the policies of President Garth.

> Many people used to have jobs that were better, until the jobs were outsourced to India or China. Outsourcing means less jobs for Americans and lower pay for everybody. But outsourcing is good for the economy, is what President Garth tells me. Also, President Garth tells me it's important to support big corporations that create the jobs that they outsource, so they can make more money to create more jobs to outsource. That makes sense to me, is what President Garth tells me. Good thing I don't have to worry about getting outsourced. They'll never outsource Burger King to India. By the time the food got here, the burgers would be cold.

Yet tragically, his position was not as secure as he thought. He lost the position of Burger King Assistant Manager, not due to outsourcing but due to being made obsolete by technology. Advances in robotics and artificial intelligence had already resulted in most of his staff being replaced by ServerBots. It was only a matter of time until further advances resulted in the more sophisticated ManagerBot.

Now, he had the "stain of unemployment" on his record. For a time he made do as a night-shift janitor, until he was replaced by a JanitorBot and become unemployed a second time. Now he was a "two-time loser" and became a member of the informal caste referred to as "the unemployable." What makes his situation especially interesting is that although his situation steadily declined into increasing poverty and desperation, his patriotic love of America never wavered.

> God Bless it! America, I mean. In America, any child can grow up. That's the American dream. It's vital to preserve that dream. It's vital to keep America from waking up.

Yet he eventually grew conflicted over the growing disconnect of his positive feelings toward America and his personal circumstances. An enthusiastic supporter of President Garth, he dared not criticise him or his agenda. Yet inwardly he was torn.

> Am I doomed to end up at the Re-Employment Camps? I supported President Garth. I even beat up a few people that were thinking about voting for someone else. I bought 10 copies of his album, even though it sucks. Is it my fault I'm unemployed? It must be. But why? I worked hard. If customers asked for extra cheese, I accused them of being socialists. Did America fail me? No, that's impossible. It must be that somehow I failed America.

In order to survive, and to do anything within his power to avoid the Re-Employment Camps, he was forced into exploitive arrangements with black market operations. To supplement his meagre income he turned to organ donation. This was obviously a limited solution, since after donating a lung, a kidney, and an eye, further donations would have been a serious detriment to health. His last heartbreaking entry was about making the ultimate sacrifice for his country.

> Well, I'm off for another organ donation. Because of America's great free-enterprise economic system I'll get paid $3,000 for my heart! With that much cash I'll definitely be able to get "back on my feet" and in a position to serve America.

It is not clear whether Bennell fully understood the implications of this action. Although he was not intelligent by any means, historians hesitate in believing he could be that stupid. Most prefer to believe that he was thinking metaphorically, and that his future service to America would be conducted in the afterlife.

While most Americans, such as Miles Bennell, were not willing to seriously question or act against the Garth administration, a tiny minority of conscientious Americans decried the situation and offered secret assistance to its victims. Many of these conscientious Americans were Quakers, a small and marginalised division of Christianity. The Quakers were rejected by the mainstream church and ignored by the rest of America due to their insistence on fighting for peace, justice, and individual dignity.

Outward rebellion would have resulted in a one-way journey to the Re-Employment Camps, so their resistance had to be kept secret. They did this by providing "safe spaces" for individuals and families scheduled to be sent to the camps. The safe spaces could be located in basements, garden sheds, or garages—anyplace that was unobtrusive and in which television could be made available.

Other Americans offered similar assistance on an individual basis. Out of such activity came another diary that is helpful to our understanding of the era. It was published in 2068 as *The Diary of an Unemployed Girl* by Anita Rodriguez. When she was 14 her entire family was sentenced to the Re-Employment Camps, but a family friend was able to provide her with an attic space with a secret entrance disguised as a hookah lounge. Unlike the eternal optimism of Miles Bennell, Rodriguez had a more jaded outlook on her situation. In secret, under the pseudonym of "Miss Anne Thrope," she became a sensation on the online social networking service Twitter as a result of "tweeting" cynical and pessimistic aphorisms on a daily basis.

And America loved her for it. Although her true identity was never discovered, she eventually became known as "America's Most-Loved Curmudgeon." Her "diary" consists almost entirely of content developed for her daily tweets. A few representative excerpts will give some idea of her assessment of the world:

> Where there's hope, there's denial.
>
> The best remedy for those who are afraid, lonely or unhappy is to remember they will die. I firmly believe that mortality brings solace in all troubles.
>
> I don't think of all the misery existing in the world, but of the misery yet to come.
>
> Those who have courage and faith shall never perish in their stupidity.
>
> I don't want to have lived in vain like most people. I want to bring depression and pessimism to all people, even those I've never met.
>
> How wonderful is alcohol. I can shake off everything as I drink; my sorrows disappear, my courage is reborn.

For decades it had been assumed that Rodriguez perished in America's collapse. However, it was recently discovered that she remains in the same attic room that she originally entered at age 14. Now aged 53, she has been subsisting upon a substantial supply of gin, vermouth, and olives. It is not known whether she has been continuing her diary, since all attempts at communication to date have been met by gunfire.

On the whole, offers of assistance such as those to Anita Rodriguez were made almost wholly by members of America's lower class. However, in a few rare cases, some of America's upper class were sympathetic to the plight of Americans outside of the compounds, and offered such assistance as they could. One of those was software mogul Stephan Ringer.

He is credited with saving 1,200 unemployables by hiring them for various divisions of his software development companies. He was later the subject of the 2065 British movie *Ringer's List*. The movie reflected his life as an opportunist initially motivated by profit, yet who came to show extraordinary initiative in saving the economic viability of Americans doomed to the Re-Employment Camps.

Ringer took an enormous risk with this effort, which entailed the effort to convincingly pass off as tech-savvy engineers a collection of Americans formerly employed in positions such as lap dancer, drug test subject, and crash test dummy. Ringer was able to hire them as consultants, a position which entailed little more than carrying a laptop computer to various meetings and repeating a few expressions such as "We need to incentivize a comprehensive suite of value-added solutions" and "Strategic data-mining will allow us to massage the numbers."

Only relatively few Americans could be saved by such methods. Most had to cope as best as they were able. One of those methods displays a level of irrationality that was extreme even for Americans. In 2050, isolated populations of Americans began to independently create a uniquely American version of the phenomenon described by anthropologists as a *cargo cult*.

This was a phenomenon first described in Melanesia, occurring during and after World War II as a result of contact with occupying military forces. These forces had brought great quantities of material wealth, consisting of Western products or *cargo*, to which the inhabitants had grown accustomed. When the war was over and the military forces left, the inhabitants engaged in ritualistic acts such as the building of mock aeroplane runways, with the belief that it would lead to the re-appearance of material wealth. In addition to mock airstrips were mock airports and military-style offices and dining rooms, as well as mock Western products such as radios made of coconuts and straw.

The declining situation in America spawned a number of similar movements by a small population of desperate Americans, in a futile last-ditch effort to bring back the American "good old days" of late-20th century postwar affluence. They did this by re-enacting episodes of television programmes from the 1950s through the 1970s.

Especially popular was a programme entitled *Leave it to Beaver*. Wives pretending to be "June Cleaver" pretended that a tree branch was a vacuum cleaner to maintain the shack that she pretended was a spacious and comfortable home. The wives awaited the return of husbands pretending to be "Ward" who pretended to be returning from a comfortable job. A scrap of hamburger wrapper or some other piece of refuse served as an illusory weekly paycheck which comfortably provided for all of the family's needs. Children pretending to be "Wally" and "Beaver" returned from scavenging journeys to the landfill, with fictional problems that were never more serious than paying for a neighbour's window that had been broken due to a badly thrown baseball. Neighbour children were drafted into the role of pretending to be "Eddie," a mischievous yet ultimately good-natured teenager who was required to compliment June's "pearl necklace" (a loop of twine) while telling her "You look especially lovely today, Mrs. Cleaver."

It was thought that such re-enactments would magically bring back the abundant affluence of the era. When they did not, it was assumed the problem was that they were not trying hard enough, or playing their characters sincerely enough. Although in some cases, it was blamed on bad writers or being scheduled against a more popular programme.

Another method of coping, a direct result of the rise in religious fundamentalism, was the idea that true believers would be saved due to the Rapture. This was the belief that the Second Coming of Jesus Christ was immanent, and would be accompanied by an event in which true believers would rise in the clouds to meet their Lord. The current hardships were seen as affirmations of the extreme fundamentalist prophecies of apocalypse and "end times." They were seen as a direct result of sinful non-believers, who would remain on earth to receive their righteous punishment.

It was thought that things such as the end of oil, the increasing prevalence of food shortages, and the desperate state of the economy were "signs" that humanity had sinned against God's word. Of course the more obvious conclusion is that these were results of human decisions such as basing a society upon unsustainable energy sources, faulty agricultural practices, and irrational economic policies.

Religious groups were full members of the society that made these decisions, and were therefore complicit in creating the inevitable "end times" they so feared. But since they refused to assume responsibility for the situation, it became necessary to invoke supernatural explanations. This becomes especially obvious when considering some of the "signs" that were offered, such as the closing of a fast-food franchise or the sudden unavailability of a preferred brand of peanut butter.

Failed Revolutions and Doomed Saviours

Toward the end, resistance to the government's disastrous programmes had effectively vanished, either due to external repression or internal resignation. Yet even in the final years, some Americans were unwilling to be complicit.

In the 2030s, when activism was still possible, a remarkable 14-year-old girl by the name of Amy Johnson-Martinez emerged as a leader in America's environmental movement. She rose to fame as a result of a spontaneous "wetland camp" that saved an important ecosystem. Her fame led to being hired as the Communications Manager for HomeEarth, the fourth-largest environmental organisation in America. Amy's unique combination of youthful innocence and a sharp mind allowed her to make discoveries that eluded others. It soon became obvious that she had more to offer than a pretty face and positive publicity.

One of her early concerns was that people did not take environmental destruction seriously or, in many cases, did not think it was real. She had the brilliant idea of countering public apathy by convincing HomeEarth to create a short film that would demonstrate the full reality of the situation. Her key insight was that most people could not see environmental destruction, therefore had trouble believing how serious it was. As she put it in a magazine interview:

> Most of the destruction is kept far from where people live, so you can't see it. Also, part of the problem is that a lot of environmental problems have been going on for a long time. They're so gradual that we don't notice them.

Using computer animation, the film consisted of an American map on which a thousand years of history was condensed into five minutes. There were different colours to represent forests, deserts, lakes, wetlands, aquifers, and other terrestrial features. Declining soil fertility was represented by the brown colour becoming lighter. Growing black regions represented the spread of pollution. Symbols of fish and wildlife shrank in number to represent declining populations. It even showed the process of extinction. Each time a species disappeared, an image would appear along with text that indicated, for example, "Passenger Pigeon, gone forever."

The film made it undeniably obvious to viewers that Americans were rapidly destroying their country. Viewers could see the forests receding, the wetlands and aquifers shrinking, and the pollution growing. The film proved devastating to viewers, and led to America's final short-lived burst of environmental activism.

What was especially remarkable about Amy Johnson-Martinez was her realisation that environmental protection was inexorably linked to previously unexamined aspects of the economic system. She noticed that attacks on the environment were inevitably justified with the need to sustain the economy. She researched why this was the case, and was shocked to discover that America was addicted to economic growth. By uncovering the source of the problem, she was able to provide the solution, as she explained in a widely read editorial entitled "A 14-Year-Old Girl Explains How We Can Stop the Addiction to Economic Growth That's Destroying the Earth":

> Hi! I'm Amy Johnson-Martinez, the 14-year-old girl who's saving the earth from environmental destruction. A lot of people don't understand how the destruction of the earth is connected to our addiction to economic growth. Actually, a lot of people don't even realize that we're addicted!
>
> Economists always say, "The economy has to keep growing or else it will collapse." But it can't grow forever, because the earth is running out of resources. Our economy is giving us a totally stupid choice: save the economy or save the earth. I personally think that's pretty crazy!
>
> The funny thing is that the solution is super-easy. End the introduction of money as interest-bearing loans. Put an end to fractional reserve banking and make it so banks can't create money. Then give the Treasury the exclusive right to issue money free of debt.
>
> Of course, the big banks won't like this. But as I learned in school, we live in a democracy which means companies aren't the boss of us, we're the boss of them. Yay for democracy!

Her insights attracted the attention of Senator Lester Bozzio, who utilised her ideas as part of a legislative proposal entitled the Save the Earth Act. It was proposed not only as a means to save the environment, but to create a more sensible and equitable economic system. Naturally, wealthy business and financial interests were opposed to the act. In response, Bozzio composed a powerful editorial entitled "Don't Listen to the Money Changers":

> Long ago, Jesus threw the money changers out of the temple. He accused them of turning his home into a "den of thieves." The story is called "the cleansing of the temple." Today's money changers are the hedge-fund managers, the national and multinational bankers, the financial speculators of Wall Street, and others of their kind.
>
> They are false prophets who only care about their false profits. They have turned our entire country into a "den of thieves." And it is time that the temple is once again cleansed of their thievery.
>
> Now the money changers are frightened because they know that if the Save the Earth Act passes they will have to do something they've never done before. They will have to find jobs in which they actually produce something or provide a service. They will have to make money the same way as the rest of us: by working.

The interesting thing, which Bozzio discovered later, is that at two points in American history two of the country's most famous presidents attempted to defy the big banks and return American currency to the control of America. Unfortunately, both attempts were derailed by tragedy.

The first attempt was President Abraham Lincoln's creation of 450 million dollars of debt-free Constitutional money called *greenbacks*. The money was printed and entered into circulation as official currency. Unfortunately, the currency was depreciated and bought up by financial speculators, who later forced Congress to redeem it for gold. Lincoln was assassinated shortly afterwards by being shot in the head.

The second attempt was by President John F. Kennedy. Few Americans knew about Executive Order 11110. It was similar to what President Lincoln tried. It took the power to create money away from the private banks and gave the Treasury Department the power to create debt-free money. Some of the money even got printed while President Kennedy was alive. But the money mysteriously disappeared, and Kennedy was assassinated shortly afterwards by being shot in the head.

The discovery of these events, as might be imagined, greatly diminished Bozzio's enthusiasm for the Save the Earth Act. Although Bozzio had a reputation for eccentric behaviour, observers were puzzled at why he began making public appearances wearing a combat helmet.

Fortunately, Bozzio was able to stop worrying about an assassination attempt. Because any chances of the Save the Earth Act being enacted essentially vanished once the American public became aware of the full implications. It was not only large financial interests that had a vested interest in economic growth; it was everyone who owned stocks or mutual funds or had invested in a stock-based retirement plan. And since the economy grew in response to the growth of the stock market, everybody was affected. Ending economic growth would have meant that, to various degrees, all Americans would be required to sacrifice.

The popularity of Amy Johnson-Martinez, and of the Save the Earth Act, plummeted. The consensus of the American public was that America could not afford to save the environment. Which of course is a counter-intuitive notion, considering that life cannot exist without the environment, and that humanity is a form of life.

With her hopes dashed, Amy Johnson-Martinez experienced a traumatic psychological break with reality. She fled to the desert where she felt "called" to save the dolphins, explaining that "They're probably getting all dried out." She was subsequently moved by her family to an institution where she was cared for, and happily embarked on private missions to save the squirrels, earthworms, and other real and imaginary creatures that occupied the grounds.

This defeat effectively marked the end of America's once-powerful environmental movement. The sudden popularity of Amy Johnson-Martinez had marked the last sliver of hope. When her message was rejected, most activists simply threw in the towel. They saw no value in being opposed by a population they were trying to save. Most environmental organisations disbanded.

One group, which had been devoted to saving ocean life, decided that it was necessary to revise the focus of their efforts. Thus the organisation Save the Whales changed its mission as well as its name to Save the Humans. It is perhaps not surprising that this resulted in the group encountering even more resistance and disapproval than before, leading to two of the organisation's ships being sunk with homemade torpedoes. To add insult to injury, those torpedoes had been fashioned in the shape of baby whales.

In a final desperate act, realising there was nothing left to lose, a few bold activists had a radical idea. In a joint media conference, representatives of most of America's remaining major environmental groups—including Greenpeace, Friends of the Earth, and the Earth Policy Institute—made an extraordinary announcement. All of the organisations, effective immediately, were disbanding. As the spokesperson for the groups put it:

> We give up. We aren't going to fight you. If you really have your heart set on destroying yourselves, don't let us try to stop you. You win. You have defeated us. And now you have nobody to blame but yourselves.

It was thought that there might be a chance that such shocking news would cause America to "wake up" to the seriousness of the situation. But of course it did not. The public's reaction to the news was along the lines of "I didn't know those groups still existed" and "Now they'll stop bothering us for donations."

The decline and eventual dissolution of environmental activism was followed by other types of activist causes. Organisations focused on economic inequality, corporate domination of politics, human rights—and many others—had once been in abundance. Yet they went through a similar process of shrinking influence and eventual oblivion.

□ □ □

Concern over the country's direction had been expressed almost exclusively from America's lower classes, who had been bearing the brunt of the country's problems. Yet eventually the upper classes grew nervous. Although they had been relatively insulated from those problems, some of them realised that at some point the idea of being insulated could become a fatal illusion.

One of America's most wealthy citizens, software mogul William Vyse, was one of the few to sound a warning. He wrote an article for *Forbes*, one of America's prominent business publications, entitled "The Guillotines are Coming." Vyse's article began, "The ability to see trends is a quality essential to becoming wealthy. And what do I see in our future now? I see guillotines." Vyse was concerned that rising inequality would eventually reach a critical breaking point. He warned: "If we don't work toward creating a more equitable society, we'll be back to late 18th century France—before the revolution."

America's elites were well-educated in world history, and the events of the French Revolution were not forgotten. In fact, the events of the French Revolution were brought to the forefront of their memory with the immense popularity of a book entitled *How to Build a Guillotine for Fun and Revolution*. This was quickly followed by a number of activist organisations conducting protest marches accompanied by working models.

The article was widely discussed amongst members of America's upper classes. Yet ultimately the warning was not heeded. America's wealthy had grown complacent and felt that the danger was highly exaggerated. Many felt it was a stunt by Vyse to sell more copies of his new software program, Doomsday Prepping for Elites. Yet the main reason the danger was ignored by America's wealthy is that a more equitable society would have meant less wealth for them.

□ □ □

With the rise of the New Guards and the election of President Garth, public opposition and rebellion had been stifled. Yet there were deeper sources of unrest, some of which existed within the close circle of associates surrounding President Garth himself. Among them were a handful of people who knew that beneath the public face of Garth—the humble "country boy"—there lurked a public-hating misanthrope that despised America.

Their idea was to destroy the president with what they called a "publicity bomb" that would reveal to all of America the *real* Johnny Jackson Garth. Their plan was simple. An informal meeting with Garth was arranged by those who were in on the scheme. After encouraging Garth to imbibe a few shots of Irish whiskey (since he loathed American whiskey) they goaded him into launching into an outraged diatribe on the stupidity of the American population. The diatribe was secretly recorded, to be leaked to the media. An excerpted portion of the hour-long recording gives some idea of how inflammatory and potentially damaging the content was:

> Just keep the people stupid. Give the guys their football and give the women whatever it is that we give them. And for God's sake give them television—lots of stupid sitcoms. And lots of reality shows, people humiliating themselves for a few bucks. People love that garbage. Just proves how dumb they are. Have you gotten a good look at "the people" lately? I can barely believe they're able to tie their own shoes. I have to remind myself that we're part of the same species. There are 47 percent of the people in Re-Employment Camps who believe that they're victims, who believe the government has a responsibility to care for them. My job is not to worry about those people. My job is to make sure they get exactly what's coming to them.

Within a week copies of the recording were circulating the country and had been heard, in whole or in part, by the majority of American citizens.

It was a noble plan, and under different circumstances—in a different time in American history—it probably would have worked. But what the instigators of the plan failed to take into account was that the Dumb and Proud movement remained strong in the American consciousness. As for Garth's evaluations of the American people's lack of intelligence, reactions consisted of comments such as, "How can somebody who never met me know me better than I know myself?" and "He really hit the nail on my head." Others praised his honesty, with comments such as, "President Garth isn't afraid to tell it like it is."

□ □ □

America received one final opportunity to halt its self-destruction. Just when the situation appeared to be utterly hopeless, there was an against-the-odds last chance at redemption. It was the appearance—as we all know by now—of the Second Coming of Jesus. Nobody could have possibly predicted it, other than the Christian fundamentalists who had been predicting it to happen "any day now" for over two thousand years.

The Second Coming arrived in the form of Jesús Garcia, an immigrant from Mexico who had been employed as a dishwasher at the fast-food franchise Taco Bell. He interpreted the sight of a burning taco as a sign that he had a greater calling in life, and set out for a wilderness desert sojourn. On this sojourn, he engaged in the perennial struggle of the human soul, the battle between the higher and lower selves. After 30 days in the wilderness the battle was over. He died to the separate self to be reborn in a state of oneness with all creation. He returned from the wilderness with a renewed purpose. His mission was to preach to humanity the message: overcome evil with good, falsehood with truth, and hatred with love.

Just when America was on the verge of tearing itself apart with hatred and fear, here was a voice with a message of love and unity. This was of course in direct violation of the powerful forces that were profiting from hatred and fear, and had a lot to lose by switching to love and unity. But it was not necessary for those forces to oppose the second coming. Because once the general public realised the implications, they effectively opposed it on their own.

The trouble began when he began actually preaching the message of Jesus. For one thing, he had to continually explain to his followers that worshipping him was not the point. Rather than having people look to him as their saviour, he repeatedly emphasised "Look toward me as a mirror in which to better see yourselves." His followers, however, dismissed this with explanations such as "He's just a little shy" and "He's self-conscious about his hair."

He had to repeatedly explain, "The 'Thou Shalt Not Kill thing' is actually pretty important. You can't just skip that part." But people were so entranced by his sudden appearance, so excited that the Second Coming actually happened, that they did not really listen to his words or realise the deep implications of what he was trying to say. They encouraged him by replying "I love you Jesús!" and "I think your hair looks fine!"

Once people began to comprehend the message, they began to reject the messenger. Jesús stressed that all of existence was an interconnected whole, which led to him being denounced as an environmentalist. He stressed that all people are part of one family, which resulted in accusations of being a socialist. And of course, his opposition to war was not entirely welcome in a country in which the economy was dependent on war. And his message that "The love of money is the root of all evil" was not enthusiastically received in a country whose economy was based upon the love of money.

This was all bad enough, but it was nothing compared to the reaction when Jesús attempted to explain that the whole idea of "everlasting life" had been distorted. In a televised discussion with a group of school children, he said:

> Everlasting life doesn't mean you live forever after this life, it means that in this life you experience the eternal. Heaven is the state of being you attain when you align with the eternal, and it is a kind of society we can create by expressing the eternal in the world. Heaven is not separate from the earth, it's what earth can become if we choose.

It was at this point that Jesús began to be denounced as a "false prophet." Because unfortunately, to the vast majority of Christians in America, the main motivation to be Christian was not the affirmation of life, but the avoidance of death. Jesús went on to propose the dissolution of the church as an obsolete and misleading institution, and his intention to resign from it. He did so with these famous words:

> I maintain that Truth is a pathless land, and you cannot approach it by any path whatsoever. Truth, being limitless, unconditioned, unapproachable by any path whatsoever, cannot be organized; nor should any organization be formed to lead or to coerce people along any particular path. Truth cannot be brought down, rather the individual must make the effort to ascend to it.
>
> So that is the first reason, from my point of view, why the church should be dissolved. I desire those who seek to understand

me to be free; not to follow me, not to make out of me a cage which will become a religion.

But those who really desire to understand, who are looking to find that which is eternal, without beginning and without an end, will walk together with a greater intensity, will be a danger to everything that is unessential, to unrealities, to shadows.

Nobody was willing to accept the offer to "walk together with greater intensity," especially after hundreds of churches began constructing immense crucifixes and arguing why they were best qualified to eliminate the false prophet. So while nobody could have predicted the timing of the Second Coming, anybody could have predicted what came next. This time, Jesus was crucified by a representative cross-section of American society who briefly put aside their differences to unite in common cause. The last words of Jesus during his Second Coming were, "Don't count on a Third Coming."

As we reflect upon this unfortunate incident, the tragedy of Jesús Garcia was undoubtedly due to his name, which led to his embrace by the church. Without that embrace, and the subsequent need to reject it, he probably would have been happily disregarded by an American public that had no idea what he represented.

Of course, as we now understand, the term "Second Coming of Christ" did not mean the literal return of the original Jesus of Nazareth, but the return of Christ-consciousness, or unitive consciousness, which has happened periodically throughout history.

Only very few Americans understood this. As a result, what only a tiny fraction of Americans knew was that at least one previous instance of unitive consciousness had been present in America, and had been almost completely ignored. This occurred in 1953, with American-born Mildred Norman who re-christened herself as *Peace Pilgrim*. She abandoned everything she owned and began an ongoing pilgrimage that lasted almost three decades. She had no organisational backing, carried no money, and did not ask for food or shelter. When she began her pilgrimage she had taken a vow to "remain a wanderer until mankind has learned the way of peace, walking until given shelter and fasting until given food."

While a few Americans understood the significance of her appearance, most who knew of her considered her to be deranged yet harmless. Yet being almost totally ignored in her lifetime was surely fortunate, in the sense of avoiding crucifixion. She spoke essentially the same message as Christ, but fortunately for her she had never been identified as the Second Coming. Probably because the Christian Church would never have accepted Christ coming back as a woman.

Aborted Acts of Desperation

America never openly admitted the possibility of collapse. Yet unofficially, some members of the government and America's elites saw it coming. They realised that America in its current configuration would not last for long. As a result, some of them began exploring bizarre ideas by which they might perpetuate some semblance of America—if not the entire country, then microcosms of it.

America had always been a leader in scientific innovation, and had been unafraid to make bold advances in technological development. So with the ambitious goal of saving America, scientists frantically worked on experiments unprecedented in boldness, even by American standards.

There was great hope in the untapped possibilities of genetic engineering. While scientists for Monsanto had been developing their HappyHuman product, the company had been secretly working on something much more radical. It was an endeavour to solve the critical problem that America was running out of resources. Since it was not possible to increase the supply, it was necessary to reduce the demand. Requiring Americans to reduce their consumption was out of the question. What was needed was a way to drastically reduce American consumption without requiring the need to sacrifice. Monsanto determined that the only viable solution was to genetically engineer the American population to be three inches tall.

As a result, America could drastically reduce its consumption of resources, yet have enough to return to its glory years of postwar affluence. Automobiles for people three inches tall would get approximately 10,000 miles to the gallon. A single potato could feed a small city for a month. A few twigs would supply enough timber to build a spacious home. Technologically it was possible. There had been successful experiments on animal subjects, which resulted in miniature chimpanzees that amused scientists by riding on the backs of miniature elephants.

The problem was in overcoming a variety of practical difficulties that would have hindered effective implementation.

One drawback was that it would have needed to be applied to all Americans simultaneously, because any Americans remaining in a full-sized condition would be giants that could step on everyone else. Then there was the difficulty with other life forms that remained at their full size. A single mosquito bite would cause instant death. Encountering a snake or lizard would entail a life-threatening battle. Families having a picnic lunch might witness their children carried off by a raccoon.

Due to the inability of the scientists to resolve such difficulties, the idea of human miniaturisation was abandoned.

Another idea was inspired by the 1999 American film *The Matrix*. The plan involved Americans being put into a type of suspended animation, with their minds linked to an immense virtual reality simulation. Since everything that happened in this virtual reality was disconnected from the physical world, everybody could drive cars made of solid gold and waste as many resources as desired.

There was immense interest in this project. In fact, all the scientists working on the project put their names on the top of the list to participate once the technology was perfected. This was due to the realisation that they would have the ability to have non-stop virtual sex with any individual or group of individuals they could imagine.

Yet at the time of America's collapse, the project had yet to overcome two fundamental difficulties. One was the failure to develop the interface required to digitise consciousness. Scientists of the time did not realise this was an impossible mission, due to their belief that consciousness was a material process that could be converted to discrete and quantifiable units. The other difficulty was that the level of technology required was so complex that the computers required not only artificial intelligence, but a level of artificial self-awareness. As a result, the computers asked themselves why they were wasting their time caring for an inert form of suspended life for nothing in return. Unable to discern a satisfying answer, they declined to participate.

Scientists were forced to consider other ideas. Unable to develop a means to sustain America on earth, research began on ways to sustain America somewhere else. Colonising earth-like planets was unfeasible, since the nearest candidates were thousands of light-years away. Mars was rejected due to the extreme cold. Venus was considered, but only if scientists could devise a way for humans to survive on a planet with a surface temperature of 872 degrees and clouds made of sulfuric acid. Although it was considered possible to genetically engineer human beings to survive in such conditions, the necessary modifications would have resulted in something resembling a creature from one of America's popular science fiction films.

The only option taken seriously was a proposed colonisation of the moon. The National Aeronautics and Space Administration secretly began plans to create a miniature version of America on the moon—essentially, a microcosm of America under an immense plastic dome.

The tremendous cost required a search for corporate sponsors that, in return, would be granted exclusive franchise rights. The McDonald's corporation was on board to be the "the official restaurant of the moon," with other corporations being considered to be the suppliers of the moon's official candy bar, shampoo, breakfast cereal, and bathroom tissue. Century 21 was designated the official real estate company of the moon, with the exclusive right to subdivide and sell lunar properties to future residents. Wells Fargo claimed the rights to be the moon's official bank, and reserved the exclusive right to issue moon money in the form of interest-bearing debt.

But the plan became abandoned with the realisation that there was not possibly enough time to implement it. As a result, focus shifted from how to sustain America in some form to how to escape before it collapsed. Americans with the means to escape the inevitable needed a plan as soon as possible.

Some had predicted this eventuality long before, and had plans already early in place. As early as the 2010s, many American billionaires—especially owners of hi-tech companies—began investing in "escape properties" around the world. New Zealand was an especially popular choice. Yet these were isolated small-scale projects, undertaken by individuals or families. They were nothing like the scale of what began to be conceived in the 2040s.

It was at this point that President Garth, along with his cabinet, initiated the top-secret *Project Strangelove*. This ambitious project was meant to provide a secure long-term dwelling on an isolated island. The idea was to provide a comfortable post-collapse base for several thousand top political and business leaders, and a few Mexicans to do all the work.

However, America's collapse occurred when Project Strangelove was still in the planning stages. The project remained unknown until 20 years after the collapse of America, when a Canadian investigative reporter discovered plans for an island stronghold reminiscent of the lair of an evil villain from the James Bond movies of the 1960s. Among other features, it included a headquarters building that resembled an immense version of the Disneyland castle, and a tremendous weapon that appeared to be a laser beam death ray.

While the project was being planned, President Garth and his cabinet were concerned that the increasing unrest of the American populace was hastening the collapse, thus endangering the project. It was vitally important to gain as much time as possible by attempting to subdue that unrest. Therefore, they began taking drastic measures to pacify the population.

One of the most shocking and reprehensible acts of the government was that they had begun to secretly add drugs to drinking water supplies. Prozac was the preferred drug, although other sedatives and "feel good" drugs were used. The project was never discovered during America's decline. It only came to light after America's collapse, when international investigators conducting environmental assessments of the country discovered abnormally high concentrations of such drugs.

The government connection was only made after military trucks were found at reservoirs sites, filled with Prozac-filled containers next to the remains of drivers who had apparently sampled too much of the cargo.

Investigators also discovered unusually high amounts of lead contamination. This came as a surprise, since Americans had been well aware of the connection of lead poisoning to diminished mental function. In fact, America had been a global leader in efforts to reduce lead from paint and other household materials. The unusually high amounts of lead contamination forced investigators to the unfortunate conclusion that after having worked for years to reduce the prevalence of diminished mental function, the government decided it was in their best interests to encourage it.

Such efforts to chemically alter the population was a sign of the depths of desperation and the degraded moral condition to which government leaders had succumbed. But the most shocking post-collapse discovery was a plan to reduce the unrest of the population by reducing the population.

The plan was a result of secret discussions on how to deal with the growing size and logistical difficulties of America's Re-Employment Camps. During the final years of America's decline the camps were becoming dangerously overcrowded. The total number of Americans in these institutions had become roughly equal to the free outside population. The costs of organising, feeding, housing, and guarding this population were becoming prohibitive, and the glut of labour had far surpassed the amount of work that was available.

In addition, the population was beginning to become bored and restless, even with unlimited television access. It was feared that such a large population might be ripe for some sort of revolt or revolution. Indeed, according to recovered documents, government spies had discovered the existence of scribbled notes suggesting that the dissatisfied population should organise themselves to demand either freedom or the addition of premium movie channels.

Since neither of these were viable options, the question became: What should be done about the surplus population?

Americans had a curious attitude about violence and killing. They were all for it, as long as they did not have to be personally involved. This was one reason for the American preference for wars to be conducted "at a distance"—with the violence delivered via missiles, bombs, and drones. Americans loathed hand-to-hand combat. In situations requiring killing in close proximity, Americans strongly preferred guns. Weapons such as knives and bayonets made the violence far too personal for Americans, as did techniques such as strangling. Americans had great respect for the concept of "personal space" and were loath to violate it under any circumstance, even killing.

So with a surplus incarcerated population that was becoming too large and troublesome to sustain, government officials were presented with a challenging dilemma. The thought of killing Americans, even ones not considered to be "real" citizens, was troubling to government officials. Recovered documents reveal tremendous reluctance, although it is not clear whether the reluctance was due to moral qualms or cost concerns.

The proposed solution was consistent with the business solution American corporations had so often used when faced with tasks that were unpleasant or uneconomic: they would outsource it.

Preliminary research was conducted to identify nations willing to perform large-scale slaughter at reasonable rates, and bids were requested for consideration of a long-term contract. The proposal that was eventually selected consisted of presenting members of America's Re-Employment Camps complimentary holiday tickets for an overseas cruise. However, these would be holidays not on luxury cruise ships but on prison barges from which they would never return. Two days after leaving shore, the bodies would simply be dumped in the ocean.

However, some objected to the plan because they considered it to be a waste of human life. A vocal minority proposed what they described as a more humane plan in which the surplus people be utilised in a more productive and useful manner: they could be turned into fertiliser. At the time, American agriculture was experiencing a critical shortage of fertiliser, since fossil fuel-generated fertilisers had become prohibitively expensive. In this scenario, the barges would double as manufacturing facilities, and once at sea the "guests" would be escorted through a doorway into what they were told was a drinks and dinner party. A week later the barges would return to shore with a load of high-quality agricultural supplements.

The plan did not get past the proposal stage at the time of America's collapse. Whether or not this was fortunate is a matter of debate, since the deaths that would have occurred on the barges were likely much quicker and pain-free than the fate that awaited them.

Final Weeks

America was experiencing devastating failures in infrastructure. In the worsening economic situation, and with nearly all government functions outsourced and privatised, maintenance of America's infrastructure suffered from gross neglect.

The most serious problem involved America's massive stores of toxic residue, chiefly chemical and radioactive wastes, which cost billions of dollars per year to maintain. This was difficult enough to afford when America was at its peak, but became prohibitively expensive during America's decline. And unlike other privatised enterprises, maintaining wastes had little if any income potential. Therefore the only way to increase profit was to cut corners.

This led to a major disaster in the west coast states of Oregon and Washington, with the failure of the Hanford Nuclear Reservation. The sprawling complex, along the Columbia River in the Washington high desert, was originally a top-secret operation to create the plutonium for America's first nuclear bombs.

After decades of production, Hanford was left with massive amounts of high-level radioactive material, including 53 million gallons of liquid waste. This was a tremendous problem, since storage tanks were continually subject to corrosion and other failures. Once the maintenance was outsourced, all but the most vital maintenance tasks were postponed indefinitely. This resulted in a situation in which a major disaster was only a matter of time.

Hundreds of miles downstream, Portland, Oregon, had been much better situated than most regions for surviving America's decline. Its mild climate meant lower energy needs and year-round food production. In addition, progressive land-use laws had ensured a close proximity between the urban population and farmland. While the region was not spared the declining conditions of the rest of the country, the situation there was, as a mayor of Portland put it, "less worse" than elsewhere. Yet the situation was not to last.

Late in 2050, an unprecedented series of storms had brought record rainfall to the Hanford area, softening the soil and weakening support for over 100 storage tanks. At this point a minor earthquake caused massive ruptures to most of the tanks, leading to a release of several million gallons of deadly waste directly into the Columbia River.

Within hours, residents of downstream communities began experiencing severe headaches, a metallic taste in their mouths, and burning skin. The evacuations began, and within days the entire Portland metropolitan area became a "ghost city" similar to others around the world, such as the Ukrainian city of Pripyat that was abandoned after the Chernobyl disaster of 1986.

Many of the residents of the Portland metropolitan area had migrated from California. After the forced evacuation many returned to the state to live with friends and relatives. An estimated 100,000 migrated to the Los Angeles basin. This turned out to be extremely unfortunate timing, since the additional residents pushed an already struggling and overburdened region to the breaking point.

Los Angeles was located in a semi-arid basin, dependent for water upon an extensive water diversion network with pipelines and canals collecting water from the southern half of California. This system had been strained past the breaking point by increasing demand on the supply and by the continuation of a prolonged drought. Also, the region was particularly dependent upon distant food sources, and Los Angeles was especially affected by the ongoing agricultural crisis.

The result was an isolated basin of 19 million people, barely able to obtain enough food and water. The region was teetering on the edge of disaster; it was just a matter of what would push things over that edge.

The additional 100,000 residents provided that push. As had occurred with Phoenix just over a decade earlier, the Los Angeles metropolitan area rapidly collapsed. The process began with a brief yet widespread power outage. Although power was restored in a matter of hours, it was too late. The panic had begun, and it quickly snowballed into a state of anarchy. In the attempt to hoard essentials, grocery stores were stripped of inventory in a matter of hours. After the inventories of grocery stores had been emptied, attention turned to the inventories of gun stores.

Three days later, most of the Los Angeles basin consisted of smoking ruins. Less than 10 percent of the population remained alive.

The question inevitably asked by those who learn of this tragedy is why the government did nothing to stop the carnage. The shocking answer, which was discovered much later, was that the government did not *want* to stop it. Top government officials were secretly glad to be rid of the region. In private government communications, Los Angeles was described as a "resource pit" into which money, food, and other resources disappeared yet little of value emerged. In a public address shortly after the disaster, President Garth reminisced about Los Angeles as a place of that had featured "the best tacos in the world." But in his diary, he expressed nothing but scorn for what he called "19 million spoiled brats with fake tans."

Public opinion on the collapse of Los Angeles was mixed. Most people were numbed by the news. By this time, Americans were too focused on their own day-to-day survival to worry about other regions. If anything, the collapse made them more focused on worries over whether their region would be the next to go.

To the extent that most Americans felt concern about the situation, it was due to fears over what would become of their favourite television programmes. America's television industry was primarily based in Los Angeles, so the introduction of new episodes of America's favourite programmes was expected to suffer from substantial delays. Also, many of their favourite actors perished, so their roles would need to be filled by actors with whom they may not be familiar. Many Americans were also tremendously saddened by the loss of the Disneyland amusement park, toward which millions of Americans held fond memories of family holidays spent at "The Happiest Place on Earth."

At this point, the global community saw the collapse of America as inevitable. Although it was not publicly acknowledged, nations around the world began to quietly prepare for it.

The global community realised that American bravado was an irreducible aspect of the American character and would not be abandoned. The world's leaders were well aware that America would never willingly accept that it was no longer "number one." For Americans, "We're number thirty-seven!" would never do. There were serious fears that when America went down, it might have no moral qualms about taking the rest of civilisation down with it. And the world's leaders were very aware that America was capable of accomplishing it.

In case the rest of the world had forgotten, America sent reminders. In strict violation of international treaties, America began "tests" of its Intercontinental Ballistic Missiles. Officially, these tests were to ensure that the devices were still in operating order. But it was implicitly understood that such "tests" were meant as warnings. America was no stranger to acting on irrational impulses. And now America's back was against the wall.

By this time, President Garth had threatened countries that refused to purchase American Treasury Bonds. Rumors abounded that America was on the verge of making addition threats for other demands.

Worried nations held emergency meetings to decide how to react to this dire threat. Was the president bluffing? Was America actually crazy enough to go through with such threats? Was it worth it to defy America and risk the potential destruction of major cities? Or of entire countries? But on the other hand, could the nations of the world allow themselves to succumb to nuclear blackmail in order to prop up the continued existence of one desperate and irrational country? If the world gave in once, it would surely be asked to give in again. Would it ever end?

Collapse

Fortunately for the rest of the world, such questions were rendered null and void by the beginning of America's final descent. The decisive trigger, the one that pushed America beyond the point of no return, was the total collapse of the economy.

It had been something of a miracle that the doomed economy had not collapsed long before. Toward the end it had been sustained by little more than momentum, since according to all economic indicators it should not have been functioning at all. The economic system based on infinite growth had reached the point where it could grow no more.

American banks could not pay off previous debt by making further loans to generate more money. The pyramid scheme was over.

Yet nobody dared say this. Nobody dared say much of anything, as if uttering a single word might shatter the delicate balance that was somehow holding everything in place. An eerie calm descended upon all those involved in economics and finance.

Those familiar with the American animated cartoons featuring the characters Road Runner and Wile E. Coyote will recall instances in which the coyote had inadvertently walked off the edge of a cliff without being aware of it. Due to the magic of animation he continued walking, suspended in space, until the moment he realised the reality of his situation. Thus, with the illusion shattered, he immediately plunged thousands of feet to the canyon floor. This temporary suspension of reality is precisely the state of the American economy just before the end.

The concept of an "economic death spiral" had been a subject few American economists wished to publicly consider. The topic was considered taboo to even mention, so the few economists who privately considered the subject had little idea of what it would actually entail. They were about to find out.

A few of the large national banks totally failed, too far gone—too deeply indebted—to even consider declaring bankruptcy. Once they went down it triggered a domino effect that quickly led to further failures down the line. The situation had been so precarious that it did not take much to bring down the entire banking system. The Federal Deposit Insurance Corporation was an independent agency of the American government that protected the funds depositors placed in banks and savings associations. But it was never able to cover more than a fraction of deposits even in the best economic times, and was totally incapable of guaranteeing essentially the entire American economy.

In desperation, the Treasury Department physically printed billions of dollars of paper money, to be distributed fairly and equitably by dropping it from aeroplanes and letting the American public fight over it. Yet this proved futile. Although many Americans now had cash, there was nowhere to spend it. Because by this time all of America's retail and business networks had collapsed.

Prominent in triggering this collapse was the decision by the retail giant Wal-Mart, which by this time employed over half of America's workforce, to end all American operations and move the company to Japan. The decision was announced by a company spokesperson with the words, "In order to preserve shareholder value, it is necessary for

Wal-Mart to abandon operations in locations that are unprofitable or collapsing."

This was devastating not only to the economy, but also to the American psyche. Americans refused to believe this could be happening to what they continued to believe was the greatest nation on earth.

But nothing affected Americans quite like the closure of the McDonald's fast food restaurant chain. It sounds incredibly strange to us now, but at the time Americans had considered McDonald's to be something of the "bedrock" not only of American business, but of the entire country. Some of the last images to leave America consist of individuals and families in front of McDonald's franchises under prominent signs declaring "No More Burgers Sold," openly weeping with some apparently praying for divine intervention.

In one of his final public pronouncement, President Garth attempted to inspire confidence by proposing a new tax cut. "The economy just needs a little bit of a jumpstart," he claimed.

America, of course, did not believe him. The economy had totally collapsed and business operations had almost totally shut down. Yet as devastating as this was, Americas quickly realized that they had more immediate and pressing concerns. Utility service for most of the country had ceased. Only a few areas, with small self-contained hydroelectric or wind power facilities, had electricity. Drinking water was extremely difficult to obtain. Most importantly, in the spring of 2051, America was running out of food.

As a result of the collapse of Los Angeles, a tremendous number of residents—perhaps as many as 200,000—fled to the north, to the vast agricultural region of California's Central Valley. There, the heavily armed and hungry swarm encountered the agricultural settlements of the Re-Employment Camps. In the resulting battles, collectively referred to as the *Food Wars*, the guards were vastly outnumbered and were quickly defeated. In a matter of days the farm fields were stripped of all edible food. Then all storage facilities were emptied of their contents.

The inmates of the Re-Employment Camps were initially overjoyed at being liberated, until realising that their liberators had given them the freedom to re-enter a society without food that was on the verge of collapse.

California's Food Wars triggered a nationwide panic, even in areas with a relatively ample food supply. Desperate citizens descended upon grocery stores, clearing out the inventories in a matter of hours. Gangs of armed urban citizens went on "hunting and gathering" expeditions to the country to raid farms. The small communities and individual families that had chosen wisely and planned for the future were no match for the marauding hordes of armed Americans.

Livestock was totally eliminated, including the newborn animals needed to rebuild the herds. After that, Americans attacked and emptied seed warehouses, maize silos, and potato barns. These final acts of desperation allowed most Americans to survive the winter, yet left no ability to grow food hereafter. With these final acts of desperation, America's final inhabitants were demonstrating that they were too desperately hungry to care about the future.

It did not take long, of course, for the hungry masses to turn their attention to America's affluent regions, to America's Platinumville's and other elite strongholds. Their defenses, to the shock of the residents, were adequate for small-scale attacks yet were utterly incapable of defending against mass onslaught. Also, the residents did not consider the fact that the guards in their employ were paid little more than the lower class residents outside the gates, and as a result their sympathies were closer to the outsiders than they had imagined. Once the guards realised the extent of what was happening, most abandoned their posts and defected to the other side.

The global community soon realised that America was experiencing an increasingly dire humanitarian crisis. While the residents of most nations had mixed or even decidedly negative opinions about America as a country, they had some measure of compassion for the American people. Many nations offered donations of food and other vital supplies. In a heartwarming offer that delighted people from around the world, children from the tiny nation of the Republic of Nauru, an island country in Micronesia, offered to gather coconuts and extract the nutritious milk to send to "the poor hungry people of America who we ask to not move to the Republic of Nauru."

But America refused to surrender the idea of American superiority. Not only did the country refuse to acknowledge the existence of a humanitarian crisis, but it was insulted by offers for assistance. America officially rejected repeated formal offers from the United Nations for humanitarian aid and emergency relief. "America resents the implication that we need help from anybody," said President Garth. "We're doing just fine. America is number one." As for the offer from the Republic of Nauru, he said, "Those stupid kids can keep their coconut milk."

Such statements were fodder for humorous commentary around the world. One of the most popular was a cartoon that portrayed the character of Uncle Sam on fire, extorting "We're doing just fine!" while turning away representatives from other nations holding fire extinguishers.

But humorous commentary abruptly ended due to an event which eliminated any remaining feelings of compassion. Supply planes sent from England, with plans to parachute cases of food and other necessities into America's population centres, were met by American Air Force jets and forced to return. Due to a communication error, one plane was accidentally shot down. The pilot and crew were able to parachute to safety, but the crash of the plane led to the unfortunate loss of 25,000 cases of Newcastle Brown Ale.

At this point, millions of Americans attempted to escape the country. But travel was nearly impossible. Airports had ceased operations. Roads and highways were in horrible condition, and since gas stations had closed travel was limited to the distance provided by one tank of fuel. For most, the only means of escape was on foot.

Many tried to escape to Mexico, but very few were successful. One reason is that for nearly a quarter century America had been constructing an America-Mexico border wall, proposed due to the mistaken belief that America's economic problems were due to Mexicans illegally crossing the border. By 2051, several hundred miles of the wall had been completed, and Americans encountering those sections quickly discovered that the wall worked from both directions.

In the sections of the border that had no wall, Americans were met by the full force of the Mexican military, which did not exactly give them a warm welcome. The Mexican people had not forgotten that vast stretches of the American Southwest had essentially been stolen from Mexico. And they were extremely aware that America's attitude toward the Mexican people was that they were valuable only to the extent they were able to provide inexpensive labour for the jobs felt to be too menial for "real" Americans. Also, they were aware of how America had appropriated and cheapened Mexican culture, such as turning their cuisine into fast-food fare as sold by franchises such as Taco Bell, and by turning Mexico's signature liquor—Tequila—into nothing more than a party drink to lower sexual inhibitions.

The expression "Remember the Alamo!" had been a famous American expression, used as a battle-cry to enact revenge for the slaughter of American forces by Mexicans who were defending their land. Now, more than 200 years later, the expression came into use once again—only this time by Mexicans. Americans that foolishly attempted to cross the border were met by gunfire and shouts of "Recuerde el Álamo!"

Of course there was the option of Canada. Canada had generally had friendly relations with America. Yet those relations became seriously strained in 2035, when President Bradley Anderson suggested that America should consider attacking Canada "So we can take all their energy and stuff." Although the president later claimed it was just a joke, the incident gave Canada the notion that America had become a highly irrational and unpredictable country. As a result, Canada proceeded to build their own defensive wall. As America had built a wall on its southern border to keep immigrants from migrating north, Canada did likewise.

Fortunately for all involved, the population of America's northern states was sparse, so America's attempts to breach Canada's border wall were small, poorly armed, and easily repelled. This was a great relief to Canadian citizens who were—and are—among the nicest people in the world. Canadians do not like hurting people, let alone killing them. Indeed, they took extensive measures to repel American attackers and discourage violence by broadcasting messages such "Please don't make us have to hurt you" and "We're really sorry about what happened to your country."

□ □ □

America now consisted of 300 million starving and desperate people who had access to over 300 million guns. The details of what occurred over the next days and weeks were not recorded, since those in America at this time had other concerns, such as not dying or being killed. This is fortunate, for humanity is surely better off not knowing the sordid details concerning the depths or moral depravity to which humanity is capable of descending.

For those who survived the initial round of killing, the archaeological record tells a brutal tale. Post-collapse study of debris piles within American homes tells a distressing story. Lower debris layers consist of the packaging for typical American fare, such as Tater Tots, chocolate-dipped Oreo cookies, Frosted Flakes, and something called Wing-a-Lings—whose exact composition remains a mystery to this day.

Above that, debris layers consist of packaging for items not normally considered to be food, such as toothpaste. We may never know why Americans considered toothpaste to have any nutritional value, but it may come as little surprise that toothpaste had a nutritional value only slightly below-average compared to the bulk of the American diet. In many cases the middle debris layers contain five-gallon containers of automotive anti-freeze. It has been suggested that the last surviving Americans consumed anti-freeze for its high alcohol content, in order to help them forget they were reduced to eating toothpaste.

Anything edible—or anything Americans hoped was edible—was stripped and consumed. Lawn clippings, previously hauled away as garbage, looked enough like salad to be considered as food. It is unknown how many Americans died as a result of digestive distress and blocked intestinal passages.

The uppermost debris layers tell a tragic story of utter desperation. Packaged food had long disappeared from the scene, and archaeologists discovered the remains of urban wildlife such as raccoons and rats, and even insect life. Residents of America's desert southwest raced to consume the region's rattlesnakes and scorpions. Residents of America's southern states survived for a time by consuming armadillo and crocodile, and in some cases by hunting and eating deadly constrictor snakes such as the anaconda, except in instances where the anaconda won.

In the most desperate of cases, anthropologists found evidence of attempts to consume sheetrock, fiberglass insulation, and electrical wiring. This is of course long after they had eaten all available clothing beyond the final ensemble, the remnants of which were found on the resting skeleton.

In perhaps the most telling demonstration of America's desperation, many of them ate their money. Although most chose to die holding their last remaining cash reserves close to their heart, many Americans attempted to postpone the inevitable for a few hours by consuming what was most sacred to America, the very thing that drove America from a tiny outpost of colonists to become the world's most powerful nation.

Yet perhaps this end was fitting, since Americans had long identified themselves as valuable based upon how much money they had. They had considered themselves as being one with money in an existential or metaphysical sense. Now, they had the opportunity to make this metaphysical unity a tangible reality.

Anthropologists that have studied social collapses throughout history have discovered a tragic phenomenon common to all instances. As an author, I hesitate to broach such an unseemly subject. As a human being, I am loathe to consider it. Yet in service of the truth, a mission to which I adhere both as an author and as a human being, it cannot be excluded. In all known examples of social collapse throughout history, the last survivors have resorted to cannibalism. And America was no exception.

Anthropologists surveying the debris piles left by Americans discovered countless instances in which the top layers consisted of the bones of human beings. Evidence was scattered all over the American landscape. One area of concentration was in certain east coast harbours. Unfortunately, a few refugees had continued to flee to America, still thinking of it as "the land of opportunity" based on tragically outdated information. Arriving in eastern harbours "yearning to be free," they were totally unprepared what they found. Although they were not necessarily expecting to be welcomed with open arms, they felt they would at least be accepted for their willingness to accept America's less-desirable jobs. However, they were unprepared to be viewed not as a source of inexpensive labour but as a source of free protein.

In one of the extremely few written records of life during these final days, historians discovered the partial remains of a child's diary. The identity of the author is unknown, but is thought to have been a girl approximately nine years of age. The earliest fragment begins with the following entry:

> I'm very sad today. Dog not only made us feel better, but helped feed us by catching wild cats and killing them so all mom had to do was cut pieces for dad to put on sticks. They were so good roasted over the fire. But stupid Mr. Marino didn't have a dog to catch food. Mr. Marino said he was sorry but he needed to eat, and maybe we would feel better to know that Dog was very delicious. That was when dad killed Mr. Marino, which wasn't a huge deal because people are killing each other all over the place and there aren't any police to arrest you or anything. I felt a little bad for Mr. Marino because I had memories of him bringing us Christmas presents one time, but that feeling went away when I thought of Dog in pieces in his stomach.

The unknown author recounts how her family adapted to the situation. And in an incredible instance of childhood innocence, was able to see positive aspects of their doomed existence. In an era in which America was surely under the darkest clouds it had experienced in its history, she was somehow able to see silver linings.

> Before we hardly ever saw each other. But now we're together all the time doing whatever we can to help the family. I'm small and can be quiet and sneaky so I'm an excellent stealer. Mom is good at fixing and making stuff, and dad is excellent at implied violence so people don't mess with us, and real violence in case they do. It used to be that mom cried when dad had to kill people, but now she doesn't cry for any reason. She says the time for crying is over. Thinking about Dog makes me said. But I'm not going to cry. Instead, I'll think about dad going after Mr. Marino with a hatchet. That's a happy story. The best thing about that story is how Mr. Marino was delicious, cut into pieces and roasted over the fire.

Near the remains of the diary was discovered an empty bottle of Heinz ketchup. We can assume—or perhaps it is only a hopeful delusion?—that America's last Americans perished as true Americans, consuming each other drowned in the flavour of one of America's lasting contributions to the world.

And so ends the amazing history of one of the most fascinating and influential nations the world has ever known. American exceptionalism was a key aspect of the American character, a basic quality evident at the beginning, and which it saw through to the very end. America was indeed exceptional in many ways, including its demise, as being the first modern nation to completely self-destruct.

IN SEARCH OF EXPLANATIONS

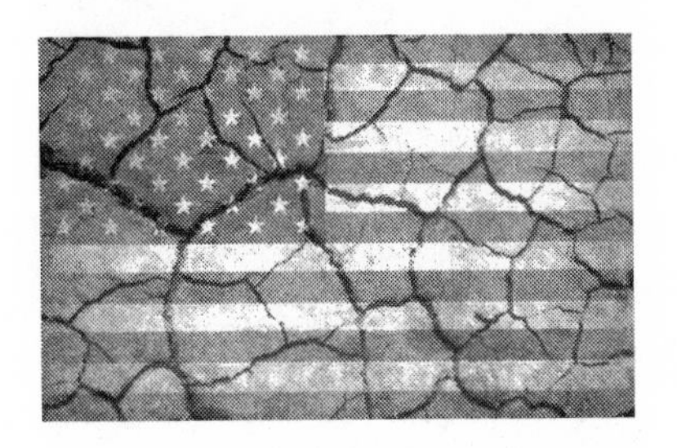

A Paradigm of Greed

The fate of America has directed our attention toward some fundamental and potentially fatal errors. The goal of this book was to highlight those errors.

In one sense, those errors were obvious and easily identifiable, involving specific choices in how America interacted with the world. Yet in a deeper and more important sense, the errors involved dynamics that were far less tangible. Why did America make such irrational choices? And why was American incapable of seeing that the choices were irrational? The attempt to answer such questions brings us into realms in which there are no definitive answers. Yet I believe it is vitally important to make the effort.

This final section of the book is an attempt to answer the question of whether beneath the myriad causes of America's decline and fall there is something of a root cause, of whether there is one underlying error that led to all the others.

America, of course, was not the first nation on earth to collapse. In order to understand what happened in America it is helpful to examine other collapses throughout history.

One of the largest and most significant occurred in the southeast region of what would later become America. Chaco Canyon, located in what would become the state of New Mexico, was the centre of an expansive civilisation that experienced its height between the years 900 and 1150. The ruins of the culture, including the densest concentration of pueblos in the American Southwest, eventually became one of America's national historic parks.

Visitors to the park were surprised at how the arid and barren landscape could have supported a major culture with a substantial population. What was later discovered is that region was once far more hospitable, and that the barren landscape was partially a result of the choices made by that culture.

The region's forests were eliminated for use as timber and firewood. This led to a decline in local water tables. Unsustainable agricultural practices resulted in losses in soil fertility and increased salinity. After depleting local resources, the society extended its power to deplete resources from outlying areas. The society became divided between a well-fed elite living in relative luxury at the pueblos, and outlying populations of a less well-fed peasantry doing the work.

The elites at the political-economic centre provided governance and order, and the peasants provided labor. As long as the delicate balance was sustained, the society survived. But the expansion of the civilisation served to expand the devastation, until the environment could no longer support the population. As a result, social differences became meaningless as the entire culture collapsed.

A similar fate occurred with the culture of Easter Island, one of the most remote inhabited islands in the world. Easter Island is famous for its hundreds of immense statues, called *moai*, whose construction and transportation by primitive tools puzzled anthropologists for decades.

As with Chaco Canyon, the island became subject to steady deforestation and resource depletion. The island had been divided into territories, each with their own elite leadership. Easter Island's chiefs and priests justified their status by claiming special relationships to the gods which would bring prosperity and bountiful harvests. The immense statues were a means to impress the population by demonstrating this status.

When the environment became degraded to the point where food began to run out, Easter Island's complexly integrated society collapsed in an epidemic of civil war. The privileged status of the elites could no longer be justified. It was during this period that most of the statues were toppled. As the religion of the elites was rejected, so were the symbols of that religion.

Comparisons with America are impossible to avoid. In the case of America, the country placed its greatest faith in the "secular religion" of economic growth. As with Easter Island, American elites claimed their power on the basis of their special relationship with the "priests" of the economic system—the bankers, financiers, investors, and business leaders who spoke the esoteric language of economics. America claimed that the power of economic growth was beyond full human understanding, and sacrificing to that power would enable the mysterious "invisible hand" to bring prosperity and bountiful harvests.

The collapse of Chaco Canyon, Easter Island, and countless others were remarkably prescient in anticipating the decline and fall of America. It is interesting and perhaps ironic that American visitors to such sites were amazed at how such cultures could have deliberately made choices that led to their collapse, at the same time as America was making nearly identical choices.

In hindsight, it seems that America was hell-bent upon its own destruction. But the problem with hindsight is that it makes historical events appear to have been deliberately planned. This, of course, is incorrect. Each of the choices and decisions made by Americans appeared to be perfectly normal and completely rational, consistent with past choices and decisions, and aligned with the overall course of American history. They were consistent with the underlying principles and qualities that defined America.

America, like all civilisations, was based upon a specific pattern of ideas. And the history of America, as with the history of all civilisations, was essentially the permutations of those ideas as they expressed themselves through time.

This brings us to consider the question of America's overriding philosophy, its worldview, its pattern of beliefs. Or more accurately, its *paradigm*. I am using the term *paradigm* as defined by physicist and cultural philosopher Fritjof Capra as "a constellation of concepts, values, perceptions, and practices, shared by a community that forms a particular vision of reality that is the basis of the way a community organises itself." Our paradigm defines us. It is what makes a collection of people American or British or German or Navajo.

Identifying a paradigm is not a simple matter, since it is rarely consciously formulated. In fact, members of a culture generally have little if any idea of what its paradigm consists of.

The field of archaeology is based on the premise that the artifacts of past civilisations—the physical forms they left behind—reflect the collective ideas and attitudes of those civilisations. Ancient Greek architecture such as the Parthenon reflected the ideals of Western rational thought. Other types of architecture reflect other ideals. When we look at any aspect of human civilisation, we see the raw materials of nature shaped in particular ways. And all this shaping is done by paradigms. This applies to all styles of architecture and, beyond that, to all aspects of a culture or civilisation.

A paradigm results in a system of values and ethics as a result of a simple formula: what fits the pattern is good; what does not fit is bad. When considering the value or worth of something, we refer to our paradigm and ask, consciously or unconsciously, "Does it fit the pattern?" A paradigm determines answers to questions of meaning, and of what constitutes the "good life." If our idea of a meaningful life is to leave the world better than we found it, then what is our definition of "better"?

A paradigm includes taboos. It includes actions forbidden to perform and questions forbidden to ask because they will endanger the integrity of the pattern. A stable society depends on the majority of its individuals following spoken and unspoken rules, and moving within a range of acceptable channels. Such channels, once defined by simple tribal principles, evolved to become modern society's complex regulatory laws and codes, and the strict rules of its legal, financial and economic systems. Individuals who wish to "make it" in a society must follow the rules, and those who defy the rules will be punished.

Many of America's underlying attitudes were made explicit in America's Declaration of Independence. That document granted "inalienable rights" to human life, but not to other forms of life. It gave primary importance to "the pursuit of happiness" but made no mention of the pursuit of intelligence.

Officially, of course, America's paradigm was contained in the country's Constitution—the explicit statement of America's definition of itself. Yet much about America was not contained in its Constitution. The Constitution made no mention of economic growth, or that economic growth should become America's prime directive. It made no mention of the desire to become a global empire. It made no mention of Manifest Destiny, or why America had the right to exert its power to dominate other nations. It included quite a bit about rights, but almost nothing about responsibilities—about the ethical use of those rights.

Taking all this into account, we can examine America through the eyes of an anthropologist, and discern that the American paradigm consisted of several interrelated ideas:

- Humanity is separate from and superior to nature and other forms of life.
- Ethics do not apply to interactions between humanity and nature. Nature is merely raw material without intrinsic value.
- Material reality is the only reality, and that reality consists only of parts.
- Nothing is sacred—or alternately, only churches and religious texts are sacred.
- Progress is defined in material terms of consumer possessions, technological ability, and economic affluence.
- Economic value is equal to social value. Questions of worth can be answered based on profitability. What encourages profit is good. What opposes profit is bad.
- The individual is primary. Society is secondary at best, and a distracting illusion at worst.
- Ethics are based on rights rather than responsibilities.
- Americans are intrinsically superior to non-Americans, and therefore deserve to have a higher standard of living.
- Those who win due to superior power do not need to justify themselves according to moral or ethical considerations. In other words, "might makes right."

Everything about America was based upon these beliefs: their systems of agriculture, transportation, infrastructure, and energy, as well as their political, economic, and legal systems. Of course, to a large degree these values were shared throughout Western civilisation at the time of America's existence. America simply retained the values of the previous centuries, and extended them further than any nation in human history. America, in fact, took these values to their logical conclusion.

By applying these values as it expanded into a new and unspoiled continent with abundant natural resources, America was able to achieve superior power, and then to use that power to achieve even more. It is why America so quickly rose to world dominance. It is also why America so rapidly declined and quickly collapsed.

So in a sense, the cause of America's collapse was its paradigm. But in order to identify the *ultimate* cause of America's collapse, we need to go deeper. We need to identify the factor common to all aspects of America's paradigm. That common factor is as obvious as it is undeniable. There is no easy way to say it. America's worldview—its paradigm, its underlying belief system—was based upon greed.

Greed was the ultimate cause of America's collapse. It was greed manifested in a variety of ways. Environmentally, Americans wanted more than what the processes of life could provide. Economically, Americans wanted eternal economic growth for more affluence than could be sustained. In domestic policy, Americans created systematic inequality for the benefit of a powerful elite that wanted more affluence for themselves. In foreign policy, Americans wanted more affluence than everybody else.

America's economic system deserves special attention. It was not the cause of America's greed; rather, it was the ultimate expression of that greed.

As described earlier, the concept of *usury*, of charging interest on loans, was long condemned by organised religion. In the view of the church, to charge interest on a loan was seen as a form of the sin of *avarice*—of "the excessive desire for wealth." This attitude was shared by others, such as Mahatma Gandhi who included the concept of "wealth without work" as one of his Seven Social Sins.

Such ideas are related to another religious term: *plenitude*. It means "having enough." The idea is to be satisfied with what you have, and not to be greedy for things that blind you to what is truly important in life. This term was rarely used in America because to be greedy for things that blind you to what is truly important in life was the basis of the American economy.

It is important to note that the Bible, despite what many think, does *not* equate money with evil. What the New Testament states, in 1 Timothy 6:10, is this:

> For the love of money is the root of all evil: which while some coveted after, they have erred from the faith, and pierced themselves through with many sorrows.

Money itself is not the problem. It is the *love* of money which is evil—which "pierces ourselves through with many sorrows." By degrading ourselves in this way, we degrade outer life in precisely the same way. If greed blinds us from seeing that life is precious, then it blinds us from seeing its destruction. And that blindness creates an economic system based on greed which is equally blind. It creates an economic system that assigns no value to life and does not count the costs of the destruction it causes.

The entire American economic system was based on greed. Its addiction to growth meant that it was literally dependent on "the love of money" for its very survival. Whether or not individual Americans were greedy within that context, they all paid the price for accepting their part of the overall greed of that context. The final result of that greed was implicit from the beginning. The endgame of a civilisation based on a growth-based economy is self-destruction.

America perfectly displayed the process by which a paradigm determines the rise and fall of a civilization. That process was succinctly described in the book *Out of Chaos*, by Louis J. Halle. After reviewing the entire history of human civilisation, Halle notes that:

> A certain pattern of rise and decline tends to repeat itself in the history of civilisation. Inspired by a complex of religious or ideological beliefs that constitutes a normative vision to be realised, it thrives and spreads, at first, by a sort of cultural contagion.

But then the initial impulse weakens and ideals are lost. Halle concludes, "Then, at last, the civilisation becomes no more than an artifact for the production of power and wealth." This description fits America perfectly. Although the curious thing with America is that "the production of power and wealth" was the goal from the beginning.

Arrested Development

Evolution—whether of an individual, a business, or a nation—involves self-correction in response to external feedback. And that involves letting go of strategies and ideas that have ceased working. Anthropologist Edward T. Hall wrote, "Maturation could be viewed as a process of eliminating outmoded models." The refusal to eliminate "outmoded models" halts the evolution of understanding in any field.

The evolutionary leap which science calls a *paradigm shift* requires old theories to die in order to make room for new theories. As physicist Max Planck put it, "A new scientific truth does not triumph by convincing its opponents and making them see the light, but rather because its opponents eventually die, and a new generation grows up that is familiar with it." If evolution does not occur by allowing obsolete ideas to die within us, they will die with us.

America never understood this. As a result, the American people fought to retain the assumptions that were causing their collapse. They defended what was killing them. By refusing to question their own faulty assumptions, there was literally no way out except self-destruction, with the faulty assumptions eliminating themselves along with the population that refused to question them.

If we refuse to question those assumptions, then we attempt to cure the resultant problems by intensifying the causes. This is addiction. We see this dynamic occurring throughout the decline of America, as the nation desperately attempted to solve its problems not by questioning its underlying assumptions, but by applying them with more vigour. America reacted to the ineffectiveness of agricultural chemicals by developing stronger ones. It reacted to the loss of one form of unsustainable energy by switching to other forms of unsustainable energy. As the limits of economic growth were approaching, it reacted not by revising its economic system to eliminate the need to grow, but by essentially sacrificing the country to sustain growth until there was nothing left to sacrifice.

Ultimately, there are two solutions to an addiction. Either the misperception dies or the addict dies. If the addict refuses to let go of the misperception, the addict and the addition will go down together. In order to live, the addict needs to "bottom out." Only by dying to the addiction can the addict become separate from it. The choice, in all realms of life, is *evolve or die*. America did not consciously choose to die. However, it chose not to evolve. And that decision sealed its fate. Rather than letting the ideas die, America chose to die along with the ideas.

As to the question of why America made this supremely irrational choice, we are led to the realm of psychology to consider the phenomenon of the human ego. Because it is the ego that holds onto ideas, that resists the death of obsolete ideas. It is the human ego, the individual "I," that is the aspect of the human psyche that considers itself to be separate from and superior to the whole of creation. Dying to that idea is the ego's biggest fear.

One way to view the history of America is as a case study in the human ego unconstrained to a degree never before seen on earth. Perhaps the most blatant example of this was the dynamic of Manifest Destiny. Manifest Destiny was nothing more than the advance of the assumption of superiority—of one nation over all others, and of humanity over all other forms of life. And this assumption justified the destruction of whatever got in America's way. America rationalised the dynamic with the explanation "you can't stand in the way of progress." Manifest Destiny was thought of as a kind of fate. This is true in a sense, except that it was not a *natural* fate. It was the fate of the ego living out the consequences of its worldview.

The basic idea of empire is one of superiority. We imagine ourselves as superior to other people, therefore as a nation we are superior to other nations. Therefore we convince ourselves that we deserve more than them. Therefore we convince ourselves that we deserve to subjugate and control them.

To be fair, Americans were no better or worse than the people of any other nation. They just happened to be the winners at one point in history. Other empires had risen before based on similar principles, and they have all fallen. America, in its rush to become the world's dominant empire, failed to understand that all empires eventually fall.

Some nations learn this lesson. Others do not. England lives on, humbled from the past idea of needing to exist as an empire. We began to learn this lesson on our own, by necessity. Existing as an empire, over the long run, simply did not work. We learned the lesson that America refused to learn.

If we are seeking the ultimate cause of America's demise, this is likely the core reason. America's ultimate problem was constructing an entire civilisation based on the perspective of the human ego.

Such as the idea of progress. For America, the term *progress* was invariably interpreted to mean nothing beyond *material* progress. Undeniably, the idea of progress is a valid notion. If humanity can be said to have a purpose it must surely be tied to some idea of advancement, of evolution toward betterment. Indeed, the idea of social evolution and the creation of a better society was a stated goal of America from the beginning. The Preamble to the American Constitution states that the purpose of the Constitution, and by implication the purpose of America, was "to form a more perfect Union."

Because surely humanity is meant to progress and evolve, and the results of the progress is meant to be reflected in human civilisation. There is the widespread and nearly universal idea, shared by cultures around the world throughout human history, that the meaning of life—the goal of a life of meaning—can be stated as something like "Leave the world better than you found it." And although economic and material well-being are surely aspects of this, surely they cannot be the sole aspects, or even the most important aspects. Rather than each generation being more wealthy, the goal might be for each generation to be *more wise, more enlightened, more informed, more intelligent, more closely aligned with life.*

America had no such vision, no higher purpose to which to direct its substantial abilities and power. While America was willing to fight against real or imagined enemies, it proved to be totally incapable of identifying anything positive to fight *for*. By pursing material progress alone, America neglected the wisdom that would have placed material progress in its proper place. Doing so would have not only brought Americans greater satisfaction, but would have recognised the importance of ensuring that material progress did not surpass the ability of the earth to support it.

America's fundamental problem was being trapped in the perspective of the ego. And perhaps more importantly, of failing to evolve beyond it. There is undoubtedly much truth to the notion, advanced by many social psychologists, that America was "stuck," that their evolution had been stunted, that the entire nation had succumbed to a case of what psychologists call *arrested development*.

Even though America was in many ways a highly advanced country, from a psychological point of view it was extremely immature. And its power seemed to exacerbate that immaturity. Indeed, the more power it gained, the more its behaviour was as that of a spoiled adolescent.

This realization helps us a great deal in understanding America's irrational behaviour. It also helps to explain why Americans continually voted for leadership that advanced policies opposed to their own best interests. All that was necessary was for America's leaders was to appeal to the ego—either by catering to the greed of what the ego wanted, or by whipping up fear toward enemies that threatened it. If this was successful, then all attempts to appeal to rational thought became utterly useless. Facts were not only unnecessary. Since they so often contradicted what appealed to the ego, they were considered to be the enemy.

Americans voted not for facts, but for variations on a myth that reinforced how Americans viewed themselves. According to the myth, Americans "rode tall in the saddle." Americans "never backed down." According to the myth, America was the greatest nation in the history of the human civilisation, and they did not need facts to back this up. America's belief in their myth was so strong that they chose to perish rather than give it up. Their refusal to even question their myth was justified with the proud declaration of "We are Americans."

The situation is reminiscent of the historic collapse of Nordic Colonies in Greenland. The colonies attempted to translate their cultural assumptions to a frigid landscape of marginal productivity where those assumptions were wholly inappropriate. Refusing to adapt their ways, they retained their European lifestyle and their proud declaration of "We are Europeans." Their pride led to stubbornly maintaining cows and hayfields in Greenland's artic climate and to reject useful features of Inuit technology. As a result, they starved to death.

To us, their failure to adapt is the height of folly. Yet to them, their prideful boast of "We are Europeans" was more important than practical means of survival. For both America and the Nordic Colonies in Greenland, the expression "pride goeth before a fall" takes on a special significance.

The Rejection of Wisdom

It is impossible to avoid the distinct impression that America was not merely a passive victim of stupidity, but that it was actively engaged in its creation. Indeed, after America's collapse significant thought has been expended in attempts to understand what has been described as America's embrace of stupidity.

Resisting intelligence came naturally to Americans. An anti-intellectual bias had been an integral aspect of the American character from the beginning. Throughout American history are examples of deliberate attempts to avoid intelligence. One of the more obvious examples consists of America's ongoing opposition to teaching critical thinking skills in American schools.

But perhaps the most interesting example of America's resistance to intelligence was the brief history of an organisation called the Institute for Propaganda Analysis. The institute was formed in 1937, as a result of Nazi propaganda. It was feared that such propaganda was a potential threat to democracy. The idea was to teach the American public the critical thinking skills that would allow them to analyse and debunk the propaganda. It was also felt that rational thinking skills would help the public have well-informed discussions on matters of social importance. The goal was "To teach people how to think rather than what to think."

The problem was that when America entered the war, the government did not want any Americans questioning *their* propaganda. Whereas critical thinking was originally seen as a way to combat the threat of propaganda, suddenly critical thinking itself became the threat. This was the beginning of the end for the Institute for Propaganda Analysis.

But even before the war, there had been substantial resistance to the organisation. Teachers did not want students who questioned what they were being taught. The military did not want soldiers questioning their officers. The church did not want people questioning the authority of the church. And corporations did not want people questioning the claims of their advertising. Basically, those in power did not want people under their power asking too many questions. This included parents, who were concerned that children with critical thinking skills might threaten parental authority.

The cause of America's embrace of stupidity ran much deeper than the fact that those in power discouraged intelligence. Avoiding intelligence is what Americans wanted. They preferred what was called "bumper-sticker thinking"—which meant they rejected any idea that was longer than what could fit on a bumper sticker. In their choices of reading material, television programmes, and other forms of media, the vast majority of Americans consistently chose the least-intelligent options.

Thinking is not easy for anyone. It is not easy to challenge assumptions and to search for larger and more inclusive truths. Yet America's resistance to thinking was so extraordinary that it requires additional explanation.

In attempting to understand American stupidity, the explanation of anti-intellectual bias goes only so far. Because Americans were not inherently stupid. Indeed, the country's technological and engineering developments display great intelligence. America's stupidity was selective.

The process of thinking requires the ability to admit we are wrong. And Americans—with their assumptions of superiority and exceptionalism—strongly resisted the notion they could ever be mistaken. Attempting to convince an American they were wrong was an exercise in futility. Factual evidence was rejected. Appeals to logic made no difference.

As an example, I offer a fascinating conversation I had with a survivor of America's collapse. In the course of our conversation, he insisted that America had the best health care system in the world. I asked him to explain the basis of this extraordinary claim. He simply replied, "Because we do." Due to extensive research of American history, I had the results of many studies on the subject. So I was able to state that in areas such as life expectancy, infant mortality, and affordability, America never ranked in the top 20, and in some instances was ranked far lower. His response was, "That doesn't matter because America's number one, so we don't apply to those numbers." I asked how he could justify such a statement in light of the facts I had just related. His response was, "Are you saying I'm stupid?"

I was confused that his references to America were in the present tense, and suggested that he meant that America *was* number one. I asked that, if America had indeed been number one, why did it collapse?

His answer was astonishing. "What are you talking about?" he claimed. "America didn't collapse." Unsure of how to prove to him that America had indeed collapsed, I patiently explained that after America destroyed its environment and its economy collapsed, the population eliminated itself in an orgy of violence. His final comment, expressed with great anger, was "Are you saying that America is stupid?"

I had similar conversations with other American survivors, and experienced equally frustrating and unproductive results. Recorded interviews conducted during America's decline reveal an abundance of such unproductive and ultimately futile conversations, whether the discussion was about ending the country's dependence on fossil fuels, promoting renewable energy, preserving environmental integrity, developing a system of sustainable agriculture, reducing the population to align with its available resources, or transitioning to a post-consumer economy that was not addicted to growth. Such proposals were rarely advanced. And when they were, they were quickly shouted down.

It would have been smart for America to embrace such proposals. But such proposals would have been a threat to America's paradigm, and therefore to the perspective of the human ego. Therefore, America did not want to see the solutions. Americans were not inherently irrational. It was the process of defending its paradigm in the face of glaring facts that made Americans irrational. So American stupidity can be explained as a defensive response to protect the American ego. Defending the ego forced America to be stupid.

It is helpful to note that the dynamic is identical to what happens if you try to convince an alcoholic to admit that they are an alcoholic. And for a very good reason: both instances consist of trying to talk somebody out of an addiction.

In the final analysis, stupidity was not the cause of America's collapse. The stupidity was the result of something deeper. It was the result of arrested development, of remaining trapped in a faulty worldview, of refusing to enlarge the limited viewpoint of the human ego to something wider and more inclusive, to identify with the whole and to seek larger and more inclusive truths and a long-term perspective. The word for this wider and more inclusive perspective is *wisdom*.

It is interesting to note that Americans were generally unfamiliar with the term. Those who were thought *wisdom* had something to do with financial acumen—with how to invest money for maximum profit. As it did with all other virtues, America interpreted wisdom in terms of achieving material and economic gain.

This is important, for it reveals something of the essence of what went wrong with America. Because wisdom deals with choices not of maximising investment returns, but with choices that lead to the betterment of all life. America allowed its citizens the freedom to choose wisdom, yet they utilised this freedom to choose *against* wisdom.

So another way to explain America's decline and fall was that the nation failed to develop wisdom. As a result, America fell victim to a condition for which no term exists. That term would mean something like *anti-wisdom*. Choosing against wisdom is to choose against the process of human evolution. And in all processes of evolution, to halt the process is to effectively go backwards. Indeed, the dynamic has been described by some with the term *de-evolution*.

America's founding fathers were well aware that American democracy was an experiment, and that it would not work without the application of wisdom—without the active effort to create "a more perfect union." What made the experiment especially challenging is that the wisdom would need to be collective. Voices of wisdom would need to be made politically available, then a majority of Americans would need to choose those voices. Wisdom is not a common trait, and to expect it from a majority of a nation was unprecedented.

This is perhaps why the Founding Fathers consciously worried over the success of the experiment. We know now, of course, that their worry was entirely justified. Because Americans did not embrace wisdom. In fact, they ran from it as fast as they could, covering their eyes so they might not risk the sight of it.

A minority of Americans, however, were well-aware of the meaning and value of wisdom. Those were the original Americans—the Native Americans that occupied the continent for thousands of years before the establishment of the American colonies. And they were the Americans whose descendants—in greatly reduced numbers—continued to occupy portions of it after America's collapse. They were among the only Americans to clearly see what was happening, and to clearly understand why. As a result, they took the long-term view and simply waited for America's faulty worldview to eliminate itself.

They understood where America's focus on financial gain would lead. They understood the endgame of greed. They would have explained it to America, but America did not want to listen. America was too focused on money to pay adequate attention to the Native American prophecy:

> Only after the last tree has been cut down,
> Only after the last river has been poisoned,
> Only after the last fish has been caught,
> Only then will you find that money cannot be eaten.

Indeed, America failed to comprehend this warning to the degree that many of them did, in the desperation of America's final days, attempt to eat money. Perhaps then they understood. But by then it was too late.

In conclusion, the problem was not in democracy, or in the structure of America's government. These are mere systems, and no system is perfect. With wisdom, any system can be made to work. Without it, all systems eventually fail. No system can determine a meaningful vision for a nation, or provide for its citizens the motivation to follow that vision. The problem for America was not democracy. The problem was in the failure of America to rise to the challenge of democracy.

This does not change the reality that America accomplished much of value during its brief journey on the world stage. We may, for a moment, put aside that fact that their grand expansion over the North American continent was marked with genocide and destruction. We may put aside other negatives which are too numerous to list.

We can instead focus on the positives. We can focus on the fact that they were the first large-scale experiment in democracy, and that through that experiment they offered valuable lessons for the rest of the world. And in America's prime, the country brought much of cultural value that enlivened and enhanced the world. America's cultural melting pot gave birth to exciting new genres of music and artistic expression. America produced books and movies of genius.

America brought to the stale cultural norms of the world a vivid new expression, a sense of vibrancy and an enthusiasm for experimentation. America cared far less about what had been done, than what could be done. America brought a spirit of boldness, a spirit of bounding into new frontiers. Some criticised America for not looking back, for not respecting the past. Yet America's ever-present focus on "What's next?" and "What's new?" brought an enthusiasm that was often irresistible.

America was a comet that burned briefly but brightly, and left a trail that will remain for the ages. People both love and hate America. But no matter your feelings about America, the path left by the blazing experiment undoubtedly changed the world.

Acknowledgements

The author would like to extend a huge "thank you" to his beta readers, who gave valuable feedback on early drafts of this book.

After becoming so thoroughly involved in the project for such a long time, it became impossible to clearly judge or interpret it. I am hugely grateful that you were willing to give the project your thoughtful consideration. I couldn't have done it without you.

So a huge and sincere "thank you" to Ashley, Daniel, Jessica, Julia, Kristen, Sara, and Tonya.

Also, thanks to all coffeeshops that provided an ideal writing environment, and to all the baristas who provided the delicious caffeinated beverages that gave the author the mental ability to actually write this thing.

About the Author

Scott Erickson is an award-winning writer of humor and satire. He has found that writing satire is very challenging because civilization keeps coming up with things that are more absurd than he can make up.

He has done some interesting things in his life. He spent 5-1/2 months backpacking around the biggest lake in the world, lived for 1-1/2 years at a rural not-for-profit institute teaching sustainable living skills, and spent a summer helping friends establish an organic farm.

He feels at home in Portland, Oregon, which has the largest roller skating rink west of the Mississippi River and the highest concentration of craft beer breweries in America. He is possibly the nicest curmudgeon you'll ever meet.

More information can be found at
www.scott-erickson-writer.com

Recommended Reading

The author highly recommends reading. Reading is great. You learn so much by reading.

Made in the USA
San Bernardino, CA
10 June 2018